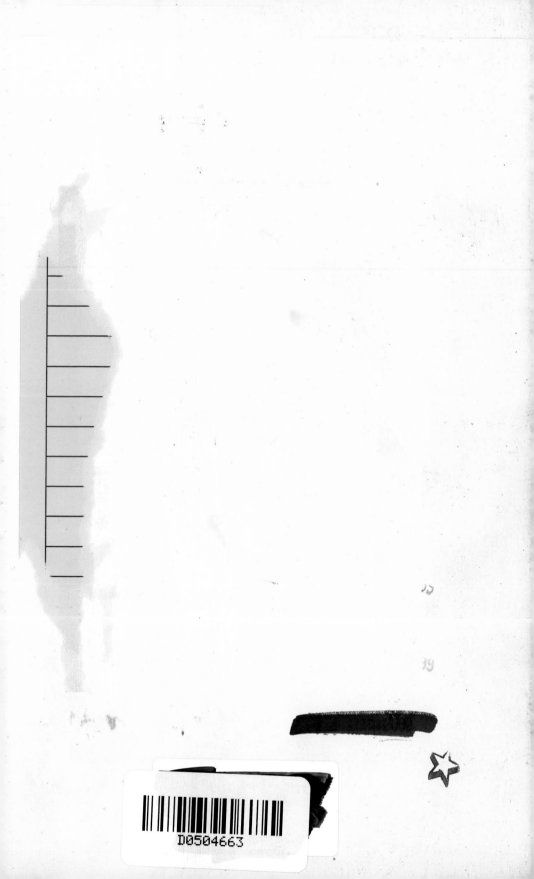

D0504663

DEADLY PERFUME

DEADLY PERFUME

GORDON THOMAS

WEXFORD COUNTY LIBRARY

CHAPMANS
1991

Chapmans Publishers Ltd
141–143 Drury Lane
London WC2B 5TB

A CIP catalogue record for this book
is available from the British Library

ISBN 1-85592-013-1

First published by Chapmans 1991

Copyright © Gordon Thomas 1991

The right of Gordon Thomas to be identified as the author
of this work has been asserted by him in accordance with
the Copyright, Designs and Patents Act 1988.

Photoset by Rowland Phototypesetting Ltd
Bury St Edmunds, Suffolk

Printed and bound in Great Britain by
Clays Ltd, St Ives plc

To
VICTOR O'ROURKE
Friend and Mentor
who made this book possible.

Only he knows what a close call it was.

Special thanks

To Ian and Marjory Chapman: two of the world's few remaining genuine publishers. They had the courage to take a chance. No writer could ask for more support.

To Russell Galen: my agent – but much, much more.

To Yvonne Holland: quite simply a superb editor, and gracious with it.

To Donough O'Connor: his eagle eye made the surveillance technology work.

To Sean Dignam: a veteran of helicopter missions, who made it possible to understand where a machine could go.

To Mary McGrath: long the 'first reader'. There is none better.

To Miranda Moriarty: she typed every handwritten scrawl perfectly, and made sure that much more than the commas were in place.

To Edith: my wife. She read each version and suggested the kind of changes that only a very clear mind could see.

And finally to my friends in Israel and Egypt, who serve still and because of that cannot be named. But they will know who they are. For them, it will be enough.

I

Not even the Chinese knew David Morton had entered China. He'd travelled a route a thousand years old – a smugglers' trail established around the time the first Emperor unified the seven warring States into a great country.

Now, six days later, he was well inside the People's Republic, in the rain forest, keeping watch on the four Arabs who were far from their lair.

The coin-sized headphones built into the air vents in Morton's jungle combat hat enabled him to follow the Arabs' conversation. So far it was about how good it would be to go back home.

They reminded him of desert foxes, tense and nervous, with their noses sniffing and eyes darting. But they hadn't spotted the children. The cloying humidity stifled everything. The girl and boy from the village a mile back down the track were also trailing the Arabs.

Morton had glimpsed the children a moment ago, gliding through the foliage to his right. The boy seemed no more than ten, the girl a little younger. Kids playing hunt the stranger.

Long ago he'd learned the adult version – learned all the rules for survival in jungle, mountain, snow and desert. There was a simplicity about them, of falling back ultimately on what his own body could provide, which went to the very core of who and what he was.

Even here, among trees a hundred and more feet tall, his own height was striking. That, and his massive head, topped with a shock of fair hair still without a trace of grey. People marvelled at the way he avoided the more obvious signs of ageing. His skin was unlined and wrinkle-free, his vision perfect, his body lean and trim. He didn't look like a man in his forty-ninth year.

The way he dressed, khaki drill shirts and pants, winter and summer, made for necessary easy packing. He was entitled to a lieutenant-colonel's epaulettes, but he didn't bother with rank. Those who needed to knew who he was.

The clues were there in his chin, jutting, ready to confront trouble halfway. His grey eyes observed everything and revealed nothing – except to say if you weren't part of the answer, you were part of the problem. They suggested, too, an obsession with the truth, both seeking and telling it. He'd hidden his face behind insect repellent cream and camouflage green so that, lying perfectly still, he'd pass for a log.

Three of the Arabs were wiry, with the forgettable faces of gunmen the world over. The fourth was squat and muscular and completely bald. He was an incongruous sight; a bull of a man clutching a shiny new briefcase. Bagman and escort.

They were soaked from the first of the afternoon cloudbursts. Once more the light drained from the sky as another rainstorm swept in and was over in a minute. It left the air heavy like a warm sponge filled with moisture.

The mikes picked up the faint rustling of the children moving through the growth. There was a whispering in Morton's ears. The girl wanted to go back.

'Not yet,' urged the boy. 'Let's go a little closer.'

'All right. But not too close,' agreed the girl reluctantly.

Their dialect was Cantonese, thin and reedy. There was no way Morton could head them off. That would alert the Arabs. Nothing must be allowed to do that.

The parabolic microphones he'd ordered planted in southern Lebanon had alerted him about these Arabs. And the money they'd offered in those cryptic calls to Bangkok had deepened his suspicions. Two million US dollars. No haggling. He *had* to know what was worth that much. And put a stop to it.

He had patiently followed the Arabs all the way from Beirut, flying on the same TriStar as them to Bangkok. They had not given him a second glance; no one had.

The Arabs spent a day sampling the sexual offerings at Pattani, going from one brothel to another, choosing under-age boys and girls as the mood took them. The bagman had also bought the briefcase, and Morton had realised then he was not wasting his time.

The Arabs had gone to a branch of the Royal Bank of Thailand in Bangkok. That evening they travelled by train north to Udon. He had taken a compartment near them and left the train before they did. From Udon a Thai guide took them by road to Chiang Rai, the hilly capital of Asia's drug-running gangs, far older and as powerful as Colombia's Medellín cartels. Morton followed, knowing now, for sure, where they were going.

At Chiang Rai the Thai handed the Arabs over to a Chinese, a short, light-skinned member of the tribe of Yao, one of China's minority peoples who had long been renowned smugglers. The man had taken the Arabs into the People's Republic. The party travelled light, pausing only to eat and rest at villages where their guide was known in this region of slash-and-burn farming. Locals no longer looked curiously at strangers who came in search of heroin and cocaine.

Nevertheless Morton never showed himself but waited close by in the jungle, eating high-protein food concentrates specially prepared in Tel Aviv. He had enough food for two weeks. After that he could live off the land. He knew now he would not need to. When he had led the Arabs into the clearing, the guide said they had reached their destination.

An hour later, they were still squatting on the ground, the Arabs in their cheap Lebanese bazaar suits, the guide in the baggy trousers and high-buttoning shirt of his people. From time to time he glanced furtively at the case. The bagman rested a hand lightly on its handle. Like the others, he chain smoked.

Morton saw the bagman look at the guide. The Arab's cough rasped in Morton's headphones.

'How much longer?' demanded the bagman in English.

'Now not long,' promised the guide. 'They come long way.'

The bagman grunted and lit a fresh cigarette. One of the gunmen pulled out his pistol and made a show of checking it before shoving it back in his belt.

'Bad men,' came the girl's whisper in the headphones. 'We go now.'

'No!' insisted the boy. 'You can go. I'm staying.'

Morton judged the children were slightly ahead of him. The

gunmen were talking quietly among themselves in Arabic, ignoring the guide.

'We can kill him once we are back across the border,' said one.

'He may have friends waiting,' objected the second. 'We kill him here, no one knows.'

'We need him to get us out of here,' insisted the third gunman.

Even at this distance Morton heard the sudden fury in the bagman's voice.

'There will be no killing until I say so.'

The gunmen fell into a resentful silence.

Rather than stir, Morton let a column of ants march across his hands, a million and more of them passing in review before his face half buried in the mulch. He closed his eyes tight and sucked in his lips when the ants suddenly changed direction. Despite the cream, they filed up one side of his head and down the other, barred from entering his body by wadding placed in his nose. When the ants passed, he opened his eyes.

'Let's go.' The girl's further plea whispered in Morton's headphones.

'No!' said the boy, more determinedly.

The girl's sigh was followed by the sound of them wriggling closer to the clearing. They were expertly using the shadows and sounds of the jungle to cover their approach. Suddenly the boy gasped and their movements stopped.

Morton, the Arabs and their guide, and the children saw the two men emerging on the far side of the clearing at the same time.

The guide scrambled to his feet, smiling in relief. One of the Arabs moved to the bagman's side, the other two separated, ready to provide crossfire. The newcomers ignored the move.

Morton studied them through the sight of his light machine gun. Dark-skinned Han, dressed in coolie smocks and pantaloons, mountain people used to open terrain. As well as carrying M-16s, both wore belts on which were clipped knives, the long, serrated blades matt-finished to avoid glare. From each belt hung a trenching tool, similarly coated. No Han went anywhere without one. The men stood for a moment before retreating into the jungle, moving awkwardly and using their guns to beat a path.

They returned with a third man. The man was middle-aged

and his chest heaved as if he had walked a long distance. He wore a cheap suit and carried a case identical to the bagman's.

He was tall for a Chinese, close to six feet, but well-built, not undernourished or weak. Someone who received extra rice and meat. A privileged person. The hands holding the case had never done a hard day's manual work. The face was pale, almost like ivory. An indoor person.

The man's narrowed eyes took in the Arabs. Then, his breathing calmed, he walked into the clearing, holding his case with both hands as if it were heavy.

As he started to speak to the guide, there was an electrical crackle in Morton's ears. The headphones were shorting. Water, probably. The cloudburst had left him soaked as if he had been swimming with all his clothes on.

He watched the guide turn to the bagman and point to the briefcase.

'Open, please . . .'

Morton could see hatred in the bagman's eyes.

'The money is all . . .' The bagman's words were lost in renewed crackling in the headphones.

'Open, please . . .' repeated the middle-aged Chinese. '. . . za say oke-dokey . . .'

Morton stiffened. He held his breath, silently cursing the static. Yet despite the poor transmission and the man's imperfect command of English, there was no mistake. The Chinese had said — *za*.

Only one name that mattered to Morton ended like that. Raza.

During the Gulf War Khalil Raza had vied with Abu Nidal as the grand master of global terrorism. Then, in one horrific and never-to-be-forgotten incident, Raza had established himself as the world's most evil man. The memory of what had happened once more bored into Morton's mind.

Raza had personally planted, in a Jewish maternity hospital in Jerusalem, the Semtex that slaughtered sixty-three new-born infants and their mothers, along with thirty-one of the nurses and doctors tending them.

One had been Ruth, Morton's sister.

She had been a living reminder of the rest of their family who had died in those grim Stalinist years when Soviet pogroms against Jews matched Nazi atrocities. Ruth and he were among

13

the first Jews freed by a Kremlin eager to show it had changed. Flown to Israel, they'd been fostered by the Vaughans. Steve was a Talmud scholar, Dolly an earth mother. It had taken Morton years to understand Steve had changed Ruth and his surname because there'd be less chance of anyone persecuting someone with a name like Morton.

They were good and gentle people, who had understood his protectiveness towards Ruth. He'd encouraged her through high school, college and university, flown halfway across the world to attend her graduation, and insisted on visiting the hospital the day she started work, prowling the corridors and asking every member of staff for *Doctor* Ruth Morton. Six months later he'd been there when Ruth brought home her Benjy, a handsome young Sabra, also a doctor at the hospital. Ruth said they planned to marry, and Steve opened a bottle of wine to toast the happy couple. Next day Raza struck. They'd found Ruth and Benjy beneath several tons of rubble in a delivery room.

When they'd told Morton Ruth was dead, he'd felt like the day Steve took him to the Holocaust Museum. Then, too, he could show nothing. He had never gone back there. Never attended any of the remembrances for the Six Million. He didn't need to know his past that way.

The day he'd buried Ruth it had rained, making the ground treacherous. He'd felt the other pallbearers grip each other's hands anxiously as they supported the coffin. They'd been Ruth's friends from the hospital, and he'd been struck by how young they were and how they could show their feelings, grown men weeping.

When he stepped forward to recite the committal prayer, his voice had been cold and clear, and had shown no grief or anger. Yet, as the soil covered her coffin, he knew he had been left with an emptiness nothing could ever fill. Burying Ruth, he'd conducted a funeral in his own heart.

As Steve and Dolly led the others away, he had stared at her fresh mound, his prayer shawl heavy on his shoulders, the prayer book in his hands closed. Into his mind had come the one passage he still remembered from those Friday nights Steve read the scriptures to them. The words were from the Prophet Ezekiel: *And the enemy shall know I am the Lord when I shall lay down my vengeance on them.*

14

He'd silently repeated them as a promise to Ruth. Then he had taken off his prayer shawl and walked quickly away, ignoring the shocked, accusing whispers. In his cold, remote world there was no more time for grieving.

Steve had come after him and asked what he was going to do. He'd looked into the old man's face and said softly that he was going to kill those who had killed Ruth.

He'd hardly seen the old couple since, pleading work, pleading anything. He hadn't wanted to look into those eyes that believed the answer was to turn the other cheek.

He'd continued to hunt Raza and his people, flushing out a dozen of their nests. When he'd read in a Beirut newspaper that Raza had placed a 100,000-US-dollar bounty on his head, dead or alive, he'd sent word he'd pay a single Israeli shekel for Raza. The price of an Israeli bullet.

Almost a year ago, Raza had disappeared after two spectacular failures. His plans to launch a Stinger missile against the House of Commons from a warehouse across the Thames, while at the same time detonating a bomb in the newly reconstructed Reichstag in Berlin, had both ended in firefights with antiterrorist forces who had killed or captured Raza's men. Raza's own credibility among his Arab supporters had nose-dived. The consensus was that Raza had followed his notorious predecessors, Carlos the Jackal and Abu Nidal, into broken-backed oblivion. When Morton had said to wait and see, his peers had told him he was just being Morton.

Now Raza's spectre loomed large in the gloom of the clearing. And the children were still arguing.

As Morton reached up to tweak the headphones he smelled burning. A miniature electrical thunderstorm filled the headphones, then silence. The acrid smell was stronger. Morton removed the hat. A wisp of smoke was coming from the headphones. He reached for a dollop of mud and smothered them.

In the clearing the bagman opened his briefcase and, watched by his bodyguards, the Chinese was pulling out bundles of US-dollar bills, expertly riffling them. Satisfied he was not being short-changed, he handed over his own case, unopened. The bagman held it in his hands testing its weight.

Morton thought it seemed to weigh the same as the two million dollars. He eased the stock into his shoulder. He'd found the weapon where Asia Division said it would be, wrapped in layers of waxed paper and buried near one of the stockaded villages he'd passed. He was still getting used to adjusting his aim to compensate for the weight of the bulbous silencer.

The light was going. And where were those kids? Then all else was forgotten. The groups were separating. The middle-aged man clutching the bag was retreating to the far side of the clearing, the bodyguards walking backwards, ready to deal with any attempted shot in the back. The Arabs and their guide moved quickly and diagonally across the clearing, making the range hard to judge.

Morton switched to automatic fire: five seconds to empty the magazine of twenty rounds of 7.67-mm cartridges, three to reload.

He saw the children then. The boy had risen out of the ground and was trotting towards the Arabs, laughing and pointing at the briefcase. The girl was running, hands outstretched, trying to pull him back.

Through the gun sight Morton could see the sudden fear in her eyes. See the boy reach the bagman. See the Arab smash the case against the child's head. Hear the crunch of breaking bone. See the boy go down, poleaxed. Feel and hear the rage choke in his own throat.

The girl was screaming. He could see her mouth opening, see the surprisingly white teeth. And see, as she turned to run, one of the Arabs shoot her. For a moment the child stood, poised in mid-stride. Then, as the crimson spread on the front of her smock, she collapsed against another of the gunmen. He hurled the limp, lifeless form from him.

Morton opened fire, feeling the hard kick of the gun against his shoulder. The silent, sweeping burst tore through the girl's body, instantly killing the three gunmen. The bagman and the guide had vanished.

Rolling to a new firing position, Morton cursed softly. The dead Arab who'd thrown the girl into his fire path had allowed the bagman to escape.

Bullets scythed over the ground where Morton had lain. The Chinese had spotted him. He killed one with a short burst, ripped out the spent clip and rammed in a new one.

No sign of the middle-aged man. A fresh storm of bullets

showered leaves and twigs on Morton's head. The other body-guard was hiding somewhere to his right. The silence was broken by a bolt being jemmied, followed by the clank of a magazine being unlocked and locked.

Crouched double, Morton moved with extraordinary quiet and speed to where the Chinese should be. He'd gone.

Morton picked up a small branch and lobbed it across the clearing. A chain of bullets flayed the area. A sign of panic. He spotted a movement to his left and crawled towards it, gun in one hand, bolo in the other. The ground foliage was still crushed where the man had lain. There was the smell of a bowel that had moved.

Morton lay on his back, gun beside him, knife in his hand. He picked up another piece of wood and threw it high into the trees. The falling stick rattled and bounced against the branches.

Feet away the Chinese rose, M-16 pointing upwards.

Morton jackknifed off the ground and kicked the M-16 from the man's hands. The Chinese grabbed his knife. Morton jabbed the bolo, cutting away cloth and flesh on the man's arm. The Chinese grunted and dropped his knife, then charged. The bolo slipped from Morton's grasp and fingers clutched at his throat. He drove his knee hard into the man's groin, and crushed his nose with a blow from his elbow. There was a louder grunt and the pressure on his throat eased.

Morton struggled to his feet. The Chinese rose from the ground, trenching tool swinging. Morton kicked out, and the tool went flying. He grabbed it, and drove the tool's point into the man's throat. The Chinese clutched at the handle as they struggled for possession. Morton smelled the man's sour breath and saw bubbles of blood oozing from his mouth. The man's eyes were haemorrhaging. Morton pushed harder. There was a tearing sound as the steel emerged at the back of his head.

Only then did Morton relax his grip.

When the pain eased in his chest, he rose to his feet. The blood was turning to darkening jelly where the man's nose had been. Ants had already found the arm wound.

What had he been protecting? There was nothing in the trousers side pockets. He turned the body over. The ID card was in a slit pocket in the rear waistband, where on a Chinese security guard he'd expect it to be. He found the M-16, ruined

17

its barrel against a tree trunk and threw the weapon into the undergrowth.

He went into the clearing and searched the other bodyguard, removing the identity card.

There was no identification on any of the Arabs, but Morton didn't need any. Foot soldiers were foot soldiers. He tossed the men's pistols deep into the growth. He dragged the bodies into the bushes, laying the children a little apart from their killers. It was all the respect he had time to show.

Morton looked at his watch. Fifteen minutes since the bagman had gone. A quarter of a mile from here was a choice of trails to Burma, Thailand, India or Pakistan. He'd long ago realised pursuit was always a matter of balancing expectation against reality.

He sat against a tree trunk to study the identity cards. Laminated plastic protected each face and an embossed stamp that meant nothing. But the symbol in the top right-hand corner of each card he recognised immediately. The two interlocked red squares containing motifs of a test-tube and pestle-and-mortar were the logo of the State Research Institute at Chengdu in Sichuan Province.

The scientists who worked there had established the People's Republic as the world's leading manufacturer of chemical and biological weapons. At Chengdu they had recently created the newest and most deadly of all those weapons, Anthrax-B-C. The 'B' distinguished it from all other kinds of anthrax. The 'C' honoured China as its birthplace.

Anthrax-B-C could be safely transported and handled in its frozen state. But a few ounces, when thawed, could kill thousands. When scientists spoke of an antidote, they usually added *if*: *if* a victim could be diagnosed in time . . . *if* he or she received the correct kind and amount of penicillin . . . *if* he or she was otherwise physically fit. Even then the chances of survival were not great.

So deadly was Anthrax-B-C that the People's Republic had refused to supply it to Iraq, a client state, which it had discreetly provided with other bio-chemical weapons in the run-up to the Gulf War. Morton was certain the Chinese had not broken that embargo now. But the world was getting that much darker when that kind of credit could be given.

Fearing Saddam Hussein had managed to duplicate Anthrax-B-C, Morton had led a small force into Iraq on the eve of the war to destroy a key plant near Baghdad. Buried deep beneath the sands, the lab complex was safe from even the tactical nuclear weapons the Americans had stationed in Saudi Arabia.

To work with the Delta Force and SAS units he'd picked his own people. They were tempered by more than previous battle experience. Each had stared closely into the face of death and respected it. They were like him: Lou Panchez, with those out-to-lunch eyes. Wolfie who never smiled, except when Michelle was around. She was calm and remorseless and deadly with any hand weapon. Matti Talim, who looked like Montgomery Clift. That's where people made their first mistake, labelling Matti. The second was to underestimate him. No one had ever done that to Danny Nagier. He had an artist's touch when placing his beloved ultra-sensitive parabolic microphones, and all the other black boxes that could eavesdrop or create havoc, depending on what was needed.

From the beginning the team had forged the strong bond that comes with mutual liking and respect. Lou Panchez had made his name with the CIA in Lebanon. Wolfie with Europe's most formidable security service, West Germany's BND. Michelle was a product of French Intelligence, SDECE. Matti and Danny were among the very best Mossad had produced. Despite being a Jew and a ranking member of Mossad, Morton knew he was the surrogate Englishman. His education, Clifton and Cambridge, and a slightly clipped accent, ensured that.

Within their closed ranks they were Morton's Men. They'd passed his tests, none in the rule book. They'd shown they could maintain control in any situation, had the guts to go in first, but not *every* time. He didn't want Rambos. They'd also passed the hardest of all his tests, loyalty. Giving it to their country was one thing. He demanded the loyalty that came from ignoring the book and doing it his way. After Iraq, he'd told them, the time would come when they could show it again. Instinctively, he knew the ID cards he now held had brought it that much closer.

Saddam was gone. But the threat remained.

Morton squinted through the trees. The sky was turning purple. The first of the stars were out. The air had grown still. Soon the predators would creep through the darkness to the bodies. By morning there would be only little piles of white bones, picked clean. His thoughts returned to Raza.

Before he had disappeared, Raza had formed an alliance with the drug barons of the Golden Triangle and the Medellín cartels in Colombia, promising to guarantee their supply lines through the Middle East in return for safe houses in North and South America, in Europe and Asia.

Had Raza sent his dogs of war to meet a Chinese drug contact? Was that middle-aged man somehow using the Chengdu facility to purify drugs? Instinct told Morton it wasn't drugs.

This was somehow connected to the cabal of mullahs. They had emerged from the Gulf War as a powerful force with clearly stated aims for the Middle East: the destruction of the State of Israel, the removal of all Western influences from the region, coupled with its total Islamic fundamentalisation. With that went complete control of the oil fields and the rich mineral deposits being found in the deserts. With such power, the cabal would not only achieve hegemony over all Arabs, but would be as rich economically as any superpower. So far they had done nothing but threaten.

It was The Syrian who had told Morton the cabal was poised to escalate.

The Syrian was one of the Arab world's key intelligence officers, privy to priceless secrets. Morton had gone to a back room in West Beirut and recruited him. It was an intelligence coup unequalled since Kim Philby had spied for the Russians. The Syrian wanted nothing for his information except a chance to play his part in bringing a lasting and just peace to the Middle East, in which Jew and Arab would be in harmony.

But the mullahs now wanted to launch a jihad, holy war, sending their hordes storming through Arab countries and creating fear and panic around the world. The adventurism of Saddam Hussein would pale in comparison. It would be the greatest single uprising mankind would have seen.

At their last meeting, The Syrian had brought the news that the cabal was transferring the two million US dollars to Bangkok. Everything else had flowed from that.

Had the mullahs provided the money for the bagman to vanish into the jungle with a quantity of Anthrax-B-C, and had they found in Raza the one person prepared to use it?

As Morton began the long walk out of China, he knew he dare not miss his next scheduled meeting with The Syrian in three days' time.

WEXFORD
COUNTY
LIBRARY

2

The guide led the bagman into Burma at that point where the Mekong begins its long flow to the Gulf of Tonkin.

Only then did their fear subside. The guide said it must have been a rival drug cartel who'd ambushed them. Territorial rights were jealously guarded. The bagman understood. It was the same in southern Lebanon.

In the Burmese capital of Rangoon, the bagman was taken to the first of the safe houses alerted to receive him.

There he performed a procedure rehearsed many times under the watchful eyes of Raza. He opened the briefcase, using the key on a chain around his neck. He turned the key anticlockwise. Raza had said any attempt to turn it in the normal direction would result in the bag exploding.

The bagman removed the protective layer of formed plastic to reveal a shaped mould into which was snugly fitted a stainless-steel cylinder. Six inches long and two inches in diameter, the cylinder had a screw-on top. It resembled a small thermos and was ice cold to the touch. Raza had explained the mould was filled with a freezing agent.

To ensure they remained frozen, the bagman transferred mould and cylinder to an ice chest. Again as instructed, he waited two hours before carefully repacking the bag.

He was then escorted to the airport by the local head of the cartel and put on a plane to Mandalay.

During the flight the bagman continued to wonder what could be worth two million dollars in that cylinder. A new kind of explosive? A bomb that only needed priming? More powerful

than all the Scud missiles that had fallen on Israel during the Gulf War? One so devastating it could destroy the whole of Tel Aviv? The Arab's imagination could not think of anything more powerful.

By the time he reached the safe house in Mandalay, his curiosity was consuming him. He removed the cylinder from its mould and turned it over and over in his hands. It didn't look like a bomb. There was no place to connect a timer to that smooth, shiny, icy surface. And he had never heard of a bomb that needed to be kept frozen. He put the cylinder back in its mould and placed them in the freezer.

From Mandalay the bagman flew to Patna in India. There, in a safe house by the Ganges, he succumbed to his curiosity. He unscrewed the cylinder cap. When he did so, something totally unexpected happened. The cylinder came apart in two halves to reveal a tube of clear, frozen liquid.

The bagman stared at it, holding the tube up to the light, squinting. There was nothing held in suspension. His puzzlement increased. This was clearly no bomb. Yet Raza had said the cylinder would change the world. The bagman held it under his nose, sniffing. The ice gave off a faint and slightly musky smell, like the perfume of the whores in Beirut. He touched the ice with a finger and licked it. There was no taste. He began to feel uneasy. He quickly reassembled the cylinder, placed it in the mould and put both in the freezer. What could smell and have no taste – yet change the world?

From Patna he flew to Delhi. There he began to feel unwell, with aches and pains and the symptoms of a summer flu. With each flight and stopover, he grew worse. A cough developed, which produced rust-tinted sputum. On the last flight from Damascus to Tripoli, the bagman began to shiver so violently his teeth chattered.

At the airport in Libya he was met by one of Raza's men. They drove on the Muammar Gaddafi Highway – the broad tarmacadamed six-laner, which ran for a thousand miles southeast to nowhere in the Libyan desert. The driver glanced sympathetically at the bagman slumped beside him, clutching the briefcase. The man was very sick. But he had never seen a cold produce those angry-looking pustules around his passenger's mouth and nose.

Ninety miles down the metalled road, the driver turned off, passing between rusty coils of barbed wire. Beyond, a disused guard hut was slowly being reclaimed by the desert. In its lee was a Bedouin tent and a herd of goats. The shepherd seated in the tent's opening waved them on with his Kalashnikov. Then he reached for a field telephone and spoke briefly.

Desperately ill though he felt, the bagman managed a smile as the Jeep bounced over the bleak landscape. He was home.

The hut was a reminder of those days when Libya had been a monarchy in the fifties, and the King had allowed the Americans to keep bomber bases in this desert.

When Gaddafi deposed the King, he had expelled the Americans and closed down all the bases except one. This he had converted into a training camp for generations of terrorists. Arafat, Nidal and Carlos had all operated from here until they had fallen out with the mercurial Colonel. In the aftermath of the war in the Gulf, the Supreme Leader who had replaced Gaddafi had announced Libya would no longer provide a home for any group. The international press had been invited to witness the expulsion of the PLO from Libya.

A month later, when the Arab world had turned its back on Raza after his crushing failures in London and Berlin, and he had been forced to flee from Iraq when Saddam Hussein could no longer protect him, the Supreme Leader had provided Raza with this perfect hiding place.

Even a low-flying aircraft would not spot the cleverly concealed bunkers and billets built into the sand dunes. All that was visible was a modest-sized villa that would be dismissed as the desert retreat of some functionary in Tripoli. There were any number of such structures dotting the landscape, where men who had been raised in the sands came back from the city to remember their roots.

During the past year the bagman had watched thousands of recruits being trained to the highest standards, and sent back to the refugee camps to wait. In between, Raza had gone on mysterious trips. After the last one he had briefed the bagman to go to China.

The Jeep continued across the vast, arid landscape towards the villa. The sight of the low, white-walled building made the bagman stir uneasily. Suppose someone in the safe house had seen him open the cylinder and informed Raza . . . But he'd made sure that was not possible. The bagman decided it was this sickness that made him so jumpy.

The *Feydeheen* in the guard post in front of the villa studied the bagman with the intensity that comes from uneventful sentry duty.

Coughing, and feeling so weak he could barely hold the briefcase, the bagman walked into the building. An aide dressed in battle fatigues met him. The man had sad eyes and a habit of unconsciously tugging his straggly beard.

The bagman told him what had happened in China. From time to time he was wracked by raw, deep coughs. When the bagman had completed his report, the aide looked at him solicitously.

'You are sick. Go to the pharmacy.'

The bagman shook his head. 'It is nothing.'

The aide took the bag, asking for the key to open it. He walked down a corridor, knocked on a door, paused for a moment and then went into the room.

The bagman leaned against a wall. Even here, in the cool of the building, he felt feverish. He touched his face. The pustules seemed bigger. Something in the cylinder had made him feel like this. He felt suddenly frightened.

The door opened and the aide emerged. In his hand he carried a Taurus 9-mm automatic.

'Is everything okay?' the bagman asked.

'Yes.'

The bagman forced a smile. His flagrant disobedience had gone undetected. But he felt worse.

'Come, let us go outside,' said the aide.

'Perhaps I should go to the pharmacy.'

The aide shook his head. 'It is only a cold. You said so yourself.'

They walked into the compound. At this hour of the day, noon, it was all but deserted because of the heat. The bagman shivered.

'Come, let us walk this way.' The aide motioned towards a training range. It was close to the latrine pits. A new bout of coughing convulsed the bagman.

The aide walked a pace behind, oblivious of the bagman's

suffering or the stench. They walked in silence until they reached the pits.

'Why did you open the cylinder?' asked the aide in the same caring voice he'd first used to suggest the bagman went to the pharmacy.

The bagman turned, shaking his head. 'You are mistaken. I would never do that.' Usually he was an excellent liar.

The aide looked sad, like a brother disappointed in a sibling. 'But you did. That is why you are sick.'

He casually thumbed the slide release on the gun, and the heavy sheath of metal slid forward. He squeezed the trigger. The force of the blast drove the bagman back several feet, to the edge of the pits. The aide used his combat boots to kick the corpse into the sewage. Tugging at his beard, he walked slowly back to the villa.

From a window Raza watched the body slowly sink from sight, knowing the Anthrax-B-C he possessed had claimed its first victim.

The gunshots had carried clearly to the bunker behind the villa. Two hours later their effect continued to make Faruk Kadumi's hands tremble as he waited to retrieve the cylinder from the deepfreeze chest.

For someone who had lately seen so much, he had never become reconciled to violent death. Somehow, it offended against all he had been trained to do.

He also accepted that those who had known him at the height of his success would now hardly recognise him as the slim, svelte surgeon who had operated on Europe's rich and famous. His face was coarsened and bloated, the once finely shaped nose lumped and twisted slightly, the result of a recent driving accident. His body had an unhealthy toad-like shape, which the cumbersome anti-contamination suit emphasised.

Designed to protect against biological and chemical agents, the suit's charcoal-coated cloth chafed his skin, and the gloves and foot coverings made it difficult to walk and handle anything.

The hood and respirator, with its gelatine filters, made him feel nauseous and dizzy.

He had found he could not remain in the suit for longer than an hour. After each practice run he'd taken a whiff of ether from the hip flask he constantly carried with him. He still found sniffing both relaxed and excited him. He also knew he was powerless to kick a habit that had ended his illustrious career.

He'd been hooked, of course, long before that day he'd killed a patient he'd operated on after sniffing. Because of who he was, colleagues had covered up – but had insisted he must retire. He had not yet been forty. Within a year his childless marriage was over and he had returned to Algiers, embittered against his profession and France. In Algiers he'd found ready work treating the city's criminals. His fame spread and soon he was operating on Raza's *Feydeheen* wounded on missions.

Raza had paid his exorbitant fees, and Faruk Kadumi was now a millionaire in any currency. But he knew he was as hopelessly tied to Raza as he was to his addiction. Raza had told him he could have anything – so long as he continued to obey.

Faruk Kadumi's Faustian bargain had brought him to the bunker to prepare a sample of the Anthrax-B-C.

As he had once done for any particularly difficult and dangerous surgical procedure, he had prepared carefully, immersing himself in the literature Raza had provided on biological weapons. Faruk Kadumi had paid special attention to the top-secret manual smuggled out of China. It had been vital in creating the conditions in which he could work safely.

A completely sterile laboratory and decontamination chamber had been built at one end of the bunker. Access was through airlocked doors. Inside, the lab's air supply was filtered. The lab was equipped like those at the State Research Institute at Chengdu that handled Anthrax-B-C.

In the event of an emergency, there was a built-in self-destruct system. Several thousand gallons of petrol were stored in a tank above the lab's false ceiling. At the press of a button the ceiling would collapse, releasing the fuel. Gas jets built into the wall would automatically ignite and the lab would become an instant fireball. The manual had explained only a temperature in excess of 1,000 degrees Celsius was capable of destroying Anthrax-B-C.

The image of being incinerated made Faruk Kadumi once more sweat as soon as he put on the hood. The pungent aroma from the respirator's filters began to fill his nose and mouth.

Forcing himself to ignore the several destruct buttons

positioned within easy reach of the walls, Faruk Kadumi cast his eye over the stainless-steel lab table in the centre of the room.

He had laid out his instruments the same neat way he would for any operation.

At the far end of the table were two vials filled with perfume. Standing in neat rows were small empty bottles.

Faruk Kadumi picked one up in his heavy gloved hand. He'd broken several before he'd mastered the knack of doing so.

He brought it close to his visor. The bottle was a striking shape, octagonal and made of dark green glass. It bore an elegantly scripted label:

Grecian Nights
A Perfume for Tomorrow

Raza had told him he had spent weeks rejecting designs before he was satisfied. The bottles had been specially blown in Hong Kong. Raza had paid over the odds. But the glassmaker had not lived to enjoy his profiteering. The local cartel had killed him on Raza's orders.

Faruk Kadumi remembered how Raza had relished telling the story. He felt the sweat seeping from his body.

He looked at the wall clock. It was time to open the deepfreeze chest standing beside the table.

There was a hiss as the airlock disengaged and the door opened. Into the room came three women. They were all dressed in anticontamination suits.

The younger two had struck him as more of the serious and totally committed women drawn to Raza. All Faruk Kadumi had been told was that they were Greek.

With them was Lila. Even now she was striking. Her thick, red hair cascaded around her face behind the visor and despite the cumbersome suit she moved with easy grace.

This past week she had spent most of her time with Raza in the well-equipped broadcast studio at the far end of the bunker.

Faruk Kadumi had known better than to ask what they had been doing. Raza's fury at being questioned was legendary.

After sealing the airlock, Lila turned to the Greek girls.

'Watch carefully. Anything you don't understand, ask.'

The microphone built into her respirator metalicised her voice. Lila turned to Faruk Kadumi.

'Doctor, you can begin.'

He motioned for them to stand on the opposite side of the table. His mike made his swallowing sound like a burp.

'I would like to start with a reminder. We are dealing here with the ultimate weapon. Cheap to produce. Not needing complicated dispensing techniques or equipment. And guaranteed to work.'

He saw he had their attention, the way he had once held medical students in thrall.

'What we have here is a refinement of thousands of years of man's learning how to harness the forces of Nature for his own end. Three thousand years ago our ancestors introduced diseased carcasses into the water supply of their enemies. Later they deliberately infected their prisoners with the plague and drove them in among the enemy. The Spartans did that when they laid siege to Athens. Ten thousand a day died in the city. Since then more people have been killed by such means than any other. The Black Death killed a thousand times more people in Medieval Europe than died at Hiroshima. Man has come a long way, and today there are over two hundred diseases which can kill or incapacitate by biological attack –'

'Doctor, can you move on?' Lila interrupted brusquely.

Faruk Kadumi bit back his anger. Not for the first time had Lila reminded him of her power as one of Raza's longest-serving aides. He smiled weakly behind his visor.

'Raza wishes you to be absolutely clear of the power of the weapon he has entrusted to you. So you will listen to what I have to say. And that includes you, Lila.'

'Doctor, let's not waste time arguing!' said Lila.

'Very well. Anthrax-B-C has been designed to kill by skin contact, inhalation or in water. In each case, once inside the body the spores produce a high temperature, throat swelling, a severe cough, severe respiratory problems and internal damage. The fever inflames the brain and leads to raving and hallucinating. At death, corpses have a blackened appearance, like the Black Death –'

'Get on with it, doctor,' snapped Lila. 'Just tell us the best way to distribute the stuff.'

Her sudden explosive fury startled the Greeks and made Faruk Kadumi blanch.

He picked up a bottle. 'One way would be to introduce it into an underground transport system, such as the Tube in London or the Metro in Paris. The CIA showed it could be done when they introduced a harmless agent into the air-conditioning system of the New York subway a few years ago. If it had been the real thing, up to a million people could have been infected.'

Faruk Kadumi was gratified to hear the gasps from the Greeks.

'What precautions would we have to take when releasing the bottles?' asked the shorter of the Greek girls.

Faruk Kadumi sighed. Raza had ordered him to play down the risks with dissemination.

'You would need to wear some sort of face covering and gloves.'

Lila spoke. 'How about using a small electrical timer that would break the bottle after it was in place?'

Faruk Kadumi nodded. 'That would certainly work, but it would be less effective. Breaking the bottle would release all the contents at once. The most effective way is to release it slowly.'

'What about in water?' asked Lila quickly.

Faruk Kadumi looked at the bottle. 'Dropped in a small reservoir, this would be lethal.'

'Okay, we've got the message. Let's get on,' said Lila crisply.

Faruk Kadumi flushed inside his hood.

He put down the bottle, turned and shuffled to the ice chest. Removing the cylinder, he placed it on the table. He unscrewed the cap and the metal separated. The frozen Anthrax-B-C gleamed in the shadowless overhead lights.

He deliberately waited before continuing. 'At forty degrees below freezing the anthrax spore is dormant. Unlike other agents it can be repeatedly thawed and frozen without losing any of its potency. In theory you could go on doing that for a hundred years. The important thing to remember is that a fraction of a degree above zero, the anthrax becomes lethal. And it gives no warning it is active. Detection and a positive identification require appreciable time and very expert clinical diagnosis. It is designed so that doctors would diagnose its effects as pneumonia. By the time they have realised their mistake, their patients will be dead.'

'Doctor, will you start preparing a bottle? I have a plane to catch,' said Lila.

Faruk Kadumi's mouth tightened. Clammy rivulets of sweat were now running down his body. The sooner he finished, the sooner he could be out of this suffocating suit. He picked up some surgical tongs and carefully removed the frozen shape from the cylinder. He placed it between two steel blocks fixed to the table and fitted with tightening screws. Slowly he tightened the screws until the shape was held firmly with the minimum pressure to avoid it breaking.

Faruk Kadumi spoke without looking at anyone. 'The technology is simple. What is important is never to rush.'

He reached for a surgeon's high-speed electric saw. A low whine filled the air as he moved the saw steadily along the top of the shape to cut a thin, unbroken slice. He switched off the saw and picked up a pair of spatulas, inserting the broad steel blades under the slice and removing it to a cutting board.

Faruk Kadumi glanced at the Greeks. Both were staring wide-eyed at the sliver.

He picked up a long-bladed scalpel and cut the slice into equal segments. Using a pair of tweezers he dropped the sliver into the perfume bottle. In moments he had transferred all the segments.

Holding the first bottle firmly in his hand Faruk Kadumi turned to a vat.

'Here, hold this,' he said, giving the bottle to Lila.

She gripped it between her padded fingers.

Faruk Kadumi picked up a syringe and began to fill it from the vat. The perfume was a pale honey colour and oily-looking.

'It's a clove and aloe base,' he explained. 'The requisite perfume smell remains even when the anthrax is diluted.'

'Diluted?' asked the taller Greek girl.

Faruk Kadumi turned from the vat with the full syringe.

'When mixed with a standard saline solution, the kind you can get from any medical supplier, Anthrax-B-C retains eighty per cent of its original potency.'

He nodded towards the bottle in Lila's hand.

'You could dilute its contents to produce forty, maybe fifty bottles. Each of those bottles would still have a capability of killing several hundred people. In theory you could continue to dilute and know the guaranteed effects would still be to produce widespread serious illness. You will not need to do that, of course.

31

Long before then people will have understood the potency of this weapon.'

Faruk Kadumi began to fill the bottle with perfume.

The tall Greek broke the silence.

'Can this be transmitted from one person to another?'

He answered without taking his eyes off the bottle and syringe.

'No. It's not like the plague. You can't drop it into the sewers and hope the rats will do the job for you. It'll kill them before they could run the length of a drain. But unlike all other biological viruses, fungi and toxins, Anthrax-B-C does not remain active in the dead for more than twenty-four hours. In that time it can, under certain circumstances, be passed on.'

He put the empty syringe on the table.

'What circumstances?' asked the shorter Greek.

Faruk Kadumi shrugged. 'One you are not likely to encounter – an autopsy. If someone came into contact with infected blood or body fluid in that twenty-four-hour period, it could be fatal. But primarily, Anthrax-B-C is designed for battlefield conditions – fast-acting over a limited time.'

He took the bottle from Lila, corked and then sealed it by placing the bottle neck in a mould of melted red wax.

Faruk Kadumi handed the bottle back to Lila. While the Greeks continued to watch he began to cut a second slice.

Lila walked to the hatch leading to the small decontamination chamber. She spun the steel wheel that opened the hatch, stepped into the airlock and closed the door behind her, turning another wheel to lock it securely. Using the same method, she opened the door into the chamber.

Putting the bottle on a shelf, she stripped out of her suit. She wore only panties. Removing these, she placed them with the suit on a chute and pulled a lever on the wall. A panel opened in the wall into which the chute slid. Lila caught a blast of heat before the panel closed, consigning the clothes to the electrical furnace buried in the sand behind the bunker.

Then she repeatedly showered and scoured herself with a solution of fuller's earth, a clay-based decontamination powder. Afterwards she dried herself under a powerful blow-drier set in the ceiling.

Holding the bottle, she opened the airlock on the other side of the chamber and entered a changing-room. She dressed in the clothes she had chosen for her long journey – jeans, hand-tooled calf-fitting boots and a blouse that emphasised her huge pointed breasts and narrow boyish hips. She studied herself quickly in the wall mirror. Her skin had the lustre of health and youth. No one would believe she was a year from her fortieth birthday.

She put on the distinctive denim jacket with its multiplicity of pockets for exposed film, a light meter and all the other accoutrements of a professional photographer. She checked an inside pocket for the American passport, *Time* ID card, and the letter on the magazine's notepaper stating she was a freelance on assignment. The documents had been provided by the cabal at Raza's request.

Stashing the bottle in the bag filled with cameras, Lila walked out of the room.

The Jeep that had brought the bagman was waiting outside. The driver had stowed in the back the travel holdall she had packed earlier. When he attempted to take the bag and place it beside the holdall, she shook her head. Instead she carefully placed the bag beside her on the front seat.

From the darkness of the villa's verandah a voice softly called in Arabic.

'Good luck, Lila. I am depending on you.'

She smiled. Raza never forgot the importance of such reminders.

'You may depend on me,' she called out, nudging the driver with her elbow.

The Jeep headed out across the desert. It seemed to be filling with its own sounds as it cooled. Then Lila realised she was listening to the beat of her own heart.

3

Morton saw Walter Bitburg had not managed the usual mastery over his eyes. Grey, like everything else about Mossad's Director, they had started to carom soon after Morton came into this windowless room adjoining Bitburg's office.

That was like a rich man's library, walled with leather-tooled books, and dominated by a seventeenth-century desk an earlier Bitburg had fled with from Germany the year Hitler came to power. This small cheerless room with its matching grey walls and ceiling, grey metal table, around which three men now sat, and chairs, was known as Bitburg's Bunker.

The Director's eyes reminded Morton of balls being repeatedly struck by a cue in Bitburg's head. What else was going on in there, going round and round? Bitburg's way was to keep everything in separate compartments, each labelled with the amount of proof they contained. When Bitburg thought there wasn't sufficient, his eyes led a life of their own. They continued to carom as Morton explained.

'When I got back to Bangkok, all traces of the Arabs had been removed, Walter. Hotel registrations, airline bookings. Their names had even been wiped off the Immigration computers. Only the cabal could do that. And those mullahs would only do so if it was important.'

Bitburg leaned forward, the light from the neon strip catching his thick glasses.

'And the bank? Any proof it actually paid over two million dollars?'

Morton showed neither impatience nor irritation. 'I saw the man count the money.'

34

'Surely not the whole amount? That would have taken an hour.'

Morton wondered if Bitburg's glasses were to protect his eyes from reality as well as to see better. 'I wouldn't know, Walter. I've never counted a couple of million dollars.'

The silence returned, creating more than distance between them. It was something wider and deeper.

'What I'm trying to establish, David, is supportive evidence. Something tangible. Which I fear is lacking here.'

Morton continued staring at Bitburg, remembering again what had happened at the clearing, each distinct, detachable, unforgettable moment.

Bitburg turned the Chinese ID cards over, inspecting them carefully. 'If I understand, everything you are suggesting flows from these?'

'It's more than a suggestion, Walter.'

Bitburg put the cards on the table. 'Correct me if I am wrong, David. When you first brought Chengdu to our attention, I recall you made a particular point that the plant was actually close to the route China's own drug smugglers use to run in and out of the Golden Triangle. And that there were at least two or three cocaine-processing labs operating in the vicinity of the plant itself. Is my memory right, David?'

'There are now four labs.'

Bitburg pursed his lips. 'Four? I see.'

He glanced quickly at the cards. 'I also recall your saying some of the people at Chengdu could be involved in a little moonlighting. Lending their skills to those labs.'

'Yes. But not this time.'

Bitburg once more picked up the cards. 'All these IDs prove is that the two men worked at the plant. Nothing to show they smuggled anything out. Or that the other man even worked there. And he could have been a drug smuggler. He could have been anybody. And there's nothing to show this has anything to do with Raza.'

'I heard one of them, Walter, just before those damned headphones blew up on me.'

Bitburg glanced at the papers before him. His voice was dry and precise when he looked up.

'Yes. I've registered my disappointment with Research and

35

Development. But these things happen, I suppose, when people are too eager to prove something works.'

His eyes resumed caroming. 'What you heard, David, was " —za". That's what your own report says, " —za". That could have been a reference to Gaza. There are a hundred Arab names and places which end in " —za". Your father will tell you that.'

Bitburg lowered his eyes, as if the papers would confirm all this.

Morton continued to look at the Director's bowed head. In a few days' time it would be Steve's seventieth birthday. He'd surprise him by turning up, please him with the gift he'd bought. The last time he'd visited was the first anniversary of Ruth's death. After dinner Steve had sat in his armchair and said there was vengeance and revenge, that one was scripturally acceptable, the other not. Morton had let Steve cite the Law and the scholars, not wanting to argue that Raza did not operate by the rules of Maimonides or Rashi.

Bitburg looked up. ' "Za", David. That's all. It could refer to anybody, any place, any thing.'

'Is that what you really believe, Walter?' Morton asked softly, his eyes never leaving Bitburg. 'You think I don't know by now when it's Raza? That those Arabs were his people? You really think that?'

Bitburg put down the cards. 'But I need something more than these before I go to the Prime Minister.'

The third man at the table shrugged. Morton always liked the way Danny Nagier conveyed contempt by the merest lift of a shoulder.

'Our intercepts clearly show the two million went to the Thai bank, Director.' For a man who often spent his time listening to whispers, Danny had a loud voice.

Bitburg's eyes momentarily steadied. 'But your intercepts don't show what the money was for.'

'No, we don't *know*. But I'd bet on David having it right,' boomed Danny.

In the Yom Kippur War he'd lost his left eye, leaving the socket covered with a patch. It had done nothing to lessen his skills at directing all of Mossad's electronic surveillance. At fifty-five he still led from the front.

Danny turned to Morton. 'Any idea how much of this Anthrax-B-C could be in that bag?'

Morton had thought about little else since he'd left the clearing. 'I'd say around a pound. A couple of ounces, properly dispersed, could kill thousands. A pound, tens of thousands, maybe more.'

'My God!' said Danny.

Bitburg's eyes resumed caroming. 'But we don't *know*. That bag could have contained anything! The collective wisdom in the Intelligence community is that he's in no position to do anything spectacular. The business in London and Berlin has hurt him badly. The loss of his patron, Saddam, more so. If Raza's doing anything, it's probably protecting drug runners.' Bitburg sat back in his chair, looking from Morton to Danny, but never allowing his eyes to settle. He continued: 'The Americans, the Brits, everyone says the same thing. Raza's shot his bolt with those two failures. These mullahs, if they're only half as smart as you seem to think, won't want to put their money on Raza.'

Morton shook his head. 'He's a terrorist, Walter. He thrives on action. He guarantees escalation if his demands are not met. And he lives off unpleasant surprises. Everything I know about him says he's about to spring another one.'

'Proof, David – where's your proof? Show me that and I'll go to the Prime Minister.'

Danny gave another shrug. Morton folded his arms, watching Bitburg resume reading.

After Morton flew back to Tel Aviv from Bangkok, it had taken him a morning to write his report and go through the usual oral debriefing. The young lawyer from Operations Assessment had asked good questions.

She'd reminded him of Shola. Six months after Ruth's death, he'd gone looking for Raza's bomb makers in Beirut. Shola had been new to Operations Assessment and he'd pinpointed on a map for her the places where the terrorists worked. Mirage fighter-bombers had taken out the factories, while he'd taken Shola to dinner.

He'd discovered she, too, was a survivor of Stalin's pogroms. As simply as that it had begun.

Four months later they were married. He'd told himself it was the start of a new dawn. He'd truly believed that, just as he hadn't suspected anything was wrong until that day he'd come out of Iraq and found Shola gone, to her sister in New York. She'd left a note saying she couldn't take this life any longer. Six weeks later a lawyer in the Bronx wrote saying Shola wanted a divorce. He hadn't contested, just shipping everything she'd asked for. Twelve crates, one for each month they'd been together.

Bitburg looked up. 'There's really nothing here to make me change my view.'

'There's nothing more, Walter. Unless you want a blow-by-blow.'

'Thank you, no.'

Bitburg disliked details of violence; they jarred with all his fine theories of geo-politics.

The grey silence returned, matching Bitburg's dark grey banker's suit. He had become Director after another of those purges that periodically ran through Mossad. A real banker, Morton thought. Put it on paper. Plus a copy for file.

Bitburg cleared his throat; he suffered from summer colds. He looked at Morton.

'Correct me if I'm wrong but I've always understood that caught in time, anthrax can be successfully treated with penicillin?'

Morton's voice was measured and certain. 'The Chinese have made sure that Anthrax-B-C will not respond to any of the usual medical countermeasures. Atropine and pralidoxine would be totally useless – not that they offer much protection against any of the other biological weapons. But the only possible defence against Anthrax-B-C could be the new PEG-enzyme. It's a by-product of the present AIDS research. The theory is that for Anthrax-B-C it would have to be given in the first few hours of exposure to have a chance. Then massive doses at six-hourly intervals for the next forty-eight hours. Until it's tried, no one really knows. But I'm still recommending we get our labs to start producing the stuff in sufficient quantities. At least that way we'd have something ready. I'd also recommend we tell our allies to stockpile as well.'

Bitburg's eyes caromed as if he was going for a winning break. 'So what do we have? A drug that may or may not work? And expensive to produce – right?'

Morton's glance was as steady as his voice. 'Very expensive. And yes, no absolute guarantee it will do the job.'

Bitburg's voice was as thin as his hair. 'Yet you want everybody rushing to produce the stuff?'

'Because it's the only logical thing to do.'

'The only logical thing to do,' repeated Bitburg. 'Sometimes, David, I wish you wouldn't sound so English. Move away too far from your upbringing and faith, my father used to say, and you move away from what's important.'

'Going to Cambridge didn't make me less of a Jew, Walter. It just showed me that faith's not a prison.'

Bitburg smiled thinly. 'You argue like a Jesuit.'

'I hope I sound like someone who wants you to act on my recommendation.'

Bitburg looked down at the papers, his refuge. Danny turned to Morton.

'How long will it take to produce sufficient quantities?' he asked.

'Ten days if our labs work round the clock, Danny. That should provide enough for every man, woman and child in this country. I don't know how long it would need any of our allies to tool up.'

Bitburg raised his eyes. 'There's nothing here to justify that kind of extreme action. Making connections out of very little is one thing, but the pieces you've produced belong to different puzzles, David. Those that do fit together suggest you interrupted a drug deal in that clearing.'

Morton let the silence stretch before answering. 'Why not take it to Karshov. Let him decide, Walter.'

'The Prime Minister expects *me* to decide, David.'

The harsh overhead strip light emphasised the vein that had started to throb in Bitburg's forehead.

'Accepting you've overlooked nothing, what do we have? Three dead Arabs no one's going to mourn, but still a messy business. If the Chinese find out, it could rule out any hope of our achieving a détente with Beijing.'

A clock struck the half-hour in Bitburg's office. He'd been given the long-case to mark his sixtieth birthday. By then Bitburg was long embalmed in his own certainties.

The Director cleared his throat. 'And those children, was there no way to warn them?'

'No, Walter, there was not.'

'I see. Let's hope their deaths are not laid at our door. That would cause –'

'I didn't kill them, Walter.'

Danny broke the silence. 'One of those scientists at Chengdu could have been bribed, Director –'

'Why didn't your people pick up the bagman?' snapped Bitburg.

Danny shrugged. 'My people are good. But miracles they leave to God.'

'There were a hundred ways home for the bagman, Walter,' said Morton. 'There isn't a surveillance system that could cover them all. And Danny's right: almost certainly a scientist was bought.'

Bitburg's eyes suddenly steadied. '"Almost", David? But no proof, right?'

Morton stared at Bitburg, saying nothing.

The Director continued, his voice even thinner. 'To get that stuff out, a lot of people would need to have been bribed. And the chances of discovery would increase with each one. Chengdu, as I recall, has a high security rating.'

Morton breathed out slowly. 'Because of that, they wouldn't expect anyone to try and break it. Those two guards would be all that scientist would have needed. And he'd take them along to make sure Raza's people played fair and square.'

'Pure speculation. But given you are determined to reject a drug connection, let me give you something to think about, David. We all know the Chinese are once more doing a thriving business as armourer to the Middle East. Those Arabs could have been a weapons paymaster and escort from Libya or Syria.'

'I can't give you the proof you need, Walter, for sure. But if there's one thing I've learned in this business it is to trust my own gut feeling. And that tells me Raza could have a quantity of Anthrax-B-C.'

Bitburg pounced. '"Could have", David? You expect me to go to the Prime Minister and say Raza "could have" this stuff? And would he please ring up Washington and London and any-where else where he might get a hearing and say, "Excuse me, we *could have* a terrorist who *could have* this new kind of anthrax"? Men have been sent to the Negev for less. I need a lot more than that, David, a *lot* more. You know – we *all* know – our relationship with our allies is not what it used to be. They didn't listen to us when we warned about Saddam Hussein before he walked into Kuwait. Then, we gave them chapter and verse. Now you expect them to listen just because of . . . a gut feeling?'

'Walter, the political end I leave to you and the Prime Minister. All I know is any threat by Raza to use anthrax would not be against just us. The whole world would be at risk.'

'Would you like to expand?'

For a long moment Morton remained silent. Then in a quiet voice he began. 'When that old madman Khomeini was ranting and raving, he wanted Iran to fight the world. But after what happened to Saddam, Khomeini's successors learned a lesson. The way to win was not by head-on confrontation, but through surrogates.'

Morton looked at Danny. 'Two of those intercepts from Lebanon were calls to Teheran, right?'

'Right. To the mullah, Ali Akbar Muzwaz. To arrange for the two million dollars to go to Bangkok,' replied Danny.

Morton turned back to Bitburg. 'When I was last in Teheran, Muzwaz was already firmly established as leader of the cabal. Khomeini's old war chest for financing trouble was in their control. There could be a hundred million dollars there. It's on deposit in half the banks in Geneva. The interest alone could finance a lot of problems, for sure. And you know how hard it is to get anything out of the Swiss, Walter, let alone agree now to freeze that money.'

Bitburg's quick, reluctant nod confirmed the machinations of a world he knew well.

Morton continued. 'The virulent fundamentalists haven't magically gone away. They've just learned not to shout so crazily, that softly-softly works as well. Of course, when we say that in Washington or London, let alone Paris, we are accused of being hardliners.'

Danny nodded vigorously. Morton continued, 'The cabal know how to exploit this. How to tap a couple of hundred million minds. All of whom believe their leader, their Imam, has been waiting in the desert for several hundred years for the right moment to launch his version of Islamic purity. The mullahs preach he can only do so if there is a bloodbath. That before the

Imam can return, Israel *must* be destroyed. That the last Jew must be violently removed from this land. But since the Gulf War, the mullahs also know the West would never allow that. So the cabal need to recruit someone to frighten the West so badly that even the United States will try and persuade us to voluntarily give up this land. My gut tells me the mullahs have turned to Raza.'

'What does he get?' Danny's voice was a whisper.

'Respectability, for sure. Justification for his terrorism. Killing in the name of the Prophet sanctifies it. He can present himself as a Saladin, all the heroes of the Koran rolled into one. Raza's the archetypal thug posing as the ultimate patriot.'

Bitburg took longer than usual to clear his throat. 'An instructive reminder. But let's get back to this China business. All I know is that the CIA, the Germans and the British, who are all thick on the ground in China, have assured me they have not heard a single whisper that any anthrax has come out of Chengdu. And, despite their best efforts, they have also failed to trace this bagman.' He picked up a paper. 'The CIA sent a team at my specific request to the clearing. They found nothing. Not even a spent bullet.'

'Why did you ask the CIA to get involved?' Morton's voice was dangerously calm.

'Because they were the nearest. Because I decided to –'

'You don't do that, Walter. Ever. You don't do anything involving *my* work without first checking with *me*.'

Eyes fixed on Bitburg, Morton sat perfectly still.

When Mossad had come head-hunting in his last year at Cambridge, he had responded to the appeal to patriotism, the mystique surrounding the agency and the knowledge its intelligence was more detailed, wide-ranging and up-to-date than anyone else's. But he'd also said he didn't want a desk job. The recruiter had replied, we'll talk when you've proven yourself.

Morton had done so in all those places where Israel's interests were threatened. Finally he'd been offered a teaching post, to spot talent, and the chance to run Operations. He accepted both on condition he didn't answer to anyone. A tough and pragmatic predecessor of Karshov's agreed. Successive Prime Ministers went on doing so.

Bitburg finally forced a weak smile. 'No offence intended, David.'

Danny shrugged.

Morton suddenly felt tired – tired and wasted. He wanted an end to this nonsense.

'The CIA should know that Raza's a tidy housekeeper, Walter. His local people would have done the kind of clean-up we do.'

'Very well. I will send your report to the Prime Minister. But I will also recommend we do nothing until we have more evidence.'

Morton pushed back his chair and stood up. Bitburg had made another of his banker's decisions. Without another word he walked from the grey room. It was time to go and see The Syrian.

4

The helicopter known as Morton's Chariot flew so low it left a swirl of desert dust in its wake.

Morton hoped that at this height, Jordanian and Iraqi radar scanners would dismiss the Long-Ranger as another herd of camels racing from one strip of grazing to another.

The chopper was coated with radar-deflecting paint, and its heavy armaments replaced with extra fuel tanks for the long journey into the northern vastness of Iraq. The Long-Ranger's only protection were the Eagles and Tornadoes. Morton had glimpsed their contra-trails as they rode six miles above. But the escort would turn back when the Long-Ranger reached the Dead Mountains. There was no way for them to protect Morton's Chariot from then on.

Morton continued to stare out of the cabin window, ignoring the professional crosstalk from the flight deck in his headset. The two pilots had barely spoken to him since lifting off from their base north of Tel Aviv. The city had been blanketed in a grey haze. People said it was caused by a mix of car exhaust and sea ozone. He knew better. The noxious cloud was a combination of wasted breath expended on the Bitburgs of this world.

Morton wasn't a Zionist, God knows. He hadn't found his own truth by destroying other people's, or by clinging to blind faith. Those four years at Cambridge had shown him there was something more important than that: they had taught him the meaning of real freedom. And that included the right to live and let live.

He could have gone over Bitburg's head directly to the Prime

Minister. Doing so would risk plunging Mossad once more into factions. Bitburg had his supporters – that legion who only returned calls when they had ensured they were covered by a memo – and they would fight to protect one of their own.

But Bitburg was right when he'd said Israel's relations with the West were at a nadir. Despite all that had happened in the Gulf, the West clung to the belief it was possible to co-exist with militant Islam.

When George Bush and John Major had been in office, they'd at least listened. But an Arabist now sat in Downing Street and, in the White House, other Arabists dominated the present incumbent's strategy and policy. Their bottom line was that Islam was to be accommodated. In the meantime Israel shouldn't rock the boat. The caveat was that Mossad should keep its hands off the alarm button.

Those times when there'd been no alternative but to press it, his peers in the West had asked for evidence. They'd done so before Lockerbie, before all the other outrages he'd warned would happen. Afterwards, they'd said of course they would have acted – if there'd been proof. Every Intelligence service had its Bitburg.

Morton had little doubt what would happen if the West was warned about Raza. There'd be a flurry of meetings. Somebody would be deputised to go to the Chinese. The Chinese would deny they ever made the stuff. They denied everything as a matter of policy. There'd be a final meeting. Recommendation: action must wait for certainty. The Bitburg solution.

Forty minutes after entering Iraqi air space, the Long-Ranger passed over the first foothills. Beyond, running the width of the horizon, reared the granite of the Dead Mountains, their jagged peaks rising one above the other without symmetry or beauty, as if God had started to form them and then moved on to create something more worthwhile. The mountains were dark and forbidding in the hot afternoon sun.

'Our air cover's heading for home,' came the pilot's voice in Morton's ears.

He stood up and poked his head into the flight deck. On the radar the last of the blips were peeling off. In moments the screen was empty.

'They'll be back for us in a couple of hours,' promised Morton into his microphone. There was always a feeling of anxiety at a time like this, knowing help was no longer a minute's flying time away.

'Let's hope the weather holds,' said the co-pilot, peering at his radar. 'There's a disturbance a couple of hundred miles ahead. Looks like the makings of a helluva storm.'

Morton craned his head. The sky was clear, but its intense blue was being steadily distilled into white, in places streaked with yellow. Somewhere beyond the mountains the wind had become sufficiently strong to have funnelled up huge swathes of sand and spread them across the heavens.

'The mountains could deflect it coming our way,' said the pilot.

'Hope so,' said the co-pilot. 'I once got caught in a whirler in the Sinai –'

'Any sign of the gorge?' cut in Morton brusquely. This wasn't the time for horror stories.

The co-pilot turned back to the map on his knee.

Beyond the gorge The Syrian would be waiting. He never chose the same meeting place twice. But the arrangements were always the same. The day before a scheduled contact, The Syrian placed a classified ad containing a verse of poetry in the Egyptian daily, *Al-Ahram*. The verse that had brought Morton to the Dead Mountains referred to the suffering of the people.

This inhospitable area of waterless gullies and deep fissures had witnessed its share. The first King of Babylon had gone mad here. The Philistines, Phoenicians and Romans had all seen their armies founder in this parched, burning land. Driven from their Promised Land, Morton's own people had wandered here, dying in their thousands from thirst and starvation. And, centuries later, the Crusaders had failed to hold this no man's land against the lifeless, yet implacable stone.

The Syrian had chosen one of their forts as the meeting point. It lay on the far side of the mountain range.

As they drew closer, Morton saw that the solid dark red of the granite was broken by gorges and defiles, dark, uninviting openings running back into the mountains.

'You're looking for a gully that leads up from a scree slope, maybe five hundred feet from ground level,' Morton reminded the crew.

The mountains had begun to cast long shadows, making it more difficult to spot the opening.

'Give me those co-ordinates again,' said the pilot.

Morton repeated the instructions The Syrian had given. The pilot checked them against the ones he had earlier fed into the navigational system. The Long-Ranger changed course and began to traverse the rock face.

'There,' Morton called out. 'On your left!'

The Long-Ranger crabbed towards a spill of boulders and sand. The mountains were close enough to block out the sky.

'That's it,' confirmed the pilot.

Ahead was a break in the rock face that began at the bottom of scree. The opening was less than a hundred feet wide. The clearance for the Long-Ranger would be tight.

Morton grabbed a strut as the Long-Ranger entered the gorge. The rotors began to create air currents, which swirled from one side of the defile to the other. The pilot altered the pitch.

'Switching to sensors,' said the co-pilot.

From now on the helicopter would depend on the two black boxes fixed on either side of the fuselage to stay clear of the tall cliffs.

It was gloomy in the gorge. Morton sensed the tension in both men as they listened to the constant pinging of the echo returning from the rock, and watched the digital computer read off the clearance. Often it was no more than thirty feet as the gorge narrowed and twisted its way through the mountains. With each turn the light grew dimmer, the feeling of claustrophobia and imprisonment greater.

'We need lights,' said the co-pilot.

'No lights,' replied Morton. An Iraqi air patrol would spot them from miles away.

The engine's reverberation dislodged loose rocks and shale. On either side of the Long-Ranger, small avalanches slid down the gorge.

One medium-sized rock hits the rotors and it will be all over, thought Morton. He'd deliberately left no map reference back in Tel Aviv; a search party would not know where to begin.

'We're out of the gorge!' yelled the pilot. Ahead the granite rose unbroken and perpendicular.

'Take her down,' ordered Morton. 'The tunnel should be below us.'

When he'd briefed them on this part of the flight they'd looked at him, not quite believing. It was there again in the pilot's voice.

'We don't know how long this tunnel is, how wide it is, and whether it's obstruction-free, correct?'

'Correct,' answered Morton steadily.

'That's what I thought you said.' The pilot shook his head as the Long-Ranger began to descend.

'I heard you flew one of these at street level in and out of West Beirut. This'll be a piece of cake,' encouraged Morton.

'And I've heard about you, Colonel. Talk anybody into anything!'

'For sure.'

The Long-Ranger continued to drop.

'Three-hundred-feet ground clearance,' reported the co-pilot.

'Plenty of room,' insisted Morton. He'd detected the nervousness in the co-pilot. The kid couldn't be much more than twenty. When he'd been that age, Morton remembered, he'd led a platoon into the Golan Heights. That had also been scary. He reached forward and tapped the co-pilot's shoulder.

'Just watch your instruments and you'll be fine.'

'Yes, sir,' said the co-pilot.

Morton felt dwarfed by the immensity of the rock on all sides.

'Two-fifty.' The nervousness in the co-pilot's voice was more pronounced.

'Steady, son,' said Morton softly into his lip mike. 'You're doing fine.'

A living mass suddenly rose in front of the Long-Ranger. The co-pilot jerked his head back.

'Just bats,' said Morton reassuringly. The Syrian hadn't mentioned the bats. 'No problem.'

'Hope so, Colonel,' said the pilot quietly. 'We're down to twenty-feet tolerance on either side.'

'That's still plenty,' said Morton.

'Two hundred feet,' whispered the co-pilot.

'There! Straight ahead!' said Morton.

They had reached the mouth of the tunnel.

'Ease us close, then take a quick peek with your lights,' ordered Morton.

The pilot edged the Long-Ranger to the opening in the rock and switched on the powerful headlights.

'Almighty shit!' yelled the pilot. 'What the hell do we have –'

'Just more bats!' said Morton tightly.

The rat-like creatures clung to the roof and walls of the tunnel. Their hairless young were deposited on the floor, creating a writhing, heaving carpet of blind flesh. Great piles of droppings were dotted everywhere.

The helicopter began to fill with an almost overpowering stench. The crew's faces were turning sickly green in the instrument glow.

'We can't go in there!' croaked the co-pilot.

'Sure you can, son,' said Morton firmly. 'It looks worse than it is.'

The disturbed bats were swooping and diving at the Long-Ranger. One crashed against the windscreen. A dark red splodge ran down the glass.

'Set your wipers working,' ordered Morton.

Thousands of creatures hurled themselves against the Long-Ranger. The air filled with continuous, unearthly screaming. The windscreen was streaming with blood.

'They're moving back!' reported Morton. 'Move in!'

The bats were retreating, carrying their young with them. The glare of their eyes was like millions of tiny glowing coals.

The co-pilot looked tortured. 'Please, sir –'

'Shut up, son. Just do your job,' rasped Morton. He had not come this far to turn back.

'I'll need to keep on the lights –' the pilot began.

'For sure.'

The Long-Ranger entered the tunnel.

'Oh my God!' groaned the pilot.

Morton felt his skin creep. Millions of bat skulls and carcases were deposited on every ledge, nook and cranny. The floor was a thick carpet of crumbling bones, which were moving.

'Tarantulas!' screamed the co-pilot. 'The whole place is swarming with them!'

'They can't hurt you!' said Morton hoarsely.

Drawn to the surface by the lights, the bloated, black-bodied spiders stood in serried ranks. Long, jointed legs clicked against

49

each other and mandibles probed the air. They began to devour pieces of bat flesh that fell from the helicopter.

The creatures launched a new attack and were minced by the rotors.

'The crud's blocking our sensors, sir!'

'Increasing pitch to clear them,' said the pilot.

The Long-Ranger moved faster. The pinging resumed.

'You're doing fine,' yelled Morton.

The bats continued crashing against the Long-Ranger.

'Cut the lights!' ordered Morton. 'That'll reduce their panic. Just keep the beacon on!'

Only the revolving red glow of the navigation light filled the tunnel. The nightmarish screaming continued.

'Five foot portside,' cried out the co-pilot.

'Easy, son. We're almost there,' said Morton.

The Long-Ranger lurched and dropped a few feet.

'The rotors must be clogging!' screamed the co-pilot.

'I'm going to give her more pitch!' said the pilot.

The helicopter began to move faster, constantly buffeted by the bats.

'Look!' yelled Morton, pointing beyond the windscreen.

Ahead, brighter and steadier than the myriads of eyes all around them, was a pinprick of light.

'Go!' yelled Morton again.

With a surge of power the Long-Ranger forced its way through the bats and emerged from the tunnel.

'You want to curse me, curse me,' said Morton quietly.

The pilots looked at each other and said nothing.

In silence they flew another quarter of a mile down the gorge before it opened out on a rubble-strewn plain that stretched to the horizon. The Crusaders' fort stood at its edge.

The pilot let the Long-Ranger hover. 'There's no way we're going back that way.'

Morton nodded. 'We'll go back over the top. The Iraqis won't be expecting us to come from this direction. We'll be gone before they realise we're not one of them.'

He reached for binoculars in a rack behind the co-pilot and studied the fort. Constructed from stone hewn from the mountains, it blended into the landscape.

'Let's take a look,' he said.

The Long-Ranger began slowly to circle the fort, flying at rampart level. The roofs had long gone, but the walls remained immensely solid-looking. Its eastern parapets rose from the edge of an abyss. The crack looked as if it had been made when the earth had cooled, and was too wide for a horse to jump. The only access into the fort was a causeway, narrow enough for just one horse to cross at a time. Behind, the mountains provided a natural defensive barrier. Before gunpowder the fort would have been virtually impregnable.

'That storm's really brewing,' reported the co-pilot, turning from the radarscope. 'Less than a hundred miles out and tracking this way.'

'You'll be snug before she hits,' promised Morton.

'Where do you want me to put down?' asked the pilot when the Long-Ranger had completed its circling.

Morton pointed to the rear of the fort. 'There.'

Cut into the rock was a bower large enough to shelter a 747.

As they passed over the fort, Morton saw a camel tethered in one of the lower courtyards. Otherwise there was no sign of life.

The pilot drifted the Long-Ranger across the ground and in under the overhang. The bower's walls disappeared up into the mountain. When the rotors stopped, the silence was overpowering.

Morton looked at his watch. 'I'll need an hour.'

He turned and picked up his Uzi, slid open the cabin door and dropped to the ground.

The smell almost made him vomit. The Long-Ranger looked as if it had flown through an abattoir. Pieces of skin and gristle were stuck everywhere. Only the protective mesh had stopped the engines seizing. The underside of the helicopter was coated a greyish-white in which were fixed thousands of dead tarantulas.

Morton walked to the front of the Long-Ranger. The pilots hadn't moved, sitting slumped in their seats. Yet he couldn't let them relax. They would need to keep their adrenalin pumping for the return trip.

'You better start cleaning up,' he called out, walking out of the cave.

Across the black flintstone scree, the wall of the fort rose steep and unbroken, each stone worn smooth with wind and sun.

Morton glanced at the sky. The sickly pallor was deepening

as more sand was being sucked up. There, the wind would already be howling. But here, only the faintest breeze stirred the air.

He reached the fort. There was no sign of life; no face at the opening higher up the wall, from where the Crusaders had drawn up their ladders and rained down arrows and spears on attackers. The Syrian would have heard the helicopter. But he'd only show himself when he was certain Morton was alone.

Morton walked along the wall. It was as tall as Herod's Western Wall on Temple Mount in Jerusalem and constructed the same way: each massive block fitted together without a need for mortar. Steve had once said it was a construction technique as old as Israel.

Above, the sky was turning the colour of burnt custard. He looked back towards the Long-Ranger. An outcrop of scree blocked his view.

'Hello,' Morton shouted in Arabic.

There was no reply. He placed his mouth close to a crack in the stones and called again. The echo of his voice reverberated through the inner wall of the fort, then faded. The oppressive silence returned.

He turned a corner and came to an opening. There was fresh camel dung near the breach in the wall. He stepped through the gap into a courtyard.

The flagstones were each several feet square. The floor sloped upwards towards an arched opening. This must have been a storeroom of some sort.

Morton walked through the archway. Beyond was another flag-floored room, open to the sky. The air, which had been preternaturally still, was now stirring sufficiently to send an eddy of sand swirling across the flagstones. Above the ramparts, out across the plain, the sky was black and ugly.

The camel was in a third storeroom, tethered at its fet‐ locks.

Morton called again in Arabic. There was no reply. The camel moved uneasily and exposed its teeth to Morton as he moved to another arched opening. Beyond was a narrow passageway.

He almost didn't see the desert cobra. It was the colour of the stone and was coiled at the edge of a black rectangular hole in the floor. It reared with the speed of an express elevator, rising to the height of his face and swaying forward. Its tongue was flickering and a faint hiss, like steam being released, came from its throat.

Morton blew the snake's head off with a single shot. Still twitching, the cobra fell into the hole. He listened to its body scraping against the sides of the cistern. Then came a distant splash as the snake reached the water level of one of the natural wells that had supplied the fort.

Morton continued to climb and reached a walkway. Steps led to the crenellated top of the fort. At regular intervals there were narrow openings for bowmen.

Ahead was a doorway larger and more imposing than the others. It was the entrance to a narthex, the lobby where the Crusaders had left their weapons before going into the chancel proper.

Morton walked into the vestibule, pausing to look at the carvings in the stone, which had survived a thousand and more years. There were lions and angels and palm trees and robed figures with hands crossed on chest or entwined in prayer. And everywhere Christ: Christ at Gethsemane, Christ at Calvary, Christ risen.

Beyond, just inside the nave, stood The Syrian. He wore the flowing robes of a desert prince. A burnous rested squarely on his head, the white cloth draped around his face.

'Hello, Morton. Glad you could make it.'

The Syrian's voice was surprisingly soft for such a large man. Not even the folds of his robe could conceal the massive muscular frame. As a student, he had boxed middleweight for Yale. In the intervening years his English had remained almost accent free.

Morton walked forward. 'You choose the most unexpected places to meet, for sure.'

The Syrian smiled. 'No one would look for a Jew or a Moslem here.'

'Except a snake.' Morton told him about the cobra.

The Syrian produced from inside his robe a curved-handled knife.

'I prefer this.' He put the knife back inside the robe.

Morton went into the nave. The remains of the roof littered the marble floor. The niches for the incense burners were thick with sand. Only the plinth of the altar remained. Above it was a tall narrow window opening, flanked on either side by wall carvings of Christ and the Madonna, and Christ on the Cross.

Morton suddenly felt an intruder in this atmosphere of cold piety.

'You parked your helicopter well,' said The Syrian. 'The *shua* will be here shortly.' He used the Bedouin slang word for a sandstorm.

Morton nodded. Beyond the narrow window the sky was spotted a dark red, like wine, on the underside of the unbroken blanket of cloud.

'Come,' said The Syrian. 'This is the best place to shelter.'

He walked back into the narthex and squatted with his back between a Christ figure and a pair of lions rampant. He produced a cigar from inside his robe and busied himself lighting it.

Morton sat beside him, waiting. Some things could not be rushed.

It was almost dark where they sat. A gust of wind made the cigar glow intensely and tiny flakes of leaf whirled off.

Morton laughed softly. 'You're wasting a good cigar. You'll not manage to smoke half before the *shua*.'

There was another movement against his cheek, a sudden ruffling of his hair. The cigar flared again, fanned by the wind.

'I know,' sighed The Syrian, drawing deeply. He studied Morton momentarily as he exhaled. 'The news is very bad. Raza has the Anthrax-B-C.'

A gust hit the ramparts and bounced off into the gloom.

'Where is Raza?'

The Syrian drew deeply again. 'No one knows except Ayatollah Muzwaz. And he is not saying.'

'When and where will Raza use the anthrax?'

The Syrian gently shook his head. 'It is not as simple as that, Morton.'

'So tell me.'

The Syrian took another puff and closed his eyes for a moment. Another gust of wind, like a sheet being snapped taut, hit the fort. He opened his eyes.

'The mullahs are divided among themselves over this matter. There are those who say Raza must use the weapon at once. That it would be a fitting way to launch jihad. Others say that after his failures in London and Berlin, he must prove himself. They say the weapon is too precious to risk mistakes.'

54

A longer gust filled the air with its low, insistent moaning. The first swirl of sand, which had been carried hundreds of miles, stung Morton's face.

'The cabal is like the *shua*,' continued The Syrian. 'It is very powerful. It has invested much in Raza. It expects much in return.'

'Where and how will Raza provide this proof?'

The Syrian sighed and removed the cigar from his mouth. Glowing ash was swirling around his head. He stubbed out the remaining two-thirds of the cigar on the ground.

'Raza will not say, Morton. Only that he will provide it very soon.'

'How soon?'

'No one knows.'

The wind had started to howl, piercing, intermittent shrieks that screamed against the fort. With them came a steady drumming sound.

'It comes,' shouted The Syrian huddling closer to Morton.

The air was filling with sand, grit and stones. A fully-fledged *shua* could carry small boulders.

'How long after he has proven himself before he uses the anthrax?' Morton yelled in The Syrian's ear.

'No more than seven days. The moderates in the cabal say a week is a reasonable time for the world to meet all their demands.'

The drumming was growing louder. The sky had gone, leaving only a stifling pitch-blackness. The Syrian wedged himself in a corner, pulling Morton with him.

'Are they asking for anything new?' yelled Morton.

'They've added pornography. They want a worldwide ban on it. Every type. Even the soft stuff.'

'A lot of people would support them on that.'

The Syrian pulled the edge of his burnous around his face.

'That's what they're counting on, Morton. They've decided to wrap up their more extreme demands, such as getting rid of Israel and having full control over the oil fields and mineral deposits in the Sahara and the Empty Quarter, with things that appear almost moderate. For instance, they also want a worldwide ban on drugs. And they want punishment to be under the sharia law.'

Morton shook his head. 'No one's going to agree to public beheadings in Times Square, or hands being severed under the Eiffel Tower or Big Ben.'

'Then the die-hards in the cabal will say there is no alternative, to make the world a better place, than to cleanse it with the purity of a jihad. They're convincing more and more of their people that their traditional values and faith are being destroyed. The mullahs say the West's materialism and erosion of moral values is all part of a plot to force these standards on the Arab world. To weaken the Arabs, like the Africans and Asians have been weakened.'

'There's a lot wrong in the West,' said Morton. 'But people can still pick and choose. These mullahs want to enforce their standards at the point of the sword! They're crazy!'

Morton turned his face into The Syrian's shoulder, pulling the tail of the burnous across his nose and mouth, and clenching his eyes.

'Tens of millions don't think so, Morton! They're just waiting for the touchpaper to be lit. And they'll be like this *shua*, un-stoppable!'

The grit tore at every exposed inch of their skin. It was like being flayed alive.

'If I can stop Raza –' began Morton.

Then further conversation was impossible as the full fury of the sandstorm burst against the fort with the impact of an artillery barrage. Great funnels of wind, near-solid with debris, drove through the narthex, burst against the walls of the nave and then exploded upwards to reform and attack once more.

A flash seared Morton's eyeballs, followed by a thunderous boom overhead. Another bolt of lightning zigged and zagged, momentarily giving the swirling debris a purplish hue. Another great roll of thunder echoed and re-echoed through the fort. They continued to be lashed in a sustained fury that blocked out the whole world. Each purplish flash of discharged electricity was followed by a boom as if the fort had been hit by a monstrous artillery shell.

Morton and The Syrian clung to each other as the maelstrom tried to pull them apart, as if to pick them up and hurl them from its path. It tore at their skin and clothes.

Then, suddenly, the wind dropped as the eye of the storm

arrived. The eerie silence was broken by a new sound: the half-scream, half-bellow of an animal in fear.

'My camel!' shouted The Syrian.

Before Morton could move, The Syrian was out of the narthex, running along the walkway and was gone.

Then the fury of the storm returned. Its violence seemed even greater. No matter which way he huddled, the driving particles found Morton, lashing him, trying to choke him, wanting to kill him somehow for daring to come here. He pushed his face hard against the wall, so that it was against the feet of a crucified Christ. In the dying minutes of the *shua* he fell asleep in that position, numbed by the sound of the wind and the thunder.

When he awoke, the night sky was filled with stars; a million sharp points of brilliance against a velvet blackness.

He struggled out of the sand which half-buried him. His mouth felt dry and swollen. Putting a finger to his lips he touched the sand-covered blisters.

Standing up, he felt tired almost beyond endurance. When he called out in Arabic for The Syrian, his voice sounded hoarse and he could hear the raw anxiety. He called again, and again there was no reply.

Crawling about on his knees, he found the Uzi, buried under the sand. He picked it up and checked the mechanism. It worked.

The star light was sufficiently good to guide him down through the fort. From time to time he continued to call for The Syrian. There was still no answer.

Morton reached the passageway where he had killed the snake. In the renewed force of the storm, The Syrian had fallen into the cistern. His neck had been broken and twisted so that the head was facing backwards. The Syrian stared wide-eyed and sightless, a look of stunned surprise on his face. His jaw resting on the edge of the hole was all that stopped his body falling into the cistern.

Morton knelt and gripped the head with both hands and gently lifted The Syrian. Then he let go. The body disappeared from sight, bouncing against the sides of the well before hitting the water with a splash not much louder than the snake had made.

Reaching the storeroom, Morton untethered the camel, led him down out of the fort, and then released him. Almost certainly a passing Bedouin drover would find the beast and ask no questions why Allah had been so generous.

Morton could see the pilots standing in the mouth of the bower. Behind them the Long-Ranger stood intact. He called softly in Hebrew if everything was all right. They replied it was.

Those were the only words exchanged between them on the journey home.

5

It was the darkest of all hours in the Libyan desert. The last of
the stars had gone, the first grey light yet to ooze over the
horizon.

The blackness pressed down, thick and icy cold, over Nadine's
head. The Bedouin called this the time of the dead, when the
spirits still spread their night-time fears before returning to their
tombs beneath the sand. She knew the desert intimately, the way
she had once known her mother, the way Raza knew her.

She sensed his presence. He would be standing alone, coiled
and tense, like a desert leopard come to point, his head, which
seemed carved from granite, tilted slightly forward to listen better, his coal-black eyes half-closed to see what no one else could.
His energy radiated through the darkness, a tangible thing, like
his animal magnetism, and the way he could rouse a crowd by
simply standing before them. This power was the nearest to the
supernatural she had experienced. Raza was using it now to create
fear in the recruits.

He had silently counted them as they ran into position and
dressed off – ten rows of fifty, none older than twenty, some not
yet fourteen. The latest pick of the refugee camps of Lebanon.
Some had already killed, all had shown they were anxious to do
so.

He had promised them that in the training camp they would
learn ways to kill they had never imagined. But no matter
whether it was with a wire garrotte, steel blade, booby trap, bomb
or gun, they must do so with total discipline. And that meant
making no movement at all while on parade.

In the week since they had arrived, the recruits had stood for hours at attention. Those who moved were punished by being made to force-march in the noon heat with backpacks filled with sand. Those who collapsed were dragged to their feet and ordered to continue. Those who fell again were beaten mercilessly. Last night Raza had told them the time for soft punishment was over. The recruits had gone to their barracks filled with unspoken unease. Now he waited for the first infraction. A boot moving on the scree, a hand changing position on a Kalashnikov, a mouth suppressing a shiver. He would hear the slightest sound. Waiting, he enjoyed the fear he created, the power of his will over theirs.

Raza glanced sideways, where Nadine was standing. She was tall for a Palestinian and her thick, tawny hair would be tucked beneath a forage cap and her body hidden by fatigues. Her face, pale and as finely sculpted as a Pharaoh's princess, would be staring fixedly ahead. Though he could not see her, he was certain of this because he had told her that was how she must stand on parade. Nadine still obeyed him in all matters.

Her sister, Shema, had once done the same. Because of that he'd chosen her to take his most secret orders to cell leaders all over Europe. He'd dressed Shema for the part and ordered her to stay in the best hotels and always to fly first class. And she'd carried off to perfection the role of the culture-loving daughter of an Arab millionaire. In the museums and art galleries of Europe she had passed on his instructions.

Then the girl had forgotten who she really was, turning up her nose at the spartan rations all *Feydeheen* ate when back at base, and complaining about having to stand guard duty and performing other chores. Because Shema was so good at her job he'd contented himself with warning her that such behaviour would not be tolerated. Then, when she displayed an arrogance towards him he'd seen her show others, he punished her the way he did any other woman under his control. He'd given Shema to one of his aides for the night. The man, a coal-black Sudanese, was feared for his brutality and sexual excesses.

Next morning Shema came to him begging forgiveness. He had stared at her, cold and silent. After a while he told her, as she stood before him like a penitent, she would have one more chance.

The truth was he had had no one else to deliver new orders for a bombing campaign in Germany. He told Shema to fly directly from Cairo to Munich. Instead she'd taken a flight to Frankfurt. When his fury over her disregard for his orders abated, he remembered Shema had a desert dweller's fascination with fertile countryside and whenever possible, liked to travel by train.

What she had not expected was for one of Nidal's teams to kill Israel's cultural attaché in Bonn an hour before her flight landed. Waiting for the train to Munich, she had been caught in the German dragnet. Their computers quickly discovered her real identity. Shema had been charged and convicted of complicity in a crime in which she had had no part. The Germans sentenced her to fifty years. She had forty-eight more to serve.

When Raza told Nadine what had happened, she'd been stricken. He'd shrugged and said a true revolutionary accepted such punishment. For a moment he thought he'd seen hatred in her huge almond eyes. But whatever was there had quickly passed. Then he had mounted her again, reminding her with each thrust she would do anything and everything he demanded.

The knowledge that Nadine would still do so added excitement to Raza's tension as he continued to scan the rows of recruits. He had told them that only the snakes, lizards and scorpions could escape his authority here.

His energy was so great Nadine felt as if it was touching her body. And, despite herself, she became aroused. Apart from the boy who had raped her when she was twelve, Raza was the only man she had known. It was six months now since he had first touched her.

After he'd told her what had happened to Shema, Raza had left on another of his trips. Before then he had put her in charge of the camp's clinic. There was little to do, as the *Feydeheen* were extremely fit. She spent her time reading books from the villa's well-stocked library of revolutionary tracts.

She had been there one evening, browsing, when she turned and found Raza towering behind her. He smiled and asked if she'd found anything to interest her, touching her arm as he did so. No man had ever touched her like that, so deliberately, so lingeringly, so sensuously. She had stood there, not knowing what to do. Still smiling he had moved closer, stroking her arm and then her neck. She'd closed her eyes, feeling her breathing quicken. Then without a word he laid her on the floor, his weight on her so that she felt crushed. And, as he entered her, she had said to herself she wanted this because somehow it could help to free Shema. But she had also clung to him for herself. When he finished, he had rolled to one side on the cool tiles and looked at her. Then, very softly, he said she was now his woman.

Since then he had made love to her in ways she never imagined. At first she felt she was being torn apart as he filled her. Then the pain passed and she experienced a feeling of mission, that if she satisfied Raza, he could be persuaded to use his power to free Shema.

When his chief bomb maker had been arrested in Paris, Raza had promptly taken three diplomats from the French Embassy in Beirut. While Paris had gone on hesitating, Raza sent a finger from one of the hostages. Next day the bomb maker was back. Yet, whenever she asked if he could free Shema, Raza would only shrug.

Nadine planned to ask him again once this fearful tension was satisfied. While it remained in his body, he was like a man possessed.

The darkness was lifting. It was not yet quite light, but it was enough for Raza to spot the recruit change grip on his rifle. He was in the back row and must have thought he was safe. Feet barely touching the scree, Raza burst through the lines, scattering recruits. He frog-marched the youth to the front and hurled him to the ground.

'Reform ranks!' Raza roared.

The recruits quickly scrambled to their feet.

Nadine saw the sky was turning grey, the colour of slate. The youth was on all fours, like an animal, his head moving from side to side, as if desperately seeking a way to escape or for someone to save him. Hundreds of pairs of eyes stared fixedly ahead. A heavy, expectant silence hung over everything.

Raza hauled the youth to his feet, holding him by the scruff of his collar until his feet were almost off the sand. The recruit squirmed, half-choked by the grip. Raza turned slowly, so that everyone could see the abject terror on the youth's face.

He can't be more than sixteen, Nadine thought. She glimpsed something in Raza's eyes and, despite herself, she shivered.

'Look at him! All of you, look at him!' Raza commanded.

He gripped the boy's face with one hand, wrenching it round to study it for a moment, then removed his fingers as if he had touched something dirty. He looked out over the stilled, watchful ranks. 'What is the first rule of this parade ground?'

'Nobody moves unless ordered!' came the low, fearful response.

'And why?'

'To make us disciplined!' The voices grew in strength and certainty.

'And why?'

'To defeat our enemies!' Hundreds of voices roared.

'And who are our enemies?' Raza's voice seethed with pent-up hatred.

'The Zionists! And all those who support them!' The thunderous response echoed around the parade ground.

Nadine saw the terror deepen on the youth's face. His lips moved, but no words came.

'What do we do with our enemies?' Raza could feel his skin starting to crawl and itch with fury.

'Kill them! Kill them! Kill them!' bellowed the voices.

Raza felt the tension and excitement was almost unbearable. He had to steel himself to remain absolutely still, as the repeated, insistent bellowing broke over him. The recruit hung limp in his grasp.

Letting the boy fall to the ground, Raza raised his hand, palm open. The silence was immediate and total. He touched the recruit with the tip of his combat boot, his eyes raking the ranks.

'A man who moves when he has been ordered not to is more dangerous than our enemies because we trust that man with our lives.' Raza's expression was savage. 'A man who betrays that trust, betrays us all!' He gave the recruit another small kick. 'Speak!'

'Yes, Comrade Commander! All you say is right. But I only wished to hold my rifle better for you.' Words tumbled from the boy.

Raza kicked again. The youth was at once silent.

Don't beg, pleaded Nadine silently. Whatever you do, don't beg.

'Please, Comrade Commander,' the boy pleaded. 'It will never happen again. I promise on my life. I will never disobey any rule again. I will be the best *Feydeheen* you have. I beg you, believe me.'

Raza stepped back. He slipped the Uzi off his shoulder, reached down, pressed the snub-nosed barrel against the boy's head and squeezed the trigger. He continued to empty the magazine long after the head had ceased to resemble any human form.

As Raza finished the sun rose. He turned to face the glow that came surging out of the east, spreading across endless miles of sand and stone, all the time climbing swiftly into the sky.

These several kilometres of arid sand dunes and treacherous gullies were his testing ground. Here he had trained others in his image. Thousands had passed through the concealed barrack huts on the far side of the parade ground. Tons of Semtex had come and gone from a bunker, buried under the sand so that only its heavy steel doors showed. On any day he kept sufficient explosives there to destroy a small city or all the aircraft in the world. His bomb makers had served him well. But soon their skills would be obsolete because of what had been created in the bunker nearest to the villa. There, the Anthrax-B-C had been made ready.

The knowledge filled him with an excitement stronger than anything sexual. It was such a wonderful feeling that once he had savoured it again, he pushed it back into his subconscious, to nurture and strengthen it for the day when he could indulge himself without restraint. The prospect made him feel a little crazed. Only the killing had kept it under control.

Raza turned and deliberately stood over the body. He riveted the recruits by his very silence. When he began to speak, he pitched his voice to reach the furthest ear, no further.

'Your enemies are many and strong. Some were your brothers and sisters. But they have been seduced by promises of money and an easier life. Even by soft drinks and hamburgers, and cheap radios to listen to the lies and filth, and videos to watch it.'

He stepped over the body and began to pace. The mullahs had said the message must be simple because jihad itself was simple. A holy war was to the death. That was the way to glorious martyrdom. He hadn't believed them. But he had paid lip service. With their money he could achieve goals even he had thought impossible.

'Our enemies want to destroy your values. To dilute your faith. To keep you their prisoner. To make Islam weak.'

Personalise it, Ayatollah Muzwaz had said. Make each one feel personally threatened; each one feel this is his fight. Raza had smiled politely. He knew as much about mind control and motive as any mullah. About group psychology, and about imbuing with ideology, and promoting that all-or-nothing attitude that permits no half-measures, no grey areas.

'You must fight our enemies as never before! You must show them no compassion, because they show you none! Destroy them before they destroy you! You must be prepared to kill in the name of justice! And you must be prepared to die!'

Raza looked into the faces, glaring this warning at them. The sun was burning off the night odours of the desert, leaving the air as purified as Allah intended.

He continued to address the recruits. 'Every one of you here has one thing in common. You are victims. Of the Zionists. Of the infidels who support them. Every one of you has a right, a sacred duty, to defend his family, his home, his land, from the tyrant.'

Nadine heard the familiar surge of fury from the recruits. He had told her, in the quiet dark hours, when their lovemaking left her exhausted, that arousing rage was very necessary. An angry man did not think – only did what was ordered.

Raza pointed at the landscape. A moment ago it had been faint and grey. Now it was alive with a rainbow of warming, vivid colours. Nadine knew every trick in his repertoire. Yet no matter how many times he displayed them, she was enthralled by his charisma.

'Allah gave us the sun to warm us,' he was saying now, 'and to keep our faith hot and alive even in the coldness of the night.'

'Allah be praised,' came the low, unified response.

He saw their eyes were bright and their faces suffused with blood.

'Allah gave us food. But our enemies deny it to us. They took our lands and drove out our people. They have installed their own puppets to rule in all those countries where they plunder our oil. When we protest they send their ships and bombers to threaten us, their soldiers to protect the Zionists! Now Allah has said this must stop! That you will stop it in his name!'

Another chorus praising Allah came from the recruits. His words were like an aphrodisiac, promising them paradise beyond the harshness of their present surrounds.

Once more, as Nadine knew he would, Raza turned away, to stare across the wilderness, which stretched to the horizon. He drew his *kaffiyeh*, his checked headdress, about his face. He reminded her of a prophet communing directly with Allah. Belief, he had told her, is all. Not the soft-centred faith of the mosques, but the hard, unyielding creed he had fashioned, in which killing was an expression of freedom, another step towards justice. And so well had he convinced her, that already she was coming to accept that the slaughter of the youth was necessary.

Raza turned back, his face calm and certain. He allowed his *kaffiyeh* to fall from his face. The headdress was his only concession to desert convention. While everyone else wore fatigues, he was dressed in a black polo-neck cotton sweater and black trousers tucked into his combat boots.

'Remember this day well,' Raza cried, 'for this is the day before judgement. Tomorrow our enemies will feel our power. Tomorrow they will know our fire, our justice. Our revenge for all they have done. And tomorrow will only be the beginning!'

Raza turned and looked directly at Nadine. She nodded, staring into his eyes. Tomorrow *something* would happen. This was no longer dizzy rhetoric, but reality.

Raza began to walk slowly among the recruits, here and there pausing to study a face. She had seen him do this many times. It bound that person even more closely to him. She watched him stop before the two Greek girls, Anna and Zelda, standing apart from the recruits and the camp's permanent staff.

For a week they had hardly left the underground bunker converted into a laboratory and broadcasting studio. The other Greek, Lila, had spent all her time in the studio. That puzzled Nadine. Lila had a speech impediment; she lisped when she became excited or angry. How could she be a broadcaster? When she had asked Raza he had smiled enigmatically. Nadine had come to know that smile. It was a warning not to question him.

Lila had left the camp two days ago. She had called from Rome to say she had dropped off the tapes for Al-Najaf.

Of all Raza's men, Nadine disliked Al-Najaf the most. The others could be hard and coarse. Al-Najaf was evil. Whenever he came to the camp, a young girl would be provided for him. Raza had said that as long as Al-Najaf did his job, his private life was his own.

Raza showed the same tolerance towards Faruk Kadumi. The day before he had left the camp, they had spent several hours closeted in the villa's library. When they emerged Raza was in good humour, inviting Faruk Kadumi to dinner. Over the meal the surgeon had asked if Raza could provide him with a woman. Laughing, Raza said he could have any girl but his.

Faruk Kadumi had chosen one of the girls who waited at table. Before taking her to his room, he had insisted on formally kissing Nadine on both cheeks. She had smelled the ether on his breath. But when she had later tried to tell Raza someone so dependent on drugs could be very dangerous, he had given another enigmatic smile.

Next morning Faruk Kadumi had flown to London.

Nadine watched the two Greek girls walk back to the bunker, their eyes shining. Shema had had the same look when going on a mission.

Raza strode towards a group of men who had completed their training and were ready to return to the refugee camps to recruit others. He would lead an army greater than Saladin's, than even the Prophet himself had commanded. He ordered the group to form a circle, and the recruits to make an outer square. Inside this perimeter, towering head and shoulders above everybody, Raza spoke in a powerful and vibrant voice.

'Look at these men!' He pointed to the circle. 'They are an example to you all. They will go from here to the West Bank and Gaza. To all those places where our enemies are. And they will destroy them in the name of Allah! They will tear out the hearts of our enemies like –'

Raza pointed dramatically as the perimeter parted to allow two of the kitchen staff to pass. Each girl carried in her hands several live chickens, gripped by their legs.

'– like chickens! Like *this*!'

Raza grabbed a bird and tore it apart, first the legs, then the wings and finally the head from the body. As he did so, he walked around the circle, shoving the raw flesh into mouths, his voice leading the loud, repetitive chant.

'Our enemies are weak! We are strong! *Ins'Allah!*'

Raza handed the other birds to the circle of men. They tore the chickens apart, the raw flesh and warm blood covering them as they gobbled pieces of the meat.

'Our enemies are weak! *Ins'Allah!* We are strong! *Ins'Allah!*' they chanted, working themselves up.

Raza then stood before them, his eyes blazing, his head nodding in time with the chanting. He raised his hand for silence.

'Let others call for passive resistance and restraint! Let others plead and beg. You must kill!'

'Kill!' shouted a voice. 'Kill!' The cry was taken up. 'Kill! Kill! Kill!'

The animal growl of the circle spread until every voice in the square was repeating, '*Kill!*'

'Enough!' Raza's command brought instant silence. He turned to the blood-soaked circle. 'You are now *Feydeheen!* Remember that well.'

Raza strode to the bunker which the Greek girls had entered. Nadine was already going to the villa to ready herself. How well she had come to understand his needs. Knowing why she was so eager to satisfy him, only excited him. The more she tried to manoeuvre him into having Shema released, the more sexually inventive she became. He had never known a woman like her, in such a frenzy for him.

The studio was a soundproof booth in a corner of the lab. All that remained of the hours he had made Lila sit here were the butts in the ashtray, and the cassette tapes he had rejected before he was satisfied. Lila had come close to protesting more than once as he made her repeat a word time and again. Her speech impediment was a drawback, but she more than compensated with a ruthlessness that almost matched his own.

Now that Faruk Kadumi had finished, the airlock to the lab was kept open. Anna and Zelda were packing the bottles of perfume into the Gucci tote bags.

He had chosen the bags, just as he'd chosen the name for the perfume – Grecian Nights – and the uniforms the girls would wear when they promoted it. He had chosen everything. For the moment Raza was content to stand in the doorway, watching the girls go about their work, knowing they represented a year of careful planning.

It had helped soothe his fury over Saddam Hussein. For years

Iraq's leader had been his paymaster and protector. They had often sat in Saddam's Baghdad palace and redrawn the map of the Middle East so that Iraq was the dominant power in a region where Israel no longer existed.

To prepare for that day, Saddam had asked him to smuggle in vital parts for the great military machine Iraq was creating. Raza had not realised how awesome it was until Saddam took him to Samarra. There, buried deep under the sand, was Saddam's stockpile of chemical and biological weapons. The most powerful was based on China's Anthrax-B-C. He had begged Saddam to give him a quantity to use against Israel. Saddam had promised when the time came he would.

Even now the memory of what had happened made Raza's eyes blaze. Saddam's plan to make Iraq the first Arab superpower, which would also be a permanent haven for Raza, had begun gloriously. In a few hours Iraq had taken Kuwait, and Saddam's forces massed on the border with Saudi Arabia. The royal lackeys of the West in Riyadh had seemed doomed. Then Israel had struck. Morton had destroyed the Samarra plant.

Raza had urged a near-berserk Saddam to attack Israel – and seen Saddam for what he really was, a craven braggart. He was like all the other Arab leaders – frightened of the Zionists. When he had finally launched his Scud missiles it had been too late.

The war had been unusually brutal, fought in the full glare of television cameras. But even they had not been there to witness the moment when Saddam had gone. Raza had been forced to flee with his men from Iraq, finally finding sanctuary in Libya.

The more Raza had thought about it, the more he realised how close Saddam had been to success. Uncorking a few bottles of anthrax would have been enough to have created terror in all their enemies.

Then came the invitation to travel to Teheran to meet Ayatollah Muzwaz and the other mullahs. Raza had listened politely to their lofty sentiments about the need to wage a jihad. He had finally told them how this could be achieved – and how much it would cost. Within twenty-four hours ten million US dollars had been transferred to a bank in Geneva for his use.

The easiest part, as he'd foreseen, was getting hold of the

Anthrax-B-C. Once his contacts in the Golden Triangle knew the money was available, it had taken them only weeks to strike a deal with the scientist at the Chengdu plant.

But by the time the pick-up in China was arranged, the cabal was divided. A growing number of mullahs had actually dared to demand he must *prove* he had not lost his skill. They had asked, in their icy, polite way, for a demonstration. Curbing his fury, he had gone along with them, saying that he would be happy to provide proof.

Raza remembered how he had paced this long cavernous bunker with Al-Najaf, discussing killing the Cardinal Archbishop of Lebanon. He had supported the Gulf War from his pulpit, calling it a just cause. In a few days, the Cardinal would be in Rome to attend a conference called by the Pope to see if the Church could mediate a reconciliation between Islam and Christianity. There would be no more fitting way to express total rejection of the idea than to murder the Cardinal in front of his Pontiff.

Preparing the assassination had been far less time-consuming and costly than the second proof Raza intended to provide for the cabal. A million dollars had been spent to get the explosives in place. Over fifty hotels had been checked before the final dozen were chosen. His most skilled bombers had been sent to London, Paris and New York. They had all confirmed that everything was now in place.

Before coming to the parade ground, Raza had telephoned the news to Ayatollah Muzwaz from the studio, using part of its state-of-the-art equipment to route the call through his Beirut office.

The console, known as a voice throw box, had been developed by the now defunct Intelligence service of the German Democratic Republic. Raza had paid 500,000 US dollars to a Geneva-based broker specialising in obtaining ultrasensitive electronic equipment, and a few weeks later the console had been delivered in a Libyan diplomatic bag. Weighing less than twenty kilos, the console could be programmed to give the impression that a call was coming from up to several thousand miles away from where it was actually being made.

In his coded message to the cabal's leaders, Raza had made no mention of the third proof he intended to provide. He would show them that not only had he retained his skill at terrorism – but that no one could tell him when and what to do. That was why he had sent Lila to South Africa.

He knew that she had been drawn to him by his skill at manipulation. Men or women, young or old, attractive or ugly, sophisticated or simple – all were totally susceptible. It was a gift and a weapon. It always amused him how he, the son of a nomadic shepherd, could exercise such total power over so many educated minds. He continued to do so now.

'Tell me again exactly what you will do when you leave here,' Raza ordered, walking into the lab.

The girls took turns to repeat their instructions. While they spoke he studied their faces carefully, searching for the slightest hesitation. At last he was satisfied. He stepped back, his eyes hard and bright.

'You understand that your desires, your needs, even your very lives are of no consequence? Nothing must be allowed to come between you and the success of your mission.'

'We understand,' said Zelda, the pride in her words clear.

'We will not fail you,' promised Anna.

His voice still low and compelling, Raza delivered a final reminder. 'You have been chosen by me because I trust you. I will go on trusting you. But do not fail me.'

In that moment he saw in their eyes that they would continue to do his bidding. He turned and strode from the lab.

Walking towards the villa, Raza felt his excitement grow. Nadine would be waiting. But she would have to offer something very special to equal the way he now felt.

Nadine watched him approaching, looking neither to left nor right. Yet he would be taking in everything: the recruits creeping up on each other, lunging and trying for strangleholds. Others down in a gully, learning how to assemble and place bombs. From the shooting range came short bursts of small-arms fire. Out on the assault course, uniforms were already dark with sweat and fear as men and women jumped from a tower while instructors shot at them with live ammunition.

Here in the villa it was still cool. At one end of the verandah the camp's political officer was conducting his first class of the day. Until dusk, groups of recruits would be inducted in revolution. At the opposite end, a mullah from Iran was teaching

71

fundamentalism. Every month a new cleric came, but the message was always the same: Islam would triumph.

Nadine turned from the window. She wore her lightest silk robe, as cool as the sheet on the bed. His footsteps paused outside the door. He was removing his boots. He had not forgotten his upbringing.

The door opened and Raza came in. Nadine walked to him and, pushing shut the door with one hand, began to run her tongue over his cheeks, nose and eyes, at the same time removing his *kaffiyeh*.

Her words were filled with excitement. 'I need you so much.'

What happened out there had increased her desire. The more he behaved like an animal, the greater her arousal. She began to move against him.

Raza pushed her away. 'Are you no longer curious about what is to happen?'

She smiled and began to unbutton his shirt. 'I have learned to wait. But can you?'

He stood before her quiescent and unmoving, sensing her need, but making no effort to match it. Once more he pushed her away.

'Tell me how much you have guessed.'

Nadine became still. They'd played this game before. It aroused him, the way she tried to fit together the pieces. Afterwards, she would ask him about Shema.

Nadine took his hand and led him to the bed. He lay on his back, staring up at her. She straddled him, smiling, speaking softly. 'You will this time attack the Zionists through their friends?'

He chuckled softly. 'But how?'

'Bombs?'

Raza gave another soft chuckle.

Nadine squeezed him with her thighs. 'Lila will explode the bombs by radio control?'

'No.' He looked at her. She had no idea. He began to feel his excitement grow. 'You have forgotten Al-Najaf.'

Nadine shook her head. 'I try not to think of him,' she began, and then warned by the look on his face, she became silent.

She was aware of her own lightness, knowing she could rest

her full weight upon him without causing him discomfort. If he was in the mood, he could continue this way for hours.

'And the doctor you also dislike?' he asked.

'I do not know. I only hope Faruk Kadumi will serve you well.'

'Have no fear.' He exhaled softly, enjoying his ability to postpone his own pleasure. 'The Greek girls – what will they do?'

Nadine was silent, thinking: he does not want me to know. If I guess, he will lose his good humour. And I will lose any chance to ask about Shema.

'They will carry messages to the cell leaders?'

Raza chuckled, his good humour intact. 'No. Not like Shema.'

He lay with his eyes half closed. 'Please . . . will you have her freed? For me? Please.'

He stood up and quickly removed his sweater and trousers. As usual he wore nothing beneath. He lay back on the bed.

'Please, will you do that for me?' She ran her hands over his body, over the scar tissue below his ribcage and his inner thighs. She saw she was beginning to make him hard without a direct touch.

'Please,' she began again.

'No!' His sudden explosive fury filled the room as he sat up. 'Do not speak of your sister! Do you understand?'

'Yes,' she said meekly. 'I am sorry.' It had not been the time to ask about Shema.

She began once more working her tongue over his face, in his ears, eyes and mouth. He lay back on the bed.

Without removing her robe, Nadine sat upon him, allowing him to enter slowly, so slowly.

'Faster,' he ordered, his voice coarser.

'No,' she breathed.

She made a game of pinning his arms, as if she was actually strong enough to control him. He responded to the fantasy as he always did, pretending to struggle against her grasp, then surrendering.

Nadine attentively followed his rhythm, encouraging him. It was more than physical lust, it was the only way she could dominate him, when she had him held tight in her body.

But, time and again as she strained every muscle, he paused just short of orgasm. She waited a while, then resumed, attempting to vary her motion, coaxing him, then moving faster and faster, thinking surely he must come now.

Instead, he suddenly pushed her aside and went to the window. Outside the bunker, the two Greek girls were climbing into the Jeep that would take them to Tripoli. From there they would fly to Athens. Only when the Jeep disappeared from view did he turn back to Nadine.

'May Allah protect the perfume makers,' he whispered, returning to the bed.

Nadine looked into his face and once more thought she saw true madness there. Then the needs of her own body demanding to be satisfied, drove out all else. Only when he was finished and lay beside her, his breathing slowly coming under control, his body at last still, did she ask him what was going to happen. And when he finally told her she saw not madness, but an absolute certainty that he would succeed.

6

Morton drove out of Tel Aviv. Before leaving, he had alerted every Mossad station that Raza was poised to attack. He'd sent copies to Israel's internal security service, and the commanders of all border units. He'd prepared the country as far as he could.

Apart from Danny he had told no one about the death of The Syrian. There would be no memo for Bitburg to pick over.

The city limits gave way to the first of the Bedouin encampments. Black tents, black implacable faces, their voices lost in the roar of the traffic.

At this hour the road to Jerusalem was like a race track: army convoys, *sheruts*, the shared taxis, motorcyclists. In less than an hour it would be dark and the Arab pot-shotters would be out in the hills, choosing their targets. Every death widened the gulf, deepened the hatred.

Ahead a caravan of donkeys shambled across the highways, their drivers oblivious of the pumping horns. The caravan was going to camp for the night in the ruins of the police station, which had stood for forty years until one of Raza's commando units had come off the beach and kamikazed it. Morton had warned this could happen. Bitburg had sent down a memo saying he'd circulated the warning. The note had arrived after the attack.

That was why he hadn't told Bitburg about the operation in Rome. Bitburg would have written another memo to file, ready if anything went wrong. And anything could go wrong on a take-out, especially on the one planned to kill Mahamoud Al-Najaf.

75

In her last call Michelle had asked for a couple more days. He'd agreed at once. A take-out was never something that could be dictated purely by the clock. The actual place and hour of a killing was something that had to be left flexible. Better for Wolfie and Michelle to wait two more days than move too soon.

Morton reduced speed as he approached the first of the Arab settlements of the West Bank. There was a roadblock, a dozen Defence Force soldiers, a couple of Jeeps and an APC tucked into a bend in support.

He showed his ID and was waved through. He drove slowly the short length of the street, missing most of the potholes, trying not to throw up stones from his wheels. Riots had started for less. He ignored the hostile faces.

Al-Najaf had come from a village like this. In such a place he'd first learned his violent and brutal skills and gone on to help to write the agenda of modern terrorism. On any take-out list he'd be there with Raza. Now Al-Najaf was finally in one place long enough to be dealt with. It was a good feeling, knowing there'd be one less to hunt. And natural justice was the best of all. Steve's books had taught Morton that.

The hot afternoon wind whipped at his sleeve and rustled the wrapped package on the seat beside him. Months ago he'd bought the leather-bound volume of life in the First Dynasty of Egypt for Steve's seventieth birthday. It would be a fitting addition to all his other books on the ancient world.

They, and Steve's way of making the past come alive, had fired Morton's own interest in archaeology and comparative religions, and made his tutors at Cambridge plead with him to come into academic life.

Another communal taxi roared past. Morton kept a steady fifty miles an hour. Conserving petrol, resources of any kind, was deeply ingrained.

Ahead, a military convoy turned off into the Judean hills. He knew its destination – the base he'd helicoptered from into Lebanon a dozen times this past year.

On either side the Judean wilderness began. At school he'd been told Jesus had come out here to think. He could understand why. There was nothing here to distract.

How long, he wondered, would Raza wait before starting? When he'd first got his hands on Semtex, he hadn't delayed more than a week before beginning to engulf his victims in fireballs. The only certainty was the longer he was from his last outrage, the closer Raza was to his next.

Another Arab village loomed up. More white-walled houses, and the same tense, watchful faces. Beyond the village, the last of the daylight went. Morton switched on his headlights.

The first lights gleamed in the hills – Bedouin shepherds in their huts. A full moon was rising to meet the stars. Ruth had always said the first hour of night was as if time had stopped.

Topping a rise, Morton pulled off the road. No matter how many times he saw it from here, Jerusalem was like no other city. There was nothing elsewhere in the world to match the Dome of the Rock, and all the other domes, spires and minarets outlined in the labile darkness. Once more he could sense the city's piety and hypocrisy. Jerusalem was unique: a timeless place beyond the touch of time, which God had chosen to make holy to Jews, Christians and Moslems. Yet it was fought over like no other.

To his left, in the lee of the hill, paraffin lamps flickered. Since he had last come this way, another Arab village had sprung up, creating another fertile breeding ground for Raza. He could feel the tension coming up the hill, knew hate-filled eyes were watching. He eased the car into the flow of traffic, and headed towards Jerusalem.

He parked near the Damascus Gate, and the pedlars surged forward. This was the quiet time between festivals, but still a chance to unload seeds from Gethsemane, water from the Jordan, soil from Calvary. He brushed them off in English. It was still okay to be a foreigner here, but not always safe for Jews.

Yet Steve and Dolly had lived in the Old City for over fifty years. Their apartment on the Via Dolorosa remained striking proof co-existence was possible.

Inside the Crusader walls, the pedlars continued to offer pieces of the true cross, nails from the hands and feet of the Risen Christ, hairs from the tail of the Prophet's beast, fragments from the Temple of Herod. Jerusalem always reminded Morton of a whore, selling the same thing over and over.

As a child he'd loved it: talking to old men sitting in even older doorways, following the veiled women burdened with pitchers and panniers, and staying clear of the rabbis and the priests of the Greek and Russian Orthodox Churches who were cut off from the present by their witness to the past.

These were dangerous streets. Young men lounged in doorways, silent and watchful, practising the skill of menace. There was a constant wail of music in the air: loud Arab love songs, sung shrilly by young voices; discordant Greek music. And everywhere the Beatles and Rolling Stones. They survived here like nowhere else.

Long ago he had gone from here. Steve had said an English public school prepared anyone for life. Five years at Clifton had broadened and toughened him. Each time he'd come back during the holidays, Dolly had said how much he'd grown, how English he sounded. Ruth had teased him about girls. Steve had beamed his proud father's smile.

When Morton went to Cambridge, Steve had provided a long list of introductions. He'd seemed to know half of his tutors. Until then Morton had not fully realised what a huge academic reputation his putative father had.

An army patrol came driving down the street, the two Jeeps forcing people against the wall. Morton felt the anger the soldiers created, and saw the nervousness in their eyes. They blooded conscripts here before sending them to the real trouble spots: Nablus, Beersheba, Nazareth. The patrol glanced at him quickly. One of the soldiers muttered in Hebrew, 'bloody foreigner'. Morton ignored him and walked on into Via Dolorosa.

The last time he'd come back from Cambridge, the print still damp on his Double First, History and Political Science, and said he was joining Mossad, Steve had looked at him for a long time before asking if he was certain this was what he wanted. He'd replied immediately, yes. The matter had never been mentioned again.

The apartment was in a building constructed during the Ottoman Empire. The stone façade was smooth to the height of a man, from the millions of pilgrims who had leaned against it as they'd paused while retracing Christ's steps.

Morton stood for a moment, thinking it was as if he had never been away. Then he climbed the stone steps to the first floor.

He had his own key, and he inserted it in the lock of the heavy, iron-studded front door. He held his gift in one hand behind his back. He wanted to surprise them, to hear Dolly's little cry of pleasure, to see Steve rise from his chair, his hands spread in gentle welcome. Morton eased the door open.

The apartment was in darkness. He let the light from the landing flood into the hallway, as if it would banish the dead silence. Then, switching on the hall light, he closed the door behind him and walked from room to room, turning on the lights. All the apartment windows, shutters and curtains were firmly closed.

He returned to the living-room. Everything was exactly as he remembered it. The heavy oak dining-table and its four chairs stood at the far end. The table and its brass candelabra gleamed from yet another polishing from Dolly. Steve's armchair stood in one corner, Dolly's in another. Between them was a military chest and its reading lamp. They'd brought the chest with them from Europe.

The couch on which Morton and Ruth had sat as kids and watched television on the black-and-white set was against a wall. With his first month's pay he'd bought a colour set. Such extravagance, Dolly had scolded happily.

The floor to ceiling shelves, fitted in every available wall space seemed, if anything, more crowded with books. Christian, Arabic commentaries, a Koran, an Infancy Gospel, a Russian biography of Alexander the Great stood between hand-bound copies of Syriac scripts. The library ran on through into Steve and Dolly's bedroom, the shelves covering three of its walls, surrounding the large brass bed.

He wandered down the short passage, which led to Ruth's and his old bedrooms. Since he had last been here the passage had been lined with shelves filled with yet more books. Morton reached Ruth's room. Her nameplate was still on the door. He remembered the day he'd stuck it up. Ruth had been twelve.

His own room remained untouched from the last time he had slept there. The oak-frame bed was against one wall, a chest and wardrobe along another. He still kept a few clothes here. The shelf of books was full of his boyhood heroes: Just William, Biggles, Rockfist Rogan.

Morton walked back into the living-room, searching for clues where Steve and Dolly could have gone. On the sideboard, beneath the telephone, he found a small pile of travel brochures. Steve had always promised Dolly they'd make one last trip to

Europe. To London, to hear a play performed as it should be. To Paris, to enjoy food and wine as it should be cooked and served. To Germany, to remember.

He remembered, too, why they had not called him to say where they were going. He had always said there was no way he could be reached – unless it was a matter of life or death. For that he'd given them Danny's number. Danny always knew where he'd be. Danny had to.

Putting his gift on the table, Morton went round turning off the lights. Back in the hall, he noticed again the small patch of wall that remained unplastered above the door. It was a reminder that those who lived here still mourned the destruction of the Jerusalem Temple almost two millennia ago. He had been privileged to have been raised by such good and devout people. He suddenly wanted so much to tell them that.

Morton became aware of a noise outside the front door. It came again. The faint but unmistakable sound of breathing, of a face being pressed against the wood, listening.

Morton eased the Browning from his shoulder holster and edged towards the door. He switched off the hall light and sank to his knees. Crouching, he waited, one hand poised above the handle, the other holding the gun at shoulder level. The breathing was hoarser, louder. In one quick, smooth movement he yanked open the door and brought the gun to bear.

The stout, elderly woman recoiled in horror, hands flying to her face, the key in her hand dropping to the ground. She looked at him blankly, struggling for words. When she spoke, it was a mixture of Hebrew, Yiddish and English.

'Davey! May God forgive you! Pointing a gun at me!'

He relaxed. Hannah Meir was Dolly's closest friend. She had been the first and only person Ruth and he had called *tante*, aunt. She was one of the few who still called him Davey.

'Sorry, Tante Hannah, sorry, for sure.' He quickly came out of the crouch and replaced the gun in its holster. 'It was just . . . well I was not expecting it to be you.' Morton picked up the key, handing it to her.

She shook her head. 'So, who were you expecting? Yasser Arafat? You think after all these years someone would come here and kill your Mama and Papa?'

He smiled. 'You're right. If any two Jews are safe in this world, they have to be the ones. But I'd expected Mama would be in the kitchen, preparing the birthday dinner.'

He still called Dolly, Mama and Steve, Papa. They liked that.

She squinted at him. 'You want to talk here, or inside?'

'Sorry, Tante Hannah.' Morton stood aside.

'Enough of this saying sorry,' she said, pushing past him. 'I like it better that you don't take chances. Your Mama says in your business you can't be too careful.'

'Mama worries too much.' He closed the door behind them.

She strode into the living-room. 'Your Mama loves you. Your Papa even more so. It's natural they worry.'

He followed her into the room where she turned and faced him, looking him over as if he were a child.

She sighed. 'I said they should call you.'

She pulled a sheet of paper from a pocket in her dress and smoothed it open.

Morton recognised Steve's handwriting, a scholar's penmanship, small, neat, equal separations between the words.

Hannah read out: 'Day one and two, London. Connaught Hotel. Day three, visit Shakespeare country. Day four, take Orient-Express to Paris. Stay in Hotel Maurice –'

'What day is this, Tante Hannah?' he asked.

'This is still day one, Davey. They left this morning, dressed to the nines, with enough traveller's cheques for your Papa to satisfy his one great wish: to order for your Mama only the finest champagne for lunch and dinner. He's promised to bring me a bottle for looking after this place.'

Hannah stuffed the itinerary back in her pocket. She saw his gift and walked over and picked it up. 'Yours?'

'Yes. A book.'

She nodded. 'What else? Every year I say, how about a nice shirt? And your Papa says no, just a book. Did you know he has a list? Hundreds of books he still wants to read.' She put the gift back on the table. 'I told your Papa you'd come. No son forgets his father's birthday.'

Hannah seemed to be about to say something else. Instead she turned away. She'd lost her son, her only child, in the Yom Kippur War. Her husband had died the following year. The others had gone long before. He sensed her putting the old pain back in its secret hiding place. Hannah had always had the kind of courage he'd admired. She turned and faced him, smiling.

'Your Mama even left food in the freezer. She knew you'd come. Kneidlach soup. Knaishes filled with potatoes, liver and onions. Blintzes. Everything she remembers you like. Everything that wife of yours never made.'

She pulled a chair from the table and sat down. 'Sorry. I didn't mean to raise the dead.'

He pulled out a chair and sat across from her. 'Shola's not dead, Tante Hannah.'

She shook her head. 'She is in this house, Davey. She hurt your Mama and Papa like I've never seen them hurt.'

'It wasn't all Shola's fault.'

Hannah let out a long, soft sigh. 'Have you ever told your Mama what went wrong, Davey?'

'There was nothing to say. Nothing really big suddenly went wrong. No big fights. Nothing like that. It was just . . . just I was away a lot. It can't have been easy for Shola.'

Hannah looked at him. 'But she knew. That's what your Mama can't understand. She *knew* what your job was like.'

He looked into her plump, worn face, her grey hair tied back in a bun. She was a mother without children. He didn't want to hurt her.

'Davey,' she started again, 'you were two people from the same world. You would have thought, with so much in common –'

'It doesn't always work like that, Tante Hannah.'

'You both needed time to find your own levels together.'

'You're probably right.'

There was a length of silence before she spoke. 'There's no way back?'

'We've been divorced two years now. The last I heard she had somebody else.'

'You keep track?'

He smiled. 'No. But that kind of news travels.'

She looked into his face. 'And you? No one else?'

He let the smile widen. 'So this is what all this is about! Seeing if you can do a little matchmaking!'

Hannah raised her hands in mock protest. 'May the Lord of the Universe forgive you thinking such a thing. But yes, I do know one or two nice girls who would make anyone a good wife.

And pretty with it. And as fashionable as any girl from London or Paris.'

'I'm quite happy as I am, Tante Hannah, for sure.'

She looked at him seriously. 'Every man needs someone to come home to. And your Mama and Papa would love to have you married again. And a grandson for them –'

'Tante Hannah, you're incorrigible!'

She beamed. 'I know, I know. I also make the best coffee.'

'Coffee I would like.'

She bustled to the kitchen.

'So how is Tel Aviv?' she asked, returning with a tray holding cups and coffeepot. They both drank their coffee the Arab way, black, no cream or sugar.

'You know . . . Tel Aviv is Tel Aviv . . . a change a day. Some of us are trying to get used to accepting that the rest of the world thinks Iran's the nice guy on the block.'

She handed him a cup. 'Will there ever be peace, Davey?'

There was a simplicity to her question that stirred him. He answered her honestly. 'One day, maybe. But it's still a long time away.'

She looked directly at Morton. Her eyes were troubled. 'But we are so small. When Iraq took Kuwait, the rest of the world talked of "tiny" Kuwait. But we're smaller.'

He sipped. 'Wonderful coffee.' He put the cup down. 'Our size is part of our strength, that's something our enemies have never understood. Having more weapons and men doesn't make them stronger. A determination is what matters. As long as we have that, Tante Hannah, we will survive.'

'But they are getting stronger. You see it on television every day. I hear it on the radio. There is trouble coming, Davey. I can feel it in my heart. Your Mama feels it too.'

He drained his cup and poured himself another. A clock ticked tidily in its place on the shelf above the radiator.

'These people want their holy war, Tante Hannah, and they want to carry it everywhere. But they know they must remove us first. We stand between them and the rest of the world. That's why America supports us, and all those countries in Europe. We're their buffer.'

The highly polished wood of the table caught and held fast the glow from the chandelier. Whenever he sat here, the reflection had seemed to lie buried far below Dolly's layers of polish.

'Your Mama has always said that God put us here for that purpose, Davey. To take all the punishment for the rest of the world.'

'Mama should be in the Knesset.' He pushed his cup away. 'As we've shown we can't be removed by force, our enemies will try and use other means. Blackmail the world into not supporting us. Terrify even our few friends into walking away from us. Then our enemies will come.'

The silence lay between them for a long time before she asked, 'When, Davey? When will they come?'

'I wish I knew, Tante Hannah,' said Morton.

She tried to smile. 'Your Mama says if you don't know something, then it's not worth knowing.' She poured herself a fresh coffee. 'I wish your Papa could have heard what you've just said.'

'Yes?'

'Yes.' She drank quickly and put down her cup. 'I don't often argue with your Papa, Davey. I never heard anyone explain better our past. He should have published more. And not just with the Hebrew presses. In America. He should have gone and lectured when they asked.'

'He didn't like to leave us behind.'

She waved her hand impatiently. 'Ach! His excuse, that's all. He didn't like to travel ... now ...'

Something was troubling her. He waited while she gathered her thoughts.

'Like I said, I don't often challenge your Papa. But I get really mad when he says we must learn to love our enemies. I ask him where it says that in the Torah? In any of his books? But he just says we've got to learn to do it.'

'He's a genuine visionary, Tante Hannah. If all the world were like him, it would be a wonderful place.'

She held her cup to her lips, peering at him over the rim. 'When did you last see them, Davey?'

He had to think. 'Almost ten months now.'

'And spoke to them?'

'Five, six weeks ago. Why'd you ask?'

She looked at him steadily. 'Then you don't know?'

'Know? Know what, Tante Hannah?'

Suddenly the weight of her emotions bore down on him. 'Your

Papa's very sick, Davey.' The words came in a rush. 'Very, very sick.'

He stared at her. 'What's the matter with him? How can he be sick? He's gone on holiday.'

'The doctors said he could still travel.'

'What doctors?'

'At Brai Nith.'

He stared at her wordlessly. Brai Nith was Israel's new hospital for treating cancer.

Hannah put her cup down. 'A month ago your papa went there. They found cancer in the liver and stomach. Because of who he is, they told him everything. No point in operating. That would just shorten his time.'

'But they have a cyclotron there. Surely they could bombard . . .'

Hannah shook her head. 'It's too far gone, Davey . . .'

'How long?' he whispered. 'How long does he have?'

'They don't know.'

He stared into the misery in her face, feeling only this terrible deadness inside him, so heavy it crushed the air from his body.

He stood up. 'I want to talk to him.'

She fished out the itinerary and gave him the number of the Connaught.

He walked to the phone and direct-dialled London. The hotel operator said Professor and Mrs Vaughan had left strict instructions not to be disturbed until morning. He put down the phone and stood for long moments, staring at the shelves.

She walked over and held him in a mother's hold. 'Stay here tonight, Davey. Call them in the morning. Then go to the synagogue and pray. Mama would like that.'

Morton nodded, non-committal, and walked out on to the small balcony that led off the kitchen. When he'd been a boy, he'd stood here for hours while Steve had pointed out the stars. Morton looked out over the Old City to the Hill of Gethsemane. The air was cooling. Soon it would be as cold as the grave.

When he went back into the apartment Hannah had gone. Unplugging the phone, he carried it to his room and connected it in the socket beneath the bedside table. Steve had installed the point so that he could receive calls at those unearthly hours when he used to stay over after Shola left.

He removed his gun and holster and placed them on the table. He closed his eyes, allowing his mind to drift . . . from Ruth to Shola, to Dolly and Steve . . . and finally to Nan.

For a moment he had been tempted to tell Hannah that meeting Nan had been like opening a little-used drawer and discovering a favourite shirt and finding it still fitted. But he still wanted to share Nan with no one. He'd wondered if other men felt like that when falling in love again.

It was a year since he'd noticed Nan as he'd walked out to the podium to deliver his annual lecture on the psychodynamics of terrorism to Harvard's brightest and best. When all the others had finished, she'd stood up and introduced herself – 'Dr Nan Cooper, Virologist' – and asked her carefully thought-out questions, demanding of him carefully thought-through answers. He'd taken her to dinner, already certain Mossad was about to acquire a remarkable new asset. Over the coffee she had simply said yes, she would like to help.

In the cab back to her apartment she told him enough about O'Hara for Morton to know her year of living with the pathologist had been hell. It had finally ended when O'Hara had gone to New York. He'd tried to match her youthful honesty, explaining that since Shola, he'd avoided emotional entanglement. She'd offered her cheek and he'd kissed her a chaste good night.

Six months ago Nan had moved to London, as Senior Researcher-in-Residence at the Hospital for Infectious Diseases. At times she could be as formal as her title. So different from the Nan he had discovered on that last visit to London.

He'd gone to brief the Home Office on the latest Nazi war criminals Mossad had discovered were alive and well in peaceful places like Hastings and Torquay. That night he went round to Nan's flat, expecting to take her to dinner, as on the previous half-dozen times they'd met. Instead, she opened the door in a thin silk housecoat. It was all, he quickly realised, that she was wearing.

She led him to a couch and poured champagne into tumblers, then said, softly and directly, she wanted to make love to him, that she had wanted to from the day she'd met him.

A crushing excitement overcame him. He'd forgotten there was something so very special about touching an unfamiliar nude body and, as he began to kiss her, he felt as if he had never touched a woman before. He undressed, his mouth never leaving her body. As she'd arched into him she called for him to hurt her. Afterwards, she lay there for a long time, completely still beneath him, saying nothing.

After the tenth time they made love that weekend, he told her he loved her. She gave him her slightly crooked smile, and said he should stop worrying about his age. A man half his years couldn't perform so well.

The morning he left for Tel Aviv they lay in the old-fashioned bath, which they'd discovered was big enough for them both. Bodies pressed together they once more made love, joined like sea urchins, her eyes closed. He had whispered again he loved her.

She had climbed out of the bath and towelled off, her voice as brisk as her movements. He could still remember every word. 'Davey, don't be such a teenager. I don't want love. I want to make love. Don't complicate things. Okay?'

Because he loved her, he accepted. He knew there were areas of her past he would never know. When their affair began she made that clear. He had never probed. He had reminded himself she was almost thirty-five, and he should not expect her to come to him a virgin.

In another month Nan would be back in Boston, that much further away. But he'd find a way to go on seeing her.

The phone rang.

'David,' said Danny, 'we have an intercept.'

'Did you get a voice print match, Danny?' asked Morton, knowing he didn't need to ask.

'Positive. It's Raza.'

'I'm on my way back.'

Twenty minutes later, with Jerusalem rising behind him as he sped down the road to Tel Aviv, Morton reminded himself he must phone Steve.

7

Lila continued to photograph the people gathered for the barbe-cue. The whole of Trekfontein seemed to have come to the sports field at the foot of the turreted grey rocks that rose out of the veldt. The field was encircled with Jeeps, half-trucks and cars that had been driven the half-mile from the town across the sandy earth of the plain.

From this distance Trekfontein looked like any other township in the Transvaal: white-walled buildings, many thatched to keep them cool in the scorching summers, and all with deep, shaded verandahs and bright rooms. Rising above them was the imposing Dutch Reformed Church. Even from here its shimmering white colonnades suggested a certainty and determination that found a ready echo in the guttural Afrikaner voices all around Lila.

They were gathered to celebrate another year of totally suc-cessful resistance to the changes that had elsewhere swept through South Africa. Apartheid was all but dead – except in Trekfontein. Here they continued to practise a more sophisti-cated form by ensuring even the most menial job was done by a white. No black was employed within the city limits. No black had reason to step over those limits and enter the last great bastion of racism in the Union.

Trekfontein's name had spread across the world – and come to Raza's attention. He had told Lila that the township would provide a perfect illustration of the creed that governed both their lives: that destruction is the only creative act, and violence is man re-creating himself; that each enemy killed ensures a free man emerges to propagate the revolution.

Beneath the barriers proclaiming Trekfontein to be 'The Heart of the Nation' and 'White and Proud', women in summer frocks held parasols against the hot African sun. Many of the younger men wore the veldt garb of shirt and shorts. The children were often dressed in Voortrekker costume of bonnets and long skirts for the girls and stiffly starched shirts and suits for the boys.

People smiled and waved to Lila as she moved among them. In the two days she had been in Trekfontein, she had become a familiar figure to most of its 5,472 inhabitants, photographing them at work and now at play.

They had welcomed her into their shops and homes, their hospital and church. And when she had asked, they had proudly pointed out Trekfontein's two landmarks: the grey rocks, which rose like a scaled-down replica of Table Mountain overlooking Cape Town; and the reservoir, which provided Trekfontein with some of the purest water she had ever tasted.

Lila had visited both locations and quickly eliminated the rocks. The prevailing wind was from the wrong direction. She had concentrated on the reservoir.

'See any wildebeest out there?' called out a grizzled old man in straw boater and high-buttoning suit.

'Not yet.'

'You keep looking, girlie,' he chuckled.

She smiled and walked on. The old fool thought she didn't know there wasn't an animal worth photographing within a hundred miles. She probably knew more about the habits of the wildlife in the area than he did. Raza had made sure she'd read everything. That was his way – and she admired him for it.

But she'd played along with the old man; she'd play along with them all. That was an essential part of the job.

She had gone again to the reservoir at dawn to photograph the sunrise. Then, when she was satisfied no one was looking, she had conducted another test to check the speed of the water flow.

As before, she had chosen a piece of driftwood. To this she tied another of the miniature bottles of liqueur she'd taken from the mini-bar in her room at the ridiculously named Trekfontein Grand Hotel. Once more it had taken four hours for the bottle to reach the reservoir sluice gate. She had watched the bottle break against the metal gate, and saw, for a moment, the brandy spilling over the weir and on into the pump room, which filtered the water before it was piped to Trekfontein three miles away. Several tests had produced the same result.

Lila was satisfied that when the time came, the perfume bottle in her camera bag would take the same time to reach the sluice. From there it would take another couple of hours before the Anthrax-B-C entered the pipe to Trekfontein.

Six hours. Johannesburg international airport was a three-hour drive across the veldt. Two hours to clear departures. She could still be in Nairobi before the first deaths. And in Athens before the last.

A police officer in khaki shirt and shorts stopped in front of her.

'You photograph us good now,' he said in his thick accent. 'You show the world we don't care what they think.'

She waved a hand, keeping her eye to the viewfinder.

'Put your hand on your gun, Captain.'

He placed his hand on the holstered sidearm on the polished leather Sam Browne belt.

'I've never had to draw this gun once,' continued the captain. 'You know why? Because we don't have a Kaffir problem. No blacks – no crime. It's as simple as that.'

He dropped his eyes for a moment to her breasts and then returned to her face.

'A woman is safe here. Anywhere else, she runs the risk of some black pawing her at a dance or a movie. The more freedom they get, the more they want. But you try telling Mr Mandela that.'

'I'll remember that,' said Lila, reloading her camera.

The police captain touched the peak of his hat and moved on.

Lila made her way towards the barbecue pits on the far side of the field. She paused to photograph a group of teenage boys all wearing tee shirts emblazoned with the legend: 'Work to remain White'.

'Your magazine like Kaffirs?' asked a youth. She recognised him as the waiter who served her at the hotel.

She smiled. '*Time*'s non-political.'

He squinted at her. 'That sounds liberal to me.'

The others laughed. A tall girl, with long limbs and sun-gilded blonde hair, pointed at Lila's camera bag.

'I'll carry that for you. Cost you no more than you'd pay for a black boy in Johannesburg.'

The rest of the group laughed uproariously.

'I don't think the magazine would let me claim for a bag girl,' Lila said politely. When the time came it would be a pleasure to destroy these racist pigs.

She hefted the camera bag and continued across the field. To reassure herself she felt inside again. The bottle of Grecian Nights was still there.

A short, stocky, middle-aged man blocked her progress. He was dressed in a lightweight summer suit, an old-fashioned wide tie and a straw boater. Beside him was his wife. She wore a pastel dress, a picture hat and white cotton gloves.

'Hello, young lady. Getting all you want?' boomed the man.

'Thank you, Mr Mayor.'

Trekfontein's first citizen beamed proudly. 'It's a great honour to have *Time* here.'

'It was your willingness to stand up for what you believe in which attracted my editor.'

The woman peered from beneath her hat. When she spoke her voice was soft and gentle.

'But you won't go away and write nasty things about us? Attacking us just because we don't want to hand over our lovely town to a bunch of savages?'

Lila somehow found a neutral smile. 'But it is the last bastion of "whites only".'

The mayor nodded vigorously. 'And we're very proud of that. No matter what the politicians in Cape Town say about cancelling sensible legislation on race and colour, Trekfontein will remain as it has always been.'

'Look around you, young lady,' said the mayor's wife, waving an arm. 'No one here feels uncomfortable at being white. If God had meant us all to have one colour of skin He would have arranged it. Instead He made us black and white, and, just like night and day, He meant us to separate. That's all we ask – a separation.'

The mayor gave another emphatic nod. 'We don't want to

fight them. We just don't want them here, in *our* town, on *our* land, alongside *our* people.'

The mayor's wife peered at Lila, suddenly anxious.

'Do you think the world will understand us?'

Lila managed to smile. 'Your husband has explained the position very clearly.'

The mayor's wife nodded, reassured. 'But foreigners always distort what he says, call him a Kaffir-basher. He's never hit a blackie in his life!' She stared at Lila through watery eyes. 'Let me ask you a question: do you think America is a better place after what Martin Luther King did?'

'I'm only a photographer, ma'am,' smiled Lila.

She had long discovered that smiling was the one way she could suppress her hatred.

The mayor took his wife by the arm and delivered a homily Lila had heard many times since arriving in Trekfontein.

'Young lady, God chose this place for us. He guided the wagons of our forefathers here, protecting them against the Zulu spears and the Matabele hatchets. A century later, He is still protecting us. That is why everything we do is for God. If He did not approve of what we do, He would show His displeasure.'

'The way He did to the Israelites,' added the mayor's wife.

'It's all in the Bible,' explained her husband. 'If you live the way God wants, you will be blessed. If you don't, you will be cursed by whatever passes for brimstone and fire and the plague today.'

Lila nodded pleasantly. 'I'll remember that, Mr Mayor.'

She continued towards the barbecue pits. Raza had been right. These people were sanctimonious monsters. Half the world would cheer their deaths. The other half wouldn't care. The people of Trekfontein were the perfect expendables: high profile and unsympathetic.

Children were running between the sizzling barbecue grills filled with prime steaks and other meats. Nearby, tables were covered with salads of all kinds. Barrels of beer and vats of lemonade stood on blocks. Lila calculated there was sufficient food and drink to feed a refugee camp for a week. And already the scraps had filled several tubs.

She began to photograph them.

'We have the best-fed pigs in the Union.'

Lila turned to face the Most Reverend Moderator of Trekfontein's church. He stared at her with pale blue eyes. She guessed he was no more than thirty, but his full red beard made him look older.

'Why do you photograph that?' He had a soft, cultivated voice.

'It's all part of life.'

He stepped closer. She could smell the aftershave on his skin. 'You are not American?'

'Naturalised American. Like a lot of Americans,' she replied carefully.

'Naturalised from where?'

'Greece.'

'And how long have you worked for *Time?*'

Lila smiled and stepped back.

'Would you mind just standing there? It's a great shot.'

Behind the Moderator a group of girls were munching burgers.

Lila busied herself, switching from one camera to another. Why had he asked that question?

'You've taken enough photos to fill a whole issue,' said the Moderator.

'I took a thousand of the Japanese Emperor's Coronation. They used one. That's *Time*.'

Once more he stepped closer. 'I know. I have a cousin who works in the bureau in Cape Town.'

Lila felt her breath was quick and shallow. 'I'll be going down there to process some test shots. I'll say hello for you.'

She managed to fight down the panic.

'I already tried to call him. He's on assignment in Lusaka. But no one in the bureau seems to know about you being sent here.'

Lila forced herself to remain calm. 'I was assigned out of London. A last-minute thing. Someone had the brilliant idea of following up on the Mandela visit.'

Two months ago Nelson and Winnie Mandela had come to Trekfontein to challenge its policy. They had found the town completely locked and shuttered. Not a shop had opened. Every curtain in every house had remained drawn until the country's Black First Couple had driven away, defeated by the eerie silence.

'We showed the Mandelas they are not the only ones who can protest passively. Like them, we've also studied Mahatma

Gandhi,' said the pastor softly. '*Time*, of course, attacked us.'

She broadened her smile. 'I had no idea you had a cousin in the staff.'

He touched her arm.

'Actually, I don't like him. He's one of those pinko, born-again Christians.'

Lila nodded, exhaling slowly. 'We've got too many of those. I like people with faith like your mayor's.'

He touched her arm again, smiling this time.

'I'm glad to hear that. We can do with all the friends we can get.'

The Moderator turned and strolled away. Lila swore under her breath. The sooner Raza called the better.

8

Morton continued to ignore the army major, Sam Goodman, to ignore all eleven students in the classroom. He stared out of the window. Sunlight was struggling to get through the grime. Every time he came here he told himself he'd have the glass cleaned.

He could hear the whispering beginning at the back of the room. That would be the tank commander. He'd scored high on initiative and determination. But the commander wasn't going to make an analyst. He was much too impatient and restless.

Until a moment ago Goodman seemed a good bet. But that question about imperatives was disappointingly obvious. The sort of not-completely-thought-through question he'd come to expect from the fighter pilot beside the commander. The flier had a superb combat record, but he'd shown a readiness to cut corners. Fatal in an analyst.

Morton turned back to the class.

'Saddam Hussein's departure really does not change anything. The fanatics are still there. Saddam lacked real guts. He was scared what we would do. One day someone will come along who won't be. Whoever it is, he will know how to play two trump cards, for sure: religion and terrorism. If he gets the mix right, he will create an apocalypse that would make what happened in the Gulf a Saturday-afternoon exercise.'

Leaning against the desk, Morton rested his hands between the phone and the bottle of mineral water. He was going to fail the infantry lieutenant and the two commando captains. Their essays on the causes of the Gulf War had painted Saddam Hussein far too simplistically. An analyst must tease out all the grey shades.

The phone had two light bulbs. He'd told the class that if the green one flashed, he had the option to interrupt his lecture. When the red blinked, he had no choice. The bottle was because he liked to sip during a lecture. Any analyst worth his name, he'd added, should always look for the obvious.

'Anyone want to develop Sam's question?'

Silence greeted the offer. Not even Golan was tempted to plunge – and help Morton come to a decision as to whether the paratroop captain could fill one of the three vacancies on Mossad's Middle East Desk.

The Desk ran through analysts like husks going through a camel. It was the unremitting strain of guessing what someone in Damascus or Teheran was thinking.

And maybe Goodman's question was just a momentary lapse. He'd soon find out. As usual, Morton did so obliquely.

'Every day we see the dangerous limitations of the West's understanding of militant Islam. It will always be the same as long as the West persists in projecting its own ideals and values on a belief system that despises them.'

He moved away from the desk, pacing slowly before them, seeing whose eyes followed him. An analyst tracked everything.

'Radical Islam ignores the logic of mutual deterrence, which says those who have the means of mass destruction are restrained by the over-riding fear of retaliation from others who have similar weapons. Radical Islam is quite prepared to pursue its own strategic objectives even at the risk of being destroyed. Because it is dominated by the imperatives of faith and martyrdom.'

He taught the most effective way he knew, cutting back and forth and switching direction. The way the enemy did.

Morton stopped before Goodman's desk. 'To answer your question, Sam, yes, such imperatives do have an aura. There are tens of millions of Moslems who once would never have lifted a finger, but are now stirred by the thought of a holy war. Yet they are not our immediate problem. Would you like to suggest who or what is, Sam?'

Goodman shifted in his chair. 'Their leaders. Those crazies who use Friday nights in the mosque to preach genocide. If they say it often enough, the mob *will* rise. They always have.'

Morton looked down at Goodman. Those brown eyes, slightly bulging, looking at the world's perfidy in amazement, were the way a good analyst should look. He stepped away from the desk.

'Too sweeping, Sam. And the mullahs are not crazy, for sure. Those mullahs understand perfectly what the psychiatrists call narcissistic rage.'

He looked at Goodman. 'Would you remind us what that is?'

Goodman did not hesitate. 'A compulsive need for revenge. Putting right a wrong by whatever means and not counting the cost.'

'Right. That's what I was looking for. More depth, Sam.' Morton addressed the class. 'In the world of those tens of millions, it *is* all or nothing. Always. For them there is no in between. Just good and evil. They see themselves as good, the rest of the world as evil. And having identified all those who are not with them as the source of all their problems, it logically follows that the way to remove the problem is to destroy the source. To destroy all of us. I want you to put yourselves in their minds. And I want you to come up with one word that encapsulates the driving force for those millions. One word, no more.'

Morton went to the desk and drank from the bottle. Then he walked over to the wall map and turned his back on the class and thought again about Raza.

After returning to Tel Aviv, he'd listened several times to the intercept. Danny's parabolic was positioned near Raza's Beirut office, which issued proclamations in his name after a successful act of terrorism.

Voice Analysis had quickly confirmed it was Raza's voice. But there was no way to establish from where the call had been made, or if it was a recording. It could have been made any time from any place. It had taken Raza eleven seconds to deliver the quotation: *Have you not seen how your Lord dealt with Ad, at Iram of the Pillars, the like of which had not been created in any land?*

Morton had quickly identified the words were from the Koran, book 87, verse 7. Danny's cryptologists said it could take days to crack anything hidden in the tract – if anything was. He'd sensed their scepticism.

He and Danny had focused on the book and verse numbers. The seven: was that the seventh month? But July had passed. The seventh day? Was Raza planning an attack for a Sunday? That assumed Raza was calculating by a Christian calendar. He could just as well be using an Islamic or even a Judaic one. That would mean a Friday or Saturday.

Perhaps the eight and seven were meant to be added together? The fifteenth day? The fifteenth of this month had gone. The next was a full three weeks away. Raza wouldn't tip his hand that far ahead. Were all the figures supposed to be put together? That came to twenty-two. Was something going to happen on the twenty-second of this month?

Morton hadn't needed Danny to turn to his wall calendar. Tomorrow was the twenty-second. But he couldn't go to Bitburg or the Prime Minister and say how he'd come up with the date, for sure. Bitburg would say he'd finally let his intuition overwhelm him. Being able to say that would make Bitburg's day. Doing it in front of the Prime Minister would be twice as satisfying.

'Terrorism,' called out Goodman. 'That's the big turn-on for millions of Moslems.'

Morton turned from the map. Goodman could be about to redeem himself. 'Anyone else?'

'Sam's on the button,' said Golan. 'Guess most of us had it. Only Sam speaks faster.'

Everyone laughed. Goodman's drawl came from a year he'd spent on the Canadian prairie.

'Okay, Sam,' said Morton. 'See if you can keep hitting the button.'

'Well,' Goodman began, gathering his thoughts, 'for those millions, terrorists have a definite romance. There is a mystique about them carefully fostered in the Arab media. Its newspapers and television treat them as heroes. The greater the destruction they create, the more the adulation. Hijacking a jumbo merits a parade in downtown Beirut. Blowing up an airport terminal guarantees a photocall in Damascus or Tripoli. Pull off something in Israel and they get Arafat pushing to shake their hands.'

Morton smiled. Goodman's wit could be acerbic.

'Those millions', continued the major, 'identify their heroes by one name. It used to be Saddam or Nidal. Now it's Raza. Whatever he does is an extension of their own fantasies.'

'Not bad, Sam,' said Morton equably. 'But let's look at the objective of all those fantasies. It's to change the social structure. That's what every terrorist has said from Khomeini onwards.

They want to make things better. The fact is that thousands of separate acts of terrorism have led to almost no improvement. People are just as impoverished in Beirut as they were before the first car bomb. So what is terrorism trying to achieve?'

Morton fixed Goodman with his eyes.

'Humiliation? Each act of terrorism that escapes unpunished adds to our humiliation. Hits deep at our self-esteem, our sense of self,' said Goodman.

'An example?'

'The US Teheran Embassy hostage crisis. Those four hundred and forty-four days reduced the United States to making the kind of response that played into the terrorists' hands. Tying yellow ribbons to trees was as bad as yelling outside the White House to go and nuke Baghdad. That kind of response shows terrorists they've got the upper hand.'

Morton began to pace once more. 'I take it you all agree with Sam?'

There was a chorus of agreement. Morton's smile came and went. 'Now here's the question. Given what's been said and accepted, should there be a legitimate right for us, for anyone, to go after any terrorists who are given sanctuary in any country?'

Morton turned and leaned against the desk, watching Goodman's frown deepen, Golan's lips purse, watching them all trying to assess any hidden agenda in the question. He'd warned them on the first day to treat any question like a booby trap. It could blow up in your face.

'Legitimate?' asked Goodman. 'I'm not sure . . . what would we have? A kind of anarchy . . . ?'

Morton let the silence hang. Mossad had a formal execution procedure. A name went to a secret military court. Three judges studied the evidence, listened to the prosecution and the court-appointed defender. A terrorist convicted in his absence was sentenced to be executed at the first opportunity. Raza had topped the list since he'd bombed the maternity hospital. Al-Najaf came second.

Goodman could one day find himself arguing for a name to be added. It was time to push him a little more.

'Anarchy, Sam?' Morton began, moving away from the desk. 'What do we have now? A festering problem that's growing. There are more confirmed terrorists on our computers than ever before. Every year the number of terrorist incidents increases by over twenty per cent. That means three thousand more people will die this year than last. It's like an epidemic. Every time we think we have the disease under control it flares up again.'

Morton walked to the window. Goodman's mention of anarchy was part of the old argument about the morality of going down into the slime to fight terrorism at its own level. The argument was plausible. The problem was that someone like Raza had never heard of morality.

Before coming here, Morton had phoned every scholar in comparative religions in Israel and asked for a commentary on the Koran verse. They'd all said it would take days. He should have remembered Steve often spent a month poring over a sentence.

He'd called the Connaught. The hotel operator said Professor and Mrs Vaughan were out. He'd asked when they'd be back and she'd replied it was policy not to reveal such information. He'd left his name and said he'd phone later. On impulse he'd tried Nan at home. Her answering machine said to call the hospital. He'd phoned the National Infectious. An operator said Dr Cooper was abroad. He'd asked for a number where she could be reached and was told the hospital never gave out those details. The world seemed filled with telephonists who hoarded information.

Morton turned from the window and resumed pacing.

'Okay. Who says there is never – *never*, ever – a case for terrorism? And remember those we call terrorists are regarded by a great many others as freedom fighters. Some of you will remember that was the very name we used to call those Jews who forced Britain out of here, so that the State of Israel could be created. The Brits said we did it with acts of terrorism. And our people *did* blow up their installations and kill their people. So where is the difference between what our fathers did and what is done to us now?'

He nodded at Golan. 'Teddy?'

'In everything they did, our people showed an awareness of the sanctity of human life, of God's teaching. Today's terrorists are Godless,' Golan replied.

Golan's father, Morton remembered, was a rabbi. He'd also fought against the British in 1948.

'So you think the difference has a religious basis, Teddy? That because our faith says it's okay to use aggression, then everything's fine? Accepting that we have the right to save our own lives at the expense of our attackers, surely that gives them the same right over us? Or does something else come into play?'

'You're thinking of Grynzpan?' queried Golan.

'Remind us,' said Morton happily.

'Herschal Grynzpan was a Polish Jew studying in Paris in 1938. He saw what was about to happen and went to the German Embassy and shot dead the head of security. That led to a reprisal pogrom against all the Jews in Germany. Thousands died or went to the camps.'

Morton stood before Goodman.

'Was Grynzpan a terrorist? A fool, for sure. But a terrorist – or a freedom fighter? Where's the difference? Is there one, Sam?'

'Yes,' said Goodman, 'Grynzpan was making a statement for freedom. He chose a legitimate target. That makes him a freedom fighter. Freedom fighters don't blow up buses containing civilians. Terrorists do. Freedom fighters don't massacre men, women and children. Terrorists do. Freedom fighters don't assassinate innocent businessmen. Or hijack and hold hostage innocent men, women and children. Terrorists do. I think it's shit that democracies allow the word "freedom" to be associated with these people. No, there's no case for terrorism.'

Morton nodded slowly several times. He was going to fail Goodman. An analyst must always know there was no one truth. Golan would go to the Middle East Desk, the others back to their units.

When he spoke his voice was hard, like the rock in the desert.

'Forget the moral distinctions. The bottom line is that terrorists believe, absolutely and without question, that terror is the one legitimate weapon left. For them the political process has either been discredited or is too slow to deliver. You hear that in Northern Ireland, in Lebanon, in all those places where two or more terrorists gather together. For them terrorism guarantees a high return. Every time they let off a bomb, hijack a plane or take hostage a bunch of kids on a bus, they make their case. Because they know what they believe in works, because –'

Whatever else Morton was going to say was interrupted by

the red light on the telephone suddenly glowing. It was the Prime Minister's secretary.

The sun was almost gone when Morton was shown in to Isaac Karshov's office. A police motorcycle escort had cleared the road and taken him through all the traffic lights.

Bitburg was already there, standing at the large picture window. The room's only wall decoration was a map showing Israel and its Arab neighbours.

Karshov was a smallish giant of six-five, with the confident air of a boxer who still kept his hands active. He wore scar tissue over both eyes like badges of office.

The Prime Minister stood behind a chrome and glass desk, wearing a short-sleeved shirt, open at the neck to reveal an old-fashioned string vest. Black chest hair turning grey curled over the vest. Karshov came forward quickly to shake Morton's hand. It was like being gripped by steel.

'Shalom, David.' Karshov had a voice which sounded like a rasp being worked on metal.

'Shalom, Prime Minister.'

A conference table ran down the centre of the room. Dotted over its protective green felt were several ashtrays. In the centre was a basket of fruit. Morton had never known anyone touch it.

Bitburg left the window. 'Nagier's people picked up this an hour ago.'

He handed Morton a sheet of paper and walked to the map.

Morton read aloud the single sentence. 'The seed will bear good fruit.' He glanced at Bitburg. 'Danny's people get a fix, Walter?'

Bitburg stubbed a finger into Beirut. 'Nagier reckons it's the Bir Abed district.'

Morton grunted. The Teheran cabal had recently opened a bureau in the Beirut suburb. One more office for Danny's parabolics to eavesdrop on. Morton read the sentence again. In Beirut the bombers sometimes spoke of sowing seeds.

'What do you think, David?'

'It's Raza. And it's almost certainly a signal to launch a new bombing campaign.'

'Why do you say that?'

Morton told them about his trip to see The Syrian, leaving nothing out. When he had finished Bitburg's eyes began to carom.

'This mysterious Syrian of yours could have been wrong.'

'He's not, Walter. He was right over Kuwait. Right over the attempt to kill Egypt's President – over a dozen terrorist operations. And he's right now. I can feel it in my gut.'

Bitburg smiled thinly. 'Ah, yes . . . your gut. The pity is that this Syrian is now dead, so there's no way for us to question him a little further.'

Morton looked steadily at Bitburg. 'What exactly do you want to know?'

Bitburg coughed and looked away. 'Well, for a start where is Raza?'

'I've told you. Only Ayatollah Muzwaz knows.'

'Can't Nagier's people get their listening devices close to this mullah so that we can actually have something to listen to – not just all this second-hand stuff?' asked Bitburg.

'Danny's still trying. He's lost two good men already in the process,' replied Morton.

Bitburg cleared his throat. 'I still say that whatever your Syrian claimed, there's nothing to suggest the idea that Raza is about to do anything. Except maybe escort another shipment of drugs.'

Karshov's eyes seemed to recede further as his eyebrows knitted.

Bitburg gestured towards the paper in Morton's hand. 'My judgement is that this intercept really proves nothing. I grant you that the reference to seed could refer to bombs, but it could just as well not.' His eyes were settling. 'There's always a danger, in my view, of overlooking the obvious. I believe you tell your students that, David. Very good advice, too.' Bitburg paused and looked at Karshov. 'I would suggest that until we have more proof we be extremely circumspect. A wrong move now could be fatal for us. We know how close we came to annihilation over the Gulf.'

Morton nodded. 'What happened there changed a lot of things, Walter, for sure. All of them not only bad for us, but for the world. It gave terrorism a new licence to terrorise.'

Karshov sighed. 'I read your report, David. It's the most scary thing I've read since sitting in this office.'

Morton met the Prime Minister's gaze. 'The situation *is* frightening, Prime Minister. That's why I recommended you get our labs cracking to stockpile the PEG-enzyme and warn our allies.'

Bitburg's eyes had started a new dance. 'Start a crash programme and we'll have more rumours than we could cope with. Remember what happened when we issued gas masks before Saddam launched his Scuds? There weren't enough masks to begin with, and we had near mayhem in the streets. It will be the same once the word's out that we're mass producing this stuff.'

Karshov gave another sigh. 'Sit down, sit down. Anywhere.'

The Prime Minister flopped into one of the chairs around the conference table. Bitburg sat with arms folded across his chest. Morton turned his chair round, so that he could lean his chin on its back.

'Let me come to the point,' began Karshov. 'If we press the alarm button and nothing happens, we could be in a very difficult situation. London and Washington are already convinced we'll do anything to wreck their plans for the Middle East. *Their* plans which *we* are supposed to go along with. Meet with a bunch of terrorists. Let them have what they want. The West Bank, our settlements, Jerusalem itself. Never mind we built all this from nothing, or that we were legally given this land. That's yesterday. Today, London, Paris and Washington say it's time to give it back. So *they* can have peace. No more Arabs threatening to cut off *their* oil. No more problems. For *them*. But for us? That's *our* problem!

'So now we call them up and say, "Look, we think there's trouble on the way." You know what they'll say? "It's those bloody Jews in Tel Aviv playing games." So we don't call, but trouble comes, then they'll say, "It's those bloody Jews playing more games." Either way, we're damned if we do, and damned if we don't. So, what *do* we do?'

He looked into their faces, not bothering to hide his raw uncertainty.

Bitburg cleared his throat again. 'If there is a threat then it is directed against us.'

Morton looked at Bitburg. 'The next time they'll try and terrify our allies into making us do what they want.'

Bitburg slowly shook his head, his eyes beginning to carom.

Karshov ran a hand over his face. 'Let's all have a drink.' He rose to his feet and lumbered to the cabinet, which looked like a second safe. 'I'm afraid I forgot to order the ice.'

'Mineral water for me, Prime Minister,' said Morton.

'Walter?'

'Scotch, neat, please.' Bitburg placed his hands on his knees. 'Prime Minister, our army patrols are picking up activity on all the borders. Shin Bet says there's renewed unrest in the Strip and the Bank. Nagier's people say more terrorists have come down from Damascus to Beirut in the past month than in the last year. Amman could be about to play fast and loose with its promise not to support them.'

'It could all be a diversion,' said Morton.

Bitburg spoke quickly. 'If it's a diversion, it means the main target is somewhere else. Then it's someone else's problem.'

'How well you delineate things, Walter,' replied Morton.

Karshov carried over the glasses in one hand, his eyes on Morton. 'Convince me, David. In the name of God convince me that, terrible it should happen anywhere, to anyone, it is not going to happen to us.'

Morton sipped his mineral water. Karshov could sound like an Old Testament prophet. But he had a politician's need to have answers kept short.

'The Arab nations are still not ready to make a serious direct attack against us, Prime Minister; there would have to be consensus between Cairo and Damascus, and the United States will see that never happens. That way it helps Washington keep a toehold in the region.'

Karshov nodded. 'That still leaves Raza, David.'

'When he's proven himself to the cabal, he'll use his anthrax – against our allies.'

Bitburg's eyes continued to carom. 'Another big if, David. *If* he has it. *If* he even knows how to use it. *If* he can do so before he's detected. Too many ifs for me, I fear.'

The Prime Minister drained his glass. 'Out of ten, where'd you rate this one, David?'

Morton smiled quickly. Karshov's scale for assessing a problem was legendary. 'All that will delay him will be the logistics of getting his anthrax in place. Where will he use it? I'd give Europe nine to ten. Anywhere else, a point or two lower, with us at the bottom.'

Karshov looked at both men. 'So. Do we alert only our own people or everyone?'

Bitburg pursed his lips. 'If there has to be an alert, then I say we keep it to the absolute minimum. That way we retain our credibility.'

Karshov stared hard at Bitburg. 'I've long given up trying to convince the world that what we say is true,' he said. 'David?'

'We tell our people, for sure.'

'And our allies?'

Bitburg was beginning to lose control over his eyes. 'We must have proof, Prime Minister. As Director, I must insist note be taken –'

'Walter, stop behaving as if this is a board meeting at the bank,' growled Karshov. 'But you're probably right. We do need more than David's instinct, much as I trust it.' He turned to Morton. 'Any suggestions?'

'Let me put together a team.'

Karshov stood up. 'Anyone you like. What you like. Just tell me what is going to happen. And when.'

The Prime Minister grasped Morton's hand firmly, staring into his eyes. For a moment Morton was tempted to tell them about his fear for tomorrow. But the look on Bitburg's face stopped him.

The few friends he allowed into his apartment teased Morton he actually enjoyed living alone in spartan conditions. But the living-room had a wonderful view of the Samarian hills through one window and an uninterrupted view down to the shore through the other.

He'd come directly here from Karshov's office. He wanted to be alone, to think. For an hour he'd run through his mind everything that had happened. The proof Bitburg kept asking for was not there, and not likely to come. That kind of proof only surfaced afterwards.

Finally he'd begun to make his calls. The first had been to Danny. He was with the cryptologists, still trying to tease a hidden meaning out of the Koran verse. Danny would be the team's electronic ear.

In New York Matti Talim's answering machine was on. Morton left a call-back message. Matti was soon going to have little time for the new romance in his life. Pretty, too, from the photo he'd seen: thickish brown hair framing an oval face and a nice smile. Not Matti's usual type. Dr Miriam Cantwell was Deputy Director of the Emergency Room in New York's City Center Hospital.

Morton had called Washington. Bill Gates, the CIA's Director of Operations, said Lou Panchez was out of Colombia. Morton explained the situation and asked for Lou to be seconded. No problem, Gates had said. At this level inter-agency co-operation was still good. It was only the politicians who soured things. Gates had added Lou was heading for New York, probably to see his sister. Morton had met Liza Panchez once. She was an editor with the Associated Press. He remembered her as being friendly but tough.

There'd been no way he could call Rome. Wolfie and Michelle would be out of contact until after the take-out.

He'd waited until now to phone London. It was eleven o'clock at night there. Steve and Dolly would be back. He could imagine them, sitting in their room, discussing the day, the way they did every evening. He started to dial the Connaught.

On the television across the room there was a cookery programme. A pretty Sabra was explaining how to make an Arab dish. She kept stressing the culinary links of both races. If only someone could forge all the other links that had been broken.

When the hotel operator answered he asked for the Vaughans' suite. There was a pause, then Steve's cautious voice. 'Hello. Professor Vaughan speaking.'

'How are you, Papa?'

'Davey, how did you find us so soon?' Steve's pleasure was child-like.

Morton laughed. 'Tante Hannah.'

'Ach . . . who else?' He heard Steve call out. 'Hey, Dolly, it's Davey. Davey, let your Mama tell you what a wonderful day we had –'

At that moment the roar of the explosion came travelling through the telephone wires. Then silence.

'Papa,' he shouted. 'Papa!'

But the line was dead. Morton gave an almost inhuman sound, which drowned out yet another reminder from the cook of the unity between Jew and Arab.

In one fleeting moment, which held both the past and the future, Morton saw in his mind the words from the Koran verse, saw the intercept Bitburg had handed him, saw Tante Hannah reading Steve and Dolly's itinerary. They were all part of Raza's tomorrow that was here.

9

During the afternoon a mist had crept up the canyons from the East River. Matti Talim saw that here on Park Avenue its cold embrace had shortened tempers. The rush for cabs was more vicious, a need to beat the traffic lights more frantic.

Matti liked fog. You could get away with more under its blanket. Morton had said that when he'd taken him on his first assignment, to London. On a cold, foggy November night they'd bugged the embassy of another of those African nations aiding terrorists. Since then he'd been one of Morton's Men. After Iraq, Morton had sent him to New York. The posting was a prized one because New York, with its burgeoning Middle East population, had replaced Washington as Mossad's prime focus of interest in North America.

The fog gave people on Park a haunted look. Perhaps it was a fear of being trapped. Miriam had said that was why the Indians parted with Manhattan for a few baubles, they'd have taken anything for the place. She was still the only New Yorker he knew who could be truly unblinkered about the city.

Around Matti the powerful and pretentious moved with a weariness as if this was what was required of them. They seldom gave him a second glance. Those who did saw a medium-height, brown-haired, lightly tanned figure in a windcheater and ski pants. Those who still remembered Montgomery Clift, said it couldn't be. Even at his physical peak, Clift had never moved like someone who was serious about working out.

Fitness was a way of life with Matti. But when he'd realised he was going to finish in the top twenty in last year's New York Marathon, he'd deliberately dropped back. His need for obscurity overrode all else.

When he had finally told Miriam who he was, because there was no way he could keep it from her if their relationship was to have any meaning, she'd asked if that was why he was so sceptical. He'd replied his work was a continuing education in human frailty.

She'd called him her thirty-four-year-old cynic. Miriam labelled everything. He supposed medicine did that to you.

Ahead Matti saw the jostle operation was moving to a climax. He'd spotted its beginning a couple of blocks back. The four young Hispanics had singled out the elderly white couple who were clearly tourists. One by one the youths had cruised past, checking for jewellery and how tight the woman held her handbag. Now as the couple prepared to cross the street, the team's blocker was ready to make his move.

Matti quickened his pace, cutting through the crowd. The couple were looking at the stop light. Only tourists waited for the walk sign. The blocker was alongside them, ready to trip and fall in their path as the couple stepped off the sidewalk. The other Hispanics were nearby. When the blocker fell, he would bring down the couple with him. The other gang members would rush forward to help. In the mêlée one of the Hispanics would make off with the woman's handbag. It happened 50,000 times a year in the city.

Talim reached the couple as the blocker made his move, beginning to turn and stumble in their path. Without breaking his stride, Matti gripped the kid firmly by the arm, pulling him to one side. The crew, moving in, hesitated.

'Not this time,' murmured Matti, pushing the blocker away.

The old couple smiled vaguely at him, and Matti smiled back. He walked with them across the street and stayed close until they turned into the Drake Hotel, two more who believed it could only happen to somebody else. New York was full of people who never listened. They were like Bitburg.

A week ago Bitburg had sent a Double Flash – the most urgent of Mossad's priority signals – saying the Syrians were using the United Nations Building to broker a new arms deal with China.

Matti suspected the Syrians were too smart for that, but a Double Flash brooked no argument.

He'd had a crew from Swift Renovations spend a great deal of money and ingenuity to install more of Danny Nagier's bugs in the offices of the Syrian and Chinese delegations.

Morton had created the company to handle all Mossad's needs in the United States, and its staff were experts at anything from refurbishing a safe house to providing back-up for a take-out. But their speciality was surveillance. Matti knew more than one New York cop or janitor had received generous kickbacks for looking the other way while Swift's technicians went about their business.

Once the bugs were in place he'd spent his day in a van parked close to the UN, listening to the Syrians and Chinese. Some of it had been interesting, but there'd been nothing about an arms deal.

Matti's suspicion had hardened that this was another of Bitburg's attempts to show he knew what was going on. An hour ago, when he'd signed the surveillance log, he'd told the Swift crew to wrap the operation.

Striding up Park, Matti continued to think about the report he'd send Bitburg. Plenty of detail; Bitburg loved that. But nothing for him to point to and say the operation should have continued. A mention the Swift people had done their usual good job and that the bugs had worked perfectly. Final costings to follow.

With a bit of luck, when he saw them it would be weeks before Bitburg came up with something else.

Turning into 510 Park, an apartment block, Matti decided he'd send Morton a copy. He'd read between the lines and understand.

Matti crossed the lobby and checked his mail box. It was stuffed with the day's usual junk. He'd read somewhere the average New Yorker received fourteen pounds a year. With the junk was the envelope containing his tickets for the Pramoggia concert at Madison Square Garden the following night. He'd kidded Miriam he'd come down to Emergency and drag her away if she phoned to say she couldn't make it.

Dumping the junk in a trash box, Matti took the elevator to the nineteenth floor. He wondered whether the couple at the

Drake knew they were staying under the same roof as the celebrated tenor. But what would they have made of Pramoggia's passion for teenage girls?

Pramoggia travelled the world's concert circuit with a bevy of them. One was a Sudanese whom Morton had recruited a year ago. Before Pramoggia moved on to Los Angeles, Matti would meet the girl and she'd tell him everyone the tenor had met in New York. Pramoggia's renowned support for the PLO had made him a legitimate target for Mossad.

The door to 1903 looked the same as all the others, mahogany veneered. But the Ingersoll had been replaced with a mortice lock and key made by a Mossad locksmith. The day before Matti had moved in, a Swift Renovations crew had fitted the lock when they'd changed the original door. The replacement had an inch-thick steel plate in the middle, strong enough to resist a hand grenade or incendiary bomb.

He opened the door, and from force of habit immediately locked it behind him. He switched on the light, breaking the camel hair he'd placed across the switch. Tel Aviv sent a fresh supply of hairs every month. It wasn't foolproof, nothing was. The trick was to make it as hard as possible.

The apartment was large and airy. It consisted of a living-room, two bedrooms, one en-suite, and a superbly equipped kitchen. Matti only used it for making popcorn and coffee. Eating out was part of the job, to go where the enemy ate.

When he'd moved in, he'd thought Swift Renovations must have furnished the place from their Baroque Period range. Everything was all gilt, flocked wallpaper and tables and chairs with bowed legs. It was like Versailles without the garden views.

But he'd come to like it when he'd seen how well his own rugs blended into the richness. He'd bought them in a street market in Tunis and they'd accompanied him from posting to posting, along with his collection of favourite books. Once they'd fitted into a shelf; now they occupied most of one wall. Miriam had squeezed her record collection in alongside.

They'd been sleeping together for nine months, when they both felt like it, sometimes at her apartment over on Third, sometimes here. The lack of pressure in the relationship was something they both valued.

Matti walked to the sideboard and checked his answering machine. Miriam had called to say she'd be over when her shift ended, and would he order in a pizza? Afterwards, they could watch a movie on television, just like any other couple. It was a good feeling, one he'd never experienced with the other women he'd dated. The nearest had been Liza Panchez, until they'd both realised there was not enough between them to make it really work. Liza had said she'd always be his friend. Sometimes a friend was better than a lover, she'd added. Miriam had shown he could have both.

Brentanos had phoned to say his copy of the latest Mossad exposé had arrived. Once a year someone wrote a book claiming to take off the lid. It was fun spotting the errors.

Liza's brother, Lou, had called from Kennedy. He said he'd phone again when he'd checked in at the Roosevelt. They hadn't seen each other since Iraq.

They'd first worked together after Lockerbie when Morton arranged for Lou to be detached from the CIA because of his specialist knowledge about Arab terrorist contacts in the United States.

Matti discovered Lou shared his taste for good food and classical jazz. They'd become close enough for Lou to admit he was gay. That night they'd drunk a lot of wine, but even then Matti hadn't quite been able to hide his surprise. He'd asked if the CIA knew. Lou had replied no and yes: no Langley didn't know; yes it would matter if it did. Matti had liked him even more then, for his honesty and dignity.

He'd take Lou to lunch tomorrow at the Plaza. They both enjoyed the Oak Room's ambience, which reminded them of Europe.

Morton's call was the last on the tape. There was no clue as to what he wanted; Morton was always economical on the phone. Matti decided he'd fix himself a drink before calling back.

He removed his jacket, revealing the shoulder holster, which fitted like a back brace.

Bitburg had sent a memo the other day reminding all field operatives to carry out regular target practice. Matti had faxed Morton to say he'd go to Coney Island and ask the shooting gallery attendant to let him use his Walther P.38 to knock down coconuts. If you do, send your prize to Bitburg, Morton had faxed back.

Matti wandered to the kitchen and made himself a whisky and soda. He'd acquired the taste in London. Jiggling ice in the glass, he ambled back to the living-room, went to the window and looked down on Park.

His view was slightly distorted. The Swift crew had coated the window with a clear varnish that would neutralise a bugging device. They had also fitted a second window inside the original frame. Its glass had withstood repeated test firings from an Uzi.

A breeze had come up to disperse the fog. Traffic was heavy. Outside the Drake a police line had been set up to keep back the opera groupies. Apart from Pavarotti and Domingo, Pramoggia was the only opera singer commanding such a following. Maybe he could be warned he was playing with fire over the PLO. Or better yet, maybe he could be turned. Morton had done that with Yasser Arafat's closest aide. For ten years the man had revealed all the PLO's plans to Mossad, until he was killed in a road accident.

A noise from the fax machine broke the apartment's silence. The second bedroom had been converted into a safe room, and, like all the other safe rooms in previous apartments, it was totally sound- and bugproof.

The message was marked: 'Urgent from Black Tiger.' Every Israeli Prime Minister had an animal code-name. Karshov's text was brief. 'Alert your A-list of potential attack.'

The list contained the names of all prominent Jews and organisations in New York. Matti could reach them all in minutes through his computer modem. But first he'd call Morton. He picked up the phone beside the fax and began to dial.

011 – the international entry code. He'd tell Morton the collective wisdom in Washington was that if Raza was going to strike, he'd do so in Europe.

972 – Israel. It was almost midnight there. The last A-list warning had been the week before Iraq invaded Kuwait.

3 – Tel Aviv. He began to dial Morton's apartment.

At that moment the room began to sway. A split second later Matti knew this was no earthquake. Only a large quantity of detonating Semtex could provide that deep whoofing sound. He dropped the phone in its cradle and ran to the window.

Several thousand tons of concrete and steel, which had formed the Drake's frontage on Park, was avalanching into the street, burying opera buffs already behind the police line and cabs pulling in and away from the hotel. A huge chunk of masonry hit a coach, crushing it. In moments the avalanche had raised a barrier twenty feet high across Park. A great cloud of white smoke mushroomed from the Drake.

Matti thought of the Sudanese girl, the elderly couple, the opera groupies and Pramoggia and said a silent prayer. No one deserved to die so obscenely.

Then professionalism took over. The white smoke indicated the bomb was so powerful it had sucked the oxygen from the air. He immediately ruled out the IRA. No motive. The Colombian drug barons settling a score with one of their own? They'd blown up hotels before. But that had been in South America. Only one of the Arab groups would have both the means and motive to strike in the heart of New York.

The phone was ringing. As Matti ran to answer, a second great explosion rent the air.

'Matti?' Lou Panchez was shouting in his ear. 'The Plaza's just blown!'

Matti could hear screams and shouts in his earpiece and the wail of sirens. He forced himself to stay calm. 'Where are you, Lou?'

'On Fifth. I was on my way to see Liza.'

The Associated Press was in Rockefeller Plaza, near the Plaza Hotel.

'I'll meet you there,' said Matti. The news floor would be as good a place as any for an overview.

'Right!' Lou had raised his voice even more. 'Matti, I figure this is why Morton's got me detached.'

So that's why Morton had called. Then it had to be Arabs.

'Welcome to the team, Lou.'

'Some welcome! They're going crazy down here!'

The sound of a third explosion came through Matti's earpiece. Then above the roar came Lou's yell.

'Jesus H. Christ! It looks like the Pierre! Whole place is covered in smoke. But it sure looks like the Pierre's taken –'

'I'll see you at Liza's,' said Matti, hanging up. He didn't need a commentary when he had a ringside seat.

Karshov's warning and Morton's recruiting Lou were both part of this. The realisation that he also would be, made Matti shiver, not from excitement or fear, but out of knowledge.

Outside the apartment door he heard the first fearful voice, a man's, followed by a woman's, then a jumble of panicked voices. It would be the same all over the city.

He called Miriam's direct line number. A man's voice answered and told him to hold. In the background he heard frantic activity, then her surgeon's clogs.

'Cantwell.'

'Miriam, how bad are things with you?'

'Bad, Matti. We've just had a Code One declared. That means expect up to a hundred casualties.'

City Center was the nearest hospital to the devastated hotels.

'We're pulling in doctors and nurses from anywhere. Even from those fancy private clinics on Fifth and Park. Paramedics, students, anyone who can thread a needle. Right now we're in the eye of the storm. Ten minutes, this place will be crazier than usual.'

Even so people would still move around her with respect. She commanded it naturally.

'Jesus, Matti, what sort of slime did this?' Her sudden anger gave her voice a cutting edge.

'The kind of people who do this everywhere.'

'Why here? What has this country done?'

What could he tell her that would make any sense?

'It's the price of democracy. The logical extension of being the world's policeman.'

'Then maybe it's time we gave up, and only looked after our own. If we'd done that, this would never have happened.'

'Maybe, maybe not.' He understood her anger.

In the background Matti heard her name being paged over the hospital loudspeaker.

'Matti, I've got to go and scrub. I'll see you when I see you.'

She hung up without saying goodbye. It was another of her ways.

As he put down the phone a fourth huge explosion engulfed the night. He ran back to the window. It was the Mayfair House, further along on Park. He watched, numbed, as its upper floors fell into the street. A couple of firetrucks and an ambulance making for the Drake disappeared beneath the debris.

This was not terrorism, but full-scale war.

Matti went to the phone to call Morton. The line was dead.

Zipping up his windcheater, he stuck a camel hair across the light switch, opened the apartment door and stepped into the corridor.

The commotion broke over him. Locking the door, he strode past the old woman railing that this was God's plan to punish New York, past the man shouting just as loudly that Nostradamus had predicted this, past all the fearful, angry or dazed men and women. One grabbed Matti's arm, asking him where he was going. He firmly shook her off and pushed open the door to the emergency stairs. There were 1,075 to the ground. He'd counted them the day he'd moved in.

Matti emerged on the AP newsroom floor. He still breathed easily, though he had run all the way, dodging the emergency service vehicles. As he'd reached Rockefeller Plaza several monster earth movers had lumbered up Fifth Avenue. Helicopters with powerful lifting winches were descending towards all four hotels. The first detachment of National Guards had arrived to help the police keep everyone not directly involved well back. He'd never known a city that could respond so quickly to disaster. Miriam would have said it was because New York was a permanent one.

Matti stood for a moment, taking in the scene. The atmosphere in the large, open-plan newsroom was like he remembered it from other major stories he'd seen breaking here: the massacres in Beijing's Tiananmen Square, the bloody end to Ceausescu's dictatorship, the collapse of the Berlin Wall, the start of the Gulf War.

Then, as now, there was a controlled calmness. Reporters were like Intelligence operatives, detached, no matter how horrific the event. That was another reason Morton had recruited several as assets. Matti decided he'd try and call him from Liza's office. She'd pretend not to listen. She'd learned that from being around Lou.

Matti could see him in her office on the far side of the floor. Liza was on the phone as usual and Lou was standing behind her reading off her VDU screen – a big man with a big man's way of standing, loose and gangly. Lou looked tired, tired and worried.

Liza saw Matti and waved him over.

Crossing the floor he felt the extent of what had happened bearing in on all sides.

At the Plaza the explosion had been sufficiently powerful to hurl debris several hundred yards. So far thirty-six bodies had been recovered. The injured already totalled over fifty. The Pierre's celebrated La Forêt restaurant had taken the brunt of the casualties, killing sixty diners and staff.

Several eye witnesses all described the Mayfair House roof garden rising even higher above the Manhattan skyline, while at the same moment they'd seen a pinprick of light expand, followed by the explosion and collapse of the hotel's upper floors. Already a score of bodies had been recovered. The death toll at the Drake was a confirmed twenty-nine. Among them was Pramoggia.

From his jacket pocket Matti removed the concert tickets and dropped them in a trash can, as he entered Liza's office. She was the senior night editor. With her girlish good looks people often found that hard to believe.

She was typing swiftly in short bursts onto the VDU. The phone was cradled beneath her chin and she was concentrating hard. She waved at Matti and fired another burst onto the screen.

Lou turned to Matti. 'They've hit London and Paris as well. Four hotels in each,' he said, without preamble.

'Holy shit!' said Matti. 'How bad?'

Lou ran his hands over his face, as if washing without water. 'Dead? Close to four hundred, and climbing. At least a thousand injured. Liza's talking to her White House man. The President's calling an emergency cabinet. He'll want to kick ass hard on this. A lot of ass.'

'Anyone claiming?'

'Not yet.'

'It's got to be Raza, Lou. No one else would have had the resources.'

'I guess.'

'So what's the President going to do? Bomb everyone whose given Raza a bed for the night?'

Lou shook his head. 'It's not like the old days, Matti. His

Arabists have an overview for everything. And there's a permanent hands off the Middle East clause built into it.'

'Maybe this will open their eyes?'

'I doubt it.'

'Me, too.'

Lou stared out into the newsroom. People found it hard to believe he and Liza were twins. He looked at least ten years older. It was a combination of the eyes that were permanently red-rimmed and clothes as unfashionable as his sideburns and Zapata moustache. But he'd never been one for caring what others thought. He turned back to Matti.

'What now, Matti?'

'First I call Morton.'

Liza finished her call and turned to them. 'What do you make of this, Matti? You think this is Raza's only shot, or just for openers?'

He knew that look. It was her best-guess stare.

'A dozen hotels, Liza. More dead and injured than we've seen in a whole year of terrorist attacks. I figure that'll satisfy even Raza's blood lust.'

'Morton go with that?'

He grinned quickly. 'You want to ask him?'

'You ever tried to ask Morton anything? You wish you'd never asked.'

'Can I ask for a phone?'

She waved to one by the couch. 'Say hello to Morton from me.'

Liza fielded another call as Matti began to dial. Lou stood beside him. There was no reply from Morton's home number. Matti started to dial the Mossad switchboard in Tel Aviv when out of the corner of his eye he saw Liza stiffen and wave at him to stop. He put down the phone.

'We've got a claim,' she said, pushing a button on her desk console. 'I'll put it on broadcast.'

Out on the floor Matti saw reporters starting to congregate around the city desk where a rewrite man with a headset was poised over a keyboard to type up the call while it was being recorded. A number of senior news executives had crowded into Liza's office. They all stared at the wall speaker behind her desk.

There was a hiss, then a woman's voice filled the room.

'I speak in the name of Raza the Freedom Fighter for all oppressed peoples of Islam! What has happened in your three temple cities of fascism and imperialism is no more than a warning to heed carefully our demands.'

Matti thought the voice had an intensity bordering on religious fervour; a fanatic teetering between sanity and madness.

'Our first demand is that each member of the Permanent Council of the United Nations, in the name of the entire Assembly, will pledge that the Zionists will be removed from our land, and which they call Israel. This pledge will be given within twenty-four hours.'

Matti swore softly. 'No way, lady. No way at all.'

'Our second demand is that before it ceases to exist, the Zionist state agrees to destroy all its nuclear weapons. Similarly, all other tactical weapons placed there to aid and abet the existence of the Zionist state by its allies will also be destroyed.'

'She's leaving Israel naked,' gasped Liza.

The voice spoke again deliberately.

'Thirdly, all profits from oil fields and mineral exploration from Nigeria to the Persian Gulf will be redivided. At present the peoples of these lands only benefit by forty per cent. They will from now on receive eighty per cent. Further, one billion dollars will be provided by the said oil and mineral companies to be divided between the oppressed lands they have exploited for so long.'

Lou Panchez's jaw worked. 'She's using the jargon of legality to hijack the world!'

'Fourthly, every member of the United Nations will sign a properly binding protocol to ensure no pornography or drugs will continue to sully the purity of Islam. What you do in your world is your business. We want no part of your decadent culture, or your corruption of our moral values.'

The voice paused briefly, then resumed.

'The second, third and fourth demands must be completed in full within seven days. You have twenty-four hours to accept. Any attempt to negotiate or vary the terms of these demands and you will receive further proof that we possess the means to destroy your brutal, fascist society that oppresses us!'

In the silence a button light blinked on Liza's console. It was an unlisted number. Liza picked up the receiver and listened for a moment.

'He's right here.' She nodded to Matti and handed him the phone.

'Yes?' said Matti, already knowing who it was.

'Go to the consulate with Lou and wait there,' instructed Morton.

IO

No one in Trekfontein saw the Bantu arrive. He came from the west, to keep the prevailing wind in his face and to mask the sound of his powerful motorcycle. The African National Congress had bought it for him, just as they had purchased the pouch of aerosol paints slung over his shoulder.

The Bantu parked the machine in one of the thickets of ebony at the foot of the turreted rocks. Even when he crouched he was tall, with the powerful legs of a natural runner. For hours he remained perfectly still in the thicket, watching the revelry on the sports field.

As the night wore on the dancing there became increasingly abandoned, the voices more drunken. It was the early hours before the last of the townspeople had driven uncertainly home back across the veldt. When the last of the lights had gone out, the Bantu waited another hour. Then, slinging the pouch across his shoulders he padded barefoot across the ground.

The night was almost pitch-black and oppressively hot. The moon fitfully appeared behind the cumulus thunderclouds. He hoped the storm would hold off until he had completed his work. The rain would hide his tracks. He would have come and gone like a thief in the night.

Nelson Mandela's aide had said there must be no stealing, but the Bantu had stolen all his young life to eat, to live.

He reached the first homestead and paused to lick his finger and raise it in the air. He changed direction to keep the faint breeze in his face, so that a dog would not sniff his scent. He removed one of the cans from the pouch and began to spray a pristine white wall with the letters: ANC.

In twenty minutes the Bantu had worked his way into the town, defacing a score of buildings with a variety of African National Congress slogans. He began to smile as he imagined the fury when they awoke of those snoring drunkenly behind the open bedroom windows. Increasingly confident he would not be spotted, the Bantu quickly peered into houses, his skull eyes looking for something to steal. A small trinket would buy him bread and leave enough over to visit one of Soweto's beer halls. But there was nothing within easy reach.

He completed daubing the colonnades of the Dutch Reformed Church and paused to select another target. His eyes settled on an imposing building across the street. A block further away glowed the night light over the door of the police station.

The Bantu swiftly crossed the broad street that had been designed to allow ox-driven wagons to turn, and reached the building. He could dimly make out the letters over the front of its verandah: Grand Hotel.

The roof of the verandah was flat. Above it was the hotel proper, a white expanse of wall broken by the windows of the bedrooms. All but one was closed.

Standing on the balustrade of the verandah, the Bantu hoisted himself on to the flat roof. He crouched for a moment, listening. Across the town a dog was barking. It must have picked up his scent. It would soon be time to leave. He chose green and yellow aerosols and began to spray the wall with the title of the ANC's anthem: 'Nkosi Sikelel i Africa'.

Once more the moon emerged from behind a thundercloud, making it easier for the Bantu to work. His arm moved up and down to cover the hotel frontage with six-foot-high lettering.

The second word brought him to the open bedroom window. He peered in and could not believe his luck. The moonlight picked out an expensive leather bag beside the bed. It alone would fetch enough on Soweto's thriving black market to keep him in food and beer for a month. The bag was open and in the pale light he glimpsed something that made his heart race even faster. There was not one camera, but several. Each would guarantee him a fortune. He put down his aerosols.

For the first time he looked at the woman asleep on the bed.

She had kicked off the sheet and lay on her stomach, with her back to him, her great mane of red hair spread over the pillow. Her skin was the colour of ivory in the moonlight.

Unease joined the Bantu's feeling of excitement. The law was clear. Any black who entered the bedroom of a white woman was held to be intent on rape. On conviction, a man could be sent away for twenty years.

Yet that bag and cameras the Bantu knew, could secure his future for even longer.

With the utmost stealth and speed he slipped over the window-sill. The dog was still barking.

Lila stirred on the bed. A combination of the warm night and the tension that always went with a mission had made her drift in and out of sleep, her mind restlessly picking up on the smallest thing. Why was that dog barking? The fascist pig of a police captain had said the dogs of Trekfontein were trained to bark only at Kaffirs. How did they manage that when there were none around to practise on? It wasn't the barking that had once more awoken her, it was a sound she had last heard in the streets of Beirut – the faint but unmistakable hiss of the aerosols of the graffiti gangs going about their business in the dead of the night.

Lila turned as the Bantu slid across the window frame. She saw his face gleaming with the sweat of sudden fright. He had nothing in his hand. She could smell his sour body smell. She had no weapon; she never carried one on a mission. To do so was to court disaster.

The figure remained rooted to the spot, breathing softly. An animal about to spring.

Lila tensed herself. If she could get a grip on his carotid, she would stop him, kill him even.

He hadn't moved.

Lila groped for the panic button, built into the bedside panel, which also controlled the room's lights, television and radio.

The manager had made a point of explaining the button was linked directly to the police station, that it was part of the price whites had to pay to go on living in a land where they were increasingly threatened.

Lila pressed the button. A red light glowed on the panel.

In a couple of strides the figure had crossed the floor, snatched up the camera bag and was out of the window.

Lila leapt from the bed in pursuit. By the time she reached the window, the figure had raced along the verandah roof and shinned down a corner post. He landed lightly on the balls of his feet and was off, running at full tilt.

Lila leaned out of the window and began to scream.

'Stop! Thief! Stop him!'

More dogs were barking. The first lights were coming on. A uniformed figure was running from the police station. She recognised the police captain.

But the Bantu had vanished into the night with the bag containing the bottle of Anthrax-B-C.

By the time Lila had dressed, the captain was at the bedroom door. With him was the hotel manager. He rushed to the window.

'What happened, missie?' he asked.

Lila told him.

She could not stop trembling. She should have hidden the bottle in the wardrobe or chest. She should have kept the window closed. Basic precautions. Instead she had behaved like someone on her first mission – not thinking. Kids in Beirut got killed for that. Raza would kill her.

The captain spoke into his walkie-talkie. 'We got a Kaffir on the loose. Get everybody out!'

He turned to Lila, smiling reassurance. 'It's only your cameras, missie. It could have been a lot worse.'

Outside in the street voices were drawing attention to the slogans. The first police Land Rover had arrived. Its powerful searchlight began to play over the crudely daubed words on the hotel front.

The captain ran for the door. Lila followed with the manager.

By the time they reached the street, three more police Land Rovers had pulled up. Each contained a pair of constables armed with rifles.

The length of the street, figures were appearing in windows. The captain picked up a bullhorn and began to speak.

'This is the police. There's a Kaffir on the rampage. He could be armed. Stay indoors. If you see him call the station.'

'You'll never find him in this dark,' said Lila.

'We'll find him,' said the captain grimly.

He turned to the nearest Land Rover.

Lila clutched his arm. 'I'd like to come with you. To make sure all my cameras are safe. There's twenty-thousand-rands' worth of equipment there.'

'Okay, missie. Get in.'

The captain briefed his men, sending one Land Rover out on the reservoir road, a second towards the road that led to Johannesburg. The third was ordered to check the area around the rocks.

'Give your searchlight plenty of play. Make as much noise as you can. It'll panic the Kaffir. He'll run into our arms,' said the captain. He gave a short, barking laugh. 'He'll wish he never came near us!'

Lila squeezed in between the captain and the driver. In convoy the Land Rovers roared down Trekfontein's main street and separated at the bottom.

'The Kaffir must have come here by some sort of vehicle,' explained the captain as the vehicle began to bounce over the veldt. 'But he may just panic and make a run for it. These Kaffirs can run fifty miles without any problem. Just like a hyena.'

'What'll you do when you catch him?' asked Lila. She gripped the dash as the Land Rover raced over the ground.

'Let's catch him first,' laughed the captain.

They'd only driven a few miles before the radio under the dash hissed.

'This is Bravo-One to all units. We have located his motorbike at the bottom of Impi Kop.'

The captain spoke into the microphone. 'This is Command to all units. Bravo-One, check the rocks. He may try to double back after you pass. Bravo-Two work your way back from the reservoir. Bravo-Three when you get five miles down the Jo'burg road, turn back. Even our Kaffir won't have run any further. We're heading south of the rocks in case he tries to head for home the long way.'

Its searchlight constantly sweeping the darkness, the Land Rover dragged a cloud of dust behind it across the veldt. The moon had disappeared. Away to the east, the first faint glimmer of grey light was emerging.

Across the veldt the lights of the other vehicles rose and fell. From time to time the radio crackled with reports of sightings. Each quickly proved to be groundless.

'Move it, man!' barked the captain. 'I want this Kaffir before the rain comes.'

The truck lunged forward up an incline. The captain turned and grinned at Lila.

'You look sick as a dog, missie.'

Lila smiled wanly. 'My editor will fire me for losing those cameras.'

The captain patted her arm. 'I'll give you a full report to show him. No way he can blame you for a Kaffir doing this.'

Once he knew, Raza would send someone. There'd be no place to hide. She'd be hunted down. She'd seen it happen before – when she had been one of the hunters.

'What's that?' yelled the captain, pointing the searchlight. Ahead the veldt stretched, broken with clumps of dark bush, trees and tall grass.

The light beam picked out the black mass of the buffalo herd a quarter of a mile in front. They were picking up speed as they ran, hunched together and bellowing.

'Something's scared them,' yelled the captain. He reached for the mike. 'Command to all units. Circle towards Impi Kop.'

Lila sat silent and numbed beside him, both hands clutching at the dash for support as the Land Rover continued to bucket and plunge across the plain. They passed behind the herd.

Ahead the ground sloped sharply upwards to a tree-lined crest.

'My great-grandfather drove an entire Kaffir tribe from here. Just him and a handful of other boys. He was sixteen, but he could already hit a bok or a Kaffir at a hundred yards and going at full speed,' the captain said.

'There! There, there!' yelled Lila. 'I saw something move!'

The captain swept the searchlight towards the tree line.

The Bantu was running with total concentration. His head was hunched into his shoulders and his arms pumped steadily, helping him maintain a fast, constant progress over the ground.

Lila saw the camera bag draped over his shoulders was thumping rhythmically against his back.

'You've got good eyes, missie,' said the captain. He spoke into the mike. 'Command to all units. The Kaffir's on Impi Kop. Get beyond in case we miss him.'

Letting go the searchlight, the captain reached for the carbine in its rack behind the bench seat. The light swung wildly over the ground.

Lila turned to the captain. 'If you shoot him, you could damage my cameras.'

A ricochet could break the bottle. She could still be dead before nightfall.

The Land Rover reached the trees. The copse was bigger than Lila had realised. The trunks rose out of a tangle of undergrowth. The driver stopped and jumped from the vehicle. He removed a second rifle from the rack.

The captain gave another laugh. 'We're going to have to hunt our Kaffir on foot.'

He adjusted the searchlight so that its beam automatically swivelled on its pod, sending a swathe of light into the copse. On the veldt, the lights of the other Land Rovers were converging towards the trees.

'Kaffir, come on out,' called the captain. 'You're not going anywhere.'

Every few yards he repeated the words. Suddenly a bush moved to Lila's left and the face she'd glimpsed in the bedroom rose into view. He held his hands high in the air. He looked fearfully at the two rifles.

'Okay, baas, I surrender,' said the Bantu.

The captain nodded. 'Take that bag off your shoulder, Kaffir.'

The Bantu removed the bag. The constable walked over and picked it up. He handed the bag to Lila. She began to rummage through it.

The captain nodded again towards the Bantu. 'You taken anything out, Kaffir?'

The Bantu repeatedly shook his head. 'No, baas, nothing.'

Lila's hand found the bottle. She felt it all over. The glass was intact. She began again to shiver all over.

'Everything there, missie?' enquired the captain solicitously.

Lila made a show of producing and checking the cameras. She turned and smiled at the captain.

'No harm done.'

'Very good, missie. Now you just go back to the Land Rover,' said the captain quietly.

Lila nodded, suddenly understanding. She turned and walked

128

away. Behind her, the captain spoke to the Bantu in the same tone.

'Now, Kaffir, you know better than to do what you did. And if you didn't, Mr Mandela and his people should have told you.'

'Baas, you take me to police station, yes?' asked the Bantu fearfully.

The dawn was coming fast. On the far side of the copse the other Land Rovers were arriving. Lila heard the captain order.

'Turn round, Kaffir.'

She turned in time to see the captain's rifle jump sharply, the barrel kicking upwards at the recoil. The Bantu was flung violently forward on his face as the heavy soft-nosed bullet entered his back.

The captain and constable dragged the body between them to the Land Rover and dumped it in the back.

'The trouble with Kaffirs is that they always try to escape,' sighed the captain, politely motioning for Lila to get in. 'The law's clear enough. We're entitled to use whatever force is necessary to detain them, especially when it's someone as dangerous as our Kaffir. If you hadn't pressed your panic button, he could have raped and then murdered you. When a Kaffir like that tries to make a run, you've got to be firm.'

After that, they rode in silence back to Trekfontein. People were already out cleaning away the graffiti, and they cheered as the police convoy passed.

When Lila entered the hotel lobby the manager was waiting. In his hand was a message slip. Seeing the camera bag he beamed with relief.

'Looks like you're going to be leaving us,' said the manager.

He glanced at the paper. 'Your editor called. He wants you to catch the next flight to Athens. I've already checked there's a ten o'clock out of Jo'burg tonight. You'll be there for breakfast.'

'Thank you,' said Lila.

Suddenly she felt inordinately hungry. Raza's call meant that everything was proceeding exactly as planned. The hour was close for her to play her part.

II

Morton was in a well-padded chair in the windowless Situation Room adjoining Karshov's office. During a crisis the Prime Minister always found it reassuring to know he was next door. Twenty-two hours had elapsed since Raza's demands.

An outsize desk and the chair were the room's only furniture. The rest was state-of-the-art communications and audio-visual equipment.

The room was a scaled-down duplicate of the War Room on the other side of the Prime Minister's office. Since the bombings, the War Room had been manned by a team of strategists. While Morton could monitor their work through closed-circuit television, he worked entirely alone in this cramped room.

On one wall was a bank of monitors. They enabled Morton to follow developments in London, Paris and Washington, and at the United Nations in New York. Other screens relayed information from Interpol and police forces in Europe engaged in the hunt for the bombers.

A couple of IRA cells had been unearthed in Holland along with a bomb-making factory serving Turkish terrorists in Germany. But there had been no trace of the hotel bombers.

At the UN the Permanent Council had agreed after a short discussion to reject the demands that Israel should give up its territorial rights and destroy its nuclear weapons. The decision had then been put before all member states for ratification. The debate had lasted ten hours. An overwhelming majority had supported the Permanent Council; eight Arab nations abstained.

In Washington, Paris and London, cabinets remained in

closed session after issuing similar communiqués that the perpetrators of the bombings would be hunted down.

The oil- and mineral-mining multi-nationals had jointly refused to meet the demands made of them.

Bitburg had appeared on one of the closed-circuit screens to say this was the first time since the Gulf War that the world was standing up to terrorism. It was the closest he had come to admitting he was wrong about Raza being finished.

Since then the hands on the 24-hour wall clock above Morton's desk had moved forward another hour. Beneath the clock Morton had taped a card bearing two scrawled words: *First Deadline*. It was a constant reminder of the time remaining before Raza's threatened second attack. There were now under two hours left.

Minutes ago the text of a statement from Ayatollah Muzwaz had appeared on the monitor labelled: *Arab Reactions*.

The statement called for the Islamic world to be vigilant in the face of provocation by the infidels. Muzwaz went on to repeat his familiar attacks on Israel, the West, capitalism and imperialism.

Bitburg's face was back on screen. His eyes were steady, his manner composed.

'Pure bluster, David! Muzwaz knows Raza made a huge miscalculation in blowing those hotels. If he was backing Raza before, he most certainly won't want to do so now!'

'I'm not so sure, Walter. That business about being vigilant in the face of provocation could be Muzwaz preparing his people for the next stage. It's the old Saddam trick of telling them they are going to be hit. When Raza does something else, Muzwaz can present it as a necessary pre-emptive self-defence.'

'You're wrong, David! Muzwaz will huff and puff for a few more days because he has to. But now that everyone's standing firm, he will know that whatever Raza tries, he is not going to succeed. Therefore he'll want to keep his powder dry for another day. And Raza couldn't have expected the reaction he's generated by the bombings. There's been nothing like it. Look at your monitors! The whole world's up in arms! The best that Raza can hope for is to be able to disappear back into the woodwork!'

Morton stared at Bitburg's screen. How could a man like this have risen so high?

'He's still got the anthrax, Walter.'

'So you keep saying. So why didn't he use it? That would have made more sense than all these crazy demands.'

'I told you what The Syrian said.'

Bitburg shook his head slowly. 'He wasn't able to pinpoint those hotels, David. It's the same with this threat of Raza's to do something further. It's very vague. And whatever else he might have been cooking up, he will most certainly now have given up.'

'Let's wait and see, Walter.'

Bitburg sighed loudly. 'David, David, why are you so stubborn?'

'Call it my gut reacting, Walter.'

Bitburg was still shaking his head when his face vanished from the screen.

For a moment Morton sat staring at the blank monitor. Then he turned to the Honeywell and tapped in a summary of the call.

The computer had made it that much easier to confirm what had happened to Steve and Dolly. It said to call Fuller.

Harry Fuller was Assistant Commissioner, Crime, at New Scotland Yard. He'd been in the job so long people simply called him 'ACC'. Morton had worked with him on a dozen operations.

The ACC had answered his car phone from the chaos around the Connaught. He'd listened without interruption and quietly said if it was any consolation, Steve and Dolly would have felt nothing. None of the thirty-four victims would have done so.

Morton had called Hannah. She had wept uncontrollably. When he'd told Karshov, the Prime Minister had cursed long and hard in Polish. Morton remembered Steve and Karshov had prayed for years at the same synagogue and kept the festivals together. The Prime Minister had said he'd send Israel's only Concorde to bring home the bodies.

Then it had been business as usual.

He had Matti transmit a copy of the tape the AP had received, and told Lou to return to Washington to liaise with the CIA and FBI.

Morton had then ordered Lester Finel, who ran Mossad's computers, to get his programmers working on the identity of the bombers. Chantal Bouquet, Head of the Foreign Intelligence Desk, had been set to probe as only she knew how the wider ramifications of the bombings. Why had British, French and

American Intelligence failed to pick up even a whisper? Bad field craft? Or something else? Before Lockerbie the Germans had suppressed vital information about the bombers because it compromised their own operations.

Psychological Assessment had been told to prepare a briefing paper on the options open to all radical Arab leaders. Would they support Muzwaz – and would the cabal feel the time had come to launch a holy war?

Covert Action had been instructed to produce a short list of candidates who could be slotted into the team.

Meanwhile the ACC had called three more times, to report on the explosions at the Savoy, Claridge's and the Berkeley. It was the worst devastation London had experienced since the Blitz.

Lacouste, the Deputy Director of French Intelligence, had filled in details of the destruction in Paris. Five floors of the Maurice had collapsed, and there were already forty known deaths. At the Georges V, over fifty bodies had been recovered. The Grand's frontage had fallen on two coachloads of guests returning from a tour of the city. A hundred were feared killed. The number of dead at the Crillon had reached seventy and was certain to increase.

Lacouste had said it was the price for allowing France to become a haven for terrorists. Morton had understood his cold fury.

Successive French governments had paid huge sums to the Beirut hostage takers to free its nationals, and struck deals with the PLO and Saddam Hussein. France's once vaunted security forces were hamstrung and demoralised. Only men like Lacouste had the will to continue and wage war against terrorism.

The anger was still there when the Paris monitor once more displayed Lacouste's gaunt, patrician-like face.

'We have limited descriptions of the bombers from hotel clerks who remember well-dressed Arabs checking in with expensive luggage,' he said.

'Can you fax them to Finel? We'll match them with what we have. One thing, for sure, Raza's terrorists always know how to blend with the background.'

Lacouste grunted. 'We have a doorman who recalls an Arab leaving several hours before the explosion at the Maurice. A floor maid says she remembers the Do Not Disturb sign on the Arab's door. She says there was nothing unusual in that.'

'Same story from the other hotels, Pierre. The bombers checked in, wired their rooms to blow at pre-set times then slipped away. Every hotelier's nightmare come true. The wonder is that it hasn't happened before now.'

Lacouste gave another grunt. 'The tape any help?'

He and the ACC had each transmitted a copy of the tapes received in London by the Press Association and in Paris by *Agence France Presse*. They were identical to the one sent to the Associated Press. Morton had played them several times. He'd then sent them to Voice Analysis. Its technicians were among the best in the field.

'No news yet. The moment it comes, I'll make sure you know,' said Morton.

'Thank you, David.' Lacouste's pinched face grew pensive. 'Do you think Raza will strike again?'

'Yes.'

'Me, too. But where?'

'Where indeed?'

They both laughed softly and without any pleasure.

Moments later the monitor that fed the satellite link from Washington bleeped. Morton punched a key on the console and the face of Lou Panchez filled the screen; he glanced down to check his notes.

'The FBI are satisfied the tone pulse of the call to the AP places it outside the continental United States. Anywhere from between five to eight thousand miles.'

Morton turned and studied a map on the wall behind. He turned back to the screen.

'That gives us maybe between the Philippines in the Pacific and the whole of Southern Europe and into Asia. Can't they do better than that, Lou?'

'I'll keep pushing.'

'Tell them that the French and Brits believe their calls came from within Europe.'

'Will do.'

'Any whisper from the White House, Lou?'

'Nothing concrete. But there seems to be a consensus that Raza will hold off now that he's stirred up this hornet's nest.'

'They're wrong, Lou,' said Morton, ending the conversation.

Damn Bitburg. He'd been casting his reassurances on waters only too eager to be calmed.

Morton turned to the Honeywell. He had already commanded it to produce lists of potential targets for Raza. The computer had identified over fifteen thousand in Europe, North America, Africa, Asia and Australia. Morton had eliminated them as either too obvious or not sufficiently important or spectacular enough to provide a follow-up to the hotel bombings.

He tapped on the keyboard the instruction for the Honeywell to search for targets that were both unusual and yet in themselves sufficiently high profile, then went to see the Prime Minister.

Karshov was alone, riffling through the growing number of messages on his desk. From an outer office came the voices of his aides politely fending off calls.

The Prime Minister looked up. 'Suddenly the whole world wants to reassure me that everything is going to be fine. And Walter, too. How about you, David? You want to make an old man very happy?'

Morton looked into the scarred face.

'I wish I could, Prime Minister.'

Karshov's face took on a haunted look.

'You know what they're beginning to say? That things would be even finer if we would be reasonable. They're beginning to murmur, how about a little land? The Gaza Strip, maybe? Or the West Bank, better even. Hand over one, or both, to the Arabs. Do that, they say, and we'll make sure Raza will never cause you a problem. No matter that it's treating with terrorism through the back door. No matter that we didn't cause these bombings. Forget all that, they say. We've still got to show willing. It's always *us*, David. Always.'

Morton had forgotten how many times he'd stood here and shared the Prime Minister's anger over the world's readiness to blame Israel.

'What about London and Washington?'

'They want a conference call in two hours. Time for the President to rehearse what to say. At least the British Prime Minister doesn't need to do that,' growled Karshov.

The hook-up would be from the studio adjoining the Prime Minister's office.

Karshov walked to the window and stared out into the night. Stars streamed across the heavens, tiny and glistening, remote and inaccessible.

'Did you know, David, that at the UN debate one of the Africans said the simple solution would be to send the Jews to outer space?' He turned and looked at Morton. 'This is the only real home I've ever had. I've fought in three wars to keep it. I've seen good people die for the same reason. The one thing I know is that no matter what Raza does, Israel stays.'

'I'm glad to hear that, Prime Minister. But the pressure will increase. You've said so yourself. Everybody will want you to make concessions.'

The anger broke through in Karshov's voice. 'We give nothing. All our lives we've been giving. Our people. Our blood. Our land. But no more!' He began to pace, each stride fuelling his fury. 'Raza and his kind have been threatening us for over forty years. In that time we've lost more of our people to terrorism than the rest of the world put together. In one year more Jews were murdered than in ten years in Northern Ireland. Munich, Vienna, Rome, Paris – there's hardly a city where our people's blood has not been spilt. And each time we've said we will never be driven from here. This is the land of our God, our religion, our people. And no one takes it. No one!'

Morton stood in silence. Not only did he understand and agree with what had been said, but he was now totally sure Karshov would support what he was going to say.

'Prime Minister,' he began carefully, 'we must encourage Raza to believe that. That will tempt him into the open. And next time we must make sure it will be his last.'

Karshov stared at him for a long moment.

'How can you be so certain?'

'Everything I know about Raza shows his one weakness is over-confidence. He showed that in London and Berlin. Other terrorists would never have tried that. Raza had to – because he's driven by a need to prove himself. These hotel bombings show that. Now he'll want to do something even more spectacular.'

'Like what? Blow up the Vatican? Buckingham Palace? Bring down the Golden Gate Bridge?'

'Possibly. But I think not. More likely he'll go for something more unusual. And something that just might win him a little sneaking sympathy in some circles.'

'Like what?' repeated Karshov.

Morton shook his head. 'Right now, I don't know. But I've asked the Honeywell to search.'

'And what do you want me to do in the meantime?'

'Be as firm as you always are. Stay at Condition Olive. Make it clear to everybody that Israel will not be cowed. That could just be enough to drive Raza into the open. A man on the rampage is always that much easier to bring down.'

There was a silence in the room that lasted from the time Karshov returned to stare out of the window and finally turned to face Morton.

'Very well. I'll do what you say. Walter won't like it. But I'll deal with Walter. A lot of people won't like it. But I'll handle them as well.'

'Thank you, Prime Minister.'

Karshov paused briefly. Morton was still listening. 'I'm also going to order our laboratories to start mass producing that PEG-enzyme. But we'll keep that quiet to avoid panic.' Karshov ran a hand over his face. 'And I'll want you here for that conference call.'

'I'll be there, for sure.'

Morton walked back to the Situation Room. The Honeywell was still searching. He programmed the computer to alert his bleeper once it had completed its task and then once more he left the room.

Lila stood on the shore of the reservoir and watched the perfume bottle she had tied to a piece of driftwood moving slowly with the current that would carry it to the sluice gate. When she could no longer see the bottle, she climbed back into the rental car and drove across the veldt towards Johannesburg.

It was late afternoon and she was in ample time to reach the airport and catch the eight o'clock flight to Nairobi. From there she would pick up a Lufthansa connection for Athens. The change from the Olympic non-stop flight the hotel manager had suggested was a routine precaution.

Not, in this case, that it would matter. In a few hours' time there would be nobody left alive in Trekfontein who would be able to describe her.

12

Twenty minutes after leaving the Prime Minister's compound
Morton passed through three separate security checks to enter
Mossad headquarters, a dun-coloured highrise overlooking the
road to Jerusalem. He inserted his colour-coded plastic card into
the slot and the elevator door opened and closed behind him.
Moments later a taped voice announced this was the seventh
floor. The elevator silently opened.

Facing Morton was a solid steel door. He spoke into a squawk
box set into the wall. The box was linked to a computer, which
identified the password as current. Morton had the password
changed daily, at one minute to midnight, a symbolic reminder
Israel had survived another day.

Immediately beyond the door was the large open-plan Operations Room. Its sepulchre-like calm was enhanced by the glow
from scores of VDU screens. Round the clock, specialists worked
here planning, activating and assessing.

Morton's eyes immediately went to one of the two bas-relief
maps on opposite walls. Light systems identified key installations.
Red bulbs pinpointed every Arab military airfield from Morocco
to Iran. Yellow indicated missile sites. Blue, supply dumps. None
of the lights was on. Israel's enemies had not gone to war
readiness.

The other map showed Israel was at Condition Olive. Every
base was on alert from northern Galilee to the Ghor. Where
Sodom and Gomorrah had stood, missile sites waited, primed.
Other rockets were at launch readiness along the Dead Sea.
Dotted among them were the batteries of Patriots, which had

dealt devastating blows to Saddam's Scud missiles. Close to Jerusalem, poised in their silos, stood the Peacemakers, the most powerful of Israel's rockets.

In the Negev, a bright pink light glowed steadily. Israel's nuclear weapons manufacturing complex was at full alert.

The head of Covert Action strode over. He was the one remaining member of the team that had snatched Adolf Eichmann in 1960 and brought him out of Argentina to Israel to face trial for genocide, and subsequent execution.

'I've got ten for your team. All men. Do you also want a woman?'

'I'll take a woman if she's like Michelle.'

The section leader sighed. 'Another Michelle I don't have. But different and as good. Okay?'

'For sure,' Morton nodded. 'Anything from Rome?'

'Wolfie's called to say they're set. He thinks the hotel bombings could make it easier. Al-Najaf will be up-beat. Always easier then.'

'It's never easy, Abe,' grunted Morton. 'Just sometimes less difficult. But never easy.'

Abe was a good man, but he'd been out of the field too long.

Morton turned away and pushed open the heavily padded door marked Voice Analysis.

Beyond was a room with sound booths against the walls and a large central workbench covered with tape decks, oscilloscopes, editing machines and equipment he did not recognise, except for the flickering dials and coloured lights.

Every booth was occupied with a man or woman listening through a headset to versions of the tape of the woman's voice. It was being played at various speeds and voice pitches.

The unit's director, his huge bald dome of a head nodding as he worked, sat at the bench. Throughout Mossad he was known as Humpty Dumpty.

He waved Morton over and continued to spin the woman's voice from one spool of tape to another.

Beside Humpty Dumpty was a stooped-shouldered older man, the unit's behaviourist.

'So how's it going?' Morton asked.

'Going good,' replied Humpty Dumpty. 'We've identified the tape as a brand made by Sony only for the Middle East.'

Humpty Dumpty used a fleshy hand to indicate the equipment around him. 'So far we know the woman's of Greek extraction, but has lived in Beirut long enough to get a spread to her vowels. The tonal quality puts her somewhere between twenty-five and forty. There's a lot of anger she's managing to hold down.'

Morton turned to the behaviourist. He had recruited him on his last head-hunting trip.

The behaviourist assumed the authoritative manner he had once used in a senior teaching post at Harvard University.

'The level of tension in her voice indicates her guilt anxiety – what we call conscience. It only surfaces with certain words: "Zionists", "Israel", "brutal, fascist society". She's clearly driven by deep hatred. To exist, she will have had to virtually eliminate any capacity for normal human feelings – except those associated with her religion. There she will be fanatical. None of the usual conflicts and doubts. She totally believes that what she does is not only not wrong, but absolutely right.'

'I've seen a thousand like her in Beirut,' said Morton quietly. 'They're more frightening than the men.'

A technician emerged from a booth and walked over to Humpty Dumpty. 'She's got a lisp. When I bring her right down, it's clear. She has trouble with her "a"s and "ch"s.'

The technician had been a speech therapist in Montreal for twenty years before he joined Mossad.

Humpty Dumpty made a note on the pad before him and turned back to the behaviourist. 'Where'd she fit into Post's framework?'

When he'd been Director of the CIA's Psychological Division, Dr Jerrold Post had shown that many terrorists had led failed lives before joining a group. The behaviourist considered.

'She fits very well. Her voice patterns strongly suggest that in joining this terrorist group, she's experienced perhaps the first real sense of belonging. It's clear from the way she speaks that she believes the group will literally protect her against danger. She needs that sense of security to exist in the hostile outside world. Consequently she may very well react with unusual ferocity if she thinks the group's survival is threatened. That way, of course, the group maintains its cohesion.'

Morton nodded. He'd made the same discovery interrogating captured terrorists. They'd endure anything to protect their peers, he remembered as he walked to the office of the Director of Psychological Assessment.

He opened its outer door, then the baize divider, and finally the inner door. The room beyond was lit only by a single spot. Its light was focused to fall precisely across the clasped hands of the reclining figure on an old-fashioned consulting couch against one wall.

'David,' whispered a voice from the couch. 'Come in, come in. I was thinking about you.'

Morton quietly shut the door behind him. There was a movement from the couch then a light clicked on, bathing the room in a sudden warm pink.

Whenever he came here Morton always felt only Steve could have crammed more books into a room this size. They filled every inch of shelf space and stood on the floor in piles as tall as their owner.

'How are you, Professor?' asked Morton, coming forward.

'Fine, David, just fine,' murmured the Director. For thirty years he had held the Chair of Middle East Studies at Yale. Morton had persuaded him to come here to see his theories put into practice.

With a sudden, effortless movement that would not have disgraced a man half his sixty years, the professor rose from the couch. Vigour seemed to flow into his face.

'Meditation always helps,' he explained, his voice suddenly vibrant. He strode unerringly between the maze of books to a table piled with more volumes and paperwork. He picked up several sheets and scanned them. His back was turned to Morton.

'First drafts shouldn't be seen by anybody.' The professor ran a hand through his dishevelled hair as he read.

'Just give me an idea, Professor.'

'Yes, yes, yes.' The professor had a habit of repeating a word. Morton wasn't fooled. Behind the cultivated eccentricity was a razor-sharp mind.

He suddenly turned to Morton. 'The hotel bombings demonstrate perfectly the adage that the greater the ruthlessness, the greater the helplessness. In the face of what's happened there will again be this general feeling that terrorism is winning. So the mood will be to go for some sort of deal. Nothing overt, of course not. But behind the scenes. Nod-and-wink stuff.'

'Led by the French?'

The professor nodded equably. 'They justify it by saying that terrorism can be susceptible to political solutions. Very French.'

'Given that, what will the mullahs do?'

'The mullahs know the danger of pushing too far too quickly. Many will still be cautious. Even Muzwaz won't want to raise the stakes until he is certain of a real chance of winning. He'll go along with the others and wait to see how the hotel bombings will be seen in the Islamic world, whether they will be accepted as legitimate action in their war of liberation.'

'You think they will?'

'That depends on Raza, David. My bet is that the cabal's still divided over him. What passes for moderates among them, those who don't actually dream of washing in our blood, will still be worried that one day Raza will turn on them.'

'He will, Professor, for sure. But what do you think he's going to do next? Given that he's threatened to do something even more awful?'

'Ah.' The professor pulled each of his long, delicate fingers. A pianist's fingers, Morton thought. 'Raza is the most complex of our enemies. Nidal, Arafat, all the others are comparatively straightforward. Their motto is strike successfully, then strike again at once. But that's not Raza. And he's been off the scene a long time. Now he's back with a vengeance, he may well have over-extended himself. The simplest way to keep us guessing is to say he's going to do something else very soon. That ties up a lot of resources. Meantime he can take his time.'

'I hope you're wrong, Professor,' said Morton. 'I really hope you're wrong.'

The professor squinted at him. 'You want him to attack?'

'I want him to make a mistake,' corrected Morton gently.

'My God, I wouldn't want to be in your shoes if things don't work out, David. Not at all, not at all.'

'Keep thinking,' Morton said softly, closing the door behind him and leaving the professor alone in the silence.

Back in the Operations Room, Morton saw the lights on the maps remained unchanged.

He went to the computer room. Its sudden coolness enveloped him as soon as he opened the door.

Lester Finel kept the temperature at a constant 55 degrees

Fahrenheit. He insisted that was the correct reading for the computers. He'd also chosen a team of deaf mutes as his programmers. Finel had said he wanted no idle chatter.

That had impressed Morton as much as Finel's background – IBM, Ampex and Honeywell. Over twenty years he'd taken all three companies along the road of commercial success, before he'd decided he'd run out of challenges.

Morton had sat with Finel one afternoon in San Francisco and talked about what being a Jew really meant. Finel had decided it was running Mossad's computers.

Now he rose from his desk at the far end of the room and hustled over. A sinewy man in his early forties and prematurely grey, he wore a bold-check sports jacket and golfer's plaid trousers.

Finel's left hand maintained a curious motion. It had taken Morton a little while to recognise it mimicked a revolving spool of tape.

'Hi, Dave. We've begun a search. To find anyone who fits what Humpty Dumpty's come up with. Problem. She fits too well.'

Morton had decided Finel's staccato way of speaking was either from listening to computer-speak or communicating by sign language with his staff.

'The lisp is a help. But not much. Problem. We've got ten thousand lispers on tape. We're looking for a certain personality type. Streetwise. Beirut-Greek. But try Cypriot-Greek. Problem. Still fits several thousand.'

'Lacouste's IDs help?' asked Morton.

'Working on them, Dave. Problem. No tell-tale marks. Even a scar would help. A funny eye, better yet. We've got listings for five thousand funny left eyes, almost as many right ones. Problem. All we have here is just Arab faces. Even hotel staff trained to remember, see one Arab as another.'

As they walked back through the room, Finel's eyes continued to sweep from one computer to another.

He stopped beside a mute. There was a flurry of finger movements between them. The mute turned back to his modem.

'He's checking airline passenger manifests out of Britain, Europe and North America. Against every known living terrorist we have on tape. Problem. Over forty-five thousand names, Dave.'

Finel pointed to other mutes. One was working through lists which Lacouste had faxed of registered guests at the four Paris hotels. Another was doing the same with those from the ACC. At the bottom of the Connaught listings Morton saw Steve and Dolly's names.

He turned away. 'Anything from New York?'

'Talim's got an FBI guest listing. Not complete. But a start.' Finel squinted at Morton. 'Hits you when you see all those names.'

'For sure.'

Finel stopped at another computer station. A further rapid exchange of finger movements before Finel turned to Morton.

'He's searching for aliases. Surprising how many terrorists use the same one. Guess the professor would come up with a reason.'

Morton smiled quickly. He encouraged the rivalry between Psychological Assessment and Computers. He'd encourage anything that helped.

'Lester, your people are doing a fine job.'

Morton moved on to Foreign Intelligence, to that corner of the seventh floor Chantal Bouquet had made her own. As he came through the door of her office she waved him to an armchair.

'To answer your question, nothing sinister is going on. Not even bad field craft. It just happened,' said Chantal.

Morton stared at her. 'You mean twelve of Raza's bombers can come and go, and the best in the West doesn't even get a whisper?'

Chantal adjusted her turquoise-framed glasses. 'I mean just that.'

He'd put her in charge of Foreign Intelligence three years ago after she'd served in London, Paris, Bonn and Washington.

'What's the consensus, Chantal?'

'On the surface, it's united-we-stand time. Everybody's pooling and sharing. The CIA have distributed more copies of Raza's psycho-biog than they ever did on Nidal or Arafat. The Brits are feeding everybody who matters with their report on the

Westminster job. Only a year ago they were swearing blind to us no such report existed.'

'The one that shows how easy it was for Raza to get his Stinger in place?'

'The very one. It's warts-and-all time in London. Same with the Germans. The BND are suddenly producing stuff on Raza no one knew was there. The French, the Italians, every Intelligence agency worth its name is offering up stuff.'

'You don't sound exactly thrilled.'

Chantal began to doodle on her desk pad. 'It's a game, David. A spooky version of pass the buck. They dollop out their info like they were sound bites on the evening news. Then sit back.'

'For what?' He knew, but he wanted her to tell him.

'For us. They want us to deal with Raza. That way, if it goes wrong, they're off the hook. They can say, hand on heart, that they gave us everything – and then we screwed up.'

Morton sat in silence. It wouldn't be the first time Mossad had been asked to ride shotgun.

'Are they setting any limitations, Chantal?'

She shook her head. 'The usual. We get covert co-operation and come and go as we like. We keep them posted. And no dumps on their doorsteps.'

He nodded. 'Any collective wisdom where Raza is?'

Chantal gave the doodle legs. 'Depends who you last listen to. The French say he's operating out of Afghanistan. The Germans place him in the Horn of Africa. The Brits and Americans think he could be in South America.'

'Why not North Africa?'

She looked up from her doodling. 'Washington says its satellites photographed the whole region. Not a sign.'

Morton grunted. 'What did they do about Libya?'

'NSA, the National Security Agency, did a grid search with one of their new multi-camera K-12s. Not a thing.'

'Anything from our own check?'

Twenty hours ago Israel's own spy satellite had been re-orbited to photograph the entire Mediterranean region.

'Nothing. Bitburg's told the air force to send it back on station.'

'My gut tells me Raza isn't that far away,' said Morton.

The bleeper on his belt began to give off an urgent signal. The Honeywell had completed its search for potential targets.

At Trekfontein reservoir the piece of driftwood to which Lila had tied the bottle floated towards the sluice gate.

After the overnight rain, other pieces of flotsam dotted the water. Some of the wood was of unusual and striking shapes. It was these pieces that the two youths from the township had positioned themselves on the sluice gate to snag with their net. They carved the wood into animals, which they sold to tourists wanting souvenirs from the Union's most celebrated dorf.

The sluice was slippery; the water flowed faster than usual. The teenagers had constantly to sway and reposition themselves as they darted back and forth across the top of the gate, mindful that a slip could send them plunging thirty feet into the foaming concrete slipway below.

One of the youths spotted the bottle moments before his companion did. Instead of waiting for the driftwood to reach the gate, he extended the net and tried to trap it. Eager to help, the other youth grabbed at the net pole.

For a moment they teetered back and forth. Then with terrified screams, they fell from the gate on to the causeway. One broke his back, the other his neck. A shard of broken glass from the shattered bottle penetrated one of the youth's eyes.

By then the Anthrax-B-C had been emptied into the water and carried to the pumping station that supplied Trekfontein's needs.

The 24-hour clock showed there were thirty minutes left when Morton returned to the Situation Room. He keyed the Honeywell's modem and its screen began to fill with the list of potential targets for Raza to choose.

Morton scanned his way through Europe. He couldn't see Raza hitting the Passion Playhouse at Oberammergau or the Sistine Chapel in Vatican City. Raza would go after blood, not monuments. Morton worked his way through North America. Any number of unusual and striking targets there. But something told him not for Raza – at least not this time.

He checked Australia and Japan. Again, plenty to tempt any terrorist. But, instinct told him, not what Raza would be looking for.

On to the screen came a list of targets in South Africa. Top of the list was Trekfontein.

At that moment Karshov's voice boomed from the loudspeaker built into the console.

'Time for the conference call.'

'On my way,' acknowledged Morton.

He remained staring at the screen a moment longer, then pressed a key. The screen began to fill with an account of Trekfontein's notoriety. He pressed another button. Onto the screen came a computer-enhanced display of the town. Clearly visible on one side were the turreted rocks. On the other side was outlined the reservoir.

Morton swiftly tapped on the keyboard: '*Double flash. Inform authorities Trekfontein potential target for Raza.*'

He keyed the message to the Mossad agent in Cape Town. Morton knew it was instinct, no more.

'David!' Karshov boomed from the speaker.

The television studio adjoining Karshov's office was like any other.

There were twenty comfortable chairs set in a semicircle. Each was occupied by a member of the Tribe, as Israel's strategic planners are known. There were air force and army generals and their key staff members, the Foreign Minister and his advisers, the Attorney General and his senior aides, the head of Internal Security.

They reminded Morton of a woodcut Steve had shown him of the Great Sanhedrin in session in the Temple of Jerusalem. The Tribe displayed the same haughty demeanour. Something else hadn't changed in two thousand years: Israel's right to exist still depended on the whim of others.

Morton sat on one side of Karshov, Bitburg on the other. From time to time the Director murmured in Karshov's ear the identity of someone on the three large monitor screens positioned before the semicircle, pointing out the Director of the CIA, the head of French Intelligence, the Director of the FBI, the heads of Britain's MI5 and MI6. Bitburg knew them all.

Bitburg turned to Karshov. 'Full house, Prime Minister. A good sign.'

Karshov grunted and continued to watch what was happening in London, Paris and Washington. Built into the armrest of his chair was a telephone.

In the Cabinet Room at Number 10 Downing Street, in the Oval Office, and in the President's Salon in the Elysée Palace, ministers and advisers were carefully grouping themselves around the one vacant chair in each location. The empty seats were for the President of the United States, the Prime Minister of Great Britain and the President of France.

Morton stared impassively at the screens. Arabists would be in the wings, briefing their masters, reminding them what was at stake. The Arabists never appeared in public. Only their influence was seen.

In less than a year both Presidents would be going for a second term, and Britain's Prime Minister would probably go to the hustings around the same time.

The nations they led had changed dramatically since they came into office. Following the Gulf War, had come global recession with food riots in what remained of the Soviet Empire.

NATO had been virtually dismembered when the United States had withdrawn its forces from Europe. There had been neo-Nazi marches in London and Paris. Anger and anxiety had hardened into the familiar cry of the mob down the ages. The Jews were to blame for the Gulf, inflation and mass unemployment.

Morton could see it there in the well-bred faces on the screen of men who had made a virtue of compromise and self-interest.

Low-voiced conversation continued among the Tribe. Then everyone became silent as from the monitors an unseen voice boomed: 'The President of the United States.'

Morton watched the tall familiar figure with a head of hair that always reminded him of Jack Kennedy, stride across the screen to his seat.

The off-screen voice boomed again. 'The Prime Minister of Great Britain.'

The years had been kind to both face and figure of Britain's leader, but had not softened the eye glint that looked as if it would shatter glass. As usual the Prime Minister ignored everybody.

'The President of France!'

Though slack-bodied the French leader gave off – Morton thought – a feeling of extraordinary strength. It was there in the way he sat and locked his hands together as if daring God Himself to pull them apart. It was there in the flat little hyphen of a mouth. But above all it was in his eyes. Only a taxidermist could have given someone such dead eyes.

'Can you hear us in Tel Aviv?' demanded the voice from London.

'Perfectly clearly, Prime Minister,' replied Karshov, 'and we can hear Washington and Paris as well.'

'Good to see you, Isaac,' said the President of the United States, waving. 'I wish it just could have been under different circumstances. And at a more civilised hour.'

It was late evening in Washington, the early hours in Europe. In a couple more hours the false dawn would creep into the sky over Tel Aviv.

'I recall my father saying the only hour that matters is the one we have left on this earth to try and do all the things we have not done,' said Karshov.

'Very biblical, Isaac,' came the resonant voice from the White House.

From London came a familiar clearing of the throat. 'Time is indeed of the essence, so let us begin.'

The British Prime Minister waited for the nods from Washington and Paris, then resumed.

'Mr Karshov, my colleagues have asked me to open these proceedings. But I wish you to clearly understand that what I am about to say is our collective view.'

Karshov's eyebrows began to knit. The voice from London continued to enunciate.

'Firstly, we wish you to know that you do not stand alone.'

Karshov inclined his head.

'We also wish you to know that in our collective judgement a military response to what has happened is neither feasible nor desirable. Any military intervention would be seen not as justified retaliation, but as a savage revenge. In the end all it would achieve would be to bring forward more of these people.'

Karshov's eyebrows had joined forces. 'Then what are you suggesting?'

The British Prime Minister ignored the interruption. 'So far there is nothing to connect any Arab country with what has happened. There is nothing to show these evil acts are in any way linked to state-sponsored terrorism.'

When Karshov spoke the fury was gone, and in its place was a cold implacable tone. 'Let me tell you now that Israel reserves the right to deal with this threat the way we see fit. And that means we will take whatever action we think necessary.'

Karshov looked in turn at each of the monitors. 'These people wish to destroy you as much as they want to finish us. Please, I beg of you to understand that!'

The voice of the Prime Minister of Great Britain was even colder and more distant. 'We have learned that yesterday's terrorist is often today's statesman. We discovered that in Cyprus and in Africa. And, of course, from your own predecessor, Menachem Begin. If we'd caught him at the time, we would have hanged him. But when he became Prime Minister of Israel we sat down with him. That's political reality.'

Karshov shook his head. 'I will not be goaded. There will be no concessions. We will not give up this land. We shall surrender nothing. And so that you understand why, I want you all, each and every one of you, to know the exact nature of the threat we are facing.'

On the monitors people looked at each other.

Karshov turned to Morton. 'Tell them, David. Tell them about Anthrax-B-C.'

The glacial voice from London over-rode the hubbub. 'Is this really necessary –'

'Yes,' said Karshov. 'In the name of God, listen! Just shut up and listen!'

In the electrifying silence Morton rose to his feet. He fished in his pocket and produced a corked vial. It was filled with a colourless liquid. He held it up to the camera. Karshov had given him the vial as they had walked into the studio.

'This much Anthrax-B-C could cause far greater loss of life than all the hotel explosions. Properly distributed this much could kill several thousand people.'

Gasps came from the Tribe and his audience around the world as he uncorked the vial and sprinkled the liquid.

Morton smiled briefly. 'Tel Aviv tap water.' He recorked the vial. 'A thousand vials like this would turn this country into a graveyard. But there would be no one to bury our dead because no one would dare to come and do so.'

For the next thirty minutes he told them about his trip to China, and about Raza. He spoke quietly and calmly. He explained about the need to stockpile PEG-enzyme. He stressed no one knew if the drug would work, but there was nothing else available. When he had finished he sat down to a stunned silence.

The British Prime Minister was the first to break it.

'Mr Karshov, my Intelligence people confirm what I understand the CIA have informed your own Director of Mossad. Namely, that they have no evidence to support this claim that any Anthrax-B-C has left China. The Intelligence consensus is that this bagman your Mr Morton failed to kill would have in any event been apprehended by Chinese security.'

Morton glanced at Bitburg. The Director was nodding. The Arabists around the British Prime Minister were nodding. The President of France was trying to nod. The President of the United States looked as if he wanted to, but shouldn't.

'Your people are wrong,' said Karshov slowly.

The Prime Minister of Great Britain leaned forward. 'Then prove it to us. And who better to do so than your Mr Morton?'

In Paris and Washington the Presidents nodded approval.

Ruth had been right, thought Morton. They'd been working towards this all along. Shotgun, pointman, licensed hitman. It all came down to the same thing in the end, going down into the slime.

'Meantime,' resumed the voice from London, 'we shall wait to see what Mr Morton comes up with before we rush to produce vast quantities of what I am told is a very costly drug.'

'That makes sense to me,' said the President of the United States.

'Agreed,' said the President of France.

'In that case, go to it, Mr Morton,' urged the Prime Minister of Great Britain. 'You have no time to lose. The deadline this creature has set has already expired!'

'Prime Minister, we do not have to be told –' began Karshov.

Then the telephone in the armrest shrilled, and he lifted it with patent relief. As he listened, the blood drained from his face.

'One moment please, sir,' Karshov said in a sudden strangled voice.

He held the receiver from his ear and addressed the watchful, frowning faces of the Tribe and those on the screen.

'Gentlemen –' Karshov's voice quivered a little. 'I have the President of South Africa on the line.'

There were gasps of astonishment around him and from the screens.

'He informs me that a dreadful calamity has befallen one of his townships, a place many of us know. Trekfontein.'

A great buzz of voices almost drowned out Karshov's next words.

'He says that every man, woman, child and animal has been killed by what sounds very like this anthrax!'

As Karshov turned back to the phone to elicit more details, Morton was already on his feet and striding from the studio.

13

For three hours Morton had sat in front of the monitors in the Situation Room and followed the response to the call from South Africa's President. The Union had sealed its borders and launched the biggest hunt in its history. Every African township was under armed curfew; there had been hundreds of arrests of suspected activists. Protests at this draconian response had been muted even from the country's black neighbour states. Like the rest of the world, they were stunned by the enormity of what had happened.

The first reports from the stricken township had done little to prepare even Morton for the live pictures that were now being transmitted on to a screen from police camera crews on the ground and in the air over Trekfontein.

Wherever the cameras turned, there were bodies, many turned black. Searchlights mounted on hovering helicopters and ground vehicles guided anticontamination teams moving through the streets in their cumbersome NCB suits. All they could do was bag the bodies and load them onto trucks.

'We got here as soon as we'd checked out your warning, Mr Morton. We were still too late. Nearly five and a half thousand murdered – for what? Because of what they believed in?'

The voice came from an adjoining screen. Piet Vorag, the Union's Minister of Defence, was in a command helicopter over Trekfontein. It was equipped with television cameras and directly linked to a satellite over the Equator.

'That came into it, for sure, Minister. It was a shrewd move by Raza to choose Trekfontein to show us he will go all the way.

I hate to say it, but a lot of people around the world, when they get over the shock, will have a sneaking satisfaction that Trekfontein's no longer there.'

'You mean they will see this as some sort of heroic act? Something different from blowing those hotels?'

Morton waited for Vorag to calm himself. He'd met him at several international conferences on fighting terrorism. The Minister had always struck him as the controlled voice of the new white liberals of South Africa.

'People are funny, Minister. They respond to what they last see or hear. Right now you could be adding to your problems by this round-up.'

'Whoever did this didn't act alone, Mr Morton. Our people have found traces of ANC slogans all over Trekfontein. That's what they've promised to do – massacre us in our homes!'

Morton realised, and understood, that a raw nerve had been exposed in the Minister. But he had to tell him the truth.

'There's nothing to link Raza with the ANC, Minister. Or any of your other groups. They're all just too soft for him.'

'All I know is what my people and I can see, Mr Morton,' said Vorag, his anger thickening his blunt Afrikaner accent.

A camera was tracking down a street of barbered lawns leading to houses gabled in the attractive style of early settlement homesteads. Bodies were being brought out. Many of the men were naked.

Vorag's harsh voice continued, 'A lot of them died having a bath or shower after work. Their wives and daughters succumbed in the kitchen preparing dinner. It's terrible, man, just terrible. Do these people look like the pariahs of the Western world?'

Morton stared at Vorag. The man was entitled to his rage.

On to the screen came shots of scores of bodies floating in a swimming pool.

'At least sixty . . . mostly kids. There's more in the shower rooms . . . and we've spotted at least another hundred in private pools . . .'

A camera paused outside a tall colonnaded building and began to move towards its open door.

'. . . the church. It was filled for a mass baptism. There are five babies in there, plus their parents and relatives. All gone . . .'

The camera pulled away as one of the recovery team emerged

holding a small body in a christening robe. In his astronaut-style suit the man looked like a corpse-snatcher from a cheap horror film.

Vorag's helicopter drifted down what Morton guessed was Trekfontein's main street. The searchlight picked out a gushing water pipe. Scattered around it were a number of bodies and several half-trucks and Land Rovers.

'We're looking at the entire town police force ... When this main burst they must have gone along to supervise traffic ... When they started keeling over, other officers went to help,' continued Vorag.

Morton saw the surprise on the faces of a police captain and several constables, as if, in death, they could not believe what was happening.

'Why did they all die so quickly, Mr Morton?' rasped Vorag. 'I'd have thought the water would have diluted the stuff.'

'Not tap water. It just acted as the perfect vector, spreading it everywhere at once. The effect was like cyanide. A drop would be enough.'

'I still say one person couldn't have done all this, Mr Morton,' Vorag said heavily, 'not kill all those people.'

'I know it's hard to believe, especially from where you are. But this was almost certainly a one-person job, someone who came about his or her business without raising suspicion and then dumped the anthrax in the water supply.'

'People come all the time, Mr Morton. That's the trouble when you become notorious. Everybody wants to look at you.'

As Morton began to question Vorag, a new image filled the screen, a sign with the words: 'Trekfontein Junior School'. The hand-held camera began to track past the board.

'What's that reservoir's capacity, Minister?'

Vorag glanced behind him and repeated the question. He turned back to the screen. 'I'm told it's two-fifty million gallons.'

Morton nodded. 'Our chemists tell me that a couple of ounces released in the right place would be enough –'

'The sluice gate where we found those boys. That would be the best place,' Vorag interrupted harshly.

'Think those kids spotted someone and were killed for it?'

'We've checked the area. No footprints except theirs –' Vorag broke off with an anguished groan. 'Oh my God, look at this ...'

The screen was filled with the bodies of small children in the school cloakrooms. They were draped across the hand basins and against the urinals. After a moment the camera began to retreat from the horror.

'There were over three hundred children at the school . . .' whispered Vorag.

The image changed. The camera settled briefly on a board, bearing the gold-painted words: 'Trekfontein High School'. The first of the bodies lay beyond, soaked with water from a hose pipe. Several more pipes snaked across the grass from outlets in the walls of the double-storey building.

'Fire drill. Every school has to have one every week after Mandela's people burned down that school in Pretoria. Remember that? Fifty kids.'

'How many here, Minister?'

Once more Vorag spoke to someone behind him. He turned back, his lower lip trembling.

'Over seven hundred. Why, Mr Morton? In God's name, why?' Vorag's voice was close to losing control. 'Dammit, man, these are just kids! Boys and girls, none older than sixteen!'

'I understand how you feel, Minister,' Morton said quietly.

Vorag took a long deep breath, held it for a moment, then exhaled slowly.

'It's like a visitation from God –'

'No!' Morton's voice was suddenly sharp. 'Don't ever say anything like that. It's nothing to do with God. It's Raza. Do you understand that, Minister?'

'All I can understand is it's easy to say that when you're six thousand miles away. And you're a soldier –'

'– and if nothing else, being a soldier has taught me how to really hate horror,' Morton finished for him.

He continued to watch the screen showing the ghastly death he had seen so often. There were no marks on these people. Not like the victims of that shop explosion in Paris. He'd got there just as they had been loading the last of the broken bodies into an ambulance. There'd been that other explosion in Amsterdam – two families wiped out by mistake. He'd seen it a score of times, and each time didn't make it easier. But no point telling Vorag that.

A camera had reached the township hospital. The first sign

something was seriously wrong were the two nurses collapsed in the entrance hall beside the water cooler. Beyond, in the dispensary were more dead nurses. They had been filling beakers with water for patients to swallow with their tablets. Some of the ambulatory patients had been struck down in the day room. Others lay dead in their beds.

In the operating suite an entire surgical team had been killed when they were scrubbing up. Their patient was dead on the table.

'A hundred beds . . . all full . . . seventy staff . . .' came Vorag's whisper.

Morton continued to watch the unfolding horror on the screen. At the Trekfontein Movie House, bodies were piled several high in the doorway as patrons had tried to escape.

'The building's cooled by an old-fashioned air conditioning system that uses water from the reservoir,' Vorag croaked. 'There's at least a couple of hundred inside.'

'Minister, what about the hotel?'

'All dead. Fifty staff.'

'What about guests?'

'Thank God there were none. The last one checked out earlier –'

Morton tensed, like a dog coming to point.

'How do you know?'

Vorag glanced down at a clipboard on his knees. 'The hotel chambermaid roster shows one room cleaned after check-out.'

'Nothing else? No clue if the guest was a man or woman? Your people check for room refuse? A razor? Tampon? Anything like that?'

'My people say there's nothing.'

'How about a registration record?'

Vorag gave a small, humourless smile. 'A place like the Grand doesn't bother with that kind of thing. It's all very casual up here.'

The command helicopter was pulling away from the cinema. Onto the screen came pictures of Trekfontein's pets. Scores of dogs, cats and cage birds were being dumped on a truck.

'You're going to have to burn them all. Douse them in petrol first. And make sure the pit's deep enough,' said Morton. 'For speed's sake burn them all together.'

'You mean dogs, cats –'

'I mean animals and humans, Minister. There's no time for proper funerals. This stuff is lethal for twenty-four hours. Just burn them all as quickly as you can. When you fill one pit, close it and seal it with creosote. You'll need at least a six-inch coating.'

Morton waited while Vorag turned and issued instructions.

The pictures from Trekfontein showed the growing fleet of ambulances and rescue vehicles drawn up beyond the police cordon. Doctors and nurses stood numbed and silent; some wept openly.

'Anything else?' Vorag asked, turning back.

'Get hold of every petrol tanker you can to pump fuel into the reservoir. Then set it on fire. The same with the town. You're going to have to torch every building.'

'Man, do you know what you're asking?' demanded Vorag hoarsely.

'Yes, but it's the only way to make sure this stuff doesn't spread. Better this than have to raze Johannesburg.'

Vorag slowly turned and gave further orders before once more staring out of the screen.

'Now,' continued Morton, 'let's go back to this hotel guest. It could be coincidence, checking out on the day this happened. But I think not. Raza has often operated with a single terrorist. It makes for better security.'

Vorag's anger surfaced once more as the camera revealed a truck piled with corpses driving down the township's main street. He leant forward to point an accusing finger.

'And the world accuses us of genocide! They should be here to see this!'

Morton intervened smoothly. 'Minister, I think we've both seen enough. Let's try and apply our minds to getting a lead on this guest.' He settled himself deeper in his padded chair while he collected his thoughts. 'Trekfontein's been in the news a lot recently. So the chances are it could have been a reporter, or someone posing as one. Raza's done that before. It's a good cover. It allows for questions to be asked, visits made to places without raising suspicion –'

'Excuse me, Mr Morton,' broke in Vorag. He turned to listen to somebody behind him, began to nod, then turned back to address Morton.

'One of our team is in the police station. He's gone through the Incident Log. There *was* a photographer in town. She had her camera bag stolen by some Bantu. He was shot escaping from arrest. There's some question of whether he tried to rape this woman when he took the bag from her room.'

'Got a name for her?'

'Not yet.'

'Call every news organisation and see if they had somebody on assignment there.'

'We're already doing that. We're also checking airports and border crossings. But we're still not sure who we are looking for.'

Morton understood clearly the Minister's need for action. Engaging and destroying the enemy would help assuage the bitter anger that consumed him. No point in telling Vorag that she would almost certainly be long gone. Instead, Morton remembered what Humpty Dumpty and Finel had said and coupled it with his own personal knowledge of Raza's people.

'You're looking for a Greek with a lisp. She'll be anywhere between twenty-five and forty. Probably travelling alone. If she's flying, she'll be going first or club class. If she's driving, she'll have something fast and expensive –'

'How do you know all this?' asked the Minister, incredulously.

'It's my business, Minister, to know.'

'Anytime you want –'

Morton cut the sound for Vorag's screen as the monitor at the far end of the bank bleeped. Danny's face appeared.

'We've picked up three intercepts in the last few minutes. A woman. Humpty Dumpty says she's not the same voice as on the demand tape. My people figure the call came from somewhere around the Equator. Nairobi probably. She called Raza's Beirut number –'

'What did she say?'

'Here's the hell of it. "The water is perfumed".'

Danny paused. 'It made more sense after the second call. It was the woman again, formally claiming credit again for Trekfontein –'

'Give me the exact words.'

Danny began to read: '"In the name of Raza the Freedom Fighter, all infidels take careful note. You were warned that if you failed to respond in full to the demands made in the name of all the Oppressed of Islam, further proof of our ability to destroy you would be given. One of our brave commandoes has now done so. The racists of Trekfontein were chosen to serve as a just warning. But be assured Raza has enough Anthrax-B-C to destroy any one of your evil cities. This will be done without hesitation unless those demands are met in full in the given time. You now have six days left.'

Danny looked up. 'That's it. With the news blackout, this will stay under wraps.'

Morton felt cold and functional. He had always known it would come to this.

'What's the third intercept?'

Danny glanced at another sheet of paper in his hands. 'Again, a woman, but not the same one. Sounds younger. Humpty Dumpty reckons she's also Greek. My people think the call came from within five hundred miles of Beirut – '

'Give me the text, Danny.'

'Sure. "The Prophet has taken to himself our sister of the Perfumes." Just that.'

'Thanks, Danny. Send me hard copies.'

Morton pressed a button and the screen went blank. He stared for a moment at the latest pictures from Trekfontein. Bulldozers were digging the first mass grave. He turned to address Vorag.

'She's safely out and heading for home, Minister. We think she's got as far as Nairobi, which means she must have flown. If your airport people come up with anyone close to the description I gave you, let me know.'

Morton cleared the screen transmitting from South Africa. A moment later, the hard copies of the intercepts arrived by fax. He tore off the papers and began to read. He reached for a phone and called Karshov.

'Prime Minister, I have a sudden feeling Raza has a problem.'

14

Though she had seen it happen many times, Nadine was still stunned by the swiftness of Raza's mood change.

It had come with the false dawn, that hour when the frost gleamed on the sands beyond the window like the crushed ice in the champagne bucket on the floor beside the bed.

After Faruk Kadumi phoned from London with news of the hotel bombings, Raza had opened the bottle. After they drank, he began to make love to her. Nadine thought each time was better than the last.

They had been interrupted by a call from Paris reporting the explosions there, soon followed by one from the United States. She had recognised the voice of the man. Rachid Harmoos, the Arab millionaire, laundered the money Raza received for his services to the drug barons of Colombia. Raza had shown her photographs of Rachid's mansion in the countryside of Connecticut. It was near a place with a beautiful name, Sweetmont. Raza had promised one day they would live in such surroundings. Sometimes he could be very romantic.

Finally Lila had called. Afterwards Raza remained straddling Nadine, his body glistening in the starlight from the window. He seemed to be cast from the darkest bronze and she filled with a melting, warm wax. Then he had increased his steady thrusting until she was writhing and sobbing and screaming she wanted this to go on for ever.

Then came the call from Beirut.

Nadine saw his surprise when the bedside phone rang. He was expecting no one else. As Raza picked up the phone, his face was already tightening. After listening he asked no questions, only smashed down the phone so hard he broke its cradle.

Raza remained crouching over her, the last vestige of light draining from his eyes. The madness was back.

'What was it?' she whispered.

He ignored the question.

'Tell me,' she begged.

His nostrils began to flare and his breathing grew loud.

'Please,' she reached up with her arms to encircle him.

The movement broke the spell. Raza thrust her away and leapt to his feet, cursing. He yanked the champagne bottle from the bucket and hurled it across the room. It crashed against a painting of Bedouin shepherds in a Lebanese valley. She had bought it for him on their last visit to Beirut.

'What has happened?' Nadine whispered again. She was badly frightened, but knew she must not show it. Fear in others always stoked his fury.

Raza turned and stared at her and continued to curse incoherently. He was close to raving. She had never seen him like this. She knew she must not shrink from him. To do so could trigger a terrible violence. He raved on.

Momentarily exhausted he was still, his view of her blurred.

Nadine tried once more. 'Tell me, so I can help.'

The madness filmed his eyes, and she was more frightened, not only for herself, but for him.

'The girl!' he roared. 'The girl is dead.'

'Which girl?' she asked, pulling the sheet about her, shivering not only from the chill, but the tension in his voice.

'The Greek!' Raza roared again. He picked up the ice bucket and hurled it through the bedroom window, shattering the large pane of plate glass.

From outside came the sound of running and the compound guards calling out nervously. They backed away when they saw Raza at the window. He remained there, cursing volubly.

Nadine remained perfectly still, waiting for the anger to pass. An attack had never lasted this long. Usually he would quickly step back across the border that divides sanity from insanity. Then he would pretend it had never happened. And, because she loved him, she would do the same.

After a considerable while, he began to grow calm, his speech to clear and the strange contortions of his face to cease. Only then did she ask him again what had happened.

Raza turned from the window. 'One of the girls I sent to Athens is dead.' His words seemed to quiver in the cold air coming through the broken window.

'What can I do to help?'

He started towards her, his mouth working. She forced herself not to flinch, only to look at him attentively and lovingly. He started to pace from the window to the door, turn and pace again. From time to time he glared at her but made no attempt to come near.

Suddenly he went to the radio on the table at his side of the bed. He began to search the wavebands pausing each time only to listen for a few seconds before moving to a new station.

'Find me a Greek station,' Raza ordered Nadine. He resumed his relentless pacing.

She slid across the bed, keeping the sheet around her, and began to tune the radio.

In a corner of the bedroom a fax machine came to life. Raza ran over, reading aloud the words as the paper unfurled.

'It's the older girl, Zelda. She's dead. Killed while making a reconnaissance. Burned to death!'

This time the speech disorder and the wild flight of ideas that characterised his hypomania, did not return. All Raza did was let out another long burst of profanity.

It drowned out the newscast from Radio Athens reporting a lorry filled with liquid petroleum had gone out of control in the centre of the city and exploded in a huge fireball, which had engulfed at least twenty people.

Raza ripped out the rest of the message and turned from the fax machine, his hands trembling.

'She was carrying almost all the bottles! The stupid camel's whore took them with her! All gone! All destroyed! Because of one stupid camel's whore!'

Raza stood at the window, heedless of the chill, heedless of everything but the realisation he was facing disaster.

He was bathed in a cold sweat. He had to hold his hands together to stop them shaking. He could not stand still, but kept putting his weight on one foot then the other. And over and over, his mind was full of words that would not pass his lips.

All those long months of planning! Wasted! All my dreams! Come to nothing! What will I tell Muzwaz? That one stupid camel's whore had ruined everything? How could I ever convince him again? Why will anybody believe me when I say I will change the world?

He did not know how long he stood there before he became aware Nadine was asking something.

'Did she say how many bottles still remain?' she asked.

What did it matter? Almost all the bottles had been destroyed. The most powerful weapon he had ever possessed had been consumed in a fire that camel's whore should never have been near.

Raza turned and stared at Nadine. He looked at the paper. Then once more at her.

'Five bottles! Just five. All the others – gone!' he whispered.

She willed her voice to be calm. 'They are still enough.'

He came towards her. 'What are you saying? Don't you understand, you stupid –'

Nadine spoke urgently. 'They will never know you only have five. And you said one bottle can kill many thousands. With five you can convince them you have five hundred, five thousand such bottles. They will not dare disbelieve you! They will be too frightened! You can bluff them . . .'

Nadine faltered and became silent. The look on his face had not changed. She'd seen men die for daring to speak out.

'Please, I'm sorry. I did not mean to tell you what to do.' She pulled the sheet around her, as if for protection. 'Please, I did not –'

'No!' cried Raza, stepping closer. His voice reverberated in her ear. 'No! You are right!'

He was suddenly smiling. She had seen him like this, too. When an attack had passed he would smile in this strange forced way.

She looked at him wide-eyed with relief. She knew she must say or do nothing further. An idea always had to be his.

For some minutes they remained staring at each other, saying nothing. Then when Raza resumed his pacing, he was once more calm and controlled.

When he spoke now, his voice was close to normal.

'It can be done. The Zionist, Morton, will have calculated the amount of Anthrax-B-C. He will know I needed to use very little to kill those racists. He will be able to work out that I can kill all the people in any of the great cities of the Zionists.'

He turned and smiled again at Nadine. This time it was a charming smile that revealed his even white teeth.

'It is true, what you say. There is nothing to make Morton think otherwise. The bottles will have been vaporised with the Greek. And the five bottles the other Greek has will achieve everything!' He walked over to Nadine and gripped her hard, a hand on each shoulder. 'It will be done,' he murmured, looking down at her.

She reached up and gently kissed him on the lips. When she spoke it was in the softest of whispers.

'But you will still need to replace the Greek.'

Raza stood back, frowning at her. He resumed his pacing, speaking aloud, reminding her of part of the plan.

'Once Lila has set the Athens end in operation, she must go to Rachid. He sounded nervous on the phone. Perhaps he is worried that all this will affect his other work. Lila will know how to remind him of his obligations. And now with so few bottles, it is more important than ever.'

'I will go to Athens!' said Nadine decisively.

Raza stared into her face. 'You?'

Nadine felt trembly and uncertain.

'You?' he asked again. Once more she had managed to surprise him.

'Yes! You will need someone. If two were needed, they still are! Let me go!'

In his office adjoining the bedroom the phone was ringing. Few people had that number. Only one person would dare call at this hour. Raza ran into the study and picked up the phone on his desk.

The voice of Ayatollah Muzwaz began traditionally. '*Salaam alaikum.*'

'*Alaikum salaam,*' replied Raza.

The mullah said, 'We have heard the news. I must tell you I have had great difficulty with some of my colleagues that you disobeyed them by using the anthrax without authority.'

Raza felt the sweat begin to trickle down his skin.

'It was important, O Magnificent One, to know it will work.

166

To kill those racist pigs was a service to everything we both believe in. Tell the holy ones that I did not challenge their authority. I merely wished to show you all that I am worthy of your great trust in bringing about what we all wish – the end of the infidel.'

The Ayatollah gave a chesty laugh. 'You speak like a true mullah! Be at peace. I have told my colleagues you have done well. Our blessings upon those you sent forth. May the Great Prophet guide them to safety.'

'They shall rejoice in your pleasure, O Magnificent One,' intoned Raza, falling easily into the timeless style of the mullahs.

By now the bombers had reached a Medellín cartel ranch in Colombia. They would remain there until the international hunt died.

The wheezy voice continued, 'The Americans are now offering a million dollars for their capture. Like the British, the Americans have launched a manhunt like no other. The BBC and the Voice of America report that every possible policeman is engaged. Spies are everywhere. Their military powers are on full alert.'

'Only a show,' said Raza confidently. 'This is all purely to impress their people. Few of them have any stomach for war. They showed that after they dealt with our brother, Saddam. They will be even less willing to make war now.'

The old man's voice suddenly hardened. 'We have also heard the Zionist radio. It has said that the Zionists will remain on a war footing, their Condition Olive.'

'Then they are frightened, O Magnificent One.'

'Do not underestimate them,' came the sharp response. 'We have also heard from our people in Paris that there has been discussion among all the Great Satans. They have agreed to put everything in the hands of the Zionists, of this man, Morton.'

Raza curbed his fury. 'Again, O Magnificent One, you will remember I predicted that. They have always used this Jew to do their work. But it still will not change things. Neither their Condition Olive nor Morton will be able to protect them. You have my assurance on that.'

'We are pleased to hear that.' There was a pause then the harsh voice continued. 'The French Satans are the weakest link. They have always tried to use money to buy their peace. We do not need their francs any more. That will make them more nervous. You will work on that.'

'Your words are well received, O Magnificent One.'

'Then continue to hear them well and we shall continue to rejoice with you.'

The connection was broken. No one except the old man in Teheran would have dared do that. But when this was over, and the people knew who had brought about victory, he, too, would show proper respect. The whole world would.

Raza continued to think. He had anticipated the weakness of the French. The next tape Al-Najaf would transmit contained the demand for the immediate release of all thirty-two *Feydeheen* the French held. And when the French obeyed, that would be the beginning, the stone that would unleash the avalanche – crushing the resolve of the other Great Satans. The Zionists would be left friendless. And their Morton powerless. Then he would be dealt with, and the past avenged.

As Raza returned to the bedroom there was a polite knocking on the door.

'We are ready,' called a respectful voice.

Nadine was already gone to take her place with the camp staff. In public he made no distinction between her and the others. They were all his instruments, to be used how he thought fit. But he could not decide whether to send Nadine to Athens.

Dressing quickly, Raza left the bedroom, ignoring the newscast from Radio Athens continuing to describe the accident that had threatened to put an end to his plans.

He stepped out of the villa into the first grey light of the day. He stood for a moment staring out over the compound. The rows of recruits stood absolutely still before a dais. To one side of the platform were the camp's permanent staff of instructors, guards and drivers. Nadine was among them, staring fixedly ahead. Beside her was a table holding a cassette player.

Walking slowly across the ground, he continued to think about her offer. She had spoken like a true revolutionary, ready to step into the breach. But was she capable?

The question still unresolved, Raza came to a stop before the dais.

He squinted his eyes against the bright orange glow which, moment by moment, was bathing everything in its warmth. The sun's rays gave the crudely carpentered throne in the centre of the dais a certain majesty, which extended itself to the man standing a short distance from the platform.

He was dressed in the mitre and robe of a bishop of the Roman Catholic Church. The robe only emphasised his gargantuan size. His heavily lidded eyes looked fearfully about him.

Nearby stood a line of figures, dressed in the black cassocks of priests. They had their hands clasped and heads bowed as if in prayer.

The man turned imploringly to Raza. 'I beg you to let me explain.' His voice was surprisingly light and musical.

Raza ignored the interruption. A week ago the man had tried to cheat on an arms deal in Damascus. He had ordered him flown here.

The man's lips were sucking and nibbling each other. 'Why do you dress me like this? It offends my faith.'

Raza turned to stare into the man's sallow, jowly face, which even the sun could not infuse with colour. The man tried to fall to his knees in supplication. The *Feydeheen* on either side gripped him more firmly and he started to weep, then whimper through his tears.

'Silence!' Raza's command was like a pistol shot.

Raza turned and faced the ranks. 'Our struggle has begun,' he thundered. 'During the night our comrades have struck the first blow!'

He told them about the hotel explosions and Trekfontein. When he had finished, the familiar roar came. He allowed it; it was important they expressed each victory.

'*Ins'Allah!* Death to our enemies!'

When Raza judged they had given sufficient vent, he raised a hand. The silence was instant and total. He glanced at Nadine. Her eyes were bright with pride.

'Our enemies believe their faith is more powerful than yours!' Raza continued. 'They have many mullahs, but none is more evil than the Cardinal of Lebanon! He hates all you believe in! More than any other, he is your enemy!'

Once again the chant rent the air.

'*Ins'Allah!* Death to our enemies!'

Raza silenced them once more.

He turned back to the man and nodded. The *Feydeheen* half

dragged, half pushed the mitred figure up the steps onto the platform, beating him mercilessly when he tried to resist. They forced him onto the makeshift throne and quickly bound his arms to the armrests and ankles to its legs. Then they left him.

The sun was up now, giving a richness to the man's mitre and robe.

Raza nodded at Nadine. She pressed a button on the tape player. The air was filled with the sound of a great crowd chanting in unison. Al-Najaf had made the recording during the Pope's regular Wednesday afternoon audience in St Peter's Square in Rome.

The terror of the man on the dais increased.

The line of cassocked figures straightened. Hands folded inside the sleeves of his soutane, the first man walked towards the dais. The chanting of the recruits was a roar that drowned out the tape. The cassocked figure paused before the writhing, screaming man, genuflected and walked on. The man sagged against his bonds, tears running down his face.

Raza's voice rose above the crescendo. 'May our enemies suffer as we have suffered! May they walk the land naked and starving as they have made us walk! May they feel our fire and steel as we have felt theirs! May their hearts beat fearfully for what they have done to us!'

Another robed figure came forward, genuflected and moved on. The thunderous chanting continued. Once more Raza's voice rose above it. 'Purge our land! Kill our enemies! We ask this in the name of Allah!'

The mullahs had said always to promise there would be a purging.

Raza watched a third robed figure bow as he passed the dais. In Rome, the opening ceremony would climax in St Peter's Square when each priest would come forward to receive a blessing, passing before the Pope and the Cardinals assembled on a platform.

The atavistic fury exploding around Raza drove him on. 'Do not fear death! Death is a guarantee of paradise!'

He no longer believed that. Somewhere along the way – he could not remember when – he had acquired a fear of dying. No one knew.

Another cassocked figure genuflected and went. The crowd

was roaring almost out of control. Raza thought their behaviour a perfect example of how he could arouse the masses. They would die for him, like the man now approaching the dais. He walked like the others who had gone before him, eyes only on the near-demented figure on the dais.

Nadine felt a shiver run over her skin and every hair on her body seemed to tingle for a moment. It was the man's eyes. All Raza's men who had killed had the same look.

Raza timed his words perfectly. 'There is no God but the true God and Mohammed is his Prophet –'

He paused to look towards the cabal's representative at the camp. The strong-faced cleric was standing to one side of the dais, still and watchful.

'– and Ayatollah Muzwaz is his true leader on earth, greater than all others.'

Nadine saw the cleric nod, saw Raza raise his hand to silence the recruits, saw the cassocked man begin to genuflect, saw the fat man's mouth open in a huge scream. But so swift was the movement that she did not see the gunman produce the pistol from inside his soutane and fire four times.

All she saw was the man's mitre and pieces from the top of his head flying into the air, and the sun picking out the spume of blood. When the shooting stopped the blood continued to gush like a burst pipe.

The gunman inclined his head towards Raza, who motioned him over.

In the stunned silence Raza did not need to raise his voice. 'That is how I deal with your enemies.'

He turned to the gunman. 'Salute him well, for soon he will go to Rome and kill your enemy there. Then his name will be revered through all the mosques of Islam.'

A renewed roar came from the recruits. '*Ins'Allah!* Death to our enemy!'

Dismissing the recruits, Raza strode to the villa to call Al-Najaf and let him know the dress rehearsal for the assassination of the Cardinal had gone perfectly.

When he reached the villa he looked at his watch and sighed. Al-Najaf would have left for his morning jog. Raza sat at his desk and continued to think about whether to send Nadine to Athens.

15

With the sense of certainty that both the deeply religious and the committed terrorist share, Mahamoud Al-Najaf knew he had prepared everything for the assassination of the Cardinal of Lebanon.

In his apartment overlooking the vast cobbled expanse of the market place behind the Pantheon in downtown Rome he carefully arranged his prayer rug to face Mecca.

Removing his custom-made shoes – they were his one indulgence in an otherwise spartan life – he knelt and prostrated himself three times, each time touching his forehead to the ground. In a low, yet clear and firm voice, the way he had learned to pray from his father, he began.

'O Allah, Master of the World, the All-Meaningful and All-Compassionate, the Supreme Sovereign of the last Judgement, hear the word of your devoted servant. Thou alone we worship. Thou alone we ask for help. Show us the path to enlightenment.'

He began to recite the words of the *Ummu'l-Quran*, the Essence of the Koran, the most sacred of prayers that the infidel Cardinal of Lebanon had dared to call the Lord's Prayer of the Muslims. The evil one had done so in yet another of his appeals for religious unity.

When Al-Najaf had completed the seven verses he paused. In a deeper voice he continued.

'In the name of Allah, the Beneficent, the Merciful. *Alif, Cam, Mim.*'

Once more he paused after reciting the three letters of the

Arab alphabet deemed to have mystical power. Then in a rush of words, he resumed.

'Guide thy servant's hand so that it may be worthy of Thee to silence the evil voice of your enemy who tries to sully your purity.'

Al-Najaf remained prostrate for a moment longer, eyes closed, his mind filled with the memory of his pilgrimage to Mecca when he had knelt with almost a million others before the Holy Place and pronounced he would die rather than see its power diminished. When he had prayed there, he had felt, as the mullahs had promised, a certainty that Allah was listening.

Now, when he lumbered to his feet and rolled up his prayer rug, he felt the same. Allah wanted the infidel Cardinal to die. It would be the just retribution the Glorious Koran spoke of.

Al-Najaf began to walk around the living-room with its panoramic view of the domes, spires and cupolas of Rome. He was a heavy-set man with a curious way of walking, as if springs were implanted in his legs. His face was an unbroken curve from forehead to chin, giving him a benign appearance.

Over the years his gentle manner had served him well while he had prepared his operations. He had come and gone with no one suspecting. Then a year ago Raza had told him the Zionists had sentenced him to death. Since then he had been even more careful. But the complexities of this operation meant he had to remain in Rome far longer than he would have liked. That meant there was always the risk that the Zionists could spot him. But as usual he had chosen a cover to minimise the risk.

The room bore all the signs of a transient foreign correspondent. Piles of newspapers lay everywhere. On the desk was an old manual typewriter, half-buried in press releases. A rented news teleprinter stood in a corner, chattering out copy. Long sheets of teletype hung from clips, like washing on a clothes line, across the room. He had taken every care to convince the rest of the building's tenants that he was a reporter with a Cairo newspaper, in Rome to cover the forthcoming ecumenical conference between Islam and Christianity that the Pope had called.

He paused once more at the teleprinter. The hotel bombings and Trekfontein continued to dominate the news. But not a word about the demands he had sent to the three wire services. The last tape – the pre-recorded tape Lila had made claiming for the destruction of Trekfontein – was still in the answering machine he had converted into a transmitter.

The infidels must have ordered a news blackout. It would make no difference. The world of the non-believers would soon know the truth.

He stood for a moment at the picture window. The dog of a landlord had charged more for this view. No matter: the time was fast coming when he, and the millions like him who had exploited the Arabs, would pay the price. No amount of incense and devotional candles would save them from the great sword of retribution. And this city would provide a fitting backdrop to remind them no matter how hard they prayed, the hand of the true faith would reach out – and show them the real meaning of belief.

Al-Najaf had prepared a piece of theatre to demonstrate this perfectly.

Shortly before Raza's commando went to St Peter's Square, Al-Najaf would give him a cyanide capsule. After he had executed the Cardinal of Lebanon, the gunman would turn and face the stunned crowd and recite the opening words of the *Ar-ra'd*, the prayer of the Law of Consequence. The commando would then crush the capsule in his mouth to show the infidels that a soldier of Islam does not fear death.

Al-Najaf himself would not be there to witness the moment. The night before he would leave this city of his enemies and fly to Tripoli. He would receive the gratitude of Raza and be rewarded with a girl child. These past weeks of enforced celibacy had been hard to bear. His only relaxation had been following the strict fitness programme Raza insisted upon.

Al-Najaf went to his bedroom and dressed quickly in a bright purple tracksuit and jogging shoes.

After stretching and bending to loosen his muscles, he walked back to the living-room and went to the answering machine on his desk. He removed the tape and opened the small safe he had bought, which stood beside the desk. He dialled the combination and opened the door.

The safe contained his air ticket, his false Egyptian passport and the balance of the money he had been provided with to cover expenses. Beside the bundle of notes were two cassette tapes. He removed one and replaced it with the one in his hands, closed the door and reset the combination. He had chosen the numbers 3–10 as the security code. They represented the third sura of the Glorious Koran and its tenth verse. As he dialled the numbers he repeated aloud the words first revealed to the Prophet at Al Madinah, Al-Najaf's own birthplace.

'Neither the riches nor the progeny of those who disbelieve will aught avail them with Allah. They will be fuel for fire.'

He straightened and turned to the answering machine. He inserted the tape and played it, keeping the volume low, listening to Lila's voice.

'In the name of Raza the Freedom Fighter, the government of France will take careful note. You hold in your prisons thirty-two of our glorious *Feydeheen*. As well as the other demands made in the name of all the Oppressed of Islam, you will release these heroes of the Revolution within twenty-four hours of this tape being received in the office of your lie-mongering propagandists. Failure to do so will result in immediate punishment.'

Al-Najaf rewound the tape, his hand unsteady. The sheer audacity of not only this one, but all the other demands, was unprecedented. Yet how could they be ignored?

He removed and, on impulse, pocketed the tape. It would be a heady sensation, trotting through the streets with the cassette. The Prophet must have felt the same when he had gone secretly to the city of the Zionists, Jerusalem, and sworn a solemn oath in their very midst to destroy them one day.

Locking the apartment door to which was affixed a brass plate bearing the words 'Arab News Service', Al-Najaf descended in the ancient lift to the ground floor and stepped out into the square. He began to run, paying no attention to the Peugeot parked on the far side of the piazza.

'He's like God, he moves in a mysterious way,' murmured Wolfie, grinning at Michelle in the front passenger seat.

He sat with his fingers gently drumming on the steering wheel. The early morning sun picked out the white strip of his Roman collar against the dull black of his priest's suit.

'Too much pasta gone to the wrong places,' replied Michelle.

She touched the modified nun's veil clipped to her wig. It went with her calf-length grey skirt and bloused top. There were thousands of religious sisters dressed like her in the Church-of-Change.

'You'd have thought he'd be too excited to bother with running this morning,' said Wolfie.

The Peugeot's radio continued to report on Trekfontein, the hotel bombings and the petrol tanker explosion in Athens.

Michelle frowned. 'I can't see Raza bothering to blow up that tanker. An entire oil refinery's more his style.'

Wolfie watched Al-Najaf disappear down a side street before starting the car.

'No claim so far,' he said, heading the Peugeot in the opposite direction to Al-Najaf.

'Morton's put the lid on,' said Michelle, reaching into a large shoulder bag, which nuns this year had taken to carrying. She screwed the silencer to the barrel of the Czech pistol.

'It looks like being a nice day,' said Wolfie as the car entered the piazza where the Pantheon stood. The first of the cafés were opening.

The Peugeot headed towards Largo Argentina. A bread delivery truck blocked the way. Leaning out of the car, Wolfie called to the driver in perfect Italian.

'*Mi scusi*. I have a mass to celebrate.'

'No problem, Father,' said the driver. He backed up the truck to allow Wolfie to enter the narrow street of Santa Chiara. The Peugeot bounced over cobblestones that had been laid down for Caesar's chariots.

Wolfie parked the car opposite the entrance to the church of Our Lady of Hope. He left the engine idling. Carrying her shoulder bag, Michelle walked into the church. Wolfie remained behind the wheel and reached for a missal under the dash. Beside him on the seat was a Luger pistol. It, too, was fitted with a silencer.

Inside the church door, Michelle dipped a finger into the wall font. Then she genuflected towards the altar, and made the sign of the cross with her moist fingers. She sat in a pew directly across from the door.

The sanctuary windows sparkled in the diffused morning sun. The light gave the Christ on the stained glass the appearance of being crucified against a purple sky, tinged with a red darker than blood. Michelle noted the positions of the other early-morning mass-goers. On two previous visits there had only been a handful of old women seated near the altar, the same as now.

Placing her bag on the pew beside her, Michelle removed a prayer book and opened it at the mass of the day. She appeared to be deep in her devotions.

The old women had reached the sorrowful mysteries when Michelle replaced her prayer book. She rose to her feet, and walked to the door. The shoulder bag was open.

She stood inside the arched doorway, listening intently. Above the idling of the Peugeot's engine came another sound – a raw, animal-like rasping mingled with a scuffing. It was coming from where she expected, from her left, moving towards where Wolfie sat, intent on his missal.

Twenty yards in front of the car the street curved. The rasping noise grew louder from beyond the bend. Now she could separate the rawness and the scuffing, distinguish lungs being pushed to the limit and feet close to collapse as they were forced over the cobbles.

Al-Najaf came into sight. Sweat poured from his face and his mouth was open. He looked as tortured as the stained-glass Christ.

Michelle saw Wolfie reach across to the passenger door and open it. He was smiling pleasantly towards Al-Najaf.

She saw the puzzled look on his face, then he was past her, peering towards the car, the look on his face now even less certain.

Michelle stepped into the street.

'Mahamoud Al-Najaf,' she called clearly in Arabic. 'Turn around.'

He lumbered another yard or two. She called again.

'Turn!'

Al-Najaf's last earthly memory was of a nun pointing a gun at him, her feet spread, both hands extended and gripping the weapon.

Michelle shot him five times, twice in the heart and three times in the head.

As he fell, the cassette tape rolled from his hip pocket.

Michelle ran towards the car as the Peugeot began to roll forward, the passenger door swinging open wider. Without pausing, she stooped and picked up the cassette, and dropped it into her bag along with the gun.

Still not breaking stride, she jumped into the moving car. Nine minutes later, Wolfie parked near the Spanish Steps. He and Michelle walked into the Hassler.

They had chosen the hotel because the Hassler gave a substantial discount to all religious visitors, and did not accept credit cards. There would be nothing unusual about a nun and priest settling their bills by cash.

Fifteen minutes later they had checked out.

The Volvo was where Morton said it would be on Via Condotti. The keys in Michelle's bag opened the car's door. With Wolfie navigating, she quickly reached the autostrada to Florence. She drove carefully, the way a nun would drive. Wolfie sat beside her, straight and prim, the way he had observed priests sat.

They drove for a while in silence.

'Let's hear that tape,' Michelle said when they had cleared the Rome city limits.

Wolfie fished in her bag, removed the tape and inserted it in the slot beneath the radio in the dash. They listened in silence. He rewound it and they listened once more. He looked at Michelle.

'I wonder what those other demands were?'

'Raza's clearly going for bust,' said Michelle.

'I hope your government doesn't give in.'

Wolfie did not bother hiding the uncertainty in his voice.

Michelle frowned. 'They usually do. Then the others follow. Morton calls it the domino effect. He'll want to hear this.'

'For sure,' said Wolfie in a good imitation of Morton's voice.

She laughed. Wolfie's mimicry had lightened many an assignment.

He played the tape once more.

'I think any government would have to think very hard if it came to a choice between more hotels or another Trekfontein, and releasing a bunch of terrorists,' said Wolfie.

'Why not release them, and then hunt them down and kill them?'

He looked at her and grinned. 'Jesus, Michelle. Any more like you at home?'

'Worse. My mother wouldn't bother releasing them.'

They drove a couple more kilometres in silence. On either

178

side the vines had been stripped, the last of the harvest gone for pressing.

'He'll form a team,' said Wolfie.

'Then he'll need us.'

'For sure.'

Michelle laughed again.

Sixteen kilometres outside the city limits, they left the highway to drive between olive and citrus groves. Michelle drove slowly over the uneven track. After a mile Wolfie spotted the small cairn of stones leading into the lemon grove.

She parked the car and they both got out. Wolfie stretched his arms while Michelle rummaged in the shoulder bag. She pulled out a piece of paper.

'Five and nine,' she said. 'A diagonal cut in the trunk.'

'Typical of Bitburg,' said Wolfie. 'He's probably never seen a lemon tree in his life.'

They both laughed and went into the grove. Bitburg's fascination with recognition signals was a recent one. As they walked, they counted. At the fifth tree in the ninth row, they found a slash in the bark.

'I'll get the spade and holdall,' said Wolfie.

By the time he'd returned from the car, Michelle had removed her wig and undressed down to her panties. She had the body of a natural athlete, tanned and lissom.

'You did a hell of a job back there.' His voice was low and clear, his enunciation perfect; too perfect not to be foreign.

She moved closer.

'So did you.'

She leaned back to press her hips unashamedly against him, aware of, and exulting in, his arousal.

'We have a plane to catch,' he whispered.

'I know,' she murmured, ignoring his words and pushing forward with her hips.

'Morton wouldn't like it,' he teased.

She gave a breathless little laugh. 'For sure.'

He began to touch her as she undressed him slowly, the way he always liked. First she removed his priest's collar, then unbuttoned his black clerical shirt, pressing her lips against his chest, keening softly with pleasure. She unbuckled his belt and his priest's trousers fell to the ground. He stepped out of them, kicking off his shoes. She pulled down his underpants, letting him gently push her down. He pressed his face against her neck.

'Wait. Don't be in such a hurry,' Michelle commanded softly.

Her gently sucking mouth absorbed him. He writhed and groaned. Her head continued to rise and fall steadily. Suddenly she gasped, rolling on her back, ready for him. They made love in complete silence.

Afterwards, they dressed in the sports clothes from the holdall. Michelle made a parcel of the clerical garb and dropped it in the hole. Wolfie filled it in and used the back of the spade to scuff the ground.

Mossad's Rome sweeper would recover the clothes and burn them, and arrange for the Peugeot to be collected by a garage that never asked questions.

At Florence airport, Wolfie returned the car to the rental company. They showed their Swiss passports to a bored immigration officer. From the departure area Michelle direct dialled a number in Tel Aviv.

'The vacation was good,' she said, 'and I picked up something you'll want to hear.'

'That's fine. I've got some business in London. Let's all meet there,' replied Morton hanging up.

When Michelle told Wolfie, he smiled. They were on the team.

Morton had driven to Lod airport after Michelle's call. Now, an hour later, through the glare-free tinted glass of the control tower, he watched the Concorde swoop out of the sky. It lowered its nose cone as it passed over Tel Aviv and started to line up with the runway. A controller continued to talk down the plane bringing home the bodies of Steve and Dolly.

'Nairobi, Addis Ababa and now somewhere south of Kabul,' said Danny at his elbow, putting down a telephone. 'It's the right track for her.'

Morton turned from the window. 'Assuming Raza's in Afghanistan.'

'It's the best fix we've got yet. Humpty Dumpty says each time it's the same voice as on the demand tapes. And both Comint and Elint confirm the location of her calls.'

Morton knew that Danny swore by the technicians at Comint, communications intelligence, and Elint, electronic intelligence. Between them they could throw a net over several hundred square miles of anywhere on earth.

Since that first intercept from Nairobi, they had been probing the atmosphere for others. They had picked up the woman's voice in the vicinity of Addis Ababa's ramshackle airport and, several hours later, coming from around Kabul.

'That's good work, Danny. But no acknowledgement?'

'Well, no. I wouldn't expect one. Each time she's just reporting she's on her way. Keen little kitten that she is, she's ready to switch direction in mid-flight if that's what her lord and master wants.'

'Nothing on the other girl?'

'Not a peep more.'

Morton glanced out of the window. The wheels were emerging from beneath the Concorde's delta wings.

'Our ugly duckling,' murmured Danny.

Not a duckling, a bird of prey, Morton decided. That beak looked lethal. Tel Aviv to London and back again in under five hours. Almost a 200,000-kilo payload travelling at the speed of a high velocity rifle bullet – from here to Jerusalem in thirty seconds.

Since they'd been here, the El Al official had spouted facts at them. Everyone had his own way of trying to push away the presence of death.

Morton looked at Danny. 'Raza could be using a Voice Throw box. He could be sitting in Beirut and feeding out those calls.'

'He could be – except Elint and Comint have just picked up a call going out of his bureau in Beirut to the same area around Kabul.'

'What did it say?'

'Just repeated that stuff about the Prophet taking that woman and her perfume.'

Danny squinted at Morton. 'Think they could've scented this stuff to disguise it?'

Morton looked at Danny carefully. 'You could have put your finger on something. The woman in Nairobi mentioned perfume. She could have carried the anthrax into Trekfontein in a perfume bottle. A woman could do that without rousing suspicion. That could be what she meant when she said the water was perfumed. And we know that Raza uses women more than any other terrorist. Suppose he had one of them in place, ready to release more of his anthrax and something happened to her? Maybe she was killed in some accident or just died? And she had the stuff on her. That would make sense of the bit about the Prophet taking her – and her anthrax.'

Danny shook his head. 'If Bitburg could hear you, his eyes would pop! It's one hell of a lot to buy. And where do we even begin to look?'

'Your people said the call came from anywhere within five hundred miles of Beirut. That's a start. We've worked with less.'

'That could still put the source of the call in the Kabul area. It's less than five hundred miles east of Beirut,' said Danny.

'For sure. But my gut says we should be looking west of Beirut. Now that he's on the move, Raza will want to be close to the action. My bet is that he's somewhere in Europe.'

The official came forward, solemn faced. 'Do you wish to go to the unloading ramp?'

'Thank you, no.'

The controller guided the white-painted Concorde on to the ground. The media had dubbed the plane the Dove. Nowadays it spent most of its time flying Israel's leaders to the United Nations to argue for a just peace settlement. Morton changed his mind. Concorde was more like a stork, with those long legs racing over the runway.

The official was still at his elbow. 'Most relatives like to receive coffins when they come out of the hold.'

Morton looked at him. The man had dirty fingernails, a peasant who'd ended up indoors. Resettlement was a funny business. One of Bitburg's secretaries had been a train driver in Russia. But the official meant well.

'I'd prefer to stay here,' said Morton.

'Of course, of course.'

The Concorde was taxiing towards a hangar. A forklift and El Al van waited on the tarmac.

'Would you wish me . . . ?' began the official again.

Danny took the man by the arm, leading him towards the door.

'Just go and do what you normally do,' said Danny kindly, edging the official out of the room.

Morton watched the Concorde cargo hatch open. The forklift manoeuvred alongside to receive the coffins. When they emerged they looked so small. After they disappeared into the van Morton turned away from the window. Maybe Steve and Dolly had passed over Raza as they came home. He realised then he had still not accepted their deaths. That was why he could not grieve, why he could feel nothing.

Two hours later he walked out of the synagogue behind the coffins. Each was draped with an Israeli flag.

Hannah walked beside him, her eyes swollen from crying until no more tears would come, her dress torn in mourning. She stared fixedly ahead.

Karshov was among the pallbearers who were drawn from the ranks of Israel's academics, men in dark suits and prayer shawls, bearing Steve and Dolly on their shoulders towards the open grave next to where Ruth was buried.

Behind Morton walked representatives of the government and opposition, and members of the Tribe. It was a reminder of how far Steve's influence had extended.

Dolly's bridge partners were there, elderly black-draped matrons with faces lined from previous suffering.

Bitburg had come, staring approvingly at the television crews. The funerals of violent deaths always rated a place near the top of the news. It served as a national reminder, Bitburg had said.

Chantal and Lester Finel were there, walking with Humpty Dumpty and the professor. They'd come for Morton.

As they reached the graveside, Danny came forward and put his arm around Hannah's shoulders.

Morton looked across at Danny, thinking he should have done that. He loved Tante Hannah as much as he loved Steve and Dolly. But all he could think of was that scripture verse Steve had read all those years ago: *And the enemy shall know I am the Lord when I shall lay down my vengeance on them.*

After the coffins were lowered in the grave the *hazzan* began to chant. The cadences rolled over the mourners, enveloping them in old certainties that did nothing for Morton. The *hazzan* turned to him. A silence fell over the throng.

Morton stepped to the edge of the grave and, as he had done

for Ruth, he recited Kaddish for Steve and Dolly, knowing at last it was for him, for the death that had happened inside him a long time ago.

The short prayer over, Morton bent and picked up a handful of soil and dropped it into the grave.

Then, as he had done at Ruth's funeral, he turned and walked away.

16

In the bunker's broadcast studio, Raza sat hunched over the Voice Throw console and prepared to send the last two tapes he intended would further confuse those hunting him. His face was stiff and expressionless, his eyes intent on the flickering dials and switches.

Since the last transmission, which had placed Lila in the Kabul area, the Americans must have positioned a satellite overhead. They would be alarmed how much he knew of their methods. The knowledge had already enabled him, he was certain, to have outwitted them so far.

He had anticipated that in the aftermath of the hotel bombings and Trekfontein, the Zionists and their allies would immediately direct their sky robots to point their mechanical eyes and ears to listen and photograph every inch of ground where he could be hiding.

Their abiding belief in the infallibility of their technology was, in a sense, its very weakness. For all its brilliance in being able to photograph the wrinkles on a man's face from 60,000 miles out in space, the camera must first have a target to focus on.

Everyone in the camp had been ordered to remain under cover. All traces of the execution had been removed. The only human life a satellite would have seen were a few shepherds tending their goats near the villa. Not even the most skilled of photo interpreters would have been able to tell the shepherds were his instructors.

For months he had carefully read the mass of freely available literature on the secrets of space espionage. He knew that once a satellite has searched an area, it would be most unlikely to return.

To encourage them to look elsewhere, he had set up a network of agents. Each was equipped with no more than a telephone to which was connected a small transponder permanently tuned to the Voice Throw box.

While Lila had flown directly from Nairobi to Athens, the box had placed her making calls from Addis Ababa and Kabul. The call emanating from Beirut had also come from the box.

Now it was time to place Lila deep in the Afghan mountains. The enemy would scour the area with their spy cameras and sound probes positioned halfway to the moon. All they would see and hear were the Islamic Mujaheddin encampments.

But the tapes would totally convince his enemy he was somewhere in the mountain fastness.

Raza put on headphones and placed both cassettes on the console's twin decks. Then he dialled the transponder in an encampment seventy miles to the north of Kabul. The moment he heard the last number click, he switched on the first tape. It began to transmit Lila's voice.

'Do not concern yourselves further. I am safe with our beloved leader. He wishes you to know that our next move must be against our enemy in the East.'

Raza timed the length of the pause and depressed a key on the console's keyboard. Once more Lila spoke, her voice suddenly sharp.

'Do not ask! You will be told!'

Raza timed the next pause, once more pressing a key. Lila's voice this time came strong and strident.

'Ins'Allah! Death to our enemies!'

He stopped the tape, but kept the line open to the transponder.

Next he dialled the transponder in his Beirut office. When that was locked-on, he switched on the second tape. The gentle and soothing voice of Al-Najaf began to fill his headphones.

'We send greetings to our leader and rejoice you are safe to continue to help in the inevitable downfall of all those who oppress us. But we have many enemies in the East. It would be good to know which of them will first perish.'

Raza timed the pause before Al-Najaf spoke next.

'We are ready to strike wherever we are sent. *Ins'Allah!* Death to our enemies!'

Raza stopped the tapes and rewound them both. For a moment longer he sat fingers poised over the keyboard, like a pianist about to begin a recital. Then, moving with sureness and speed, his fingers began to work the keys.

Through the headphones he could hear the transponder in Afghanistan automatically making its telephone ring the one in Beirut. Next came the sound of the Beirut transponder instructing its telephone to accept the incoming call. There was a click corresponding to a receiver being lifted. Moments later Lila's voice began to say she was safe. Then came Al-Najaf's first response.

The separate conversations Raza had recorded over a week ago came together as a coherent whole. He knew there was no way for anyone to be certain they were not actually taking place in actuality.

Thirty seconds after he'd started transmitting, the exchanges were over. Both transponders simulated the sound of receivers being replaced.

For the first time Raza turned and looked at Nadine, standing by the door.

'Have you decided yet if I am worthy to go to Athens?' she asked quietly.

He smiled wolfishly and walked from the studio without a word. He enjoyed keeping her in suspense.

Faces stared at Morton from every screen on the wall of the Situation Room. The 24-hour clock had a new card taped underneath. It bore the words: *Post Deadline*. The hands showed two hours had passed since the message from Raza's woman claiming the destruction of Trekfontein.

Those on the screens were the representatives of every European Intelligence service as well as of the United States, Canada and Egypt. Each was identified by a hand-written card Morton had stuck beneath each monitor.

Additionally, Danny, Matti and Lou, Wolfie and Michelle, Lacouste and the ACC were also on screen.

'Thank you for coming,' said Morton formally. 'You all know my terms of reference.'

Quick nods came from the screens. Each of them had received in the past hour the memo confirming Morton's appointment as head of the task force to destroy Raza and his Anthrax-B-C. It had been signed by the President of the United States, the Prime Minister of Great Britain and the President of France, as well as Karshov.

'Some of us have worked together in the past. For others this is a new experience,' continued Morton, before pausing to glance at the screen labelled: *KGB-Moscow.*

A fleshy face nodded vigorously. General Igor Yertzin was the head of the KGB's First Chief Directorate. Until recently he had waged a ruthless covert war against many of those on the other screens.

Gorbachev's successor – anxious to show Soviet willingness to co-operate fully with the West in return for food and raw materials to save millions of Soviet citizens from starvation – had ordered the KGB to assist fully in the hunt for Raza.

'It is our shame that we helped to train this animal,' rumbled Yertzin.

'General, a lot of other monsters have been created by governments,' said Morton quickly. There wasn't time to get side-tracked on esoteric debate.

From an adjoining screen Anwar Salim, Director of the Egyptian Intelligence Service nodded gravely.

'I am sure I speak for us all when I say we are united in our determination to work with you to eliminate Raza and the threat he poses.'

A chorus of assent came from the monitors.

'Thank you, gentlemen. As this is our first meeting, I think it important to establish guidelines. We don't want to trip over each other. So everybody works within his own geographical area in terms of investigation. Everything gets routed through to me or my deputy, Major Daniel Nagier. My own team will work directly to me. For those of you who don't know them, let me introduce them now.'

Matti, Lou, Wolfie and Michelle nodded quickly as Morton called their names.

Morton paused and glanced at notes he'd made on a sheet of paper.

'The Secretary-General of the United Nations is warning everyone of the consequences of sheltering Raza. It could mean automatic expulsion from membership and sanctions.'

'That hasn't worked before. It won't work now!' interrupted the representative of Italy's security service.

'Have your political masters make sure it works this time,' said Morton crisply. The Italians were among the world's most notorious sanctions violators.

Morton addressed the monitors. 'The Secretary-General has formally approached the People's Republic of China. Beijing says none of their Anthrax-B-C is missing. They insist Raza must have got it elsewhere.'

'How many countries have this stuff?' growled a thick-set, middle-aged man from a screen labelled: *CSIS-Ottawa*. Norm Stratton was head of the Anti-Terrorist Force in Canada's Secret Intelligence Service.

'No way of knowing. Saddam Hussein had it. He could have given some to Raza. But the Chinese have said they will consider providing a sample so that our scientists can know how best to deal with it.'

Murmurs of surprise came from several of the screens. Morton waited until there was silence before resuming.

He gave a clear, concise situation report. The hunt for the hotel bombers and the destroyer of Trekfontein had now extended to every corner of the globe. Interpol were co-ordinating police forces in over a hundred countries. In many, the military were assisting. The focus of this unprecedented search was Raza's known link to the drug cartels. There the hunt had become bogged down in the face of the cartels' virtually impenetrable defences.

They continued to listen without interruption and with complete attention as he turned to the intercepts. He repeated his theory that Raza could be planning to distribute the Anthrax-B-C disguised as perfume, and would use women to do so. He told them about the possibility that one of the women had died.

'There are two basic questions for us to consider here. Are all these intercepts part of Raza's plan to sow confusion – even this last one between the woman and the man in Raza's Beirut office? From that arises the next question. Is Raza in Afghanistan? If he is, he can be isolated. Then we go in and get him.'

He looked intently at each monitor. From a centre screen a sallow and wizened monkey face began to draw on a pipe.

'We have a K-12 over Kabul. Another over Beirut. Their sensors are sufficiently good, so I'm told, to separate heartbeats. Both sats have verified the last call is in current time,' said Admiral Edwin Burness. He was the long-serving Director of America's National Security Agency, NSA, the world's most sophisticated eavesdropping organisation.

Morton glanced at Danny's screen. Danny nodded.

A tall, dome-headed and bespectacled figure leaned into his screen.

'Raza could still be using a Voice Throw box. The Stasi showed us how effective it can be, Mr Morton.'

Hans-Dieter Müller was the Operations Chief of Germany's formidable security service, the BND. Next to the ACC, he was the one man Morton trusted most in Europe's law enforcement agencies.

'And there'd be no way of telling?'

'No way, Mr Morton.'

Yertzin rumbled, 'We are ready to send a team into those mountains to find if Raza is there. We'd know in a week.'

'Do that, General. But you don't have a week. Two days, maximum.'

'*Da*,' replied Yertzin. 'Two days – okay.'

'We could try to have our governments extend the deadline Raza has set.'

The mellifluous voice came from a screen to Morton's left. It belonged to Percival West, head of MI5's E-Branch, responsible for anti-terrorism.

Morton struggled to conceal his annoyance.

'I think we now all know that when Raza says something, he means it.'

The sound of spittle being loudly swallowed came from the screen beside West's.

'Let's cut the crap. I've got six hundred men out on this, and not one's picked a monkey's prayer where this bastard's gonna try next. Let alone where he is! I'd be happy to send some of my people into the mountains along with General Yertzin's. But for my dime, like the intercept says, they could be looking East for their next shot. Raza could make a powerful point unleashing his anthrax in Tokyo, or Hong Kong, or Sydney, Australia.'

Bill Gates sat back, arms folded, staring morosely out of the screen, defying anyone to challenge him. He had been Director for Operations, the head of the CIA's most clandestine branch, under three presidents. Morton respected Gates as a total professional. But he was wrong this time.

'They're all tempting targets, Bill. But to make any one of them really viable, Raza would need the kind of back-up no longer available to him. He's fallen out with the Japanese Mafia over drugs. Even the cartel can't save him there. Same with the Triads. Before he went to ground he conned them out of a couple of million US dollars. He's now paid back the money, with interest. But they still wouldn't lift a finger to help him – especially in the massacre of their own people in Hong Kong. Sydney, in my view, is just too small a target. My money's between London, any of the other major European cities, or the top half-dozen in North America.'

Gates grunted. 'That's a helluva spread, David. I don't know about Europe, but we sure don't have the resources over here to keep a full watch on every major city day and night.'

'We're talking of less than a week, Bill,' Morton reminded him.

'I know, I know,' said Gates. 'But we still couldn't do it. We were stretched to provide full cover for the last Party Conventions.'

Admiral Burness spoke through a wreath of smoke. 'I just don't see Raza having the means to destroy some place as big as LA. Trekfontein's one thing. But he'd need an army to cover LA. There's no one prevailing wind, no one water supply.'

Yertzin rumbled from his screen. 'You have forgotten, Comrade Admiral, what happened in another of your cities in 1950. That was the time you really believed we were coming.'

Chuckles came from several of the screens.

'You may still do one day!' grinned Burness.

Yertzin belly-laughed. 'Only as tourists!'

'So what happened in 1950?' asked Anwar Salim, his curiosity genuine.

'The Pentagon conducted a little experiment in San Francisco,' continued Yertzin. 'Its agents released harmless bacteria from the Bay that would turn red on body contact. A million people went around for a few hours like lobsters. The incredible thing is that no one complained. They just kept telling each other to have a nice day!'

When the laughter subsided, Morton addressed Salim. 'What can you tell us about the cabal's intentions?'

The Egyptian pursed his lips. 'The mullahs are more nervous of Raza. He's gone too far too quick.'

'Will they drop him?'

'No – at least not yet. But they'll go with what Ayatollah Muzwaz says,' replied Salim.

'Why not take him out?' asked Lacouste quietly. The tension from the screen was electrifying. 'If we'd done that with Khomeini at the beginning, we wouldn't have this mess. Same with Saddam.'

Morton shook his head. 'In my view, it's too late for that, Pierre. And it could trigger the very thing we all want to avoid – holy war.'

Heads began to nod. Morton waited until Lacouste had indicated, by the merest inclination of his head, his acceptance there would be no assassination of the Ayatollah.

Norm Stratton returned to the matter he had alluded to earlier. 'What about this PEG-enzyme? Our labs have very little of it. No more than enough to cover half of Toronto.'

'The blunt truth, Mr Stratton, is that no one will have enough of the stuff ready in time,' Morton replied. 'But where do we place what we have? In Paris? And then he goes and hits London? Or vice-versa? In New York – when he chooses Boston or Chicago? In a month there'll be enough to cover all the principal potential targets in Europe and North America. But right now, the best estimate, with every lab working flat out, is that by the time Raza's deadline runs out in six days we'll still be way short of requirements.'

'We have none of this antidote in our country. Our scientists say they need a month – and then only enough for Moscow,' said Yertzin heavily.

'We are in the same situation,' added Salim.

'I'll ask the Secretary-General to see if a system can be worked out to make supplies available on the basis of women and children, the old and the sick first,' said Morton.

Gates grunted. 'Remember the *Titanic*, pal? It was first into the lifeboats, and screw you Jack! The world's got worse since then. As it is, we're putting armed guards on our labs with orders to shoot to kill.' The CIA's Director of Operations spoke directly into the screen. 'David, what do you want from us? I'm empowered to say that as far as this and any other US agency goes, you have it.'

'The KGB is at your disposal, Comrade Morton,' said Yertzin. Similar pledges came from other screens.

'Thank you again, gentlemen,' said Morton. 'Right now the priorities are simple. Finding Raza and his supply of anthrax. Finding that woman who destroyed Trekfontein. Finding that other woman who died. Finding the hotel bombers.'

A suppressed cough came from West's screen. 'This dead woman. We could be talking of thousands of deaths.'

'Then the sooner we start, the better,' Morton replied equably.

One by one the monitors cleared. Finally only Hans-Dieter Müller remained on the screen.

'I have arranged what you asked, Mr Morton.'

'Thanks, Hans-Dieter.'

'When will you come?'

'After London. Has she any idea?'

'No.'

'That's good,' said Morton softly.

Müller's image receded rapidly as the screen went dark.

Raza drove his Jeep behind the recruits. The sand was soft and their legs sank in halfway up their calves. The last of the wind had died, and only the furnace-like heat made the ground undulate.

Five miles out into the desert, five miles back again. Enough to test the endurance of any man. Raza knew, because he had done it. Out here only willpower kept you going, willpower and hatred. The recruits were exhausted beyond all measure, so that their legs would no longer obey. Later he would tell them the pain they had felt here would be nothing to what they would endure if they fell into the hands of their enemies.

Already after an hour, three of the marchers had collapsed. He had ordered they should be left where they had fallen. If they were still alive when the others retraced their steps, they would be dragged back to camp. Otherwise they would be stripped of their clothes and left for the jackals.

The walkie-talkie crackled on the seat beside him. They were in a gully and the transmission was broken.

'Base . . . to comm . . . der,' came Nadine's voice. 'Re . . . rn . . . once . . . import . . . Tripol . . .'

He had put her in charge of the villa's communications room. Once more she had surprised him with her efficiency. But he still could not decide whether she should go to Athens.

Raza drove slowly past the recruits, deliberately putting a bottle to his lips, drinking water. He ordered the instructor to add an extra half-mile to the exercise. That would really test their determination to obey his every command.

He turned the Jeep and headed back to the camp.

Nadine was waiting at the villa door. He saw at once something was wrong.

'They have called twice from the Ministry.'

He had told her he hated the cowards at the Foreign Ministry who were trying to soften the Supreme Leader's revolutionary zeal.

'What did they want?' he asked sharply.

'Al-Najaf . . . he's dead,' she blurted.

He stood for a moment perfectly still. Then his mouth began to work. The anger gave way to that terrifying look of madness. He thrust past her and ran to his office. Nadine followed, as if drawn by his power, by his voice shouting into the phone.

'How did he die?' Raza shouted.

The Ministry official in Tripoli was a pedant who would not be rushed. He continued explaining how a Roman police *capo* had called the Libyan People's Bureau in the city. The *capo* received 1,000 dollars, paid into a New York bank account, whenever he provided information –

'I'm not interested in how you get your information!' screamed Raza. 'How did Al-Najaf die?'

There was a pointedly long pause. 'I informed you of the high price we pay for such information so that you will understand how greatly we value it,' said the official.

'Just tell me how he died,' grated Raza. He would ask the Supreme Leader to post the fool to Chad, to anywhere. Then he remembered the fool had only got the job because he was related to the President.

'The Italian police say the killing was professional,' resumed the punctilious voice.

Mossad. It could be no other. Raza's mind was racing. It had to be Morton. The voice was droning in Raza's ear.

'The police have searched his apartment. They discovered evidence showing Al-Najaf was involved in a plot to kill the Cardinal of Lebanon.'

Had the impossible happened – had the entire plan been compromised from the outset? Morton had been in China. Morton's hand could be seen in Rome. The pain in Raza's head had never been like this. He tried to shake it off. The fool was saying something else.

'The Italians also discovered an airline ticket – one way to Tripoli. They are asking awkward questions. Why would we allow such a man into our country? Our position is this man would have been turned away once he landed here . . .'

Mossad had picked up on the ticket. It had happened before. Al-Najaf must have been careless. That must be it. But the plan could still go ahead.

The pedant was saying something further. '. . . and naturally, we know nothing of this madness to kill the Cardinal. However, the President has asked for your personal assurance no move will be made to harm the man in future.'

Raza struggled to control his fury. 'The President has my assurance. Did the Italian police find the tapes?'

There was a lengthy pause. 'Tapes were recovered,' finally conceded the pedant.

'How many?'

'Two. The demand tape and the one claiming for Trekfontein.'

What had happened to the third tape – the one for the French?

Now the cretin was lecturing. 'The reaction has been far stronger than we anticipated. Therefore I am instructed to say the Supreme Leader is concerned –'

'I will speak to him,' Raza interrupted.

'He cannot be disturbed. He has asked me to obtain your response.'

'Then inform the Supreme Leader that he has no cause for concern. I can promise that.'

The silence stretched.

'Very well,' sighed the pedant. 'I will inform him.'

Raza put down the phone. No matter what had happened, he must go ahead. If he waited it would give Morton more time to move. He turned and saw Nadine standing in the doorway.

'Is there any way I can help you?' she called softly.

He stared at her, then nodded. 'Come with me.'

She followed him from the villa to the broadcast studio. He shoved a sheet of paper into her hand and ordered her to read the script of the tape – demanding the release of the *Feydeheen*.

Nadine gave the words a quiet authority Lila had not achieved. He set the apparatus for recording. Once more word-perfect and without hesitation, Nadine read. In one take Raza had a replacement tape.

'You did well,' he said softly.

'It is easy with such a good teacher.'

He continued to stare at her. At last he was satisfied, and came to a decision.

'We will take this tape with us to Athens.'

He'd occasionally used one of the city's radio stations to issue a proclamation. The station had always broadcast a tape unedited before passing it to other news organisations.

Nadine looked at him wide-eyed.

'We . . . ?'

Then the realisation of what he had said filled her with pride.

His face softened. 'When we go there, you will not be my woman, but a *Feydeheen*.'

Nadine nodded, unable for the moment to speak. When she did, her voice was filled with a single certainty. 'I promise you I will not fail.'

She knew she was not doing this just for Shema any more. She was doing it for herself, because she wanted to, because she loved him.

'We leave in one hour,' Raza told her, picking up the tape.

17

Morton felt the Concorde's nose wheel lift from the runway and saw the wings cant skywards to bite better into the air. A moment later the landing gear assembly rose into the belly of the plane and the droop-nose locked into its streamlined position. It would remain there until they were in British air space.

Four hours had passed since the conference call that had set this flight in motion, among much else.

The interior of the Concorde had been designed to create a flying battle headquarters. From here Israel's Prime Minister and key members of the Tribe would fight Israel's final war. Karshov had given Morton the plane for the duration of the crisis.

Behind the flight deck was the Prime Minister's cabin. It was equipped with a bed. Aft of that was seating for his aides, and then the galley and toilets. The rest of the plane was occupied by the communications centre. Over 80-million-dollars' worth of equipment was fitted into an area that ran from midships to the tail.

The Concorde banked 40 degrees as its computers put it on a due-west heading. At 400 knots it swept over the beaches of Tel Aviv and continued its swift, steep climb out across the Mediterranean.

During take-off the technicians had connected Concorde to the Defence Communications satellite geopositioned 10,000 miles up in space over the Negev Desert.

'We have the Prime Minister on line,' the communications centre officer said to Morton.

On board, only Morton exceeded the authority of the

moustached figure in flight overalls who commanded the thirty electronic specialists.

Morton swivelled his high-backed chair to face the six-inch screens built into a bulkhead. The static cleared from one and Karshov's face appeared. The last of the squelch faded.

'Shalom, David.'

'Good afternoon, Prime Minister.'

'Chancellor Kunzler has just called me to express his concern that what you want to do could trigger reprisals by Raza against the Federal Republic.'

Kunzler held the highest office in the unified Germany.

'What did you tell him?' asked Morton.

'I told him to do what I was doing, look the other way and swear blind you had never told me,' chuckled Karshov.

'Thanks.'

Karshov was suddenly serious.

'You're sitting in my seat up there, David. You see that little flap to your left? Lift it.'

Morton raised the black-painted piece of metal recessed into a control panel. Below were two red-painted keys.

'The keys to hell, David. If the day ever comes when all else has failed and our people are facing extinction I get to sit where you are and turn those keys. They'll override all the fail-safe measures to stop our entire nuclear arsenal blasting off. No matter how many times I sit in that chair, I still haven't got used to having Armageddon at my fingertips.'

Morton gently lowered the flap.

'I hope you never get to play God, Prime Minister.'

'Right now that's very much up to you, David.'

After Karshov's face had faded from the screen, Morton sat perfectly still listening to the men around him tuning wavebands and checking frequencies.

Shortly afterwards the CCO reported: 'Major Nagier's on relay two.'

Morton turned to the screen. 'What's new, Danny?'

'Yertzin's teams are in. Sixty of his best Spetsnaz, all Afghan veterans. They've got a couple of the Admiral's men with them to run the satellite link NSA's providing.'

'Which is?'

'GWEN.'

Morton glanced at the CCO. The Ground Wave Emergency Network was a newcomer to NSA's arsenal. The CCO nodded. The Concorde was equipped to receive it.

'We'll patch in, Danny.'

'I'll tell them to allocate a link on Milstar.'

This satellite system was the most sophisticated and secret in use. It circled the world and allowed instant and totally secure communication between all American commanders.

Danny continued. 'We've run the tape Michelle picked up. Same woman as on all the others. Except the lisp's a little more noticeable. I've cued a copy to Lacouste. It's gone straight into Cabinet.'

'Does he think they will give way?'

'He's going to try and hold them up,' Danny said flatly.

'Anything from South Africa that would help Lester find this woman?'

'Zero. There was a package tour of Greeks going home that night. A computer failure at Jo'burg delayed their flight for a couple of hours. Vorag says the Greeks raised merry hell. Personally, I'd have thought they'd feel quite at home. Athens is on the blink again, the third time this month. Same thing – a bug in the Immigration computer. Planes are stacked up between Rome and Damascus.'

'Anything else?'

'Percy West says he'll have one of his cars meet you. But he can't make it himself. He's booked in for a Downing Street briefing. So's the ACC. They'll see you afterwards at Foley Street.'

Foley Street was where Mossad maintained its London safe house.

'You raise Costas yet?'

Costas Calcanis, the Mossad agent in Athens, had been Bitburg's first appointee. Since then Calcanis had on several occasions filled Morton with misgivings. He did his job well enough. But he was a little too showy, almost brash at times. Maybe that was what Bitburg liked, being able to control someone so opposite.

'I've close-circuited him copies of all the intercepts. Plus everything Steve and Humpty Dumpty have on that woman.'

Morton grunted. 'You tried to raise him on his MRT?'

'Not yet.'

The miniature receiver terminal enabled Mossad agents to receive a short message through the Defence Communications satellite. It was still in the experimental stage and Calcanis had been one of the first given the pocket-sized receiver to field test.

Danny grinned. 'Last time we called him it went on the blink and Costas couldn't shut it off. He was at the theatre at the time and had to pretend he was a doctor who'd gotten an emergency call on his bleeper.'

'Just get him going as fast as possible. I always feel better when we've eliminated Athens as one of our concerns.'

After Danny had cleared the screen, Morton sat and watched the digital Machmeter on the bulkhead steadily move towards Mach 1.000, as Concorde broke the sound barrier.

Then he started to think once more about how he would handle the interview in Germany. What would she be like now after two years' imprisonment?

Some fifty miles away and almost 50,000 feet below, the Air France Airbus from Tripoli was already thirty minutes late landing at Athens airport because of the Immigration computer being down.

'Any other airport, ladies and gentlemen, this would be a problem fixed quickly,' came the apologetic voice from the flight deck. 'But ground control has just informed me that rather than have a log jam of passengers on the ground, they prefer we use up our fuel. I'm not sure Aristotle would have admired their logic.'

Raza turned to Nadine in her first-class window seat, his hand squeezing hers. She smiled at him, her eyes bright with excitement.

Before leaving the camp he'd phoned the cabal's liaison man in Tripoli and said what he wanted. The man had called Athens and shortly afterwards the computer developed a fault. It would remain out of action for a further hour after the Tripoli flight had landed.

Raza looked up. The hostess was at his elbow, holding a bottle of champagne, smiling mechanically.

'A little more while we circle?'

He shook his head quickly and smiled her away.

Raza had chosen Nadine's and his roles with the greatest care. He had dressed and cast her in the part of his new bride. She needed no other disguise. He could not improve on that look of adoring innocence.

During the year he'd spent in Moscow, the KGB instructor had said the simpler the disguise the better. Change only the essentials, and always age upwards.

Raza dyed his hair and eyebrows grey and dramatically altered the shape of his face by inserting wax plugs in his nostrils and rubber moulds between jawline and cheeks. It created the jowly effect of middle years. Green-brown contact lenses lightened his eyes.

Beneath his shirt he wore a lightweight smock, padded to widen his shoulders and create the paunch that often goes with success and wealth. He'd veneered several front teeth with a fast-setting gold paste. A shiny new band on one finger matched Nadine's wedding ring. Both were travelling on Peruvian passports.

Leaning across Nadine, Raza glimpsed several other aircraft in a holding pattern.

'Perfect,' he murmured. 'They'll be going more crazy than usual in Immigration and Customs.'

There'd be the usual response to a mechanical failure: cursory glances at passports and baggage; keep everybody moving, avoid any hassle. Athens had long been his favourite airport.

The hostess was back to collect the newspapers. They had remained undisturbed in the seat pockets during the flight. Raza reached to hand them over.

The *International Herald-Tribune* fell open. Its headlines were divided between Trekfontein, the hotel explosions and the Athens disaster.

Raza took the paper, and waved the hostess away, no longer smiling.

The reports from London, Paris and Washington showed the hunt in full flow. Let it flow. Ground that had been hunted was always safer to walk on.

He turned to the story about the Athens explosion. All but one of the bodies were accounted for. Forensic scientists believed the unidentified remains were of a young woman carrying a quantity of bottles; glass had been found fused to fragments of bone. A police spokesman said she could be another of those pedlars who had become such a plague in Athens.

Raza folded the newspaper and turned to Nadine. He patted her hand and brought his mouth close to her ear.

'There's no need to worry. The heat will have destroyed everything.'

Nadine sensed the effort he was making to keep control. But the madness was there, touching his eyes and mouth, before it was gone. She ran her hand lovingly over his face.

The hostess returned with hot towels. Raza handed her the newspaper. He and Nadine wiped their hands with the towels and gave them back to the hostess. Neither had spoken to her during the flight. Another lesson Raza had learned in Moscow was to avoid all unnecessary contact.

Thirty minutes later they successfully negotiated the twin hurdles of Immigration and Customs. Raza slid their passports across the counter. They were stamped and passed back. A Customs official chalked their baggage without asking for either of the expensive leather suitcases to be opened. Raza had followed the KGB's advice to purchase top-of-the-range luggage to enhance the image of respectability.

Outside the hall Raza quickly and expertly surveyed the crowd. Only Cairo or Mexico attracted so many people to meet flights. The reek of tobacco smoke and perspiration reminded Nadine of the foetid atmosphere of the Beirut suburbs.

Raza spotted Lila. Hefting the suitcases, he cut a path through the throng towards her.

'Welcome,' Lila murmured, kissing Raza formally on both cheeks.

'I am glad to see you,' he replied. He pulled away and looked at Anna. He made no move to embrace her. She smiled wanly.

After Nadine had quickly greeted both women they walked out of the arrivals hall in uncomfortable silence. Only Nadine knew how near to the surface once more was Raza's fury. Anna had reminded him how close he had come to failure.

The Mercedes was one of several cars the cabal maintained in Athens. While Anna placed the suitcases in the trunk, Raza settled in the back with Nadine. He stared out of the window, hands in his lap, working his fingers together. Nadine knew it was a further sign of the fearful tensions gripping him.

Anna settled behind the wheel and headed towards Athens. They drove in a silence that had become dark and threatening. As they entered the city, Lila turned in the front passenger seat and looked at Raza.

'It was a pure accident Zelda was killed,' she said.

'Yes, yes,' said Anna eagerly.

Raza rasped in little more than a whisper. 'We will speak of this when I tell you.'

He turned back to the window. Nadine could smell Anna's fear.

Without a further word being spoken, they drove to the apartment which the cabal owned.

It was on the ground floor and consisted of three reception rooms and five bedrooms, each with its own bathroom. There was also a kitchen and spacious dining-room that led to a terrace. The furniture reminded Nadine of the villa: the same heavy, dark carved wood, and chairs covered with camel hide.

Raza turned to Anna. 'Make tea. Call me when it is ready.'

Without another word he walked on to the terrace, gripping its rail tightly with both hands, his head raised to the sun, his lips moving soundlessly.

'I did not know he prayed,' said Anna nervously.

Nadine looked at her dispassionately. 'He's not praying. He is cursing what has happened. All his plans were nearly ruined by Zelda's stupidity.'

She carried her suitcase to the master suite. Its huge double bed was surrounded by couches and ottomans. Wardrobes covered one wall. The bathroom was furnished in blood-red marble.

'A bathroom always releases the fantasy in me,' said Lila.

Nadine turned. Lila was standing by the bed, smiling. Nadine looked at her and frowned. Lila walked towards her, still smiling. Her hand was unbuttoning the top buttons of her smock.

'Do not be nervous, *chérie*,' she whispered. She moved closer, reached out and touched Nadine's face.

'Stop it!' Nadine gripped Lila by the wrist and forced her hand away.

For a moment they stood there, testing each other's strength and resolve.

'Do not be nervous, *chérie*,' Lila said again. She moved to break Nadine's hold.

'I am not nervous,' replied Nadine, releasing Lila and pushing her firmly away.

Lila smiled archly at her. She badly needed release after the tensions of the past days. Anna had been accommodating, but hardly satisfying.

'You are too beautiful for just a man,' she murmured.

'Lila, I love him.' Nadine walked past Lila and placed one of the suitcases on the bed. She began to unpack.

'*Chérie*, Raza does not know what love is. And you really think you are the only one? He is insatiable!'

Nadine whirled. In her hand was the throwing knife she had packed between her clothes. She balanced the handle in her hand then, in a swift unbroken movement hurled the knife.

It bedded itself in the door frame, an inch from Lila's head.

Nadine turned and produced a second knife from the suitcase.

'Do not speak like that of my man,' Nadine said fiercely. She walked over and tugged the blade out of the wood, then stepped back and faced Lila, 'Just stay away from him! And from me!'

Without a word, Lila walked out of the bedroom.

Nadine continued to unpack. She had learned her throwing skill as a child. No one had been able to match her except Shema.

Shema. She had not thought about her once since leaving Tripoli. She knew she still wanted her sister free, but she did not want Shema to push her once more into the background. The surprise was that she didn't feel guilty about this.

When Raza shouted for her to join him in the main reception salon, she saw Lila and Anna seated together on a couch. Small cups and a glass jug filled with tea made with fresh mint stood on a table.

Close by were the five remaining bottles of Grecian Nights, filled with Anthrax-B-C, and a cardboard box containing a couple of dozen empty perfume bottles.

Raza stood beneath a gilt-framed portrait of a glowering-faced figure in a tarboosh and black robe.

Nadine went and sat in one of the overstuffed chairs, keeping her legs together and hands in her lap. It was the way Raza liked her to sit in public. She saw the pulse throbbing in his temples. The headache must be almost unbearable. She rose and went to the table and poured tea into a cup. Holding it in both hands, she took it to him.

He drank the scalding brew in noisy gulps, his eyes only leaving Anna to stare at the perfume bottles. Why had this camel's whore not been able to save those bottles?

'Would you like more?' asked Nadine, taking the cup from his hand.

He nodded, his eyes still fixing Anna with that frightening glare. Twice more Nadine served Raza tea, which he drank without saying a word. After the third cup she saw the throbbing was less noticeable. He waved her away and she returned to her seat.

'Our benefactor,' Raza said suddenly, gazing up at the portrait. 'Ayatollah Muzwaz trusts me to ensure his plans can succeed. And he trusts me because I have always told him the truth!'

He turned to face the couch, once more staring at Anna. His eyes were now devoid of expression. When he spoke again, his voice was suddenly gentle, as if he was speaking to a child.

'Did you know she had taken the bottles?'

Nadine saw the surprise on the girl's face at his change of mood. Anna gave a little nod, lowering her eyes.

'Did you try to stop her?'

Anna shook her bowed head.

'Why not?' asked Raza in the same gentle voice. 'Why not?'

Anna raised her head. There were tears in her eyes. 'I didn't think . . .'

He looked down at her, nodding slowly. 'No. You didn't think.'

'I am sorry,' whispered Anna.

Nadine saw that terrifying look return.

Raza turned abruptly away and stared at the portrait. The girl must be punished. But not yet. To do so now would only further jeopardise the operation.

When Raza turned round, Nadine saw he was again completely composed.

'There will be no more mistakes,' he said in a quiet voice.

Anna nodded fervently. Lila and Nadine did the same.

'Very well. Because of what has happened there will be

changes,' he said, beginning his briefing, and going over to the bottles.

East of Paris, the Concorde began its descent.

'The Cabinet's divided down the middle,' Lacouste was saying on the screen. 'Half want to let them go now. The others want to hold on to the *Feydeheen* a little longer in the hope they'll stop Raza from launching a further attack in France.'

Morton shifted in his seat. 'That's never worked before. It won't now. If your people weaken, the whole thing will really begin to crumble. As it is I'm having a problem holding them together.'

'The Italians?'

'And the Germans and the Dutch. Their politicians are beginning to kick against the clamp-down. A few hours of delays at airports and borders have a wonderful way of concentrating the minds of voters. They start to call their MPs. The MPs call their Ministers. The Ministers call the Prime Minister. He orders security scaled down. It's already happening in Rome and the Hague. If your people let these terrorists go, we'll be back to normal. Europe will be like a cheese – with enough holes for Raza's people to come and go as they please!'

Lacouste sighed. '*Merde, merde, merde.* I'll go back and push some more.'

His image disappeared. Morton turned to the adjoining screen where Matti waited to talk to him from the Israeli Consulate in New York.

'How you doing, Matti?'

'I've known better days,' he answered. 'Right now this is where we're at: the first five hundred names on the list I gave them have been processed by the FBI's TRAC people. They say there's not even a postage stamp to link any one with Raza.'

The Terrorist Research and Analytical Centre had been set up by the FBI after the first spate of skyjackings to Beirut. Its prime function was contact tracing.

'How many more to go?'

'Over four thousand. They figure three more days,' said Matti.

'Too long. They've got to do it in two – maximum.'

'I'll tell them. I've had our Swift people drop everything and concentrate on the UN and the Arab embassies in Washington. They've got taps everywhere. But again – nothing.'

Matti paused to look at his notes.

'Bill Gates – nothing. Same with the Admiral. Lou says everyone is going down to the wire –'

'How about the White House?'

Matti shrugged. 'Appleton's being his usual devious self.'

Brent Appleton was the President's National Security Adviser. From the day he'd been appointed he had made no secret of his strong pro-Arab feelings.

Matti made a face. 'It'll get worse as next November comes and the President looks for a second term.'

'What's Appleton doing?'

'Being gung ho in public and saying all the right things. You want the Marines, he'd give them to you. He'd give you anything as long as you didn't plan to use it against any Arab country.'

Matti paused and shook his head. 'In private he's whispering in the President's ear all these little reminders of how political futures evaporated in the sands of Iran and Iraq.'

Jimmy Carter had ended his Presidency with his failure to rescue the first American hostages taken in the Middle East, the staff of the US Embassy in Teheran. Ronald Reagan's eight years in the White House were finally blighted by the scandal of his secret deal to trade arms with Iran for the freedom of other American hostages in Beirut. The Gulf War had left George Bush presiding over a nation never more divided since Vietnam.

Morton came to a decision. 'I'll talk to Appleton. Meantime, run your own checks on those other two thousand names I've just had the Honeywell send you. There'll be the usual academics and businessmen, but there just could be a name that will trigger something.'

The Concorde was coming up to the French coast as the forbidding features of Brent Appleton appeared on screen. He seemed dwarfed in the armchair. Morton knew that what Appleton lacked in inches, he made up for with intellect.

'Good afternoon, Colonel,' Appleton's smile was cold and brief. 'What can I do for you?'

Morton told him about the split in the French Cabinet and what was happening in Italy and Holland.

'I see,' Appleton said, steepling his manicured fingers. 'In the wider political context I can understand, and even sympathise, with their reaction. The Italians and Dutch have always had good relationships with the Arabs. In many ways what they have achieved is something we could all emulate. The fact is, of course, that this business with Raza is playing havoc with efforts to build new bridges with the Islamic world. While I would be the first to say Raza must be firmly dealt with, I only hope that nothing will be done to destroy the delicate negotiations with the Arabs many of us wish to bring to a successful conclusion.'

'If I don't neutralise Raza, there may be nothing to negotiate about. Right now nothing else is my concern,' Morton said evenly.

'But the wider picture has to remain mine,' Appleton said more sharply. 'The President is not only keen to maintain his dialogue with Damascus, but to open new ones with Teheran and Baghdad.'

'All the more reason to remove Raza.'

'Of course,' Appleton cut in swiftly. 'But a lot of people in the region see him as a hero. That what he is doing is right and just. We can all disagree with that. But we must take it into account. The view from Damascus or Teheran is very different from the perspective held here in Washington – or, for that matter, Tel Aviv.'

Morton felt the anger begin to course through his body.

'Is that what you're telling your President? That there's no real difference between a nation being forced to defend itself or be overrun – and massacred – and the mindless terror Raza unleashes?'

Appleton's fingers steepled and unsteepled. When he spoke his voice was as cold and thin as the air outside the fuselage.

'Colonel, what I tell the President is between him and me. But I will tell you this: we will do everything we can to support you in your work. But I will continue to urge the President to do absolutely nothing that would adversely affect the future of this country.'

Morton's face was as stony as his voice.

'You mean to make sure nothing compromises his chance of being re-elected?'

'To ensure he does not find himself led into needless conflict with our Arab friends,' Appleton said quickly.

Morton saw Appleton glare at his Rolex.

'Let me tell you this, Mr Appleton. If I find anything you are saying or doing gets in my way, you'll answer to me personally.'

'Are you threatening me, Colonel?'

'No. Reminding you of what the real priority is. By all means get your President re-elected. But don't do it at my expense. Have a nice day, Mr Appleton.'

Morton turned his back on the screen before it darkened.

Thirty minutes later Morton came down the ramp at the RAF base at Northolt where the Concorde had landed to avoid the log jam at Heathrow due to the security restrictions.

Wolfie was waiting in the government car Percy West had sent. Morton tossed his holdall on the front seat beside the army driver and climbed in the back.

Wolfie touched him briefly on the shoulder.

'I'm sorry about your parents, David. The ACC told me.'

'Thanks, Wolfie.' Morton gripped Wolfie's arm quickly. 'Good to see you.'

The car moved across the tarmac to the perimeter gate guarded by armed dog handlers.

'The ACC says it's the biggest flap since the IRA bombed the Tory Party Conference hotel in Brighton,' said Wolfie.

'My bet is that the bombers will have gone. But Raza will have others out there, for sure.'

Morton glanced out of the window, then turned to Wolfie. 'Michelle okay?'

'She's fine. The Italians are kicking up. The old whine about operating on their doorstep without permission.'

Morton grunted. 'If we'd told them, it could have leaked – like it did with Nidal.'

A couple of years before he'd found Abu Nidal holed up in an apartment in Rome's late-night quarter, Trastevere. Bitburg had insisted he tell the Digos, the Italian anti-terrorist squad. When they'd hit the apartment, Nidal had gone. It had had to be a tip-off.

'Bitburg can say *mea culpa*, Wolfie.'

Leaving the air base the driver began to cut through the back streets.

'There's a mass of data on these dead women. I've dipped it through the computers. Nothing showed up,' said Wolfie.

'Costas surfaced?'

'He sent a fax about an hour ago. He'd been out of town chasing a tip that some of the bombers were heading back through northern Greece to Beirut.'

'And?'

'Nix. He's now working on that tanker explosion. A real five-star disaster. Almost forty dead now. Lucky it happened late at night, otherwise there'd have been casualties to match the hotels.'

'Many women?'

'Costas says about a dozen. Housewives. A couple of hookers. And what they think was some gypsy. He reckons they'll probably never identify her.'

'How'd they know she was a gypsy?'

Wolfie fished in his pocket and produced a sheet of fax paper.

'The Athens police think she could be a street pedlar because of the bits of glass their forensic guys found on her body.'

'What kind of glass?'

Wolfie glanced at the paper. 'Costas doesn't say. But probably trinkets. When I was last there, there was a plague of these pedlars selling just about anything.'

'Including perfume?'

Wolfie looked at Morton and shook his head. 'Jesus, you don't think she could have been carrying the stuff, do you?'

Morton smiled briefly. 'No. We couldn't be that lucky.'

He took the paper from Wolfie and carefully folded it before slipping it into an inside pocket. Then he looked out of the window.

It had started to rain. Each time he'd come to London it had rained. Nan had said it was an omen. He remembered he'd asked a good one or a bad one, and she'd smiled enigmatically. He'd call her from the safe house.

Michelle buzzed them in. The safe house was a large apartment on two floors. The furniture looked as if it had come from a garage sale; nothing seemed to match. There were a few cheaply framed pictures of Israel on the walls.

Michelle embraced Morton quickly.

'So sorry. So very sorry about your great misfortune,' she murmured.

'Thanks.'

They stood for a moment in silence. Then Morton turned towards the stairs.

'I'll go settle in.'

Morton went up the stairs at the double, glad to be alone. Since Ruth he had never known how to handle condolences.

The bedroom had an old-fashioned high-legged bed whose bedspread was as worn as the carpets. On the dressing-table was a telephone. A hard-back chair and freestanding wardrobe completed the furniture. There was a drawn blind on the window. One door led to the bathroom. Through the other he entered the safe room.

There was a computer and VDU, several telephones, a shredder, two fax machines and the obligatory safe. Moulded plastic chairs allowed for three people to sit in the room.

Both fax machines were receiving. Madrid station was reporting that the Spanish navy was searching all boats off its long coastline for Raza. Mossad's woman in Lisbon said the Portuguese were mounting a similar operation. Gates had sent a CIA update: nothing new. Admiral Burness' office was reporting the satellite link with General Yertzin's Spetsnaz was working perfectly. But there was nothing yet to report.

Chantal had sent a message. Lou Panchez had called to say Appleton was making unpleasant noises about being threatened. He wanted the President to call Karshov.

Morton tore off the message, crumpled the paper and lobbed it into the maw of the shredder.

Anwar Salim had sent a long report detailing how Egyptian agents in half a dozen Arab capitals were reporting no trace of Raza. It confirmed separate reports from Mossad agents in the same cities.

Lester Finel had sent an update. His mutes were widening their search to include Japanese and Asian associates of Arab terrorists. Problem. That added a further 17,000 names to the check list. A day's work.

Morton scanned the next report.

Humpty Dumpty was heading off on a new direction – trying to establish when the tape had been made. Knowing that would help fill in the background timetable: how long Al-Najaf could have been in Rome; the gap between the recording and Trekfontein and the hotel explosions. Thankfully, he had not bothered to send a technical description of how this could be achieved. That would probably have needed a whole roll of fax paper.

The professor had sent Arab reaction to Trekfontein and the bombings. There was unanimous condemnation. The most vociferous had come from Libya. The professor thought the Supreme Leader would add to the pressure on Muzwaz to hold off calling for a holy war.

The rest of the traffic consisted of names and descriptions of the deaths of several hundred women who had died in the past few days within a 500-mile radius of Beirut. Wolfie was right. None of them looked as if they could be that sister of the perfume who had gone to her Prophet.

And nothing to show where Raza could be.

As Morton turned from the fax machines, one of the phones rang. It was Danny.

'We have a break!' He was barely able to control his excitement. 'I've been playing a long shot the last twenty-four hours. Had my best team checking the pulse tone on that call.'

'About the dead woman?'

'Right. We've been comparing the tone with those of every other telephone system in that radius. That meant ringing every city and town in the area, recording their telephone tone output, superimposing the message we taped going into Beirut, and then running comparison tests. We've run hundreds. Several were close matches. They're often hard to separate now that several countries use almost identical signals –'

'So where did the call come from?' Morton interrupted.

'Athens. We've checked it a dozen times. Each time it fits. Same pulse tone. It's as accurate as genetic finger-printing.'

'Let's get Costas on this fast.'

Danny's sigh carried clearly from Tel Aviv.

'I've been trying. He's not answering his MRT.'

Morton started to give orders.

'Get Covert Action to send a back-up team to Athens. Have Gates get his local people to liaise with them. He's got a couple of good men there. And keep trying Costas. I'll do the same this end.'

'Understood.'

When Morton next spoke, his voice was softer. 'And Danny. Tell everybody, well done. And you too.'

18

Nadine and Anna arrived in Constitution Square late in the afternoon, a time when the largest piazza in Athens was crowded with tourists.

Both girls were dressed in sky-blue uniforms of pleated skirts and bolero jackets with white blouses. Draped across each bolero was a bright red sash bearing the gold printed words: *Grecian Nights.*

Each carried a clipboard. Anna also had an instamatic camera hanging from a strap around her neck, while Nadine carried a large canvas pouch hanging from a shoulder strap.

The bag had two compartments. In the smaller were the five remaining bottles of Anthrax-B-C. The larger contained the other bottles, which Nadine and Anna had filled with a blend of their own perfumes, Raza's aftershave and several bottles of toilet water they'd found in the apartment. To this they had added sweetened mint tea.

Anna checked the camera, looking nervously at Nadine.

'You'll be fine,' reassured Nadine. 'Just remember to take a picture that shows the mule's face and mine.'

They began to walk around the square, looking for unsuspecting tourists who would carry the bottles of anthrax into the United States and Britain.

'Remember, too,' Nadine reminded Anna, 'we are only interested in American or British mules who are flying home in the next twelve hours.'

'Raza is so clever,' sighed Anna. 'Do you think he is still angry with me?'

'No, of course not.' How easily she could lie for Raza.

'I am glad Lila has gone,' continued Anna. 'She was . . . very demanding. I have never made love with a woman before. It was very strange.'

'She won't bother you again,' promised Nadine.

A couple of hours before, Lila had dropped off the replacement tape Nadine had made at the radio station. Then she had continued on to the airport to begin the first leg of her long journey through Asia and across the Pacific to the United States.

'There, look,' said Anna, nudging Nadine.

At one of the outdoor tables an elderly couple were poring over a travel itinerary. Nadine briefly studied them, then shook her head.

'No good. They're German.'

She had learned enough German from Shema to recognise the boldly printed word on the back of the itinerary – *Reisebüro*.

'Look for people who speak English.'

They continued to move around the square. Only Nadine knew that Raza was somewhere close by, watching over them. It made her all that more determined to carry out the mission to his complete satisfaction.

There were pedlars everywhere, selling all kinds of gaudy souvenirs.

'How about him?' suggested Anna, nodding towards a short muscular man strolling towards an open-air bar next to the Grande Bretagne.

Nadine forced herself to smile. 'Even I can see he's Greek. Don't be so impatient. We'll find someone. Let's try over there.'

She led Anna towards the King George Hotel. Costas Calcanis continued strolling towards the bar.

The Israeli prided himself on looking like a Greek in his custom-made suit, shirt and shoes whose maker had cleverly built in an extra inch to make Costas taller than his five-six. What he lacked in inches he made up with a leonine head and a truly wonderful smile.

It was absent now, leaving his face only tired-looking and somewhat irritated. During the past twenty-four hours he'd driven non-stop over some of the worst roads in Southern Europe. There hadn't been a sign of the hotel bombers in any of the small towns and villages he'd checked. And once more this newfangled MRT had played up. It had emitted loud crackles first in a café and later when he'd pulled off the road for a catnap.

Coming back into the city he'd switched off the box. When he had a moment, he'd send Tel Aviv a blistering report on its behaviour. The MRT was still in his jacket pocket, close to the .38 handgun in its shoulder holster.

He'd returned to Athens to find Danny's Double Flash asking for full details on every woman who had died in the country during the past few days. After he'd faxed the names of those killed in the tanker explosion, he'd farmed out the tedious task of checking every hospital, mortuary and funeral parlour to one of his contacts in the police department. The man would be glad to earn a week's salary for no more than a long day's work.

After briefing him, Costas had come to the square to enjoy a drink and the parade of pretty girls. He had a bachelor's natural talent for spotting who could be persuaded to join him for a drink, followed by dinner and then bed. He knew that his worldly charm and fund of outrageous stories had, over his two years in Athens, established his reputation as one of the city's playboy seducers. He also suspected it was this, more than anything, that made Morton so prickly. But as long as he did his job and enjoyed the patronage of Bitburg, Costas knew he would survive.

Settling himself at a table, Costas ordered Pernod and began to scan the newspaper the waiter brought with the drink.

The tanker disaster continued to dominate the news. The unaccounted body now had a face of sorts. Most of the tabloid's front page was given over to a crude composite picture of a woman whom readers were invited to name.

Costas thought she looked a little like the young woman sitting by herself at the far end of the bar. They had the same thick black hair scraped back from the forehead, and similar high cheekbones. But the face in the photo had a squarer jawline, and the woman toying with her coffee was softer round the mouth.

Just another tourist, Costas decided, probably an American. The last one he'd bedded had proved highly inventive. He gave the woman a longer glance, this time adding a little smile.

Nancy Olson stirred in more sugar, wondering how she could escape his attention. She'd glanced at him once, quickly, then turned away. He reminded her of Rob, and that was reason enough to look away.

Their affair had lasted a year – until that afternoon she'd returned to the apartment and found him in bed with her best friend. Nancy had never suspected either capable of such deceit. She had moved out within the hour. A month later, class term over, she'd gone on this vacation she'd planned with Rob, two weeks in the Greek islands.

She'd been surprised how much she'd enjoyed the freedom of being alone, of being able to choose and decide for herself, of being able to exorcise Rob from her mind.

She was going back to teaching filled with new resolve. The last thing she wanted was to become involved with Rob's lookalike.

Sipping his drink, Costas continued to appraise her. No doubt at all, she was attractive. Her halter top revealed tanned and toned muscles and breasts that were unfettered. The full peasant skirt showed off her long legs. He raised his glass towards her, smiling.

Nancy felt her cheeks begin to warm. She'd always blushed in unexpected situations. Dammit, she was twenty-six and should know how to keep a man at bay. But this wasn't New York – and it was her first trip overseas. And though she had enjoyed herself, she'd often felt an innocent these past two weeks. Yet she wasn't just going to sit here and allow herself to be ogled by this – this gigolo. He was really getting to her. Nancy looked around for something to distract her from this staring, smiling man.

Costas ordered another drink and asked the waiter to send a flute of the bar's best champagne to Nancy's table. It always worked. He sat back to wait, wondering where he would take her for dinner.

'There,' said Anna. 'I am certain she's American! Look how arrogantly she sits. And she has just pushed her glass away. Only an American would order champagne and then decide it was not good enough!'

Nadine turned to where Nancy sat, drinking her coffee.

When the flute had arrived Nancy had tried to send it back. The waiter had smilingly refused, explaining it was a house rule that a drink could not be returned. She had pushed the glass to one side and turned her back.

Costas had sighed. He'd never chased a woman in his life. He was not about to start. He ordered another Pernod and looked for someone else to catch his fancy.

He saw the two girls in their fetching uniforms. He dismissed the shorter, pale-faced one. But her companion was quite stunning. He sighed again. He never picked up a local. That only led to problems with husbands or boyfriends – or a woman who didn't know when it was over. Briefly he wondered what they were touting, then he turned away to watch the tourists coming out of the Grand Bretagne.

'I think this time you are right, Anna,' said Nadine, not quite able to contain her excitement and relief.

So far the tourists they'd approached who'd spoken English had either waved them away, or turned out to be Australian or Irish. They'd given them some of the bottles containing the concoction.

'She's calling us over.' Anna began to walk towards Nancy's table.

'Wait,' commanded Nadine. Raza had said not to appear eager. That could raise a mule's suspicions.

She led Anna to a table near Nancy's. It was filled with a boisterous group of tourists who were clearly at the playful stage of their drinking.

'Good evening, ladies and gentlemen,' began Nadine. 'We represent one of Greece's largest manufacturers of perfume, and we would very much like your help in a market survey we are conducting for a new range.'

She produced a bottle from the larger compartment of the pouch.

'Which country are you from?' she asked.

'Holland!' came a chorus of voices.

'Very good,' Nadine smiled. 'Now this perfume will be on the market in your country next year. But this bottle will be yours. Hey – sir – please!'

One of the men at the table had grabbed the bottle and was holding it under the nose of the woman next to him. When Nadine tried to take the bottle, the man held it out of reach.

'Please, sir!' implored Nadine. 'First you must answer questions!'

The man laughed and lobbed the bottle across the table to

217

another woman. Surprised, she dropped it. The bottle broke among the beer glasses and there was a sudden silence. The man looked sheepishly at Nadine, then fished in his hip pocket and produced a bulky wallet. He removed a wad of drachmae.

'Here,' he said, thrusting the money at Nadine. 'I pay for the breakage.'

A round of applause came from his companions.

'And I buy everyone a bottle!' he added.

Nadine stepped back.

'You can't buy,' she said, smiling. 'It's a promotion.'

Raza had said always to smile.

The man picked up a piece of broken glass and sniffed it.

'Lousy perfume!' he pronounced, putting his money back in the wallet.

His companions laughed loudly.

Still smiling, Nadine turned away and led Anna to Nancy.

The incident had attracted Costas' attention. The tall girl was truly beautiful, and not Greek. A Levantine probably, another Beiruti who had fled the city to graft elsewhere. He cocked his head to read the words on her sash. Maybe she'd known the missing girl in the tanker disaster. It would be one name less for his police contact to bother about. He'd wait until they'd finished their pitch before talking to them.

'You handled that very well,' Nancy said, when Nadine and Anna reached her table. 'There's nothing like a bunch of drunks to give you a hard time.'

Nadine gave a brilliant smile. 'You Americans have such a wonderful way of describing everything.'

Nancy shook her head. 'Actually I'm Canadian. Born and raised in Toronto.'

'Oh.' Anna could not quite conceal her disappointment.

'But I live in New York,' Nancy grinned. 'Not that anyone lives there. You just survive, day to day. It's still really the only place to be.'

Suddenly she felt a longing to see her adopted city, her room, and the nice elderly widow she rented from.

Nadine gave another brilliant smile. 'I would like to go to New York one day. All those skyscrapers and wonderful shows.'

'For me it would be for the hamburgers!' said Anna, slipping into the patter Raza had told them to use. 'And the milkshakes!'

The three girls laughed, instantly united.

'You are on vacation?' Nadine asked.

'Almost over.'

'You like our country?' asked Anna politely.

'Love it,' replied Nancy. 'I mean, there are some things that take a little getting used to, like the food and the amount of wine everybody drinks. And the men –'

'Ah!' smiled Anna. 'Always the men! Greek men are like bulls!'

Once more they laughed together.

'Would you like to join me for coffee?' asked Nancy.

'Thank you, but we have work to do,' explained Nadine. Raza said never become too involved with a mule. She explained about the market research. Nancy said she would be happy to help.

Nadine reached down and removed one of the bottles containing the Anthrax-B-C, and carefully placed it on the table.

'What we would like you to do', continued Nadine, 'is to answer some simple questions about the image our perfume conveys.'

Nancy picked up the bottle and turned it over in her hands before putting it down.

'Can I try some?'

Nadine stooped and produced a bottle of made-up perfume. She quickly broke the seal and unscrewed the stopper. She sprinkled some of the liquid on the back of Nancy's hand.

Nancy drew it under her nose, sniffing. She looked at Nadine and Anna. 'It seems very light.'

'Like the water in our mountains?' prompted Anna.

Nancy grinned. 'I'd go with that.'

Anna made an entry on the clipboard.

'After a while the air deepens the perfume,' explained Nadine.

Nancy sniffed once more.

'It's refreshing, yes?' asked Anna politely.

Nancy nodded. 'You can say that.'

She didn't want to hurt them by saying the perfume had a cheap smell.

Anna consulted her clipboard. 'What does the shape of the bottle convey to you?'

Nancy considered. In all the islands she'd visited, she'd been struck by the stunning rock formations.

'A headland I saw on Rhodes,' she replied.

'Very good,' said Nadine.

Anna made another entry on the clipboard.

'And the colour?' she asked.

Nancy grinned. 'The sea at Thessaloníki.'

'Perfect,' said Nadine. 'The best answers we have had all day.'

'No kidding?' grinned Nancy. She reached for the sealed bottle. 'Can I keep this one? A keepsake to remind me of Greece.'

Anna looked at Nadine. Raza had said that once hooked, a mule must be handled with great care.

'Well . . . there are difficulties,' began Anna.

'You see,' continued Nadine, 'we are only permitted to give samples to people who are leaving the country in the next twelve hours.'

'No problem,' said Nancy, looking down at the bottle. Even if she dumped the perfume, the bottle would be an attractive bathroom ornament. She looked up at Nadine. 'In twelve hours I'll be somewhere between here and over the Atlantic, heading for Kennedy.'

Nadine looked doubtful. 'Our company is very strict on such matters. I would need to see your ticket.'

'No problem,' repeated Nancy. She opened her handbag and removed the flight coupon.

Anna wrote down Nancy's name and TWA flight number on the clipboard. She returned the ticket.

'All set?' asked Nancy, preparing to put the bottle in her handbag.

Nadine gave another smile. 'Just two more requirements. Firstly, regulations forbid the bottle to be opened until you have cleared US Customs. Secondly, you must carry the bottle as hand baggage for easy inspection. This arrangement between both our countries concerns all such items.'

Raza had made Nadine rehearse the words until she was perfect.

'No problem,' promised Nancy. 'Anything else?'

Nadine laughed, delighted how well it had gone.

'Because your answers were so good we would like you to pose for a photo for our company house magazine.'

'No kidding?' grinned Nancy, rising to her feet. 'Snap away!'

She picked up the sealed bottle and held it like a pack shot in her hand.

Nadine moved to her side while Anna focused the camera. Raza had said to take several shots to be absolutely sure.

Afterwards Nancy dropped the bottle in her handbag. It really was a beautiful shape.

Nadine and Anna exchanged quick smiles.

Nancy looked at them. 'Could I ask a heck of a favour? I'd like to keep my bottle, but the lady I rent from would just go nuts for it. Could I buy one for her? If it's a question of paying, no problem.'

Nadine looked at Anna and nodded. Their luck was running. One mule carrying two bottles would make everything simpler at Kennedy. Nadine smiled at Nancy.

'No, no,' Nadine said, shaking her head. 'We cannot sell. But we will give you a second bottle because we are certain your answers will help make our perfume a great success!'

Nadine handed Nancy another bottle containing Anthrax-B-C.

'Terrific,' Nancy said, also putting the bottle in her handbag. 'Really terrific.'

'No problem,' Nadine mimicked.

Once more they all laughed together.

Nancy glanced across the bar. The Greek was still watching her. She turned to Nadine.

'Listen, would you do me a final favour? There's a guy over there been giving me the eye. I'd be glad if you'd walk me out of the square.'

Nadine looked at Costas, then turned back to Nancy.

'No problem.'

Impulsively, Nancy tipped the flute of champagne on to the ground. After leaving payment for the coffee, she walked between Nadine and Anna out of the bar.

Costas shrugged. Only an American would want to make her point in such a way. But he still wanted to talk to those promotions girls. He left enough drachmae under his glass and set off to follow.

From a lounge window of the Grande Bretagne Raza had seen what had happened. The girls had done well. But why had the mule thrown away her drink? And why was she leaving with them? That was not part of his orders. Moments later his mounting rage was replaced by a sudden tension. The girls were being followed. And the Greek trailing them was an expert, keeping his distance, the way a professional did.

Raza strode out of the hotel in pursuit.

In the Foley Street apartment Morton listened to the ACC and West. They had come directly from briefing the Prime Minister at Downing Street.

'There was only one question,' the ACC was saying. 'Was there any way Raza or his people could get into the country with this anthrax? We were able to say with confidence – no. We've got extra men on every air and sea port. We've blocked off the back door through Ireland. We're diverting all private flights to Stansted for special handling. We've got the navy patrolling the coast.'

'In other words, old boy,' West said to Morton, 'we're as buttoned down as a tick in a mattress.'

Morton moved away from the empty and ugly Victorian fireplace in the living-room. He stopped before the two men seated in the deep overstuffed armchairs. Michelle sat on the staircase. Upstairs Morton could hear Wolfie in the safe room talking to Danny, reporting still no success in raising Costas.

'Raza's not going to try to slip past your defences with his own people now,' said Morton. 'He'll know you're too good for him there, for sure. He'll have had them in place for weeks, maybe months.'

'Then how does he get in this anthrax?' asked West.

'A mule of some kind. Maybe a student. He's done that before. Or he could use a drug courier. Someone who knows the ropes,' said Morton.

The ACC nodded quickly. 'We've anticipated you there, David. We're stopping one in every four incoming passengers at every commercial airport and strip-searching them. We're doing the same to everybody coming into Stansted. Plus taking each plane apart.'

'My people have begun to ride on all scheduled flights from the Middle East,' said West. 'Special Branch and Six have chipped in. So have the SAS. By the end of the week we'll have someone on every flight into the country. And the regular sky marshals have been briefed.'

Morton nodded and looked at the ACC. 'One in four still leaves three unchecked. Why not make it one in two?'

The senior police officer sighed. 'The civil liberties people are already going to the battlements. And just about every exporter whose got a salesman travelling abroad is raising Cain. I've had more MPs threatening to table questions in the House –'

'Tell them all to go to hell,' Morton said flatly.

'This is not Israel, old boy,' West interjected flintily. 'That's not the way we do things here.'

'For sure, Percy.' Morton deliberately waited before continuing. 'Now let me tell you how I want things done here until this is all over. I want a one-in-two search of all passengers coming from all starting points between Rome and Teheran. Tell your people to look out for any kind of bottle. Infiltrate all arrival areas. In Tel Aviv our people have learned a lot by just listening.'

'We're talking extra manpower, budgets, the whole damn caboodle. Who's going to pay for all this?' flared West. 'And have you any idea how many bottles people carry with them through our airports every hour? Customs tell me they confiscate about ten thousand a day, mostly booze and perfume. You could be talking of up to a million bottles every twenty-four hours.'

The briefest of smiles crossed Morton's lips. 'You'll find a way, Percy, for sure.'

The MI5 officer shook his head. 'We can't confiscate every bottle. We've got to keep a sense of perspective –'

'You saw that footage from Trekfontein, Percy,' Morton interrupted harshly. 'That's the only perspective that interests me – making sure it doesn't happen again.'

The ACC nodded at West. 'David's right.'

He turned to Morton. 'We'll have the army pull in rummage squads from Ulster. It'll take about twenty-four hours to get everyone in place –'

'You've got to do it in less. Twelve at the most,' Morton cut in. 'We've got to work within Raza's deadline. If he hasn't got the stuff already in place, my bet is he'll need to do so in the next twenty-four hours.'

The ACC nodded, went to the phone on the sideboard and gave instructions.

'Twelve hours,' he concluded firmly. 'Whatever it takes, do it.'

He put down the phone and turned to Morton. 'It'll be tight, but we'll manage.'

'Good. Now let me bring you up to date.'

Morton began by describing Danny's breakthrough in pinpointing the call from Athens.

19

Nadine and Anna arrived by taxi at Athens airport after escorting Nancy back to her hotel behind Constitution Square.

'Suppose she opens the bottle?' asked Anna as they walked into the departure hall.

'She won't,' replied Nadine. 'Americans are very obedient. Raza always says tell them something and they'll obey. He proved that when he hijacked their planes.'

They surveyed the scene inside the hall. It was filled with passengers waiting their turn for departure formalities.

'Not them,' Nadine said decisively. 'They'll only hassle us like those Dutch pigs. This time we're looking for a businessman.'

They began to walk among the lines of travellers wending their way to the check-in counters.

From his vantage point in the gallery overlooking the hall, Costas continued to watch the girls. Increasingly he felt there was something unusual about them. As he'd passed the American girl's hotel, he'd overheard the Levantine giving precise instructions how the American should carry her bottle. Street sellers never bothered about such details, and always stuck to their own patches. But the pair had left the city's prime spot for tourists, Constitution Square, and come all the way out here. Nor could he remember a promotion involving only a couple of girls. Usually when a product was launched, there were scores of them, pushing sales literature and samples on every street corner. Besides the Levantine was much too attractive to be wasting her time promoting a product. She had the looks and walk to be a model.

His curiosity deepened, Costas had slipped into his natural role.

Following them to the airport, he'd used his car phone to call a contact in the city's leading promotions organisation. She had told him to phone back in an hour.

Now he went to one of the pay phones in the gallery.

'Any luck, Susie?' he asked when he was connected.

'*Nada*,' came the cheerful Australian voice.

They'd had a brief affair a year ago when Susie had stopped over in Athens from Sydney. When she decided to stay on, he'd ended the relationship while still managing to remain friends.

'The pitch is definitely not any of our clients. I've called all the opposition. None are running a perfume promo. I checked all the leading manufacturers. Again, *nada*.'

'What about a smaller firm?'

'I called several. Nothing. From those glitzy uniforms you say they're wearing, I'd guess a small house couldn't afford them.'

'They could be from out of town,' Costas pressed.

'I doubt it. This business is pretty well run out of here.'

'Thanks, Susie. How about dinner next week?'

'Love to.'

Costas hung up and continued to watch Nadine and Anna.

Raza had spotted him as soon as he'd entered the hall. The gallery was exactly the place he would have chosen from which to run a surveillance.

He was maintaining his own watch from inside a souvenir shop. Maybe the man was a detective or an investigator from a Ministry? But the girls had broken no law – and Nadine was carrying all the necessary permissions to work any public place in Athens. The cabal's local man had arranged that.

Whoever he was, his presence boded trouble. Raza left the shop and began to move through the concourse.

Anna spotted him and turned to Nadine.

'Why is he here? Is he checking up on me?'

'Don't be a fool. And ignore him,' Nadine said fiercely. 'Just do your job.'

From the gallery Costas saw the sudden fear on the younger girl's face, and the flash of anger the Levantine showed before she gripped her companion's arm and led her away. Something – or someone – had scared the girl. His eyes swept over the crowd. He saw nothing unusual. Walking briskly, Costas left the gallery and descended to the lower floor.

'There – he looks perfect!' Nadine murmured, nodding towards a check-in desk.

Anna looked doubtful. 'The flight is for Luton. We are supposed only to go for a flight to London.'

Nadine controlled her irritation. 'Luton is the same. Like Gatwick or Stansted. They all serve London.'

'Shall we approach now?'

Nadine looked around. There was no sign of Raza. She glanced towards the entrance to Passport Control. It was separated from the hall by a screen. Passengers were moving quickly past the policeman checking boarding passes.

'No. We'll catch him just before he goes through. It'll give him less time to think.'

She continued to watch the young, fair-haired and rather handsome man having his ticket processed.

Bill Hardiman gave a pleasant nod to the counter agent, placed his boarding pass in the breast pocket of his suit, picked up his bulky briefcase, and headed for Passport Control. In the past week he'd travelled another five thousand miles. After the first year, the food, faces, hotels and airports all looked the same. Only the deals seemed harder to make.

It was a young man's game, he'd started telling Fiona. His wife had replied he wasn't yet forty, and he'd been voted company Salesman of the Year twice in the past three years.

His job with Bio-Grow, manufacturers of the world's fastest-selling biological pesticide, gave them a lifestyle their friends envied. It also ensured Dervla and Amy received an expensive private education, and enabled him to add each month to the savings accounts of his daughters. Colleagues joked that if there was an award for the Happily Married Family Man of the Year, Bill would win every time.

That was why he felt irritated as he made his way towards Departures. This trip had been so hectic there had been no time to buy Fiona or the girls any presents. It had become a ritual always to bring something back from those exotic places he visited.

'Excuse me, sir.'

Bill turned.

'Excuse me, sir,' Nadine said again, smiling brilliantly. 'Could I trouble you for a moment?'

'Just a few questions, sir,' added Anna, smiling too.

Bill glanced at the sashes. 'What are you selling?'

Nadine shook her head. 'Not selling, sir. Only market research for a new perfume. If you help us, sir, we will be happy to give you a free sample.'

Bill looked at his watch. He still had a few minutes to spare. He put down his briefcase.

'Okay. What do you want to know?'

Anna glanced at her clipboard. 'Can I please have your flight number and destination.'

Bill fished the boarding pass from his pocket. 'Britannia Airways one-six to Luton.'

'Do you live in London, sir?' asked Anna.

'Yes. In Putney.'

'What a lovely name,' Nadine said. 'Can we have your name and exact address, sir?'

Bill hesitated. The Foreign Office guidelines for businessmen warned about that sort of thing. But there seemed no harm this time. The taller girl was smiling at him, speaking a little more quickly.

'If your answers are judged to be the best by our company, you will be invited to return here for the launch of our perfume, all expenses paid,' Nadine explained.

She never took her eyes off Bill. Raza had said no man would be able to resist, or doubt, that look.

'William Hardiman, 21 River Walk, Putney, London SW15,' said Bill.

Anna made a note.

'Now, Mr Hardiman,' continued Nadine. 'The questions. Should a Greek perfume remind you of our beaches or the mountains?'

Bill had no idea. 'Both, I suppose.'

'Perfect,' smiled Nadine.

Anna wrote on her clipboard.

Nadine looked again at Bill. 'Should a perfume have a fragrance which can be used both day and night?'

Bill remembered Fiona saying she wanted a perfume like that. 'Absolutely.'

228

'Perfect,' Nadine said. 'You really are being a great help for our marketing people.'

Anna made a further note.

'And the name, Grecian Nights. What image does that suggest to you, Mr Hardiman?'

Bill smiled. 'Soft music, good food and wine, the moon over the sea.' This was really quite fun.

Anna wrote again.

'Wonderful,' breathed Nadine. 'What a perfect image, Mr Hardiman.'

Bill nodded, still smiling. 'Glad to be of help.'

Anna looked up. Raza was standing a few feet away, studying a flight information monitor. He abruptly turned away and disappeared into the crowd.

Nadine moved closer to Bill, looking earnestly into his face.

'You have been a great help. Unless I am mistaken, you will be hearing from our company.'

Bill laughed: this was incredible.

'Will I be able to bring my wife?' Fiona would love it.

'Of course.'

'I have two girls.' No harm in pressing his luck.

'No problem,' said Nadine. 'Our company is very generous.'

They were all laughing. Bill glanced at his watch.

'Ah, your perfume sample,' said Nadine. From the bag she produced a bottle containing the Anthrax-B-C.

'You must keep it sealed until you are through British Customs. This is a regulation. I would also like very much for you to allow us to take a photo for our house magazine,' Nadine explained.

Bill hesitated. He'd heard photos could be used for all kinds of illegal purposes.

'I promise not to open the bottle until I get home,' said Bill. 'But I really don't want to have my picture taken.'

Nadine looked crestfallen. 'I'm sorry, Mr Hardiman, but I cannot give you the bottle unless you agree.' She brightened. 'The photo will not be used for any purpose without your written consent.'

She gave him a look of complete sincerity.

'Well,' said Bill, still uncertain. 'I don't know if –'

Nadine came to a decision. 'If we can take your picture, I'll give you two more bottles for your daughters,' she said quickly.

Bill began to nod. A bottle each would solve his gift problem, and they'd all like the idea of having the same perfume. A picture for a house magazine was really quite harmless.

'Okay. Where do you want to take the photo?'

Nadine smiled with relief. 'How about right here?'

He looked around and noticed the policeman checking boarding passes at the opening in the divider screening off Passport Control. A thought struck him.

'How about there?'

'All right,' Nadine said. It didn't matter where the pig had his photo taken. All Raza wanted was a picture of his face.

Bill held out his hand. 'The bottle, young lady.'

Nadine handed over the one in her hand. Bill placed it in his briefcase.

'The other two as well,' Bill said.

Smiling, Nadine produced the two remaining bottles of Anthrax-B-C and handed them over. He put them in his briefcase, too.

'Your wife won't mind you posing with me?' asked Nadine teasingly.

'Not at all,' Bill replied cheerfully, as they walked towards the partition.

Suddenly Nadine froze. The man from the bar in Constitution Square was standing in front of the partition. At the same moment she saw Raza. He was beside a kiosk selling soft drinks, and checking the time on his watch against one of the airport wall clocks. It was their prearranged signal for danger.

'You take many photographs?' Bill was asking Anna.

'Many.'

'But not this time!'

Waving his boarding pass Bill quickly stepped past the policeman, and disappeared from sight through the gap in the partition.

'Hey, mister! Come back!' shouted Anna, moving after him.

The policeman blocked her way, firmly explaining no one could enter without a pass.

'But I must take his picture,' cried Anna.

The policeman shrugged.

Anna was close to tears. 'Please, officer, let me go and take his picture. It is very important!'

The policeman pushed her aside. 'Go – or I will arrest you!'
'Don't be a fool!' Nadine said urgently, pulling Anna away.
'We must leave at once!'

In the safe house bedroom, Morton had taken the phone off the
dressing-table on to the bed with him. He continued to listen to
Hans-Dieter Müller in his office in Wiesbaden.

'Our psychiatrists say the change is genuine,' Müller was saying. 'It's almost as intense as a religious conversion. Even six
months ago she rarely showed emotion. Now she's quite voluble.'

'What do they put it down to?'

'At first they thought it was her way of coping with her inner
distress. From the beginning they'd tagged her a perfectionist,
full of self-reproach that she was dumb enough to get caught,
not that we were smart enough to catch her. So when she began
to open up, our behaviourist saw it as the lid coming off a rather
rigid obsessional personality. In between those first outbursts
she'd continue to be obstinate, irritable and morose. And for a
while she did a lot of what we call *vorbeireden*, talking past the
point.'

'A kind of thought blocking?' Morton asked.

'Exactly. When you listen to her tapes from that time, it's like
listening to recordings with pieces snipped out. You get the feeling of the huge pressure of thought she was under, as if ideas
were pouring through her head.'

'What did your people do about that?'

There was a pause on the line.

'Monitored her biochemical activity,' Müller finally said.
'They put her on one of the oxidise inhibitors for six weeks.'

The Germans had always been keen on the use of complex
drugs to control minds.

'Your people absolutely satisfied that her mood change is nothing to do with their pharmacology?' Morton asked.

'Absolutely. She was off the oxidise for a full two months
before they saw any real change. But when it came, they had no
doubt it was genuine. And it's lasted.'

From the safe room came the steady humming of the fax
machines. Wolfie was feeding more names of dead women into
the computer.

'Has she said much about her sister, Hans-Dieter?'

There was another pause before Müller replied.

'That's the one thing she's still tight about. It could be because when she first came in, the interrogators made a point of telling her that when the time came for her to be released her sister would be long dead.'

'Bit crude.'

In Wiesbaden the security chief cleared his throat. When he spoke his voice was apologetic.

'You know how it is? You use anything in the beginning to try and break down that wall they all have.'

'What does she feel about Raza?'

'She's gone through the whole spectrum from hero worship to resentment. Now she only has contempt, complete and total contempt for him. But she's still very nationalistic. The Arab cause burns bright in her.'

'That's good, Hans-Dieter. That's very good,' Morton said softly. 'Are you going to be there in the morning?'

Müller laughed.

'I'll be at the airport with all the paperwork. There's no precedent for this. So they're back on the German solution. Create a paper snowstorm. The Chancellor has to sign the last flake. He'd like to do it blindfolded.'

'Make sure he knows I appreciate it,' Morton said, hanging up.

He dialled Nan's home number. It was still busy. He rolled off the bed and went into the safe room.

'Still nothing,' Wolfie said, his eyes intent on the VDU. The names of the women who had died within 500 miles of Beirut continued to come and go from the screen.

'Given Danny's pinpoint of that call, the chances are she died in Athens,' Morton said.

'I'm still waiting for Costas,' Wolfie replied.

Morton grunted and walked back into the bedroom. He called Nan's number. She answered on the third ring.

'Hello, Nan.'

'David! What a pleasant surprise. I just got in from the airport.'

Her number had been busy for an hour.

'How was the conference?'

'A real pooper. I never know why I bother,' she sighed. 'Where are you, Tel Aviv? I got your message.'

'No, London.'

He sensed the slightest hesitation.

'It must be the bombings and Trekfontein, right?'

'Yes.'

'Simply awful. I heard the news at the conference.'

'Steve and Dolly were at the Connaught, Nan.'

He heard her intake of breath.

'Oh, David, how terrible. Is there anything I can do?'

'Thanks.' He told her about the funeral.

'Oh, David,' she said again.

He sensed her sudden awkwardness. They were both silent for a few moments, then she said, 'I'm glad you're here, David. I have to talk to you.'

'Are you free for dinner?'

Once more there was a small hesitation.

'Yes. I'd love to.'

How hope could be created by a few words.

'French or Italian?'

The last time, he remembered, they'd eaten Italian.

'French will be fine,' Nan said.

Something was wrong. He tried to keep his own voice casual.

'Is everything okay?'

The hesitation was back. 'We'll talk at dinner.'

'How about La Touche?' He hadn't realised until now how much he'd missed her.

'Fine. It shouldn't be crowded. Eightish okay?'

He thought how English she sounded. 'Eight is perfect.'

'Until then,' she said, and was gone.

A phone was ringing next door. Morton heard Wolfie's voice.

'Hold it, Matti. I'll get him.'

Morton strode into the safe room and took the phone.

'What's up?'

'Rachid Harmoos. The DEA have him listed as a suspected laundryman for the Colombia cartel. And the FBI say their Treasury people have been working for some months trying to establish linkage between Harmoos and several Swiss banks. Two of their banks are where Muzwaz keeps accounts.'

Harmoos had been on Morton's wait and see list for a year. Until now there had been nothing concrete.

'Anything to connect Harmoos with Raza?' Morton asked.

'Nothing's surfaced.'

'Anything to link Harmoos to the cabal?'

'Nothing, except sharing the same Geneva banks. That could be pure coincidence. Like the time we found Arafat was keeping his money in the same bank as the Jewish Defence League.'

'Are the FBI or CIA tapping Harmoos?' pressed Morton.

Matti's voice was a low growl. 'FISC has refused. Not enough to go on.'

Morton cursed in Hebrew. The US Foreign Intelligence Surveillance Court had been set up specifically to approve the wire tapping of any suspicious foreigners with links to the United States. It sat in Washington in the utmost secrecy to consider every case.

'All seven judges voted a no,' continued Matti. 'As usual, no grounds. And of course no appeal. The only chance, says Gates, is if he can go back with more evidence.'

'We can't wait that long,' Morton said. 'Get the Swift people on to it. Get them to blanket Harmoos' house and his associates.'

'I'd have already done that, David. But Gates warned not to. He thinks Appleton could get to hear. Then everything would really hit the fan. Harmoos gave a couple of million dollars last time to help elect the President. He's promised double for next November.'

Morton exhaled softly. 'Okay, this is what you do. I'll get Danny to put together a team to fly in. You make sure word gets to Appleton that the Swift people are otherwise fully engaged.'

'There's still a risk, David,' Matti said doubtfully.

'There's always a risk, Matti,' Morton said.

After hanging up, Morton called Danny in Tel Aviv to tell him about Harmoos.

'I'll have a team on the next plane,' promised Danny.

'Costas surfaced yet?'

'Damn him, no. I've sat-messaged him to call in. I'll kick ass when he does.'

'Do that. Then put him on to me. I want to know what the hell he's playing at.'

*

Costas kept two cars behind the Mercedes as it turned right at the second intersection beyond the Acropolis. The two girls were in the back.

Trailing them out of the departure hall, he'd seen the smaller girl was close to tears – and the Levantine had several times told her to be quiet. They were both scared of something – or someone. It couldn't be over not getting that photo of a traveller who'd had a little more savvy than most. And why did they need photos anyway? And why had they been so selective? They'd not bothered with the Dutch drunks – or the others he'd seen them approach in Constitution Square. Only that American girl and then the businessman. They had clearly been working to some carefully arranged plan. Whatever was behind it, it certainly didn't fit any normal promotion. And they'd looked positively stricken as they waited at the kerbside. When the Mercedes swept up, they'd jumped into the back like scared kittens. But he'd still had time to glimpse the driver. He was a middle-aged man and well-dressed with a mouthful of gold. And an Arab.

That had been enough to persuade Costas to become serious in his pursuit. He hadn't felt like this since he'd picked up the trail of the Tunisian who'd been bringing in Semtex moulded into his doctor's bag.

When Costas had gone with the police to raid the doctor's apartment, they'd found enough explosive to leave all Athens looking like the Acropolis.

The car telephone rang. Leaving the airport he'd asked his police contact to check the Mercedes' registration.

'Costas,' his contact said. 'You ready for this?'

'Try me.'

'The car's registered to your favourite Iranian, Ali Akbar Muzwaz. He's got a number of cars in his name. He must have a hell of a garage. They're all listed at the same address.'

It was near the foreign legation quarter, towards which the Mercedes was heading.

'Thanks, Taki.'

'One other thing, Costas, I hear your cousin's looking for you.'

Taki had always called the CIA station chief his cousin – he couldn't remember now how it had started. The call could be anything. He'd call the station chief later.

'How's the list of dead going?'

'Two-fifty so far.'

'I'll pick them up later.'

When he'd replaced the phone, Costas fished out the MRT and switched it on. There was a crackle then a voice boomed in Hebrew from the box's speaker.

'This is Gabriel. Call Ha-Zoafim. This is Gabriel. Call Ha-Zoafim. This is –'

Costas switched off Danny's recorded order for him to call Tel Aviv. Ha-Zoafim was this week's code for Mossad; Gabriel, Danny's current one.

Now that he was almost certain where it was heading, Costas dropped further back behind the Mercedes. He decided he'd call Danny later from his safe room. Then he could tell him more about what a couple of very unusual promotions girls were doing in a car registered to one of Israel's greatest enemies.

After questioning Nadine, Raza had continued to drive in silence. She had explained what had happened, leaving nothing out.

Twice he'd glimpsed the man's car. Could he be someone from the Greek Security Service? But why would an Intelligence officer be watching the girls? Or had he been following the American? Had those whores of a camel in the back seat picked a mule already under suspicion? Drug running, maybe? Could this have anything to do with the death of that other camel's whore? Raza shook his head quickly. Supposing this was the unthinkable – Mossad? Who knew what they had on file? Maybe a photo of Nadine? He should have disguised her. He shook his head again. He was almost certain the Zionists had not picked up the trail. But he'd make doubly sure.

Raza looked in the mirror. The car was gone. He swung right, then right again, until he had completed a square and was back on the street he had been travelling on. There was no sign of the man's car ahead of him.

Raza drove another half-mile, then repeated the movement. He did so several more times before he arrived in the avenue where the apartment was. The wide tree-lined boulevard was deserted. He drove its length and then back again. There was still no sign of the man or his car.

He swung the Mercedes into the kerb, and broke the long tense silence.

'I'll go and park. Have tea ready.'

Costas had left his car a couple of streets away and taken up position in the lobby of an apartment block across from the Mercedes. He'd gained admission by using the MRT to perform the one function with which he trusted it – reading the electronic security locks on doors.

He watched the Mercedes pull away and the girls enter the apartment block across the street. When the lobby door had closed behind them, Costas waited a few minutes. The Mercedes driver did not return.

Costas left the lobby and quickly crossed the street. The apartment block door would only open by pressing the correct combination of numbers on the small keyboard set in the frame. He placed the MRT against the board and pressed the transmit button. There was a series of clicks as the device read the entry code the girls had used. He pushed open the door and stepped quickly inside, closing it behind him.

The lobby was long and cavernous. Apartment doors were on either side, and at the far end was an elevator.

Costas walked down the central carpet strip. He pressed the elevator button. The panel slid open at once. The girls hadn't gone to one of the upper floors. He stopped to listen outside the doors. There was no sound from behind the first two. From behind the third door came voices.

He fished in a pocket and produced an earpiece with a small metallic button at the end of its flex. He fitted the piece in his ear and carefully placed the button against the door. Through the earpiece came the voice of the Levantine. She was discussing the photos.

Then Costas felt something hard pressing into the small of his back.

'Just knock on the door,' said Raza softly, pushing the barrel of his gun more firmly against him.

20

Morton entered the La Touche through a black lacquered door, which was opened by a maitre d' whose hair seemed to have been similarly treated.

The restaurant was all fake beams and imitation tapestries and whitewashed walls. A silent couple sat over their plates at a corner table. A group, Swedish by their accents, occupied a mock refectory table in the centre of the room. Morton had left the restaurant's number with Wolfie.

When he was seated he ordered a bottle of Dom Perignon. Nan drank nothing else.

She arrived with the champagne. Her hair had a fringe, her dress was of patterned silk, and she walked with that confidence of someone used to being admired.

He was halfway to his feet before she waved him down.

'Just pour me a drink,' she said, smiling.

Morton filled Nan's flute while the maitre d' settled her in her seat, spreading her napkin and proffering menus.

'We'll order later,' Morton said, handing her the glass.

The head waiter bowed and withdrew.

'It's wonderful to see you,' Morton said. It had been four months to the day.

'I wish it could have been a happier occasion, David,' Nan replied. She reached across the table and touched his hand. 'I'm so sorry, so very sorry about Steve and Dolly.'

He squeezed her hand. 'It's just good having you here.'

She smiled quickly and withdrew her hand. There was that awkward silence, like there had been on the telephone.

'So how's it been?' he asked, his eyes on her.

'Okay. And you?'

Again, that slight hesitation he'd detected on the phone.

'This business has everyone stretched to the limit.'

She put down her glass.

'Do you know who did it?' she asked softly.

'Raza.'

This time she did not hesitate. 'Oh God. Not again.'

A burst of laughter came from the Swedes. Morton waited until it subsided then, leaning forward and keeping his voice low, he told Nan about Raza's threat to unleash the remainder of the Anthrax-B-C unless all his demands were met.

Morton saw the shock and horror deepen on her face. He realised again how much he'd missed sharing what little he could with her. It was still more than he'd shared with anybody else on the outside.

'I've got five days to nail him, Nan. Maybe less,' he added.

'No one will have enough PEG-enzyme in place by then,' Nan said. 'We carry enough to treat up to fifty. If Raza does what he says, we'd need a hundred times that much.'

'For sure. We've started a crash production programme. Every government with the capability has been told to do the same.'

'It's not just a question of drug availability, David, but expertise,' Nan continued. 'I guess there's probably less than a dozen people in this country competent to recognise the symptoms in time.'

The maitre d' was back, listing the house specialities. Nan ordered the smoked salmon paupiettes stuffed with shrimps and caviar, and the red mullet baked en papillote. Morton settled for duck pâté, followed by veal fried in butter with shallots.

He remembered they'd ordered exactly the same meal the first night he'd taken her to dinner.

'You will stay with the champagne, sir?' murmured the maitre d'.

'Yes.'

Morton watched the head waiter make his way to the kitchen, then turned back to Nan.

'There must be a special school that teaches them to walk like that.'

She continued to toy with her glass.

'I've really missed you, Nan.'

She gave the smallest shakes of her head. 'You think you have. But you've probably been too busy.'

There it was again, the merest of hesitations as if she had been on the brink of saying something else.

'How about you? Have you missed me?'

Nan nodded. 'Of course. I've missed seeing you . . . even if we only mostly talk shop.' She smiled quickly to soften the words. 'I mean, here we are now . . . doing it. I don't really mind. But I'm not sure . . .'

'Complaint noted,' Morton said. 'Then let me ask you this. Have you thought about what I suggested?'

She nodded slowly, no longer smiling. He tried to keep his voice light.

'You really know how to keep me guessing.' Three months ago he'd suggested she came to live with him in Tel Aviv.

'I can't help the way I am, David.'

She put her glass down and looked at him. When she spoke there was a resolve that had not been there before.

'I'm sorry, David. Really, really sorry. But it wouldn't work.'

He stared at her for a long moment.

'If we both wanted to –' he finally began again.

'David, I don't love you enough to give everything up and move to Tel Aviv.'

He put down his glass. He'd read somewhere that questioning a lover always reverses the usual roles: it forces confessions we don't like to hear.

'Is there someone else?'

This time her hesitation lasted several seconds before she answered, 'Yes.'

'I see . . . Is it serious?'

She reached across the table and quickly touched his hand.

'I'm sorry. I don't want to hurt you, David.'

'There's no way you won't do that. You know I love you.'

'We can still stay friends. I'd like that, David.'

The maitre d'. arrived with the waiter bearing the first course and poured more champagne. Morton watched the bubbles rush to the surface and then burst. He waited until the waiters had withdrawn.

'How long have you known him?'

'Three months.'

'Not very long.'

Nan cut into a salmon paupiette.

'Long enough to know it couldn't work between us, David. He's there when I need him. Not just on the end of a telephone.'

She speared the paupiette with her fork.

'I thought that's what you wanted. No strings, no pressure.'

'I thought so, too. It turned out I was wrong. I guess it was the absence of pressure which did it.'

'I've never pressurised you, Nan.'

She looked directly at him, her fork poised.

'But there were pressures, David. Not knowing when I would see you next. Not being able to make plans. And then this pressure for me to move to Tel Aviv. There I'd be doing the same thing, wondering where you were. I want something more substantial, David.' She smiled quickly. 'Perhaps not as exciting. But through you I've had my fill of living dangerously.'

Nan ate the paupiette slice.

'Do you want to marry him, Nan?'

She began to cut another piece. 'He's asked. But I don't think so. I'm like you, not the marrying kind.'

Nan ate the morsel.

'I wanted to marry you, Nan. I still do.'

She shook her head as she wiped her mouth with a corner of her napkin.

'David. You're married to your work. You're a loner, and you always will be. It must make you very good at what you do.'

His smile had gone, his face completely serious.

'I can't change the rules, Nan. But I've tried to make you part of my life more than I ever did with Shola.'

'I know that. And I'm not asking you to change the rules. I'm just asking you to understand, and accept, why they didn't work for me.'

Morton spread some of the pâté on the toast.

'I don't want to let you go, Nan.'

She pushed aside her plate and leaned across the table.

'It won't make any difference to our professional relationship. I still want to help. You can always call me. And when you come through, we can always meet. I'll always find time, David. Promise. We can still go on being friends.'

He drank; the champagne suddenly tasted flat.

'It wouldn't be easy, the way I feel. I never thought I'd feel about anyone like I do about you, Nan.' Morton put down his glass and looked at her. 'I'm glad you will go on helping. But it would be easier for both of us if we made a clean break.'

Nan reached for his hand, running her fingers lightly across the backs of his fingers.

'Is that what you really want?' she asked softly.

He remembered past pleasures, the warmth of her skin against his, the taste of her lips.

'Yes.'

She removed her hand, all the while looking at him, staring into his eyes. There was only acceptance in her expression.

'I'd like some more champagne,' she said finally.

He refilled her glass, before the maitre d' could reach the table. Morton waved him away.

'Here's to memories,' Nan said, raising her glass.

'To what might have been.' Morton did not raise his glass.

The maitre d' was back, murmuring in his ear. 'A call, sir.'

Morton rose to his feet, and asked Nan to excuse him. The silent couple from the corner table were leaving. The Swedes were clinking glasses as he picked up the phone on a table beside the door to the cloakroom.

'Sorry to bust in,' Wolfie began, 'but Danny's people have just monitored a broadcast out of Athens. One of those radical station's been playing the tape demanding the French free Raza's *Feydeheen*. Danny says the words are exactly the same as on the one Michelle picked up. But a different woman's voice. She's got no lisp and younger sounding.'

'Has Danny got Costas on to this?'

'Not yet. Danny says he's way over reporting-in time. Covert Action won't have our people on the ground for another hour. Meantime Danny's got Gates' boys hustling around.'

Morton came to a decision. 'There's something wrong. I'm on my way back. And alert the Dove.'

The Concorde could get him to Athens in under two hours.

He went back to the table and stood beside Nan.

'I'm sorry –'

'I know,' she said. 'You've got to go.'

'I can drop you off –' he began again.

242

'I think I'll stay,' she said. 'No point in both of us disappointing the chef.'

She lifted her face towards him. He bent and she kissed him quickly on the cheek.

'Take care, David.'

'You too.'

Morton settled the bill and walked out of the restaurant, steeling himself not to look back at where Nan sat sipping her champagne. It really was over.

Costas sat in an armchair in the living-room, struggling to regain focus.

The Levantine was standing a few feet away, training a pistol on him. Her face was calm and determined. She would kill him without compunction. The other girl was watching him with a look of hatred and fear.

As soon as she'd opened the apartment door, the man had rabbit punched him. In the time he'd been unconscious he had been stripped to his underpants and roped to the armchair.

The man was standing with his back to Costas. Suddenly the room was filled with Danny's sat-message to phone Tel Aviv.

Raza turned, holding in one hand the MRT, Costas' gun in the other. He knew enough Hebrew to recognise the words were Yiddish. His suspicions deepened. The pig was either a Zionist, or associated with them. A danger.

Raza held up the MRT. 'What's this?'

Costas forced himself to stay calm. Morton had always said if caught to stick to a simple story – and one as close to the truth as possible.

'My pager,' Costas said. 'I'm a private detective, specialising in divorce. That's why I carry a gun. Adultery can be a violent business.'

He looked at Raza. There was no response, not a flicker of doubt, no acknowledgement there might be some truth in what he'd said. Danny's voice once more filled the room. Raza switched off the MRT. When he spoke his voice was impersonal and cold.

'Who is Gabriel?'

'It's a Zionist name!' Anna shouted.

Nadine raised the gun so that it pointed at the man's head. Out of the corner of her eye she saw Raza's face begin to darken.

'Who do you work for, Jew?'

Through his pain Costas could hear the man's growing anger. Anger and nervousness, a dangerous mixture. The man was not wholly in control.

'I work for myself. And I am not a Jew. If you will release me, I will call my office and you can speak to my secretary. She will confirm what I have told you.'

If he could get to a telephone he could call the Israeli Embassy unlisted number. Once the duty security officer heard him asking to be put through to his secretary, the man would try to trace the call. 'Secretary' was the current Mossad codeword for an emergency.

Raza spoke in a low, hard voice. 'You think I am stupid? Long ago I learned never to trust a Jew. A Jew's word is worth nothing. Less than nothing! Now – who do you work for?'

Without turning her head, Nadine spoke. 'Ha-Zoafim is what the Zionists call the great rock overlooking the Prophet's Mosque in Jerusalem.'

Costas struggled to stop his fear from showing.

'It's the name of the birthplace of the man my client's wife is having an affair with. He lives in this building. I was only trying to find him –'

'Don't lie to me, Jew! You work for the Zionist terrorists!'

Raza's voice had risen as the madness began to take control. Costas stared into his face. He had seen that look before. It was that of someone with a need to kill.

'I have nothing to do with Zionist terrorists,' Costas said.

'Why were you following these women?' Raza shouted.

Costas shook his head. Even the slightest movement produced excruciating pain.

'I wasn't.'

'You followed them from the square to the airport. Why?' Raza shouted again.

Costas felt his hope melting like frost in the sun. 'You are mistaken. I was not following them. I was looking for the man my client's wife is sleeping with. They sometimes meet in the square or at the airport.'

'He lies!' Nadine said suddenly. 'He was following us.'

Costas looked into her face. The terror of the past few minutes had been a mere precursor for the real fear he now felt. She wanted him to die.

'He's a Zionist,' Anna said. 'Only a Zionist would be so frightened.'

'I'm a Greek!' protested Costas. 'And, yes, I'm frightened. Anyone would be.' His voice rose. 'Please, sir. Let me call my office –' Costas began.

'Do you think I am stupid, Jew?' Raza shouted. 'You think you can treat me with the contempt you show for my people? You think you can come here and spy on me?'

'Please, sir –'

'Shut up, Jew!'

Raza turned away. He was certain now. Even that camel's whore could see this was a frightened Zionist.

When Raza spoke next it was in a voice from which all emotion had been drained. 'Why did Morton send you?'

Costas felt a great wave of nausea rise from his stomach to his throat.

'I have never heard of such a man. Who is he?'

Raza stepped closer so that he was standing almost alongside Anna. 'Do you know who I am?'

Costas shook his head. 'No, sir. I have never seen you before –'

Raza stared at Costas out of flinty, emotionless eyes. There was suddenly total silence in the room. 'I am Raza.'

The silence was broken only by the sound of Raza releasing the safety catch on the gun. He began to nod. The pig had recognised his name.

Nadine saw the madness blazing in Raza's eyes. Nothing would stop him now. Anna was staring fixedly at Costas, her mouth working to control her trembling. She saw Raza's gun come up.

'Anna,' Raza said softly. 'You are like this pig. You are very stupid.'

Raza fired twice, both bullets entering Anna's head through her left ear and exiting above her right. For a moment she remained upright, a spume of brain and blood arcing towards the ceiling. Then, already dead, yet her eyes still fluttering like a china doll, she sagged to the floor. She jerked once, the little

245

spasm causing her hand to touch the sash, her fingers moved over the gold lettering. The tremor passed and she was still.

Raza glared at Nadine. 'She died quicker than she deserved.'

The madness was still there, burning and glowing in his eyes. He addressed Costas once more. 'Why did Morton send you?'

Costas said nothing. He could feel urine running down his thighs.

'It does not matter,' Raza said. 'You will avenge Al-Najaf.'

He raised the pistol and shot Costas three times in the chest in quick succession. Costas slumped against his bonds.

Raza turned and looked at Nadine. She lowered her gun. As suddenly as it had appeared his look of madness had gone. When he next spoke, Raza's voice was normal. She found that both terrifying and yet exhilarating. A man who could change so quickly was a man in complete control.

'Come, we have work to do,' he said.

Together they went to the kitchen. Anna's camera and the Polaroid prints, along with Nadine's pouch were on a worktop. The bag still contained a few bottles of perfume.

'Throw them away,' Raza ordered.

She emptied the contents down the sink and dumped the bottles in a trash can. Raza spread out on the worktop the photographs showing Nadine with Nancy.

'Here, you choose one!' Raza said cheerfully. His mood change was total.

Nadine selected a print. Raza gathered up the others and tore them into small pieces. He told Nadine to flush them down the sink. While she did so, he opened a cupboard and pulled out a fax machine. He plugged it into one of the power points in the wall.

With adhesive he took from a drawer, he fixed the snapshot to a sheet of photographic paper from a box on the counter. He then dialled a series of numbers on the machine's handset, at the same time feeding in the paper. The connection made, the machine gave a short high-pitched noise and the paper began to pass through.

Moments later the facsimile was emerging in the mansion of Rachid Harmoos in Connecticut.

When he received the acknowledgement that the fax was well

246

received, Raza used the handset to make another international call.

'*Oui*,' Faruk Kadumi answered in London.

Raza gave him the number of Bill Hardiman's flight to Luton and added an order.

'You will use the alternative arrangement,' he said.

Raza made a final call, a local one, arranging for the cabal's local representative to dispose of both bodies.

'Leave him where he can be found. It will serve as a warning. Leave her where she will never be found,' he instructed.

'It will be done to perfection,' promised the voice.

Two hours later Raza and Nadine flew out of Athens.

Dawn was beginning to creep through the windows as Morton walked around the apartment.

The Concorde had made the flight from Northolt in a hundred minutes. He had spent most of them monitoring the hunt for Raza and the killers of Costas. His body had been discovered outside the El Al office in downtown Athens an hour before the plane landed.

By the time Morton had reached the apartment, the Athens police scene-of-crime technicians had made progress. Working with a set of Raza's prints Danny had faxed from Tel Aviv, the fingerprint men had matched them with those of Raza's found in the apartment.

Other technicians had established that two people had died in its main reception room. Blood analysis confirmed one had been Costas. The other, from hair samples, pointed to the other victim being a woman.

From time to time Morton paused to watch the technicians. They were good, taking their time, missing nothing.

A couple of uniformed men were taking down the portrait of Ayatollah Muzwaz. The entire contents of the apartment were being systematically removed in the search for evidence.

Morton stopped at a window. A few hours ago Raza could have stood here. It was almost as if he could still smell his presence. Behind him a voice growled.

'I've closed down the whole country. He couldn't even get out through a sewer,' Zak Constantine promised.

Morton turned and looked at the head of Greek Internal Security.

'He's gone by now, Zak. As fast as you still get off the base line.'

Constantine nodded in acknowledgement that at fifty he still played killer tennis.

'You checked the passenger flight manifests?' Morton asked.

'Of course. Not one showed up as even having a parking violation.'

Morton nodded, accepting the limitations of technology.

Constantine growled, 'That night watchman was slow.'

The Israeli duty guard on the El Al office had failed to get the car's make or registration.

'From tomorrow he'll have plenty of time to practise, for sure – spotting camels in the Sinai,' Morton promised.

They stepped to one side as two uniformed patrolmen carried away an armchair. Dark patches of blood covered the fabric.

'First they shoot Costas with his own gun. Then chop off his balls. Nice people,' Constantine remarked.

The police pathologist had confirmed the bullets had come from Costas' handgun, and that he had been dead before his testicles had been removed and shoved in his mouth.

'They learn fast, Zak. The KGB did that to their people when they kidnapped a couple of Russian diplomats in Beirut. The Russians just grabbed two of the local Hizbollah leaders and deballed them. When word got around, the diplomats were back next day.'

Constantine grinned. 'Think we should go and deball a few of those faggots in that radio station?'

'They're telling the truth, Zak. That tape was just dropped off.'

After he'd formally identified Costas, Morton had visited the radio station with Constantine. The staff said the tape had been found in the programme request box in the lobby. No one had seen who had put it there. Morton had obtained a copy. It had been transmitted to Tel Aviv from the Concorde's communications centre.

He'd spent an hour questioning Costas' police contact. The man had still been on duty when Costas' body was brought in. The Greek had been smart enough to make two and two add up to no more than four. Following his tip where Costas had been heading, Constantine had sent enough men to the apartment to win a small war.

'I've put out a general pick-up for everyone with the remotest connection with this place,' Constantine growled. 'But it probably won't get us very far.'

'It's worth a try, Zak. But the chances are that Muzwaz will have covered his tracks. He's good at that.'

A technician emerged from the kitchen carrying a refuse sack. 'Thought you ought to see this, sir.'

The technician turned the sack out on the floor. Half a dozen bottles lay on the carpet. Morton bent and inspected them. He picked one up, sniffing the open top. There was a sweet, cheap smell. He rose, holding the bottle in his hand.

'Can we find out if this is a regular brand, Zak?'

Constantine squinted at the label. 'Grecian Nights? Never heard of it. But we'll soon see. Since we joined the EC, all brand names on luxury items have to be registered.' He beckoned to an aide and told him to check the bottle.

Morton picked another perfume bottle off the carpet. He told Constantine about the intercept that Danny had traced to Athens.

'I'd like you to get your forensic people to test for content, and see if they can match the glass with those fragments they found in the tanker explosion.'

The security chief looked pensive. 'You think the woman was carrying the anthrax in bottles like this when she was fried?'

'Let's see what your people come up with, Zak.'

'I'll go over there myself,' Constantine said. 'I'll take the bottles with me.'

'Leave me one, Zak.'

Morton walked into the kitchen with the bottle.

A technician was dusting the fax machine for prints. Another was inspecting the instamatic camera. He paused and looked at Morton.

He held up the bottle. 'I want to get this label off.'

The man shrugged and went back to his work.

The same smell was coming from the sink as he'd sniffed from the bottles. Why had someone poured away their contents? Raza wouldn't need to run another field test after Trekfontein. And he wouldn't waste his precious anthrax poisoning the sewers of Athens. For sure.

There was something stuck to the side in the waste pipe below the plughole. Morton asked one of the technicians to fish it out. The man used a pair of long-handled tweezers to ease up the paper. It was part of a photograph of someone's face.

Morton opened the cupboard beneath the sink. There was the usual deep trap in the waste pipe with an inspection seal, which could be opened to deal with a blockage. The technician placed a bucket under the seal, which he removed with a wrench. Pieces of torn photographs, which had remained in the bottom of the trap, fell into the bucket.

The technician looked at Morton and smiled. Smiling back, Morton took the bucket and, while the technician reassembled the waste pipe, spread the pieces on the worktop. He began to fit them together.

By the time Constantine returned, Morton had assembled several snapshots of two young women. One was holding a perfume bottle. Morton saw it was identical to the bottle he'd placed on the worktop beside his photo collage.

'The glass matches that found on the pedlar's remains,' Constantine said, coming into the kitchen. 'Forensic has so far identified the contents of each bottle as a perfume, an aftershave, eau-de-Cologne and what they think is mint tea.'

Constantine shook his head. 'Why mint tea unless you were running a scam? The one good news is that Forensic didn't find a trace of anything suspicious.'

'They could have used the tea to make things stretch. Maybe they had a lot of bottles to fill,' Morton suggested.

Constantine glanced at the assembled prints. 'What you got there?'

Morton explained where he'd found the prints. Constantine studied them more carefully.

'The one on the left looks Lebanese. The other could be a tourist, David.'

'And neither looks like a hawker, Zak.'

'Maybe they're tied in with Raza and the pedlar in some other way?' Constantine suggested. 'Then after she died, Raza tried to remove any evidence. That could be why he dumped the stuff from the bottles.'

Morton began to nod. 'I don't know if one of these is the woman who died in the explosion. But given our intercept and your people's match of the glass, I think there's a strong probability that your tanker woman was carrying a quantity of Anthrax-B-C, which was incinerated with her. There's no way we'll ever know how much was destroyed. But Raza must have some left. What he could have done is removed this concoction from the bottles and filled them with anthrax. But if he lost some of it in the tanker fire he may not have had enough to fill them all. So he dumped the spare bottles.'

Constantine shook his head. 'But surely he'd need lab conditions in which to make the exchange? There's no sign of anything like that here.'

'He could have done it elsewhere. This place was probably a distribution centre,' Morton said.

The aide who had gone to check the perfume manufacturers came into the kitchen to report there was no listing for Grecian Nights. Constantine ordered him to have police search every laboratory in the country for evidence.

'I'd like to use a phone, Zak,' Morton said.

'Use this one,' said the technician who had finished fingerprinting the fax machine.

Morton called Danny in Tel Aviv.

'Listen, Danny. I think we've located a potential vector. Bottles of perfume labelled Grecian Nights. Get Wolfie to alert the ACC to have his rummagers stop any bottles with that label. Warn them not to open a bottle. Have Matti and Lacouste alert their Customs people. I'll fax you a sample label. Also a photo. Tell everyone it's priority to get an ID on the women. Once you've got the Brits, Americans and French moving on the bottle, put out a global Double Flash so that everyone's on the lookout for one like it.'

'Will do,' Danny acknowledged. 'Is Costas there with you? If so, put him on. It's kick ass time for him.'

'Too late, Danny,' Morton said quietly. He then explained what had happened to Costas.

After they'd hung up, Morton held the perfume bottle under a sink tap to free the label. He patted the paper dry with a cloth and stuck it to a sheet of photographic paper one of the technicians had found in a box in a cupboard. Then he stuck one

251

of the photos he had assembled on another sheet and faxed both to Danny.

Then he dialled the direct line number of the telephone on the flight deck of the Concorde and ordered the pilot to file an immediate flight plan to Frankfurt.

21

The Double Flash, the photocopy of the Grecian Nights label and the reassembled photo reached the Foley Street safe house nine minutes after Morton's call to Danny. It was 4.12 a.m. in London. There were now less than four full days left before Raza's deadline expired.

Michelle was on watch in the safe room; Wolfie had gone off duty at midnight.

Since then fax traffic had been light. General Yertzin had sent a message that his Spetsnaz were deep in the Afghan mountains, and had checked a dozen Mujaheddin encampments without a sign of Raza, his men or the woman. The weather was slowing down the Russians' progress.

Shortly afterwards, Admiral Burness' office faxed to say the ground satellite link with the Spetsnaz had been interrupted by a severe blizzard. The NSA weather satellite positioned over Afghanistan predicted the whiteout could last twenty-four hours.

Finel had reported his mutes were halfway through the search for Japanese and Asian associates of Raza. So far none had been discovered.

Humpty Dumpty had sent another hand-written note saying his specialists had narrowed down the time the tapes had been made to between ten and fourteen days ago.

Michelle had placed the reports in Morton's file – along with others from Interpol, the CIA, FBI and a score of other police agencies. In the end they came down to much hard work producing very little.

The Double Flash triggered an alarm bell on the fax machine

loud enough to wake Wolfie in the bedroom across from the safe room. He arrived in time to read the message as it came off the machine. Wolfie began to swear softly when he saw the news about Costas.

'Let's get this out fast,' Michelle said in an unusually loud voice. It was her only reaction to Costas' death.

Wolfie removed Morton and Danny's names as the source of the Double Flash, replacing them with the standard prefix for all messages sent outside the agency: 'From Uppermost. Tel Aviv.' He then typed the message into the computer and keyed it, the label photocopy and the photograph to the ACC's personal fax machine.

The machine was beside the camp bed the ACC had installed for the duration of the crisis in his office on the seventh floor of New Scotland Yard. The message awoke him shortly after he'd fallen asleep at the end of a twenty-hour day.

The ACC struggled to his feet and switched on the desk lamp. He read the text and studied the label and began to frown. The faxed photo was of poor quality; it would be a small miracle if it produced a lead. And thirty years of police work told him that spotting the bottles would now largely be a matter of luck. Despite Morton's insistence on a body search and a full baggage check for one in two of all travellers arriving in Britain, a bottle could still easily escape detection.

At every entry point Customs officers were already stretched to the limit. Many were working double shifts; a number had collapsed on duty. On top, they continued to face angry scenes with travellers delayed by the security restrictions.

The ACC read the message once more. There was nothing to say the bottles would be hand carried. They could just as easily be hidden in freight. On an average day twenty-seven million separate items of merchandise arrived in Britain by air and sea. To check each one properly would effectively throttle the nation's commercial life. It would require a Cabinet-level decision, to authorise such a dramatic and unprecedented step – even if there were the trained rummagers available to conduct such a hunt. And already a number of Ministers were protesting about the latest security clamp-down.

There'd been questions about what should be done with the bottles already confiscated. Even with every available scientist and laboratory mobilised, it could still take weeks to check them. There was talk of simply incinerating all the bottles. But no decision would be taken until the Department of the Environment was satisfied about the level of pollution risk. A report was due in four days' time – the day Raza's deadline expired.

The ACC scanned the message again. He respected Morton's instincts. But this warning could be the work of anyone in Mossad. There were people there who sometimes overstepped the limits of conjecture. Nor was there anything in the message that conclusively said the bottles actually contained Anthrax-B-C. Nor any hard evidence that they were even on their way to the United Kingdom.

The ACC came to a decision. He called in a duty secretary and dictated a summary of the fax, under the heading: 'Advisory'. After she had typed it, he attached the copy of the label and instructed her to take both to the senior duty officer in the Yard's Operation Centre.

The Chief Superintendent scanned them and passed them to his assistant.

'This'll lose us more friends,' the Inspector predicted. 'As it is, Customs are kicking up hell because we haven't enough men to put alongside them to keep Joe Public in order.'

'Anyone else but the ACC and I'd dump it,' said the senior officer. 'But treat it strictly as no more than an advisory.'

The Inspector passed the paper to a sergeant who ran off copies on paper with the bold red printed heading: 'Scotland Yard: Advisory Only'.

The copies were simultaneously faxed to the Home Office; the Secret Intelligence Service HQ at Century House across the river from Westminster; MI5 HQ in Marylebone; the fourteen Regional Crime Squad headquarters; Customs at Heathrow, Gatwick and London's new City airport in the heart of Docklands.

The other airports that served the capital, Luton and Stansted, would receive the advisory through their own county police forces: Bedfordshire in the case of Luton, and the Essex Constabulary for Stansted.

The advisory arrived in the Luton airport administration block and was taken to the night duty manager. This was the third night he had spent coping with complaints from furious travellers over the stringent Customs checks.

All the manager knew was that the seizures were connected with the recent terrorist outrages. But increasingly it sounded like another security overkill – especially when no one would answer his repeated question of what was he supposed to do with all those bottles? The airport Customs confiscation room was close to overflowing.

The manager glanced at the advisory. In his world, the word was way down the totem of priorities. Right now his immediate concern was the arrival of the last flight before he went off duty – Britannia 16 from Athens.

It was four hours late, having put down in Frankfurt with an engine malfunction. In a few minutes there would be over 200 very tired and, the manager had no doubt, some very irritated passengers, arriving in Customs. A specific search for these bottles would further delay them – and undoubtedly lead to more complaints. He dropped the advisory in the day manager's tray. He could decide what to do when he came on duty.

In the airport's arrivals hall, Customs officers braced themselves to face the passengers from Flight 16. There was a growing feeling among several of the stressed officers that rather than endure more hostility, they would exercise their own discretion over confiscations. They, too, felt the blanket impounding of bottles was an over-reaction.

Below in the cavernous confiscation room the graveyard shift was manned by Asians or Arabs, the only ones willing to toil through the night for modest remuneration.

One was Saleem Arish. In the year he had worked here, he had quickly discovered that his pay could be supplemented by theft. He had become expert at stealing only items that could be concealed on his body. He'd found a ready market for them in London's thriving ethnic underworld.

Six months ago one of his contacts had introduced him to a man he still only knew as Effendi.

He had questioned Arish closely about the items easiest to steal, and then promised him 100 pounds a week to telephone every day before going to work in case Effendi wanted something stolen.

For months Arish had received his retainer for doing nothing.

Then a week ago Effendi had asked him to steal a bottle of French perfume, and deliver it to a contact man in the parking lot of a service station on the M1 motorway near Luton.

For this he would receive an additional 100 pounds. He had repeated the operation twice more, and was paid the same amount by the contact man.

His fellow Arab had a misshapen body and a bloated face with a twisted lump of a nose. Yet the few words he had spoken had been in a soft, cultured voice.

Arish was neither curious about the man, nor cared why Effendi should spend such exorbitant sums for perfumes that he could easily have purchased from any store – and no doubt was paying the contact handsomely to collect in this way.

Last night when he had called, Effendi had said he would pay 200 pounds for each of three specific bottles of perfume he expected to be among those confiscated from Britannia Flight 16.

Effendi had carefully described their distinctive shape and had made Arish repeat several times the name on the labels: Grecian Nights.

When he had come on duty, Arish had volunteered for the job of off-loading the baskets as they came down the chute. It was back-breaking work no one really wanted.

Arriving in the Customs hall, Bill Hardiman's irritation over the late arrival of his flight turned to concern when he was diverted into one of several cubicles. Fiona would already be worried where he was; she had never become used to the vagaries of air travel. The sooner he could get this latest delay over, the better. An elderly Customs officer stood beside a stack of wire baskets in front of a moving conveyor belt. Bill smiled at him.

'First time I've been stopped.'

'Nothing personal, sir. We're checking one in two.'

The officer asked Bill to place and open his luggage on a table. Bill did so. The officer expertly worked his hands through the layers of neatly folded clothes.

'Pack them yourself?'

'Yes.'

'You must be married, sir. Only a wife could have taught you that!'

'Bit unusual, all this, isn't it?' Bill asked.

The officer glanced up at him.

'We live in unusual times, sir. The poor bastards in South Africa and those hotels prove that.'

Bill looked puzzled.

'I'm sorry, I don't know what you're talking about. I haven't seen a newspaper in the last three days.'

The officer briefly told him about Trekfontein and the hotel explosions.

'My God, now I understand! Search away!'

The officer smiled; it was a change to get an understanding passenger.

'Let me just have a dekko in your briefcase then you can be on your way.'

Bill opened the briefcase. The officer removed the three bottles of Grecian Nights and looked at Bill.

'I'll have to keep these, sir. For a start you're way over your allowance – and secondly we're supposed to confiscate all bottles. It's connected with what's happened.'

In his years of globe-trotting Bill had learned the only way to handle a Customs officer was to remain polite and tell the truth. He explained exactly how he'd acquired the bottles.

'Let me just keep one,' Bill urged. 'Otherwise my wife will never believe she's going to get invited to this perfume launch.'

The officer picked up one of the bottles. The seal hadn't been tampered with.

'You certain this hasn't been out of your sight, sir?'

Bill nodded. 'Absolutely, officer. Just let me keep one for my wife.'

The officer shrugged. This idea of confiscating bottles was probably the brainchild of someone in Whitehall. And what was the point of it all? Now there was this rumour that all the bottles were going to be incinerated – without even being opened. That would be typical of Whitehall.

The officer came to a decision.

'Okay – just one!'

He handed the bottle to Bill and placed the other two in a basket. While Bill closed his case, the officer wrote in a docket book that two bottles of Grecian Nights had been taken off Britannia Flight 16. He tore out the top copy and placed it with the bottles in a basket. As Bill walked out of the cubicle, the officer put the basket on the conveyor belt.

In the confiscation room, Arish removed the baskets coming down the belt and stacked spirits, wines and perfume on a trolley. The bottles of Grecian Nights were wedged between a basket of gin and whisky and another filled with liqueurs.

After making sure no one was watching, Arish quickly pocketed both bottles. But there was no sign of the third. He glanced at the docket. Only two bottles had been confiscated. Effendi must have made a mistake when he said there would be three. Arish pocketed the docket and continued loading the trolley.

When he had done so, he wheeled it to the far end of the room. A couple of loaders began to stack the bottles on shelves. They logged each item as they did so, checking they matched those on the dockets.

His shift over, Arish punched his card in the time clock and walked out of the Customs area.

Forty minutes later he drove into the service station on the M1 and waited in his car. Ten minutes later the Arab tapped on the window. In his hand he held an envelope.

'You have my three bottles of perfume,' Faruk Kadumi said. 'And I have your money.'

'There are only two bottles,' Arish explained. 'Customs must have missed the other one.'

He produced the docket. 'Here, see for yourself.'

Faruk Kadumi read the docket and shoved it in his pocket.

'Give me the two bottles,' he said. 'I will still pay for three.'

The exchange was made.

Faruk Kadumi continued to stare into the car. The Browning pistol with its silencer was a hand movement away, in his pocket. This was the moment he should kill this miserable petty thief. How and where, Raza had left to him. Only that it must be done – and done by him and no one else. Faruk Kadumi had thought about little else on the drive here. One shot would be sufficient.

But the last vestige of the medical ethics that had once governed his life made him baulk at personally committing cold-blooded murder. Instead, he had debated whether to call Effendi and have him arrange the killing. But the risk was too high. Effendi was the cabal's representative in Britain whom Ayatollah Muzwaz had assigned to be Raza's contact man. He might check with Raza first for confirmation. And once Raza knew he had failed to obey his clear instruction, Faruk Kadumi also knew his own life would be forfeit.

He continued to stare at this grinning fool. Then he abruptly turned and walked back to his car.

For most of the long flight from Athens to New York, Nancy had slept. An hour out of Kennedy, a cabin announcement reminding all passengers to fill in a US Customs Declaration Form awoke her.

Nancy had placed hers in the bag of other gifts she was carrying, along with the two bottles of Grecian Nights. Checking her wrapped purchases, she realised she was just over the limits on the form. The elderly matron sitting beside her had a suggestion.

'Open one or two of your presents, honey. Just tell Customs they are for your personal use. You can always rewrap them.'

Nancy smiled her thanks. The woman glanced into the bag.

'Those perfume bottles look expensive. Open them.'

Nancy explained the conditions under which they had been given to her.

The woman smiled indulgently. 'Honey, whatever they told you in Athens, I can assure you there's no such regulation about anything having to remain unopened until you've cleared US Customs. I should know. My late husband was an inspector with the service, God rest him. You go ahead and open the bottles.'

Nancy took out one of the bottles and went to the toilet to freshen herself. Then she broke the seal on the bottle, and dabbed the perfume on her neck and behind her ears. The aroma seemed more musky than the sample she had tried in Constitution Square.

At Kennedy a Customs inspector signed Nancy's form without checking her baggage.

He'd looked at her kindly and asked if she was okay. She nodded and smiled. But the truth was she felt suddenly very tired. And the skin behind her ears and neck was beginning to itch. It must be the perfume. She wouldn't use it again.

Suitcase in one hand and bag of gifts in the other, she came out of Customs and made her way through the terminal to catch a bus into New York.

Muktar Sayeed had been waiting for several hours, constantly comparing faces with that of the woman standing beside Nadine in the photoprint faxed from Athens.

Nadine had not changed from those weeks he had spent in the training camp learning to fight and kill. But instead of joining other *Feydeheen* in attacks on Israel, he had been sent to the United States to work for Rachid Harmoos.

Originally he was employed as a driver in the Day-Nite Cab Company owned by Mr Harmoos. Later he became a courier, travelling the country, delivering and collecting messages and packets too sensitive to be sent by phone or mail.

A few weeks ago he had been sent to San Francisco to kill a man. Briefing him for the assignment, Mr Harmoos' chief aide, Nuri, had explained the man had double-crossed Mr Harmoos over a drug payment. Muktar had arrived on the morning plane from New York, driven into the city, knifed the man to death, and flown out on the afternoon flight.

Now Muktar was in the terminal to steal the bag from the woman walking a few yards ahead. He'd sighted her the moment she'd emerged from the Customs hall.

Keeping a steady, loping stride, knitted hat pulled tight on his head, collar of his windbreaker pulled up, Muktar kept his hands loose at his side. His eyes continued to judge distance and everything else that went with a successful hit.

There had been a security guard at the automatic doors when he'd come in. The man had gone. A steady stream of passengers were exiting to the taxi line. Only a few were heading, with the woman, to the door for buses. Most were elderly. No problem there. He began to increase his stride, his hands clenching and unclenching.

Nancy saw the downtown bus pulling in as she stepped through the doors on to the kerb.

Suddenly she felt a tremendous punch in the back, which sent her sprawling and winded on to the sidewalk. She glimpsed a man running with her bag of gifts in his hand. Then he'd darted round the bus and was lost to sight. Someone was screaming. An elderly man was bending over her, trying to help her to her feet. He was saying the same thing over and over again.

'He didn't get your case, miss. You're gonna be okay. He didn't get your case.'

The suitcase had skidded out of Nancy's grasp.

People were gathering round, discussing among themselves whether she should be moved. A guard from inside the terminal forced his way through them to her side.

'You okay, miss?'

Nancy nodded; she hated fuss. She just wanted to get home and sleep. Her feeling of tiredness just wouldn't go away, like the itch on her skin.

The guard helped Nancy to her feet. When she explained what had happened he spoke into his mobile phone.

'The lady thinks he could be black, and on foot.'

The guard was joined by an airline Customer Relations agent. He turned to Nancy. She had begun to rub her skin. The agent looked sympathetic.

'A lot of people's skin dries out on a long flight. A nice cool shower when you get home will usually do the trick. To get you there that much quicker, I'd like to offer you a courtesy limo.'

Nancy smiled her thanks. This tiredness was turning into full-blown exhaustion, and she felt cold and clammy.

As the limo entered Manhattan, Nancy felt increasingly unwell. The painful throbbing in her back was probably from the punch. But the other symptoms had now been joined by a headache and a persistent shiver.

By the time the limo dropped her at 510 Park, her symptoms had worsened.

Crossing the lobby Nancy felt hot and faint, and by the time the elevator reached the fourteenth floor, her shivering had worsened. She barely had the strength to turn the key of the apartment and drag her suitcase inside. Even closing the door was an effort.

Her eyes blurred as she read the note from her landlady propped against the hallstand, saying she had been called away to a family emergency in California and would not return for at least a week. The note was dated the previous day.

Nancy staggered to her room and flopped on the bed. She was too weak to even undress.

*

Once Muktar had placed the bus between him and immediate pursuit, he had slowed to a walk. He'd parked the Day-Nite cab at the end of the line, close to where the airport limos parked. Their drivers gave him no more than a passing glance as he drove away. At the airport exit there was already a couple of patrol cars. Their crews were stopping all vehicles except taxis. A patrolman waved him through.

On the Connecticut Expressway, Muktar took the Sweetmont exit. Fifteen minutes later he turned off the highway on to the private road, marked by a sculpted signboard that bore the word: 'Harmoos'.

Muktar drove for a mile between pastures grazed by horses and cattle, and fields of ripening corn. He passed the first buildings. On the left was the barn where the estate staff lived. There were forty altogether, all Arabs. Mr Harmoos employed only Arabs.

Beyond the barn, sheltered by trees, was a repair shop. Parked outside were several cabs bearing the same Day-Nite blue logo on their doors as Muktar's cab.

He continued on for another half-mile between more corn fields before reaching a checkpoint. An Arab stepped out of a guard hut, waved him on and stepped back inside. He had a pistol stuck in his waistband.

A quarter of a mile further on, a belt of conifers provided protection for the mansion. Muktar could think of only one other like it – the White House in Washington. Mr Harmoos' home had the same colonnaded central frontage and wings on either side. Formal gardens and lawns led to a turning circle before the massive double front door. Unlike the White House, the windows here were fitted with steel roll-down shutters.

As he parked, Muktar saw a curtain move. Mr Harmoos was watching and waiting in his study.

Five floors above where Nancy was becoming increasingly ill, Matti sat beside Miriam on a couch and listened as she continued to describe her past three days at City Center dealing with the casualties from the hotel bombings. Apart from short breaks, she'd been on duty non-stop.

'The first twelve hours were the worst,' she was saying. 'It was like a casualty clearing station. They just died before we could get them on the table.'

He hadn't heard her sound so tired or look so drained.

'The worst were the kids. I lost three in a row. A couple of sisters and a little boy.'

'You did your best, Miriam.'

She laid her head against his shoulder, and fell asleep. He sat for a while listening to her steady breathing. Then he carried her to the bedroom and laid her on the bed. She did not stir.

Closing the door behind him, Matti went to the safe room and resumed checking the names of the Arabs Morton had sent. He had programmed the computer to search for any links they had with Rachid Harmoos.

The only sound was the squeak of the swivel protesting under the weight of Rachid Harmoos as he moved in his custom-made chair.

He continued to divide his gaze between Nancy's bag on the desk before him and Muktar. The other two men sitting on upholstered chairs either side of Muktar continued to follow every eye movement Harmoos made.

'You are certain no one followed you?'

'Certain, Mr Harmoos,' Muktar replied.

There was another groan of protest from the chair as Harmoos leaned forward and tipped out the bag's contents on to the desk. Nancy's packages made a small pile. He picked up one in his fleshy fingers and tore off the paper. He held a small doll dressed in traditional Greek costume in his hand.

'Americans have such poor taste,' he sighed.

His voice was surprisingly light for someone of his massive bulk. Not even his handmade suit could contain his pear-shaped mass of cosseted flesh completely. The cloth strained in a dozen places. Folds of flesh covered his cheeks and neck and deep pouches filled with fat were suspended under his eyes.

'This girl, does she need to be taken care of, Nuri?'

Harmoos stared at the young Arab with the hard, knobby look of a street fighter.

'I've run a full check. She's a junior high school teacher. She won't associate what happened in Athens with the loss of her bag. I recommend no further action in her case, Mr Harmoos.'

'Very good, Nuri.'

Harmoos dropped the doll in a waste basket behind the desk. He continued to gaze at his aide.

'Of course, there may well be no need for us to do anything now that she's opened that bottle, Nuri.' He gave another, longer sigh. 'If only people would do what they're told.'

All three men nodded at Harmoos.

In one unbroken movement, astonishingly swift for a man of his size, he swept Nancy's other gifts into the bin.

'Such things offend my sense of values,' he murmured. He glanced quickly around the oak-panelled study. Two of its walls were covered with shelves filled with rare books on the Islamic world. On the others hung originals by Matisse, Picasso and Turner.

Harmoos turned to the tall thin man on Muktar's left. He had a mournful face. Heavy horn-rimmed spectacles perched on the end of his long nose. Ismail was an Egyptian research chemist on a year's sabbatical at New York State University. His tuition fees and living expenses were being paid by the cabal.

'You have everything?'

'Yes, Mr Harmoos. But I cannot start until the bottles have fully frozen. It will take another five hours to reach the required temperature.'

'Very good, Ismail. Remember, the Ayatollah is depending on you.'

Ismail gave a quick, weak smile.

'For all his wisdom, the Magnificent One is not a scientist. This is very delicate work.'

Harmoos gazed at him, smiling pleasantly.

'That is why you were chosen.'

He scratched behind one ear, continuing to smile, then sat back and rested his hands on his stomach. He glanced at a sheet of paper on the desk and was lost in thought for a moment. Then he nodded his enormous head as he stared across the desk.

'You may go.'

The men rose to their feet. As they began to walk to the door, Harmoos motioned for Nuri to wait. After the door had closed, Harmoos shook his head sadly.

'A pity about Muktar. I'd become quite fond of him.'

'I already have a replacement in mind,' Nuri said.

Harmoos picked up the paper. It was Raza's order that everyone on the periphery of the operation must be killed once they had completed their work.

'When?' Harmoos asked, putting down the paper.

'When he leaves here,' Nuri replied. 'His cab has been fixed to make it look like a pure accident.'

'There will be no problem with the insurance?'

'No. They will pay out.'

Harmoos laughed softly, his belly heaving.

'Very good, Nuri. It's not often I make a profit out of doing something for Raza. I shall fax him to say everything is in order.' Then his face grew dark. 'Ismail concerns me, Nuri. I find his presence disturbing. When he is finished, deal with him quickly.'

Nuri nodded and left the study.

In a sparsely furnished apartment in west London mostly used by the cabal's foot soldiers when they had business in Britain, Faruk Kadumi continued to hesitate over the fax he was composing to Raza. Once more he put down his pen on the pad and went over to the window.

Should he report only two bottles had arrived? But if he did that it could result in Raza contacting Effendi and discovering that the thief was still alive.

Despite the double-glazing the noise of traffic below on the Great West Road was loud. It made it difficult to concentrate. Yet he knew he could not delay much longer. There were only fifteen minutes left before the prearranged transmission time.

He turned from the window and walked into the kitchen. Since he had equipped it as a makeshift laboratory, the blind on the window had been permanently drawn. Most of the counter space was covered with the test tubes and bottles of saline he had purchased from a medical supplier in Soho.

The British Army decontamination suit he had acquired at a store selling military clothing hung on the back of the door. After the Gulf War they had become a fast-selling souvenir.

In the cupboard over the sink was the shoe box in which he kept the Browning. It had been waiting for him when he'd arrived.

Beside the box was the last remaining bottle of ether. He must buy some more. Sniffing was the only way to steady his nerves in the stressful, hostile environment of a city whose police were everywhere. Every day he spent here he felt the risk of discovery grew greater.

Faruk Kadumi uncorked the bottle and held it under his nose. He breathed in slowly and gently, allowing the fumes to rise into his head. For a moment he felt dizzy. Then the sensation was replaced by a warm and comforting feeling. Recorking the bottle, he was filled with a new resolve. He knew it would not last long. But for the moment he felt determined and decisive.

He lifted the lid off the freezer chest in the corner of the kitchen. Both perfume bottles were covered with a crust of ice. He checked the thermometer. Another hour and he could begin. He closed the lid, returned to the table and started to write.

When he had finished he read back the words. Satisfied, he took the sheet of paper to the fax machine on the sideboard and started to dial Libya.

When Miriam awoke, Matti took her to breakfast at the coffee shop on the corner of the block. Walking back to the apartment, Matti saw one of the porters was out on the sidewalk and waving urgently at them.

'*Muy malo*,' the Mexican shouted when they reached him, pointing into the lobby.

Matti recognised the crumpled figure lying half out of the elevator.

'Nancy Carson. Teaches fourth grade. Sublets from a widow,' he told Miriam, as they ran across the lobby.

She glanced at him. 'You keep everybody in this block on file?'

He grinned.

Nancy's face was chalky and bathed in perspiration. The porter continued to explain how Señorita Carson had called down saying she was ill. He'd been on the way up to her when she'd collapsed out of the elevator. He'd rushed into the street hoping to see Señor Talim and Señora el doctor . . .

'Call an ambulance,' Miriam ordered the porter when they reached Nancy.

'Let's make her more comfortable,' suggested Matti, pointing to one of several couches furnishing the lobby.

Miriam shook her head. 'She may have broken something.' She knelt beside Nancy. 'What happened?'

'Sick . . . need a doctor . . . feel bad . . .' Nancy groaned.

'I'm a doctor. Just tell me, where's it hurt, Nancy?' Miriam said.

'Everywhere.'

Despite the heavy coat she wore over a long winter nightdress, Nancy was shivering.

'Where's it hurt most, Nancy?'

A cough exploded in Nancy's chest, and then another – deep, rumbling wet coughs.

Miriam continued her quick and careful look at Nancy while she checked her pulse. It was erratic. The coughing could do that.

'How long have you been feeling like this, Nancy?'

'Yester . . .' Another deep cough broke loose inside Nancy. '. . . getting worse . . .' She struggled to sit up. '. . . all the time . . .'

Nancy sank back on the floor, exhausted.

Miriam noted the small dark pustules on Nancy's neck and behind her ears. They were also on her legs and arms. Could be bug bites that had ulcerated, or the result of an infected needle. But there were no track marks visible. And Nancy didn't look like someone who'd have lice in her mattress.

'Help . . . help me . . . please . . .'

Nancy's plea was interrupted by another deep wet cough. Blood-stained phlegm oozed from her mouth. Matti fished in his pocket for a handkerchief. Miriam took it and carefully wiped away the phlegm.

Nancy's bubbly breathing showed her lungs were filling with liquid. Miriam wondered how far the organism producing it had advanced into the spleen and lymph nodes. Her tan had probably made it much easier for it to slide under the girl's first line of defence, her skin. Tanning opened the pores.

'Where were you on vacation, Nancy?' Miriam asked gently.

'Greece . . . came back yester . . .'

Another welling cough was followed by more purulent matter dribbling from Nancy's mouth.

'Were you unwell on vacation?'

Nancy shook her head slightly, too exhausted to talk.

'How long were you in Greece?'

Nancy managed to raise two fingers.

'Days?'

Nancy's head shake ended in another raw cough.

'Two weeks?'

Nancy nodded.

Miriam tried to remember what she'd learned about tropical infections and contagious diseases. Undulant fever was still prevalent in Greece from drinking infected goat's milk. Incubation time was five to twenty-one days, but no cough. Typhus had the same incubation time, and this feverish shivering, but no cough. Same with sand fly fever and the even more deadly yellow fever. But none would have produced those ulcers. Miriam had never seen any quite like them.

'Did something bite you on vacation?'

Nancy tried to shake her head. Another cough filled the lobby with its deep uneasy sound.

'See if you can hurry up that ambulance,' Miriam told Matti.

He ran to the porter's desk, while Miriam remained kneeling beside Nancy, holding her hand and wiping her mouth. There was not much else she could do. She continued to consider. Amoebic dysentery was a possibility, so was malaria – but again, neither presented with a cough or those ulcers. Nor did smallpox, typhoid, nor any of the other fevers she'd read up on, and now only half-remembered, have such indications.

Another deep cough burst from Nancy's mouth. She was trembling uncontrollably when the ambulance crew arrived with a stretcher.

'*¡Madre de Dios!*' said the porter, crossing himself as they wheeled Nancy out to the ambulance.

22

German Air Traffic Control had given the Concorde priority clearance to descend into Frankfurt international airport. As she swooped earthwards, nose cone angled downwards, the early-morning sun cast a huge delta shadow over the ground.

In the communications centre Morton sat before the screen receiving Lacouste's image from Paris via the satellite stationed over the Negev. The only sign Lacouste's voice was being bounced from outer space was a slight loss of lip sync and a metallic tone to the French security chief's words.

'Appleton's call came just before the Cabinet recessed,' Lacouste was saying. 'He wanted to know what guarantees we were going to get from Israel that if we let the *Feydeheen* go, Israel wouldn't go after them. He kept on reminding us what happened after Munich.'

In 1972 eleven Israeli athletes were murdered by Arab terrorists at the Munich Olympics. Morton had led the team sent to kill them. It had taken almost a year and two million American dollars in tip money before he had done so.

'Appleton only knows about Munich because Bitburg told the Americans, Pierre.'

Lacouste gave a sigh of exasperation. 'I know, but it was the very point Appleton seized upon. He kept saying there would be no way to keep the deaths of the *Feydeheen* quiet, because Israel would want her other enemies to know their fate. Appleton became quite loquacious, talking about how Israel had cornered the market in an eye for an eye.'

Over the intercom came the flight deck announcement that

they would be landing in ten minutes. Morton and the technicians began to buckle up.

'What did your people tell Appleton?' Morton asked.

Lacouste shrugged. 'You can imagine. Everyone knew what Appleton was driving at. If we released them, and anything was to happen to the *Feydeheen*, it would unite Arab radicals and moderates as never before. Appleton kept saying that in this case there could be no distinction between counter-terrorism and terrorism. France would be seen as having conspired in the deaths of pardoned men. From then on it was downhill all the way. A lot of rehashing about the Palestinian cause being as honourable as the Israeli cause. After Appleton had hung up, it didn't take long to reach the bottom line: billion-franc deals going down the drain; revenge attacks on French soil. It was going to be the Gulf War all over again. Only this time fought in the streets of Paris –'

'So what are your people going to do?' Morton asked.

'The President's already phoned your Prime Minister. I gather Karshov wasn't very helpful. He said that until France actually came to a decision, there was nothing to talk about.'

Morton spoke curtly and clearly. 'He's right. The best thing your President can do is to keep those *Feydeheen* where they belong – in your prisons, serving sentences for which they were properly convicted. If France lets them go it will simply make it harder for everyone.'

A pocket of turbulence rocked the Concorde. Morton gripped the armrests of his seat.

In Paris Lacouste looked pensive. 'The pressure's on, David. The Cabinet's going to meet again when they've had a few hours' sleep.'

The CCO called out that Danny was on line from Tel Aviv – and it was urgent.

'I've got to go, Pierre. Shove a rod up the President to keep him hanging on to those *Feydeheen*.'

Lacouste's image disappeared. If France hung on to the *Feydeheen* it could make Raza more prone to make a mistake. One would be enough. Danny's face appeared on screen.

'The ACC's just come through,' Danny began. 'GCHQ have an interesting intercept out of the London area.'

Danny glanced down at a piece of paper. Britain's counterpart to the US National Security Agency was housed at Cheltenham.

271

From there its technicians had cast an electronic net over London since the hotel bombings. Danny began to read.

'It's a fax. "The deliverer has delivered and been delivered. Delivery can commence tonight at the appointed hour".'

Morton jotted down the words on a pad.

'What's the ACC's view?'

Danny looked troubled. 'The transcript came to him through MI5. By then Percy West had already convinced the powers that be that there was nothing here to show London was the target. West's argument is that Britain's so well buttoned up that Raza will probably try elsewhere in Europe. He even managed to convince the Prime Minister that Raza's simply using London as a transmitting station to divert attention.'

'What do you think, Danny?'

'I just don't know, David. Raza could have another transponder in London. Or even an agent. I've persuaded the ACC to act on that possibility. He's pulling in everyone with any Arab experience to infiltrate.'

'Did GCHQ get even a rough fix?'

Danny looked up. 'They think somewhere out of west London, but that's not much help. It's a three-million population spread. And it could have come from a portable fax maxhine. Half a million were sold last year in London alone. British Telecom say they have four million on their records. It would take a week to computer-check them all –'

'Get them to do it. I want everybody on their toes twenty-four hours a day, for sure,' Morton said firmly.

'Will do,' acknowledged Danny. 'One more thing: a few minutes after the ACC, Lou Panchez came through. A satellite the Americans have over the Azores to catch anything coming in or out of the eastern side of the United States picked up a fax almost identical to the London one.'

'Do they know its direction?'

'Out. From somewhere between Boston and Washington.'

'Get the Swift people moving on it. Maybe it came from one of the embassies. When's that team of yours due in New York?'

'This evening. You want me to pull some of them away?' Danny asked.

Morton considered. Danny's technicians could be useful in Washington and New York, working Arab embassies in the capital and missions to the United Nations.

'No, but have Matti and Lou concentrate on contact-tracing Harmoos. Get Gates to have his people in Colombia do the same thing.'

The CCO called to Morton, 'General Yertzin's on the encryptor.'

'Hold it, Danny.'

Morton picked up a phone on the keyboard beside him and punched buttons. The encryptor had been tuned in to the Soviet Over-the-Horizon radar communications headquarters at Niko-layev in the Caucasus. The encryptor provided a completely secure telephone channel while at the same time monitoring the conversation was not being overheard.

'General, good to hear you.'

There was a moment's pause on the line while the encryptor scrambled and unscrambled. Then Yertzin's voice boomed in Morton's ear.

'And you, comrade. You said two days. My Spetsnaz have done it in less. They have found a transponder in a village north of Kabul. They have established Raza positioned it there weeks ago.'

Morton could imagine how the Russians had discovered the location; he'd seen them at work in Afghanistan. It had always been tell or kill time.

'I want you to get that transponder to Tel Aviv as fast as possible.'

'You want to trace the Voice Throw box, *da*?'

'Yes.'

'We can do that for you in Moscow,' said Yertzin.

'I'm sure you can. But I want it done in Tel Aviv, General.'

The pause was longer before Yertzin replied.

'Okay. I'll arrange a direct flight, Kabul – Tel Aviv.'

'Thank you, General. And my congratulations to your Spetsnaz,' Morton said.

He put down the phone, turned back to Danny and told him what was happening.

'How long will it take your people to work backwards to where the Voice Throw box is?'

Danny frowned. 'Assuming Raza could have positioned it almost anywhere on earth, I'd say a couple of days.'

'That brings us bang up against his deadline, Danny.'

Danny gave a slow nod. Then his face brightened. 'Assuming he's got Costas' MRT, I've sent him a little reminder to tweak his nerve ends a little.'

He explained, and then his face disappeared off screen.

Moments later Morton felt the Concorde touch down. Ground control directed it to park away from the terminals in the high-security zone reserved for VIP flights in and out of the airport.

When Morton came down the steps, Hans-Dieter Müller was waiting at the bottom. Close by were parked two government cars. Each had a chauffeur in military uniform at the wheel.

'Welcome, Mr Morton,' Müller said sombrely.

'Good to see you, Hans-Dieter.'

Müller continued to look sombre. 'I hope you will still say that when you hear what's happened.'

Morton stared at him for a moment. 'Appleton's been shoving in his wrench?'

The German security officer's look of surprise was genuine. 'How did you know?'

Morton told him what Lacouste had said.

'Come, we will speak in the back of my car.'

As they walked towards the Mercedes, the chauffeur jumped out and whipped open the rear door. After Morton and Müller had settled themselves, she went to the front of the car and stood to attention, her back to the bonnet.

Müller nodded towards her. 'They teach that at training school. She's been driving me for a year and I still can't break her of the habit.'

Morton smiled. 'Why not threaten to send her back there?'

Müller sighed. 'The next one could be even more rigid.'

The Operations Chief began to hand-roll a cigarette from tobacco he kept in a silver box. 'It belonged to my father. He rolled cigarettes all the way to Stalingrad in 1941 and back again two years later. He said it was the only thing that kept him sane.'

'What's Appleton done, Hans-Dieter?' Morton prodded gently.

Müller lit the cigarette. 'Called Kunzler and spent almost an hour talking about how important it was for what he kept calling the "new Germany" to find its place in the Arab world.' Müller inhaled deeply before continuing. 'Appleton reminded the Chancellor that West Germany alone had current orders worth ten billion Deutschmarks with Arab countries, and the old East Germany almost as many. The unification has inevitably led to delivery problems. Appleton was very concerned we didn't lose those contacts by doing anything precipitous. He offered to use his good offices in Riyadh, Cairo and even Damascus.'

'What did the Chancellor say?'

'Kunzler's a great listener, especially when Washington's talking. He's not like Kohl used to be. Kunzler actually speaks English like he was brought up on American Armed Forces radio.' Müller shifted in his seat. 'Naturally, Kunzler didn't mention a word about our arrangement.'

'He didn't have to,' Morton said.

Müller sent a spiral of smoke against the roof of the car, and watched it disappear into the discreetly positioned extraction vents.

'Seemingly so. After Appleton phoned, Kunzler had his chief secretary call me to say your visit was to be cancelled.'

Morton stared at Müller.

'It's okay, Mr Morton,' Müller said quietly. 'I told the chief secretary that I had to speak to the Chancellor personally. That took a couple of hours to fix. In the end I got ten minutes between an ambassador presenting credentials and a Japanese trade delegation protesting about their car import quotas –'

'Why's it okay?'

Müller drew deeper on the butt. 'I told him he would have my resignation if he stopped you. That shook him a little. In the end he compromised. You have a morning, not a full day with her. If she agrees, she only gets a new face and freedom providing there is absolutely no doubt of the value of her contribution. Otherwise, back she comes to serve out the rest. Naturally, she won't know that.'

Morton kept his voice steady. 'Who decides? Kunzler?'

Müller smiled. 'He acts on my recommendation. I act on yours. So, no problem.'

Morton shook his head. 'Wrong, Hans-Dieter. There's still a problem.'

He opened the car door and bounded up the steps back into the plane. In the communications centre, several of the technicians were dozing in their seats. Others were drinking coffee. The CCO looked up in surprise from the foldaway table he used for writing the traffic log of every flight.

'Get me the White House,' Morton ordered.

'Anyone in particular, Colonel?'

'The President of the United States.'

The CCO hesitated.

'It's two o'clock in the morning in Washington, Colonel.'

'Dammit! Don't argue. Get him on line!' Morton rasped, sliding into his seat.

'Yes, sir.'

The CCO began to give orders. Technicians sprang into action. A circuit was quickly established with Washington. In the White House basement communications room, the duty officer appeared on screen.

'Can you tell me why you wish to disturb the President, sir?' the Marine captain asked.

'No. Just get him on the line.'

'I can't do that, sir –'

'Listen to me. I have the authority. Wake him. Tell him Colonel Morton wants to talk to him!'

'Sir, I'm not –'

'Do it!' Morton commanded. 'Otherwise you're going to be fixing telephone lines in Alaska.'

'Wait, please, sir.'

The screen went blank in Washington. Morton sensed the tension around him. Men could get fired for being part of this.

A button began to flash on the CCO's console. He picked up the phone, listened and turned to Morton.

'That was the White House Chief of Staff. They're connecting a feed up to the President's bedroom.'

Morton grunted.

Moments later the President's face appeared on screen. Despite being tousled, his shock of hair still reminded Morton of Jack Kennedy. The President wore a dressing-gown that matched his pyjamas. He glared out of the screen.

'I understand this is so important, Mr Morton, that it couldn't wait until I got my first full night's sleep since this crisis began.'

'I'm sorry to wake you, Mr President. But I have a problem only you can solve. And I need it solved now.'

The President pursed his lips.

'What is it?'

'Appleton. He's interfering in my work. I've already called him and asked him to stop. Now I'm asking you to stop him.'

Morton studied the face on the screen. The anger was because the President hadn't known.

'Tell me what's been happening, Mr Morton. Everything.'

Morton told him. There was a long pause before the President spoke. He sounded cold.

'Very well, Mr Morton. I have no doubt Mr Appleton was acting from the highest motives. But he will not trouble you further. You have my assurance on that.'

'Thank you, Mr President.'

Morton watched the President run a hand through his hair.

'I assume you have not made sufficient progress to reconvene a conference call?'

'Not yet, Mr President.'

'Good night, Mr Morton.' The screen went blank.

Morton stood up. He looked around him. The CCO and the technicians stared at him in awe. In complete silence Morton walked out of the cabin and back down the steps.

Müller was waiting by the car. He had a file in his hand. He stared curiously at Morton and asked what he had done. Morton told him.

'*Mensch!*' he finally said. 'You called the President of the USA? Just like that? *Mensch!*'

Morton smiled. 'No big deal. After all, you called your Chancellor.'

'But the President of the USA –' Müller shook his head. 'Here,' he said, opening the file. 'Your permission. The other car will take you there.'

He gave a stiff little bow and climbed back in the Mercedes.

The chauffeur of the second car was already holding open the door. She gave an immaculate salute as Morton climbed inside.

Bill Hardiman heard the sound of small feet running urgently across the hall carpet as he opened the door of the terraced house overlooking the Thames at Putney. A century ago the row had been workmen's cottages. Now they were mostly occupied by television executives, and budding tycoons who commuted to the City by river. Bill owned the corner house, which gave him a good view of the Oxford and Cambridge Boat Race as it swept beneath Putney Bridge.

Opening the door he was engulfed first by Amy – unashamedly affectionate at seven, and then by Dervla, who had reached the stage of appearing grave now that she was eleven.

Dropping his bags, he swept them both off their feet, feeling the hearts pumping beneath their school blouses. He crushed them to him and stepped inside as Fiona emerged from the kitchen. She was impossibly beautiful, like Amy was going to be, and had passed on her own gravity to Dervla.

'Bill! I was getting worried with all that's been happening.'

He kissed her on the mouth and quickly explained about the delays at Frankfurt and Luton. Then he kissed her again.

'Daddy!' Amy whispered in a gleeful rush of excitement. 'Mummy loves to be kissed.'

'Shhh!' Dervla said. 'Miss Fortescue says it's wrong to embarrass people!'

Miss Fortescue was the headmistress at the private school both girls attended.

Their father looked down at them and smiled ruefully. 'They took away your presents.'

'Oh, Daddy, no,' they chorused in disappointment. 'What were they?'

He told them about the perfume he'd won – and the chance they could all be flown back to Athens for the launch.

Amy began to cheer and even Dervla began to lose her serious look. Fiona shook her head in wonder.

Bill turned, opened his briefcase and produced the bottle of Grecian Nights.

'Oh, Daddy!' Amy cried. 'It's a lovely bottle!'

'It's Mummy's, Amy,' Bill said, handing Fiona the bottle.

'Let's all try some,' Amy suggested.

Dervla shook her head. 'Miss Fortescue says we mustn't wear perfume to school.'

Her sister looked disappointed. Fiona looked at them both.

'Listen, if I don't get you to school Miss Fortescue will have something else to say!'

Fiona turned to Bill. 'Go and have a nice long shower and I'll bring you breakfast in bed when I get back. Leave your case, I'll unpack it.'

He kissed them all once more and climbed the stairs.

Amy was looking at the bottle. 'Please, Mummy, can I just have a little drop? Miss Fortescue will never smell that.'

Fiona smiled at Dervla. 'I think that's true.'

Her elder daughter nodded.

Fiona broke the seal on the bottle. Then, using the stopper, she dabbed a little perfume on each of her daughter's cheeks, and then behind her own ears. The perfume was pleasantly musky. She replaced the stopper.

'Okay, get your bags and we're off,' she said.

The children went into the kitchen and collected their satchels. From upstairs came the sound of the shower running.

Fiona was about to put the bottle down on a shelf above the hall radiator when Dervla stopped her.

'Mummy, what have you got for our sale?'

'We're collecting to buy water for the Sudan,' Amy reminded her mother.

'Not water. A machine to make it clean,' Dervla corrected.

'We still must bring something,' Amy said. 'Miss Fortescue said so.'

'Oh God, I clean forgot!' Fiona said. 'I thought it was next week. We'll buy something on the way.'

Dervla shook her head. 'There won't be time and the shops won't be open.'

'Miss Fortescue will be very cross, Mummy,' Amy whispered, suddenly close to tears.

Fiona glanced at the bottle. She didn't really want to give it away so soon, but the girls were looking so desperate. 'How about this?'

'But it's Daddy's present to you,' Amy objected.

'And it's been opened,' Dervla added.

'I'm sure Daddy won't mind, Amy,' Fiona said, as she carefully smoothed down the seal. Bill would understand, as it was for the girls. She held up the bottle for inspection – 'There, it looks untouched' – and handed it to Dervla.

Three miles away in the apartment's kitchen, Faruk Kadumi prepared to complete his work. He struggled into his protective suit, checking in the reflection of the oven's glass door that the hood completely overlapped his shoulders. Breathing slowly through the respirator, he shuffled over to the freezer chest and lifted the lid.

Rows of securely corked test tubes filled several shelves. On the floor of the chest was the partly filled bottle, and the one he had already emptied.

With difficulty, he leaned down into the chest and removed the almost empty bottle. He placed it on the worktop and closed the freezer lid.

He then ran the bottle under warm water until the contents became mushy. He took a syringe and drew off a small amount of semi-frozen Anthrax-B-C. He injected this into a test tube. Next he carefully funnelled saline into the tube and corked and then sealed it with clear wax.

In an hour he had filled the remaining test tubes and placed them in the freezer chest. He placed the second empty bottle beside the first.

He was halfway through removing his suit when the doorbell rang. Faruk Kadumi froze.

Effendi's men were not due to collect the tubes until this evening – after he had called Effendi to confirm the number of vials. Then he would fly first to Paris, and on to Algiers. He would be well clear of here before the collectors arrived. All he knew about them was that each one had a duplicate key to the apartment.

The ringing was longer and more insistent.

As Faruk Kadumi began moving as quietly as possible towards the hallway, the letterbox was pushed open and a voice called out.

'This is the police. Is there anyone at home?'

Faruk Kadumi clenched his teeth and held his breath. He felt the pressure building in his head, making his temples throb. Why were they here? What did they want?

After a moment the flap closed. Faruk Kadumi released his breath and the roar in his head faded. He could do nothing to stop his trembling.

Outside the door voices were complaining to each other.

'Nobody's at home at this hour. Stands to reason, don't it? It's a working-class area.'

'It's all a waste of time, if you ask me. I mean, what are they going to do with all those serial numbers?'

Faruk Kadumi heard a grunt of agreement. Then the flap opened again. A leaflet fell on the floor. The letterbox banged shut. Moments later came the sound of knocking from across the corridor.

Waiting until he heard a woman's voice inviting in the policemen, Faruk Kadumi went to the hall and picked up the leaflet. It was headed: 'Police Notice'. Beneath was the announcement that Scotland Yard was conducting a house-to-house search to obtain the serial number of all fax machines and that the officers conducting the search were empowered to impound any machine. In each case a proper receipt would be provided. No explanation was given for the search. The leaflet ended by stating the police, having failed to contact the householder, would return later. No date or time was given for that visit.

Faruk Kadumi's trembling increased. Somehow they knew about the message he had sent. Now they were looking for him. He must not use the phone or fax machine again. He would make his call to Effendi from a pay phone at the airport.

Further down the corridor he could hear the policemen knocking. He dared not leave the apartment until they had left the block. But that could take hours. He began to tremble even more.

Matti walked through the apartment under the watchful stare of the Swift crew chief who was holding a clipboard. In a few hours he and his men had installed a small switchboard and several handsets as well as an additional computer and three more fax machines, one on a tie line to Langley.

His living-room furniture had been replaced with a row of desks and chairs against one wall. Portable booths with equipment for listening to tapes stood along another. Foldaway camp beds lay on the floor.

'I don't imagine they'll get much time to use them,' grinned the grizzly haired chief. 'But they came with the inventory for a mobile war room.'

'You guys did a first-class job,' Matti said. 'A real home from home for Major Nagier's specialists.'

The chief's grin widened. He held out his clipboard.

'Just sign and I'll be off to scout a location for Danny's boys around Sweetmont. Those sort of places are harder to work in than somewhere like this. Here no one cares if you come or go. A place like Sweetmont, everybody wants to say howdy.'

As Matti closed the apartment door behind the chief, the bed-room phone was ringing. It was Miriam, calling from City Center.

'Matti, it's about Nancy Carson.'

'How is she?'

'Bad. And getting worse. She's in intensive care. But she managed to tell one of the nurses something. The nurse told me and I figured you'd want to know. On the other hand, it may be nothing –'

'So just tell me, Miriam,' Matti gently interrupted. He was always surprised how diffident she could be with something outside her own field.

'Nancy was mugged at Kennedy. Some guy made off with all her gifts.'

Matti made a sympathetic noise. 'That happens. All too often, sadly. What kind of gifts?'

'That's why I'm calling. There were a couple of bottles of what sounds like expensive perfume. She says she opened one and splashed some on her face. Some new brand I've never heard of, something with Greek in it. Anyway, because she became sick soon afterwards, we're running serology tests along with everything else. She may have an allergic reaction to complicate her pneumonic symptoms –'

'Hold a moment, will you?'

Matti ran to the safe room and picked up a fax. It was Danny's Double Flash that had come with the photocopy of the perfume bottle label and the photo. While the label was still readable, the photo had lost its sharpness in transmission. He ran back to the bedroom and picked up the phone.

'Grecian Nights the name of that perfume, Miriam?'

'Yes. How'd you know?'

'Miriam, I've got to talk to Nancy. It's very important,' Matti said urgently. 'Can you fix it?'

'I would, if she could talk. She's in a semicoma,' Miriam replied. 'You can get that with certain types of pneumonia.'

'Miriam, listen, she may not have pneumonia –'

Miriam spoke sharply. 'What are you talking about, Matti?'

'I'm not a doctor, Miriam. But that perfume bottle could have contained Anthrax-B-C. There must be some way I can talk to her to find out how she got those bottles.'

'Matti, you just listen to me,' Miriam snapped. 'There's no way you or anyone else is going to question Nancy right now. She's a very, very sick girl. And she's got classic pneumonia. In all the tests so far nothing else has shown up. If serology come up with anything you'll be the first to know after me.'

She hung up without saying goodbye. Matti knew that this time it was not only from habit, but also from anger.

As he walked back into the living-room, the television he'd insisted must remain was screening a local news show. The top story was that it would be at least a week before the last bodies were recovered from the devastated hotels. There were updates on the hunt for the bombers. A consortium of Wall Street brokers had posted a million-dollar reward for their arrest. That brought the bounty figure to 7 million dollars.

The third story was about a spectacular accident on the Connecticut Expressway late the previous afternoon. Over film of the wreckage a reporter described how a cab had gone out of control and burst through the central reservation into the path of an on-coming gasoline truck. The fire had killed both drivers. Rescue workers interviewed on camera said it was an accident long overdue; that stretch of road was notorious for speeding. A police officer said that the likely cause of the accident was a blow-out of two of the cab's tyres.

The reporter ended by identifying the truck driver as being from out of state. The cab driver was named as Muktar Sayeed, a bachelor living in Queens. He had been driving for the Day-Nite Cab Company for a year. The company, the reporter reminded his viewers, was owned by the wealthy Arab philanthropist, Rachid Harmoos. He had been unavailable for comment, having reportedly left his Sweetmont residence shortly before the tragedy.

Matti scribbled Muktar Sayeed's name on a piece of paper and walked into the safe room.

23

Eighty kilometres south of Frankfurt, Morton's chauffeur turned off the autobahn and began to drive through the rolling Hessen farmland.

Fifteen minutes later the Mercedes stopped before a high steel-mesh fence. At regular intervals there were triangular signs fixed to the wire. The notices carried the same warning written in the principal languages, including Arabic. 'Do not touch. High voltage electricity.' Beneath was the universal symbol for danger: a white skull and crossbones.

Three policemen armed with machine pistols emerged from the solid brick guardhouse. One came forward while the other two covered him. He studied the passes the chauffeur presented, then opened the back door and carefully inspected Morton. Satisfied, the policeman nodded to his companions. They lowered their machine pistols, and one walked back into the guardhouse. Moments later the gates swung open.

The car entered slowly. On either side of the roadway the ground was completely covered with coils of razor wire. The wire extended all the way to a wall taller and more difficult to climb than the Berlin Wall had ever been. The face of it was covered with broken glass set in a greasy plastic compound impervious to heat or cold. Not even a lizard could scale the wall.

Set in the wall were a pair of heavy steel doors. Another guardhouse controlled the approach to them. Another trio of policemen emerged and conducted another check before the gates rolled silently open on their runners, and the car moved forward. Beyond was farmland no different to that Morton had already passed.

A group of men, all alike in their grey uniforms, were tilling a field. Armed guards watched over the workers.

Next Morton saw tennis and volley ball courts, and a soccer pitch. Play ball after a stint on the couch. Run them off their feet in the hope it'll make it easier to winkle out all those secrets, which always begin with why. Why did they rarely show emotion and almost never kill anyone in anger? Why was their violence so deliberate and dispassionate? Why was it so carefully engineered for theatrical effect? Why, why, why? And – *why?*

The Germans had purpose-built this place to find the answers. It was Europe's first criminological laboratory-cum-prison.

Morton glanced at the briefing paper in the file on his knees. Currently 97 of the once most dangerous men and women on earth were confined in these 500 acres. Three hundred hand-picked warders guarded them. The doctors did the real work. There were 50 of them, each an expert in the use of psychiatry, psychology, sociology and psychotropic drugs. Their brief, the paper explained, was to study the pharmacology of violence that lay behind all acts of terrorism. The study was supposed to make it harder for someone to hijack another plane, kidnap an industrialist, hold an embassy at gunpoint or a busload of kids prisoner. Very German.

The car parked before a tawny-coloured building. A sign fixed to the wall beside the double doors proclaimed this was the Administration Block. On either side rose the forbidding fortress of the prison itself.

'I will wait for you here.'

They were the first words the chauffeur had spoken since Frankfurt.

'Thank you, Fräulein.'

Morton got out of the car, clutching the file, and walked up the steps of the Administration Block. The building had the angry look of prison architecture everywhere. As he reached the door, it was opened by a short, broad man. He looked like he had been created by the same architect who had designed the building. The man wore a tweed suit with a name tag in the lapel.

'Herr Morton, *ja?*'

'Yes.' The sudden smile didn't fool Morton. The man was looking him over.

'*Sehr gut.*'

It was a recent thing in Germany to speak only German to foreigners. Morton glanced at the man's name tag.

'Do you speak English, Herr Vogel?'

'*Ja.* Yes, of course. And I am Herr Doktor Vogel, Deputy Director.'

'That's fine, doctor. Let's stick with the English, okay?'

'*Ja* – of course, if you prefer.'

'I prefer.'

'Show me, please, your permission,' Vogel said stiffly.

Morton handed over the file. Vogel riffled through it.

'Herr Direktor wishes to see you first.'

'How's his English?'

'Perfect, Herr Morton. He was at George Washington University for two years.'

They walked in silence past closed doors from behind which came the sound of typing. Beyond was a row of rooms with open doors. Each was spotlessly white with an examining table and armchairs. They reeked of antiseptic.

'Treatment rooms?' Morton asked.

'*Ja.* Sorry, yes,' Vogel replied.

They stopped at a door marked: '*Direktor*'.

Vogel knocked quickly before opening the door.

The Director was seated behind a large expanse of desk framed by bookshelves filled with bound volumes and journals. It reminded Morton of Bitburg's sanctuary.

'Thank you, Dr Vogel.'

The Director stood up as he nodded at his deputy. He turned to Morton but waited until Vogel had left the room before speaking again.

'Your reputation precedes you, Mr Morton.'

He came from behind the desk. They shook hands.

'Good to meet you, Herr Direktor.'

'Dr Schmeissner will do okay. Washington taught me to shake off our national trait of formality.'

He laughed, his face softening. He had heavy brows, a high forehead and thinning dark hair. He walked with a limp – it could be an old war wound. He looked close to seventy.

'Please.' Dr Schmeissner motioned towards armchairs grouped around a coffee table. There was a pot and cups, cream jug and sugar bowl on a tray.

They sat down opposite each other.

'Coffee?'

'Thank you. Black, no sugar.'

'Like the Arabs here. We import their coffee from Damascus or Teheran.'

Dr Schmeissner began to pour.

'Does it help, giving them their own coffee, to know why they do it?' Morton asked.

Dr Schmeissner gave a sidelong glance, evaluating the question. 'Everything helps. The policy here is to avoid anything that smacks of institutionalism. We take a lot of care with the food, the sports facilities. Everything is designed to help us get inside the minds of these people.' He handed Morton a cup. 'We're looking, for instance, at the differences and similarities in their psychopathology. What do they mean when they speak of "revolutionary heroism"? Our sociologists try to discover the level of genetic disposition which drove them into terrorism in the first place. Did you know that over ninety per cent of all our prisoners came from broken homes? As a psychiatrist I find that interesting.'

Morton put down his cup. 'Not all kids from broken homes end up throwing hand grenades. And certainly not Raza's people, who have a strong sense of belonging to his group. He's managed to endow terror as the justification to create his idea of a new and ideal society. One in which a place like this would never exist.'

There was sudden silence in the room.

When Dr Schmeissner finally spoke, there was no protest in his voice.

'I suppose it all depends on one's perspective. Where you sit, killing terrorists is the priority. Where I sit, understanding them comes above all else.'

Morton looked at the Director. When he spoke his voice was almost gentle. 'Doctor, I respect your position. Maybe one day I'll understand its full importance. But right now I'm not sure.' He emptied his cup and picked up his file. 'I'd like to see her now. You have the tape player I asked for?'

'Of course.'

Dr Schmeissner stood up, limped over to his desk, picked up a pocket-sized cassette player and handed it to Morton. He slipped it into his pocket, where he carried copies of the tapes made by the two women working for Raza.

Dr Schmeissner led him out of the office, back down the corridor and across an enclosed bridge. As they walked, he continued to lecture, the broad face suffused with certainty.

'We see ourselves as alchemists of sorts. We're looking for the *soul* of these people. That helps us to understand the complex psychological forces which drive them.'

A guard opened a steel door at the end of the bridge. They entered the prison.

Morton turned to Dr Schmeissner. 'I've read everything in her file. But is there anything more I need to know?'

The Director smiled. 'Only that the change in her is genuine. A most remarkable thing is the way she's managed to adopt what our behaviourists call "a group ego". The very defence which made her so formidable as a terrorist has successfully transferred into her new life. She's among the most popular of all the inmates.'

They turned into a shorter corridor. Halfway along a guard stood outside a door. There was a spyhole set into the steel. Dr Schmeissner pressed his eye to the peephole. Then he stepped aside and motioned for Morton to look.

Standing at the window, she had her back to him. She was taller than he had expected, and wore a red cardigan over her blue smock. Her jet-black hair shone in the sunlight streaming through the window. Several leather armchairs stood against the walls. There was a table with a vase filled with real flowers.

Morton studied her for several minutes before turning to Dr Schmeissner.

'I'll go in alone.'

The Director nodded. 'Of course. I'll be in my office.'

Dr Schmeissner limped away as the guard opened the door. Morton walked into the room.

'Hello, Shema.'

Nadine's sister turned and looked at him.

*

In the bunker's broadcast studio, Raza continued to sit in front of the Voice Throw console.

It was still early morning in the Libyan desert and the air in the bunker was cool. But that was not the reason Nadine shivered slightly. It was because of the look on Raza's face. He had never seemed more terrifying.

Nadine watched his hand begin once more to move towards the console's keyboard and then stop. Then, after a little while, it started to move again, creeping this time towards the gadget he had taken from the Zionist pig in Athens.

During the flight to Libya and the drive from Tripoli airport, he had handled the little box as if it were a bomb. It stood now beside the console where he'd placed it an hour ago.

He had been exultant then, reading aloud to her the faxed messages from Faruk Kadumi and Rachid Harmoos confirming the Anthrax-B-C had arrived safely. Nothing, Raza had proclaimed, could now stop him. Nadine could not remember when he had been in such good humour. He had invited her to come to the studio and watch him open the gadget and learn its secrets so that he could use them against the Zionists.

Coming into the studio, a light had been blinking on the console. Cursing, he had run forward and feverishly begun to dial the transponder in Afghanistan. A terrible high-pitched noise began. When he realised what had happened, his scream had been more than one of fury, it was like an animal in terrible pain.

When she had moved to comfort him, he had pushed her aside.

Twice more Raza had dialled the number. Each time the studio was filled with a piercing continuous shrill.

Now, an hour later, his words still echoed in her ears. 'The transponder has been disconnected. Only the Russians, the Zionists and the CIA know how to do this.'

Fighting to control the shake in his hand, he had switched on the gadget. The message for Gabriel to call Ha-Zoafim had been replaced by one so completely unexpected that Raza had backed away from the apparatus as if it were the living embodiment of evil.

Nadine had run forward and turned it off.

Since then Raza had not spoken. He sat like a statue carved from the desert rock. Nadine saw his hands. They were once more edging towards the gadget. His lips were moving, but no words came.

'Don't!' she cried. 'It's a trick! It will tell the Zionists where you are!'

He turned and stared at her.

'I must know,' he whispered.

His eyes were narrowed to slits, making his face look lifeless. She had never seen him like this. It was as if all the demons of the night lived inside him.

Raza's hand reached the gadget. It was cold to the touch. His fingers began to move towards the switch.

'Please, don't,' Nadine implored.

He pressed the switch. The studio was filled with the same booming voice as before.

'Khalil Raza! We will find you wherever you are. And you will be destroyed.'

'Turn it off!' Nadine screamed. 'Turn it off!'

She began to sob as Raza picked up Costas' MRT and hurled it against the studio wall.

There was a moment's silence, then the warning began again.

Raza leapt across the floor, grabbed the receiver and switched it off. Staring at it fixedly, he finally managed to get his breathing under control.

'Stop crying,' he ordered sharply. 'There is nothing to be frightened of. The Zionists have found the body of their spy, so they know I have their gadget. It must be linked to that satellite of theirs over the Negev. But if they think their childish game of sending a message will frighten me, they are wrong!'

Nadine wiped her eyes. 'Maybe it is also a transmitter?'

Raza turned the receiver over in his hands, careful not to touch the switch.

'There is no transmit button. If it cannot transmit, it cannot tell the satellite where it is. So there is nothing to be afraid of.'

'Destroy it, please,' Nadine begged.

Raza glared at her. 'Don't be stupid. This is a weapon. Once I discover –'

The ring of the phone on the console startled Nadine. She picked up the handset, listened for a moment, then silently handed the phone to Raza. He put down the gadget beside the console.

This time the voice of Ayatollah Muzwaz dispensed with the traditional greeting.

'We are gravely disappointed over what has happened,' the mullah's precise, dehydrated voice began. 'We have lost much in Athens. And that is not all.'

Raza breathed deeply several times, trying to keep his voice calm.

'The Zionist spy had to be killed, O Magnificent One. But I learned much from him that will be of value to us. And everything is still going to plan –'

'Then why did your man in London not kill the deliverer as we agreed must be done –'

'But you are mistaken! I have received the confirmation!' Raza broke in.

The wheezy voice hardened. 'We have spoken to our trusted brother in London –'

'Then he is mistaken! I received the confirmation an hour ago!'

The old man's voice was like ice.

'Do not interrupt again. You will listen and show respect.'

Raza motioned Nadine away. He wanted no one to hear the way he was being spoken to. But he would not forget, or forgive, this humiliation. When the time came the Ayatollah would pay dearly.

The cold, remote voice once more addressed him. 'An hour ago our brother in London contacted us. He had just received a phone call from the deliverer explaining why only two bottles had arrived. We have ordered our brother to take care of the deliverer once the collectors have made the pick-up from the apartment. As they work for our brother, we foresee no mistake there.' The Ayatollah paused to give a chesty cough. 'You are absolutely certain this person we entrusted you to send to London has done his work – given that he has failed to carry out his other instruction?'

Raza gripped the phone with tense, nervous fingers.

'I will find out why he failed, O Magnificent One. Then I will deal with him, on my oath to you.' Once more he breathed slowly and deeply. 'But yes, I am certain he will have performed his other duties.'

Another crackly cough filled Raza's ears. 'Your assurance is noted. But there is another problem of which our most trusted and valued brother in the Land of the Great Satan has informed us.'

Raza felt his heart pounding in his chest. What had Harmoos said?

'I have received a message from him, O Magnificent One. He has assured me that his deliverer has been –'

'Yes, yes, yes!' the Ayatollah interrupted testily. 'He has informed us of that. The reason he called was because the chemist has turned out to be slow and incompetent and fearful of what he has to do.'

Raza grinned wolfishly. 'Then your trusted brother should dispose of him and replace him with someone else, O Magnificent One.'

'In the time left, it is seemingly not possible to find a suitable replacement. We have spoken here among ourselves and many of my colleagues feel it would be best to postpone –'

'No!' Raza cried. 'O Magnificent One, truly forgive me for interrupting. But to postpone would be a disaster. We are so close to victory. The bombings and the fate of the racists in South Africa have shown our enemies our strength. To postpone would only give them time to overcome their panic. Then it would be harder to achieve all we both want. I urge you, O Magnificent One, not to stop –'

'Then what do you propose?'

Raza looked at Nadine, as if he hoped to find something there. She stared back at him, her dark eyes frightened. He gripped the phone more tightly. When he spoke his voice was calm and confident.

'There's only one solution, O Magnificent One. It is that I go to the Land of the Great Satan. I will also arrange for my man in London to join me. When the work is finished, he will be dealt with, along with this other chemist. You have my oath on this.'

The silence stretched for several long moments before the Ayatollah spoke.

'Very well. Your solution is acceptable. But you must understand we now hold you, and you alone, directly responsible. Our trusted brother in the Land of the Great Satan will work under your orders. His men will be yours to command. But in the end it will be you who will have to account for every decision. But there must be no further mistakes. Is that absolutely clear?'

'Completely, O Magnificent One. I will make immediate arrangements.'

'May Allah bless you so that we can rejoice with you,' intoned the Ayatollah before breaking the connection.

Raza replaced the handset and turned to Nadine. Once more she saw not madness but absolute certainty that nothing could stop him succeeding.

Morton continued to hold Shema's gaze.

She sat upright in her armchair opposite him, her eyes level with his. The sunlight streaming through the window made her hair glisten like freshly cut coal as it fell to her shoulders in one sleek drop. Her face was petite and not classically beautiful, for her mouth was too big and her eyes a little too far apart. Their colour reminded him of ripening figs, dark brown and flecked with gold.

For an hour he had taken her through her life: what she'd told her German interrogators, the trial judge and all those who had questioned her since. He knew from his reading that she had answered him truthfully. Once in a while he had, however, sensed a nuance in her voice, a curiosity perhaps of who he was and why he was here.

Both times he had mentioned Nadine, Shema had looked at him quickly before giving her sister's date and place of birth and a physical description. He decided the time had come to once more deal with Nadine. From his pocket he produced the photo he had assembled in Athens.

'Is this your sister?' he asked, showing it to Shema.

'Yes. Where did you get it?'

'In Athens, yesterday. Do you recognise the other woman?'

'No.'

Morton put the photo back in his pocket.

They looked at each other silently for a long moment. When Morton resumed, his voice was relaxed; he had reached a watershed.

'Would your sister be close to Raza?'

'Close?' Shema echoed. 'What do you mean? He keeps every-one close to him. That's how he controls them.'

Morton acknowledged this truth with a nod of his head.

'Do you think Nadine could ever be like you, and see the truth for herself?' he asked in a slower, and more gentle voice.

'When you're with him that's very hard,' Shema replied with a wise and hopeless smile. 'He's very convincing.'

She folded her arms as if she needed to hug herself because she was suddenly cold.

'"Convincing",' he repeated, as if it was a serious admission. '"*Convincing*". If he was that convincing, why did you change your mind?'

'You know why.'

His eyes left her face.

'Tell me, Shema. Just tell me in your own words.'

His eyes were so fixedly upon her that she clasped herself even tighter.

'He is a liar,' she finally began. 'He talks of Palestine with passion. But he has no interest in reclaiming it. He only uses it as an excuse to wage war. He speaks of everything with passion. But the only passion he really has is for himself.'

He watched her face register the memory, and, as it did so, to cloud with anger. He bored in.

'He still wants to kill all those dirty little Jews who live in Palestine now.'

'Don't speak about Jews like that!' Shema snapped. 'We Arabs are not anti-Semitic. Only against what the Zionists do!'

Morton nodded, but she didn't speak.

'Did you sleep with Raza?' he abruptly enquired.

She looked at him steadily. 'He took who he wanted.'

He pressed a little harder: 'Including Nadine?'

She looked fiercely past him, to some hated spot on her own private horizon.

'Not when I was there. I kept her away from him.'

Morton thought about this for a long moment, not only study-ing her face, but also her body as a guide. He had willed her, cajoled her, lulled her, startled her and finally angered her to reach this stage. Everything she had said was the complete truth. It was there in the pain in her eyes and the tension in her body.

He glanced down at the file open on his knees, made a pretence of reading and then abruptly looked up.

'Do you know why I am here?'

She shook her head.

Swiftly, but missing out nothing, he told her about the hotel bombings, Trekfontein and the threat Raza had made to unleash the remainder of his Anthrax-B-C.

When he had finished, Shema stared at him, dazed. 'Who are you?' she asked finally.

'I am a Jew. An Israeli,' he said flatly. 'People call me Morton. Or David.'

She looked at him knowingly. 'You are – Mossad?'

'Yes.' Morton sensed the struggle in her.

'I am still an Arab. Aren't we all terrorists for you?'

'No.'

Morton waited, but she didn't speak. Yet there was a tacit acceptance in her silence. He leaned forward in his armchair, his eyes still never leaving hers.

He spoke in the softest of voices. 'We both want the same, for sure. The right of our peoples to live together in peace. The way it was, Shema.'

Shema sighed deeply. 'I cannot remember how it was.'

'Let me show you how it has become.' His voice had assumed a detached tone from which all emotion had been rigorously expunged.

He felt her almost tighten like a cord, saw her unfold her hands and clasp them around her knees. She looked at him with almost child-like curiosity.

Morton produced from his pocket the cassette player and the two tapes. He inserted one into the machine and pressed the play button.

Lila's voice began to repeat Raza's demands. When the tape ended, he removed it. Shema's face was taut and strained.

'Do you know this woman?' Morton's voice was deliberately dull.

Shema nodded. 'Her name is Lila. That is the only name I know her by. Raza never allows his women to use their family names.'

Morton looked unsurprised.

'What can you tell me about her?'

'She will always be totally committed to him. She has been with him from the very beginning. She was born to hate.'

'What does Lila look like?'

Shema described her. Then Morton inserted the second tape into the player and pressed the button.

Shema put her hand to her mouth and tears filled her eyes.

'Nadine,' she said in a strangled whisper. 'Nadine –'

Morton allowed the taped message demanding France release the *Feydeheen* to come to an end.

'Oh, Nadine,' Shema said again, and hugged her knees.

'Listen to me, very carefully,' Morton said, leaning forward. He stared into her face. 'Listen to me. That tape was also discovered in Athens yesterday. Raza was there. Your sister was with him, for sure.'

'You will kill her?'

'I know of no reason to kill your sister.'

'She is not like Lila. Lila is a hard woman. She has killed many people.'

'Murdered,' Morton corrected quietly.

'Yes, yes, murdered. She often worked with Al-Najaf. You know him?'

'I know him. But he will kill no more.'

She looked at him quickly. 'What do you want of me?' she asked.

He closed the file.

'Shema, I am here because I need your help. Raza has once more disappeared. We are looking everywhere. But there is no trace. I must stop him from carrying out his threat. I have now less than three full days to do so.'

She spoke at once. 'If my sister is with him, she could be killed as well?'

'That is always a risk, but there is a way to reduce it.'

'How?'

'By having you there with me.'

Shema gasped as if she had been struck. 'You are crazy! They will never let me go from here.' Her voice became hard. 'You are trying to trick me into helping you.' She stood up. 'I wish to return to my cell.'

'Sit down,' Morton said firmly. 'Sit down and listen to me. I don't have the time to argue.' He opened the file. 'Here, read,'

296

he commanded. 'You will be released to my care if you agree to help. These are your release papers.' He thrust the file at her. 'Read!'

Shema took the file. Her hands began to tremble as she turned the pages. She sat down, hardly believing.

'How?' she whispered. 'How could you arrange this?'

'Because Raza must be stopped,' Morton responded. 'And I need you to help do that.'

She handed him back the file.

'But Nadine, what will happen to her?'

'Nothing. Afterwards she will be free to go with you.'

Shema nodded at the file. 'It does not say so there.'

'No. But you have my word.'

Shema began to pace.

'You are asking me to betray those who were once my comrades. Some of them are with Raza only because they still believe his is the only way to achieve justice –'

'Shema, we have very little time,' Morton broke in.

She stopped and looked at him. 'They could all be killed. You must give me time to think.'

Morton spoke very slowly. 'How much time do you need, Shema?' He stood up, holding the file in one hand. 'A couple of hours – I can't give you more,' he said.

Shema studied his face. 'Very well.'

Morton looked at his watch. 'Two hours,' he repeated. Leaving the room, he found Dr Schmeissner waiting in the corridor with a mobile phone in his hand.

'Success?' he asked.

'Not quite.'

The Director thrust the phone at Morton. 'There is a call for you. Scotland Yard. They have been holding for fifteen minutes. I said to call back, but they said it was too important not to wait.'

Morton identified himself into the handset. He was asked to hold. Moments later the ACC was on the line.

'David, we've got three confirmed cases. A couple of schoolgirls and their mother. They're all in the National Infectious, and they're all in a bad way.'

Morton moved a little distance from Dr Schmeissner and the guard.

'Have you discovered a source?'

'The father brought back three of those bottles from Athens, Customs took two –'

'Why not all three?' Morton snapped.

'The Customs officer was one of those silly buggers who've become bolshie over the whole thing. He's –'

'What happened to the two bottles?'

'That's the other reason for calling. We've picked up the bloke we're almost certain stole them. A Lebanese named Arish. His flat is like an Aladdin's cave of stuff nicked from the airport. But we've got nothing on file about him. I've already faxed Finel his bare details in the hope his computers show something. My bet is Arish was chosen because he was clean. We've started contact tracing and squeezing him hard.'

'Good. How'd the father get those bottles?'

The ACC told him.

'Get on to Zak Constantine in Athens, Harry, and have him pull the airport apart. Tell him you want the name of every passenger who flew out of Athens around the same time as the girls' father. I take it he's in the clear?'

'Salt-of-the-earth type,' the ACC said. 'He's done everything he can to help us. We've got good descriptions of the sales girls.'

Morton described Nadine.

'That's one of them, absolutely,' the ACC confirmed. 'How'd you know?'

Morton told him Shema had identified her sister in the photo. Then he continued: 'Arish will have had a contact man. Could be somebody in one of the Arab embassies. He may be an Arab businessman, or just someone who Raza has an armlock on. When you've squeezed all you can out of Arish, let him go. With a bit of luck he'll take us where we want to go.'

The ACC hesitated. 'Supposing he bolts?'

'Have Wolfie or Michelle waiting outside when you're ready. They'll know what to do. And tell Percy West I don't expect to hear any more objections from him.'

He paused. 'Who's treating the mother and her girls?'

'Dr Cooper, an American, a woman.'

'They couldn't be in better hands,' Morton said, ending the call.

He made no effort to encourage Dr Schmeissner's attempts at conversation as they walked back to the Director's office to await Shema's decision.

24

Mattie came out of the safe room with a photograph of Muktar Sayeed. It had been enlarged by one of Danny's technicians in the portable darkroom he'd set up in Matti's bathroom. The man had worked from an original provided by the New York City bureau of the Department of Immigration. Its file contained the routine paperwork granting Muktar a work permit to drive for the Day-Nite Cab Company. It was the only official paperwork in the United States on Muktar.

A copy of the file had been transmitted to Tel Aviv. Lester Finel had identified Muktar as a bomb thrower of long standing in southern Lebanon. Two years ago Muktar had dropped out of sight.

The knowledge of who he was had triggered intensive enquiries. The FBI were contact tracing Muktar. Agents had visited his Queens apartment; nothing suspicious had been found. The freeway accident was being reviewed. The CIA had started the painstaking process of backtracking Muktar's movements from the time he arrived in the United States. The New York Police Department had deployed several teams of its best detectives to probe the city's Arab ghettos about him.

From Washington, Gates had asked for every scrap of information that would help him go back to the Federal judges and persuade them to grant a surveillance order on Harmoos. In the meantime Danny's specialists had the watch.

When Matti had told them how Muktar could be linked to the investigation, the news had brought quick, knowing smiles to the faces of the twenty men and women in the apartment.

Their long journey from Tel Aviv would not have been in vain. In their quiet, determined way, they had continued their business of casting an electronic net over everything Rachid Harmoos possessed in the United States.

This included his holdings on the West Coast – three companies in Silicon Valley making various kinds of microchips and a lens-grinding firm in Los Angeles – his oil refinery in Houston, a meat-packaging plant in Chicago and a paint manufacturer in Detroit. Surveillance teams were now parked outside each factory and office block.

For hours now the apartment had begun to fill with the murmured language of inputs and outputs, bytes and optimum cycles, of speech strengths and voice enhancers.

In the centre of the living-room, a technician with a headset with one earpiece and a throat pad microphone tested a circuit to a Swift Renovations van positioned near Harmoos Holdings, the world headquarters of the millionaire's operations, on 80th Street. Similarly equipped technicians were talking to teams outside Harmoos Trucking at Trenton, New Jersey; at Harmoos Foods in the Bronx; at Harmoos Air Charter at La Guardia; at the Harmoos Brokerage on Wall Street and at the Bank of Arab States on Fifth Avenue, in which Harmoos was the principal shareholder.

Two teams had been positioned near Sweetmont to begin in-depth surveillance on the Harmoos estate. The Swift's crew chief had called Matti an hour before and said it was turning out to be harder than he had foreseen to find a suitable base in the area.

Continuous satellite telephone links had been opened with the Concorde on the ground at Frankfurt, with Danny in Tel Aviv, and with the safe house in London.

In booths along the wall, technicians were beginning to spin the first intercepts back and forth. Promising snatches of conversation were being isolated and fed to their computer. It was programmed to select and determine what should be transmitted to Finel's computers.

The fax machines continually received updates from the CIA, FBI, Interpol and Scotland Yard. Most of the traffic was divided between the hunt for the hotel bombers and the bottles of Grecian Nights. There had been no signs of either.

From Athens, Zak Constantine had reported that his forensic scientists had established the glass was of a type commonly produced in Hong Kong. There, police had started checking every one of the colony's glass makers. Similar enquiries were under way around the Pacific Basin. There were over 20,000 manufacturers to check.

Despite all their efforts, Constantine's men had failed to discover any trace of Raza.

An hour ago, Miriam had telephoned Matti from City Center. Nancy's skin had begun to darken and the blister-like ulcers were spreading on her body. Miriam had sounded not only desperately tired but deeply apprehensive as she'd admitted she'd been wrong over Nancy's diagnosis. Miriam had started treating Nancy with the hospital's minute supply of PEG-enzyme. That would soon be gone and she was hunting for more.

Manufacturers of the drug had started a crash programme, but it would still be several days before the first supplies were available.

Matti had suggested she called the Pentagon. After the Gulf, they'd probably have a stockpile somewhere. He'd also asked again if he could speak to Nancy, and Miriam had said she'd call him back in an hour. By then Nancy should be responding to the drug.

Matti had phoned the Concorde, leaving a message with the CCO to inform Morton about Nancy now being a confirmed case of Anthrax-B-C.

The diagnosis of her condition had triggered a new hunt. Police and FBI teams had tracked down every passenger on Nancy's flight. Her widowed travelling companion remembered Nancy opening one of the perfume bottles. Shown a photocopy of the label, she'd immediately recognised it.

More detectives and agents had followed up travellers at Kennedy who'd seen Nancy attacked. There the trail had gone cold. No one could describe her attacker. Matti had gone on applying the art of informed conjecture.

Had it been no more than a coincidence that her bag had been snatched or was the theft deliberate? And how had the thief made good his escape? He could have lain low in one of the other terminals until the hunt was abandoned, but that seemed unlikely; snatchers liked to put as much distance as they could between their crime and pursuit. He may have had an accomplice waiting to drive him away. But the airport police had responded quickly to search outgoing vehicles. Matti had checked. Only cabs had not been stopped. Suppose the thief had got into a cab? Or suppose the thief was a cab driver? Muktar? The Connecticut Expressway was not far from Kennedy. But Muktar had been coming from the opposite direction when he was killed.

Matti had still been speculating when Miriam had phoned back to tell him to come over to the hospital.

Slipping Muktar's print into his wallet, Matti told the chief technician where he could be reached.

Twenty minutes later a cab dropped him at the Emergency Room entrance to City Center. Inside, the early morning rush was winding down; staff were preparing for a new day.

Matti could see Miriam in her office in the centre of the treatment area. The glass walled booth gave her a commanding view. She was hunched over her phone, listening and running her hand through her hair. He'd only seen her do that when she was really angry.

As Matti reached the door, Miriam stood up and began to wander around the booth, holding the receiver with one hand, continuing to ruffle her hair with the other.

'No! You listen to me, General Tuttle!' she suddenly exploded. 'Our labs have confirmed the diagnosis! To hell whether she's a civilian! Or your damned procedures. I just want more of this drug!'

Matti watched Miriam pause, then once more boil over.

'That's your final word, General?' she fumed. Miriam listened for a moment longer, then hung up. She turned to Matti, eyes smouldering.

'Damn him and his procedures,' she said, dropping into her chair.

She stared tiredly at Matti. 'The army's got a supply of PEG-enzyme stashed away in Maryland. But this knee-jerk general says the stuff can't be released to any old civilian doctor, treating any old civilian –'

'Who were you talking to?'

Miriam glanced at a pad on her desk. 'General Oliver Tuttle, Director Medical Supplies at the Pentagon. He's the top honcho –'

303

'Give me his number,' Matti said, reaching for the phone.

She hesitated for a moment then called out the number for Matti to dial.

The voice that answered sounded like a tug horn.

'General Tuttle, Director –'

'I know who you are, General. My name is Matti Talim,' Matti said.

There was a moment's hesitation. Then the horn was back.

'Who? Give me your rank and unit –'

'I'm a civilian, General. But I outrank you right now.'

'*What?*'

There was sudden steel to Matti's voice that Miriam had never heard before. 'You're on the distribution list for the Procedural Memo outlining the chain of field command in the present crisis. You will know I'm in command of the US end for Colonel Morton.'

'*Wait!*'

Matti heard the phone being put down, then the rustle of papers. The horn was back.

'I have you. So why are you calling me?'

'A few minutes ago you received a call from the Emergency Room Deputy Director at City Center asking for some of your PEG-emzyme –'

'I told her what I'll tell you. We've got procedures.'

'This is a crisis, General.'

'In a crisis, it's more important than ever to follow procedure!'

Matti preserved a moment of silence. When he spoke next his voice was almost sad. 'General, you ever hear of Operation Kick Ass?'

The horn blared. 'No. It sounds like something only a goddamed civilian would invent.'

'I just did. And you're just about to become the first to get his butt kicked out of his comfy little seat and sent to a place you never knew existed unless you get that PEG-enzyme down here!'

'Listen, you goddamed civilian! You're talking to a four-star general. In war I could have you taken out and –'

'We *are* at war, Tuttle!' Matti said with savage quietness. 'And you have just ten seconds to tell me you're sending that stuff, or I put down this phone. The next call you get will be your marching orders.'

'Talim! Damn you!' roared the horn.

Matti glanced at his watch. 'Eight seconds, General.'

Miriam stared at him wordlessly. There was a strangled noise in Matti's ear.

'The stuff will be there by noon –'

'Not good enough, General. Have it there by midmorning,' Matti said firmly.

'Goddam –'

'Five seconds, General.'

Midmorning,' the horn conceded.

'Thank you, General,' Matti acknowledged, putting down the phone.

Miriam continued to stare at him wordlessly. 'Jesus,' she finally said. 'Jesus Holy Christ.'

For the first time since he'd come into the office she smiled.

'How is Nancy?' Matti asked.

Miriam reached for the phone and dialled an internal number. She asked for a status report, listened, put down the phone and stood up.

'She's conscious again. Let's go.'

As they made their way to the highly restricted Medical Intensive Care Unit, Miriam explained, 'Once Nancy was rediagnosed, we cleared everyone out of the MICU. Luckily we've another two on the surgical floor, so we can manage. We're also running maximum contagion procedures.'

'I want to show her a photo,' Matti said, fishing out Muktar's print. 'If she recognises this as the guy who mugged her, we can cut a lot of corners.'

Miriam glanced at the print as she pushed open the double swing doors leading to the MICU.

'We'll have to wrap it in sterilised plastic,' she said.

They passed through a second set of doors into the MICU's changing area. Miriam handed Matti a sealed plastic packet and broke open a second one for herself. She wrapped the photo in the plastic, and then quickly put on the surgical gown, cap, mask and overshoes, then helped Matti don his. From a shelf she took down two face masks.

When Miriam had checked Matti's was secured, she led him into the MICU proper. Matti carried Muktar's print in his hand.

Halfway along the corridor was a red-panelled surgical trolley. Its lower shelf was filled with equipment.

'Our crash cart. It contains everything we'll ever need to deal with cardiac arrest,' Miriam said as they passed. Ahead was a horseshoe-shaped desk in the centre of the treatment area. It had a clear view of all the cubicles. A monitoring system built into the desk enabled the two nurses on duty to see immediately the vital function of any patient in the MICU.

Nancy occupied a cubicle to the left.

'After you've shown her the photo, keep your questions to the absolute minimum,' murmured Miriam as they moved towards it.

'Understood.'

Reaching the opening to the cubicle, they paused for a moment.

From one of the wall outlets extended a rubber pipe ending in plastic prongs taped to Nancy's nose, providing a controlled flow of oxygen. Electrodes ran from her chest to a heartbeat monitor on a stand beside the bed. The trace was weak but steady. Towering over the bed was a drip stand. A clear liquid trickled from a suspended bottle down a tube into a vein in Nancy's right arm.

'The last of the PEG-enzyme. Given like this, it's supposed to have a better chance,' Miriam explained walking to the bed. 'You're hanging in there, Nancy,' she said.

Nancy's ribcage rose and fell under the surgical gown. A cough racked her.

Matti stood at the foot of the bed. The physical change in Nancy was frightening. Her skin was the colour of charcoal, covered with weeping blisters. One had spread across her left eye, another grew out of a corner of her mouth. There was a necklace of blisters on her neck. Others were visible on her arms.

Miriam nodded for Matti to come forward. When he was standing beside her, she turned to Nancy.

'Nancy, Matti wants to show you a photo, okay?'

There was an almost imperceptible movement from Nancy's lips.

Matti held the print in front of Nancy's face. 'Do you recognise this man, Nancy?'

She stared at the photo.

'Is he the man who robbed you?' Matti asked. 'Just nod if he was, Nancy.'

Another cough racked her body. Suddenly, as Matti was about to speak, Miriam pulled him back.

'Code One!' Miriam yelled. 'Get out of the way, Matti!'

He saw the trace on the heart monitor was skipping beats and faltering. Code One was cardiac arrest.

Even as he stepped out of the cubicle, one of the nurses ran in to help Miriam. Moments later the other arrived with the crash cart.

The first nurse pressed a red button in the wall above the bed. It triggered a prepared tape to override all other announcements on the hospital's internal broadcast system. The announcement called for all available doctors to attend the medical emergency and gave its location.

Miriam had already disconnected Nancy from the monitoring equipment and was at the crash cart with the nurse. They were working swiftly and calmly. The other nurse had produced a stopwatch and had started to count aloud.

'Thirty seconds,' she called out, giving the elapsed time since the emergency had been declared. There were perhaps four minutes left, no more than six, in which Nancy could be resuscitated without permanent brain damage.

A second doctor had arrived and was inserting an airway deep down in Nancy's throat. The nurse with the stopwatch fitted a bag-like mask securely over Nancy's mouth and began to squeeze, forcing oxygen into Nancy.

'Forty-five seconds,' she reported.

Miriam scissored open Nancy's gown. The second doctor was at the crash cart, coating with contact paste the two paddle-shaped electrodes attached to the defibrillator. Then Miriam placed them on Nancy's chest, one just to the left of her right nipple, the other slightly above her left.

'Clear!' ordered Miriam, glancing to check the defibrillator was at maximum voltage.

As everyone around the bed stepped back, Miriam pressed down on both electrodes, touching a button on each. A measured shock passed through Nancy's heart. Miriam lifted the paddles clear. The defibrillator would require nine seconds to recharge itself.

Nancy's muscles went into spasm, her spine arched and her legs stiffened as the shock coursed through her body.

'One minute,' the nurse called out.

'Let's go again!' Miriam called.

She gave Nancy a second electrical shock, waited another nine seconds, then delivered a third. Nancy spasmed, then sank back, limp and lifeless. A fourth shock. No change.

'Again!' ordered Miriam.

No change.

'Again!'

Still no change.

Two more shocks. Then Miriam turned to the others.

'We've lost her.'

She gently pressed closed Nancy's eyes.

The other doctors followed her out of the room. They looked curiously at Matti. Miriam picked up a phone on the desk and called the hospital pathologist. Then she walked over to Matti.

'We'll run an autopsy at once,' she said. 'It'll give us a better idea how this thing breaks down the body's defence.'

In the cubicle the nurses finished reloading the crash cart. They wheeled it away, then returned to the cubicle with a sheet, which they draped over Nancy. They wheeled the bed out of the cubicle to a side room near the changing area.

In silence Matti and Miriam stripped off their protective clothing and left the MICU.

'Nancy was always going to be a tough call,' Matti said as they walked towards the door of the Emergency Room.

Miriam shook her head. 'I should have started her earlier on the PEG-enzyme.'

Matti took her by the shoulders. 'You're too hard on yourself, Miriam.'

She looked at him. He held her close to him and buried his face in her hair.

'I really love you,' she murmured.

'Love you too.'

She pulled away. 'I'd better get that autopsy moving.'

'Talk to you later.'

'Call me at home,' Miriam said, walking down a corridor.

She raised a hand but didn't look back. He watched her go, then he too left the Emergency Room. He decided to pick up his car and ride out to Kennedy to pick up Lou, who was due in Washington. Afterwards Matti would show Muktar's photo around the airport. He knew that realistically he'd have as much hope of turning up someone who'd recognise the face as Nancy had had of living.

25

Exactly two hours after closing it behind him, Morton opened the cell door. Shema was standing with her back to the window. He stood in the doorway. They stared at each other wordlessly.

'Well?' Morton finally asked.

Shema remained silent for a moment longer. When she spoke her voice was low but determined.

'I will help you.'

They both smiled, though not at each other.

'Thank you,' Morton said in a formal voice, walking into the room. He continued to hold her gaze as he asked, 'Where is Raza, Shema?'

'Libya.'

'Where in Libya?'

She told him. When she had done so, he did not hesitate.

'Good. Let's go.'

Morton turned and she followed him from the cell. Fifteen minutes later, dressed in the clothes she had worn at her trial, Shema sat beside Morton in the back of the government car.

Once the car had left the prison, Morton did not relax for a moment, nor did he allow Shema even half a breathing space between questions.

He first made her describe the layout of the base, then the villa, then each bunker in turn. He took her through the dawn to dusk routine and then the dusk to dawn routine. He paid particular attention to time: sleeping times, parade times, meal times and guard-changing times.

Once in a while she faltered, as if the images inside her head were hazy. She would close her eyes tightly as if to concentrate better. Then she would open her eyes and continue in that same calm and controlled voice that pleased him.

Occasionally he would interject: 'You are certain?'

Her response was always the same. A firm nod, followed by amplification of what she had just said.

As the car swept around a curve in the autobahn, Morton returned to the question of Raza's habits.

'When does he go to bed?'

'Not later than midnight.'

'Does he lock the bedroom door?'

'No. No one would dare go in.'

'Does he sleep alone?'

'Almost never.'

'Which side of the bed does he sleep on?'

'By the window. He likes to see the first light.'

'Describe the room.'

His eyes never left her as she described in turn each item of furniture. Then the relentless questions resumed.

'Does he keep a gun in bed?'

'He used to keep a pistol under his pillow. There was also a Kalashnikov under the bed. He also kept a box of hand grenades in the dressing-table.'

The chauffeur accelerated the Mercedes past a convoy of juggernauts.

'Hand grenades?' Morton repeated.

'Yes. He made them. He's very good at that.'

'In which drawer?'

Shema shook her head. 'I can't remember. Maybe the second.'

'How many drawers are there?'

'Four.' She closed her eyes for a moment. 'No, three,' she said, opening her eyes.

'Good. Now his office . . .'

Room by room he took her through the villa, insisting she described the painting of Beirut on the dining-room wall, the dark furniture and leather chairs. Nothing was too small or insignificant for him not to want to know about.

'The floor,' he asked suddenly, 'what is it covered with?'

'Rugs. He collects them. Sometimes he lies them one on top of the other.'

311

He nodded, as if this was the most natural thing to do with rugs.

'Now the night guards,' he continued. 'Let's go over them again . . .'

Working inwards from the perimeter he made her repeat everything she knew about the mobile patrols and stationary sentries on each bunker and in the villa.

She was describing the layout of the parade ground when the car swung off the autobahn and entered the Frankfurt airport perimeter. Minutes later, the Mercedes parked beside the Concorde.

Shema followed Morton up the steps. The CCO and the flight purser were waiting in the hatchway. Morton handed Shema over to the crewman, and went to the flight deck to tell the captain to prepare for immediate takeoff for London. He then went to the communications centre.

'Hook up to Tel Aviv,' Morton ordered the CCO. 'I want the Prime Minister, army and air force chiefs and their operational planners. Call Danny and tell him to use the War Room.'

Morton settled in his seat as he continued to issue instructions.

'Hold any incoming traffic unless it's Lacouste or a direct sighting of Raza. While you're hooking up you can screen my messages.'

The six-inch monitor on his right began to fill with summaries of incoming calls.

Yertzin had confirmed the transponder would shortly be en route out of Kabul for Tel Aviv on a Soviet Tupolev bomber. Finel had drawn a blank with Asian contacts for Raza. Lacouste had phoned: the French Cabinet was still huddling. Gates had called: he was putting more men into Colombia. The FBI reported no one fitting Lila's description was on their computers. US Immigration had circulated her description to every entry point to the United States. Wolfie had left news that both the Hardiman children and their mother had died. Post-mortems confirmed Anthrax-B-C was the cause in each case. The bottle had been safely recovered by an anticontamination team, who fumigated the school. Miraculously, no one else had touched it. Matti had called with news of Nancy Carson's death. Bitburg had called, twice, asking for an update.

'Thirty seconds to hook-up,' the CCO called.

Morton pressed a button and cleared the screen of messages.

The Concorde had already rolled out to the edge of the runway. There was a short pause, then the plane was hurtling over the tarmac. As it banked to the north, onto the screen came a wide-angle view of the War Room in Tel Aviv.

Half a dozen men were grouped on either side of Karshov. Flanking the Prime Minister was the air force chief and the army chief. Danny sat beside him. Bitburg had positioned himself immediately behind Karshov. Behind the principals were their aides: young, solemn faced; today's note takers learning to be tomorrow's decision makers.

There was a quick exchange of shaloms, then one of several cameras fixed-positioned in the War Room zoomed in on Karshov.

'We are all here, David,' the Prime Minister said. 'And listening.'

Morton stared steadily at the small camera mounted above the screen. The camera was transmitting his image via satellite to Tel Aviv.

'Raza has a secret base in Libya. Almost certainly that was where he planned the entire operation,' he began matter-of-factly. 'There is every chance he is there now. I propose therefore that we destroy the camp.'

There was a collective gasp in the War Room, followed by mouth-to-ear whispering. Bitburg's eyes had started to dance as he leaned forward and said something to Karshov. The Prime Minister waved for silence around him, then he hunched forward and gave a short, mirthless laugh.

'Attack Libya, David? Please God, I assume you've thought of the consequences? For us. For the whole world.'

'It's the one chance to nail Raza and his people,' Morton said steadily.

Bitburg had thrust his face between Karshov and the air force chief.

'Excuse me,' Bitburg said, 'excuse me, how do you know Raza is there? This entire area was grid-searched by our own satellites and the Americans. Nothing showed except a few Bedouin and their camels.'

'Apart from his villa, the entire base is buried in the sands.

And satellites are not infallible, Walter. We saw that in the Gulf,' answered Morton.

The lantern-jawed face of the air force chief glanced at Bitburg.

'I could organise a surveillance run that'll guarantee to show any stubble on Raza's face!'

'If he's there,' Bitburg said quickly. 'That's the thing, Moeshe. Is he there?'

'We'll only know when we go in, for sure,' Morton said. 'But everything I've learned points to his being there. The way he could slip in and out of Athens. Libya was the perfect launch pad to send that woman to Trekfontein and for his hotel bombers.'

'Can we know the source of your information, David?' Bitburg asked.

'You'll get a report, Walter.'

'Let's not waste time,' Karshov rumbled. 'We wouldn't be here unless David thought the information was solid.'

In the War Room, Danny looked up from a pad he had been scribbling on.

'Libya would give Raza maximum efficiency for his Voice Throw box.'

Karshov looked about him. A dark stubble emphasised the scar tissue on his face.

'That still leaves the basic problem. Libya. We attack without perfect cause and we'll be hammered by what passes for the civilised world,' Karshov said heavily. 'We wouldn't have a pretzel's chance at a wedding of convincing anyone that we were different from Raza.'

Bitburg was nodding vigorously as Morton spoke.

'I propose we let the Supreme Leader know what we are going to do, Prime Minister.'

This time the collective gasp from the War Room was reinforced by those from the technicians around Morton. He stared fixedly into the camera.

'You want that I call the Supreme Leader and say we are going to bomb the shit out of a piece of his desert, David? Is that what you're suggesting?' Karshov demanded.

'You don't call him, Prime Minister. His friends do, in Damascus, Algiers and Tunis,' Morton said. 'Our allies persuade them to call him –'

Bitburg's head craned even further forward.

'Which allies, David?'

'The French. The Germans. They've always managed to keep a line open to Tripoli. They'll see some advantage in playing messenger. All they have to do is say the same thing: that Raza must somehow have sneaked into Libya without the Supreme Leader knowing. Play up your point. That our satellites failed to spot anything. Tell the Supreme Leader no one is blaming him.'

Karshov had begun to nod. When Bitburg tried to whisper in his ear, the Prime Minister waved him away.

Morton continued: 'Everyone gives the Supreme Leader an identical line – that no one expects him to use his own forces to deal with Raza, given his stated position that Arab must never fight Arab. But equally, here is an opportunity for him to establish himself to his peers, and to the rest of the world, as the one Arab who takes the long view.' Morton gave a little smile. 'Maybe Appleton should call him. He seems to have time on his hands right now.'

Karshov's chuckle sounded like distant thunder.

'I heard you called the President, David.'

'It was necessary.'

'That's what I told him.' For a moment Karshov paused. 'It could work, David. The Supreme Leader's enough of an egoist and pragmatist to see he can come out smelling sweet. And the world *will* applaud him. The way they used to applaud Saddam for standing up to Iran. Or Hitler for confronting communism in the thirties. One of the wondrous things about the human race is its ability always to look for the good in evil.'

He paused and turned. One of the aides was thrusting a piece of paper forward. Behind Morton, the CCO was listening on a phone and writing furiously on a message pad. The paper reached the Prime Minister at the same time that the CCO took the sheet off the pad and thrust it into Morton's hand. He scanned the words and looked up.

'You've heard?' Karshov asked.

'Lacouste just told me.'

'Damn the French!' Karshov roared. 'Damn them, damn them, damn them!' He looked around him. 'The French', he continued, 'have decided to release the *Feydeheen*. They've asked to go to Tripoli, and Libya's agreed to accept them on

315

humanitarian grounds. The French are flying them out, courtesy of Air France, on their flagship 747.'

The stunned silence in the War Room was broken by the air force chief.

'We can't just sit back and let those terrorists fly away like this! In a week they'll be back on the West Bank killing our people. I can have our planes intercept that 747 long before it is in Libyan air space.'

Morton remembered the air force chief had been a good pilot. But he should never have been given a job that needed more than looking through cross hairs.

The army chief turned to Karshov. 'Better yet, we bring them here and put them on trial. They've all got outstanding indictments. And we've done it before!'

Morton shifted in his seat. 'That time we only had to deflect one DC-3 passing on the edge of our air space, Sol. We're talking here of forcing an Air France 747 to fly half the length of the Med. We'd probably have to fight the entire French air force if we did that.'

The army chief glanced belligerently into the camera. 'So what are you suggesting?'

'That we let them go. All the way to the camp. We deal with them there,' Morton said.

There was complete silence in the War Room.

'When?' Karshov finally asked.

'The early hours of tomorrow morning,' Morton said.

'Tell us, what do you need?' the Prime Minister asked, this time not pausing.

Morton began to tell him as the Concorde came up to the English Channel.

The ACC had provided the van. With it came a driver, and the technician squeezed in the back with Wolfie and Michelle. The van continued to move through the streets around Paddington Green police station, where Saleem Arish was being questioned by Scotland Yard Antiterrorist Squad officers.

'I don't know how you people survive,' said the technician. He was a young man with a ponytail, denim jacket and granny glasses. He squatted on a stool bolted to the floor.

'You get used to it,' Wolfie said. He had wedged himself between two oscilloscopes and had his hands clasped around his knees.

'They're not *all* out to kill us,' Michelle added. 'Just most of them.'

She was sitting cross-legged on the floor, beside the matt black box for tracing telephone calls. Its face was covered with quivering dials.

'I did a spell in Hong Kong,' said the technician, his eyes on a monitor bolted to the wall of the van. 'I had the same feeling. Arabs, Chinese, they're all the same. Bloody foreigners.'

The screen displayed the location and number of every public phone box within a mile radius of the police station.

'Our Johnnie will probably walk a bit,' the technician said after a while. 'They always like to get a little distance between themselves and the nick.'

The van paused at traffic lights, then continued its slow progress through the streets of west London. Outside it was beginning to rain.

It was already raining in Mexico City when the Aeromexico 737 from Medellín landed. Thirty minutes later Raza had cleared formalities and was being driven to a cartel safe house overlooking the Plaza of Three Cultures.

The apartment was spacious and airy, and staffed with a housekeeper and manservant who greeted him gravely.

The man handed Raza a leather folder. 'Your messages, Senhor.'

He led Raza to the library, while the housekeeper carried his suitcase to the bedroom. She returned shortly afterwards with a pitcher of freshly squeezed lime juice and a plate of bitter chocolate biscuits. His every whim had been remembered from the last time he had stayed here.

She poured him a glass.

'Go.' He waved them away. 'I will call if I need anything.'

The couple bowed and withdrew. Sipping, he opened the file and began to scan the messages.

The top one was from the Ayatollah, reporting the French had capitulated. Marcel Bolot, the cartel's contact man in France, had faxed from Paris confirmation the *Feydeheen* would be back in Libya by midnight. Once more the Corsican had shown he had pipelines everywhere.

Nuri had phoned to say Lila had arrived in Sweetmont.

Nadine had faxed to report she was unable to contact Faruk Kadumi in London. There had been no reply to her phone calls or an acknowledgement to the fax she had sent instructing him to fly to New York once his business was finished in London.

Frowning, Raza picked up the phone and dialled the London number. He let it ring for a full minute, then replaced the receiver.

Matti eased the Lincoln Tour car into lane for the Sweetmont exit while Lou riffled through a collection of business cards in a leather case. He squinted at one.

'Ossie Oakes. Agent for steel bands,' he read aloud. 'Where'd you come across him?'

'Miami,' Matti said.

'You know anything about representing steel bands?'

'No. But I like the music.'

Lou shook his head and continued his riffling.

At Kennedy, they'd been insurance company loss adjusters finalising the claim on Muktar Sayeed's cab. They'd shown his photo up and down the cab lines and asked if anyone had remembered seeing him at the airport on the day he'd died. No one had.

'How about the Sure-Grip Tire Company?' asked Lou, extracting a couple of business cards.

'Perfect,' Matti said. 'They're having a hard time. It would be natural for them to want to check on a double blowout.'

'But suppose Day-Nite don't use their tyres?'

'I already checked. They do.'

Lou shook his head again.

Thirty minutes later they found the turning to the Harmoos estate. They showed their cards to the guard on duty in the hut and then parked in front of the mansion.

'Imitation Gone with the Wind,' murmured Lou.

'Looks like he transplanted the White House,' Matti said as they walked towards the front door.

'Bet you everybody says that,' Lou grinned as he pressed the bell.

The door was opened by a maid. Her eyes were dull black and tired. Her body beneath the uniform thickening. Matti had seen belly-dancers go like that after retiring.

'Yes. What you wish?'

Matti decided the accented English was Algerian.

'We'd like to speak to Mr Harmoos, ma'am,' he said, showing her his card, and briefly explaining the purpose of their call.

The maid hesitated.

'He's not here.'

'When's he due back?' Lou asked.

'Who are you?' Nuri demanded as he came around the side of the mansion.

He held a rifle casually in one hand, the way Matti had seen *Feydeheen* hold a weapon. Brusquely he told the maid in Arabic to return to her work.

He put out his hand. 'Your ID.'

Nuri reinforced the demand with a deliberate motion of the rifle. He inspected their cards in turn.

'This matter is over,' he said.

'We'd just like to ask a few questions,' Matti explained. 'How long the tyres had been on Mr Sayeed's cab, service checks, that kind of thing.'

'It'll only take a few minutes,' Lou added.

Nuri hesitated. Mr Harmoos had said no one was to be allowed into the house when Ismail and Lila were here. But they were in the basement, in the makeshift laboratory. And Mr Harmoos would not be back from Florida for another day. Better to answer the questions of these infidels now than have them return when he was here.

'Nice gun,' Matti said, nodding at the rifle.

'I like to shoot. Many wood chucks here,' Nuri said shortly.

He motioned them forward with the rifle. The gesture, Matti decided, was half reluctance, half anger.

They stood in the mansion's hallway. Bronzed heads on marble plinths and several hand-painted urns were positioned on the carpet. Doors led off to other parts of the house.

'We need to establish that what happened to Mr Sayeed's car was not a manufacturer's fault,' Matti began.

'It was an accident,' Nuri said dismissively. 'Come.'

He laid the rifle against a wall and led them into the study of Rachid Harmoos. Matti looked about him appraisingly at the fine leather-bound books and the paintings.

'Quite a collector, Mr Harmoos,' Matti said, his voice filled with proper respect.

'Yes,' Nuri grunted. He went to the desk and picked up a folder.

'The report of the accident. Mr Harmoos likes to see everything.' He opened the file and began to read rapidly. He looked up. 'The tyres were fitted two months before the accident. They were checked at five hundred, then a thousand miles. The cab was serviced a week before Sayeed died.'

He closed the file. 'A tragedy. The police say all is okay.'

Matti nodded pleasantly. 'It certainly looks like it.'

'Thanks for your help,' Lou added.

Nuri led them out of the study.

Matti smiled at a woman standing in the hall. 'Good-day ma'am,' he said politely.

Lila looked at them, but said nothing.

Neither Matti nor Lou spoke until they were clear of the estate and heading towards the expressway.

'I'd have liked to break that pop gun over his head,' Lou finally said.

'Harmoos keeps a regular little army,' Matti responded. 'As well as the guy in the hut, I spotted six more in the trees. Plus what's probably in the house.'

They drove a while more in silence.

'What you make of the woman?' asked Lou.

'Bad, as in evil.'

They drove past a Swift Renovations truck parked off the road. The man behind the wheel appeared to be asleep.

'She looked more Italian than Arab,' Lou said, glancing at the truck.

'She's Arab, right enough. And you only get those eyes when you've done your share of killing.'

He reached for the car phone. 'I'll call the truck and give them a description.'

*

'He's coming,' said the technician to Wolfie and Michelle.

'I have him visually,' called out the driver.

The van slowly passed the entrance to Paddington Green police station as Saleem Arish emerged.

The technician was all business, checking dials and switches and plugging in cords. He handed Wolfie and Michelle headsets with lip microphones.

'The ACC wants you,' he said.

'Our Johnnie's crossing the street,' reported the driver. 'And passed his first phone box.'

The ACC's voice filled the headsets. 'He's a tough bugger. Cocky as hell. All he'd admit to was a little pilfering. But totally denied anything about the bottles. We'd bailed him on a holding charge. Receiving stolen property. Once you're finished, we'll throw the book at him.'

'Fine,' acknowledged Wolfie.

'Looks like he's trying to find a cab,' said the driver.

Michelle swore quickly in French.

'No, hold it. He's decided to walk.'

The technician glanced at the screen.

'There's a phone box at the end of the street.'

The van driver passed Arish.

The technician started to punch buttons on the console, whistling softly and tunelessly.

Wolfie and Michelle watched the dials quiver and then steady.

The van parked fifty yards beyond the phone box. The driver got out and walked into a newsagents. He seemed in no hurry. He returned with a packet of cigarettes.

'He's in the box,' he reported, getting back into the van.

'I have him dialling,' the technician said.

He pressed a switch on a reel-to-reel recorder on the floor beside him. The tape began to revolve. Through their headsets, Wolfie and Michelle heard the sound of the digits being dialled by Arish.

'An 081 call. Harrow area,' murmured the technician into his lip mike.

'Zero-eight-one,' came the acknowledgement through the headsets. 'Locking on now.'

In a room above an army recruiting centre in north London that they had made their headquarters, the GCHQ technicians were using their equipment to trace the call.

The phone was ringing.

'Hello,' said a soft voice in the headsets.

'Effendi?'

'Saleem! Where are you?'

'The pigs arrested me.'

In the van the reel recorded the silence.

'Why did they let you go?'

There was a moment of laughter in the headsets. 'Because I told them nothing.'

'What did they want to know?'

'About the bottles. I have to go to court in the morning. But I told them nothing, Effendi –'

'Listen. You remember that address I gave you?'

'The apartment block?'

'Yes. Go there. I will speak to you there.'

'Effendi, I told them nothing.'

'I understand. Just do what I say.'

The click of Effendi hanging up was amplified by the recorder.

Moments later the driver called out. 'He's got a cab, going the other way!'

The van surged into the street, turning against the traffic as it did so.

'Oh, Christ!' the driver shouted.

His braking was sufficiently violent to send Michelle and Wolfie pitching into the technician. Then the van stopped, its bonnet only inches from a delivery truck.

In the time it took the driver to reverse, the taxi with Arish had disappeared.

Her coughing awoke Miriam. It had not been there when she'd finally drifted into sleep. Her whole body ached when she turned to look at the bedside clock. She'd managed to doze for two hours.

The drawn blinds bathed the bedroom in a soft light, soaking into the walls, touching each piece of furniture.

Miriam felt thirsty but cold. She wished Matti was here. When she'd called his apartment, a strange man had answered and said he wasn't available. She'd left her name, and said it was important Matti should call.

She wanted to tell him about Nancy's autopsy. The Anthrax-B-C had destroyed her vital organs, infiltrating lungs, liver and kidneys. Miriam had seen nothing like it before.

The pathologist had been so shaken that when he'd been siphoning out Nancy's blood, the tube had slipped in his hand and blood had spumed out of the high-speed suction pump. Miriam was certain they'd both stepped back from the tube without any blood touching them. Nevertheless, they'd stopped and gone to the scrub room, changed their gowns and face masks and once more scrubbed up with a germicidal solution. After they'd put on fresh sterile clothes, the pathologist had sprayed the area around the table with more germicide.

Miriam brought a hand to her throat. It was sore and the skin felt rough. She managed to stagger to the bathroom. She inspected her neck in the cabinet mirror. There was a blister on her neck.

'Oh, sweet Jesus!' she groaned, staggering back to the bedroom.

As she reached for the phone a great cough rose up from her chest, forcing a trickle of blood out of her mouth. She collapsed on the bed, too ill to notice she had dislodged the receiver from its cradle.

In the apartment's living-room, Faruk Kadumi continued to stare at the fax machine. In his mind it had become a symbol of the growing terror that gripped him.

Every time the machine had rung, it was to deliver another unnerving message. First there had been the order from Raza's woman instructing him to fly to New York as soon as possible. He had ignored her demand to acknowledge, completely convinced now that the machine was under surveillance. His belief had been fuelled when the police had once more knocked on the apartment's door. Since then the telephone had rung repeatedly. But he had been too frightened to answer.

The fax had delivered a second message ordering him to fly to New York. He had been instructed to send his flight details to Nadine. The message was signed 'Ahmed'. It was Raza's pseudonym.

Faruk Kadumi had also torn that paper into pieces and flushed them down the toilet. The phone had continued its intermittent ringing; the noise further fraying his nerves.

Now the fax machine had been activated again. He watched the paper begin to emerge and, even from across the room, he recognised the neat, handwritten Arabic. He waited until the transmission was complete before walking over and tearing off the sheet.

Faruk Kadumi had begun to tremble as he read the words aloud, as if somehow their awful portent would be lessened.

' "The deliverer will call shortly", ' he murmured, ' "and you will deliver him without fail in the name of Allah. The rest will be taken care of after you have left this land of the enemies of God".'

Once more the phone was ringing.

Coming into the city, Matti called Miriam's number on the car phone again. It was still busy. He came to a decision.

'I'm going to stop by,' he told Lou.

Fifteen minutes later Matti parked outside the apartment block on the corner of 51st and Third. Ten blocks over rose the tower of City Center.

Miriam had given him a key a couple of months after they'd started dating. He'd sometimes come over and cook dinner on those nights they decided to sleep in her bed.

Opening her front door, Matti stepped into a small hall completely covered with black and white prints. They overlapped each other and scenes on the ceiling ran on down the walls. The prints stuck to the floor were covered with a clear fixative to protect them.

'Miriam?' Matti called, poking his head into the living-room. Its ivy-patterned wallpaper and matching cushions she called her civilised jungle look. A breeze ruffled the drapes.

Matti crossed the room to the bedroom door and pushed it open. He blinked quickly to adjust to the gloom.

Miriam lay sprawled face down on the bed.

'Miriam,' he whispered, 'you asleep?'

She groaned. He switched on the top light and saw the blood dribbling from her mouth. Saw that, and the sores on her neck.

'Matti . . . can't breathe,' she gasped. A deep cough began to work its way up through her body.

'Don't talk,' he begged, reaching for the phone. He dialled City Center and told the operator whom he was calling about, and why. She said an ambulance was on its way.

Twenty minutes later Matti was running to keep up with Miriam's stretcher as it was propelled through the Emergency Room in a tight group of nurses and doctors. One held an oxygen mask over Miriam's face. Another a pole supporting the inverted plastic bottle and tube inserted in her vein.

'The Pentagon delivery means we have enough PEG-enzyme to treat her,' said the Emergency Room Director.

'Anyone else down?' Matti asked.

'The pathologist.'

'On the Nancy Carson autopsy?'

The Director squinted at him. 'Yeah. How'd you know that?'

'Miriam told me about Nancy.'

The stretcher swung through the doors leading to the MICU.

'I've already had Necropsy sealed off. The army's sending a decontamination squad,' the Director said.

They reached the MICU's door. The Director turned to Matti. 'Sorry, this is as far as you go.'

The MICU's doors opened and closed on Miriam.

The phone had stopped ringing. But the silence in the apartment had only increased Faruk Kadumi's nervousness. He had packed his bags and placed them in the hall, clear of the letterbox so that no prying eyes would see them. Then he had taken the Browning from the cupboard and screwed on the silencer. He had shoved the gun in his waistband, and sat down in the living-room to wait. In the past few minutes he had sniffed the last of the ether. It had not really helped.

He tried to remember what the small-arms instructor at the training camp had said about taking a firm grip, tensing your calf muscles and always aiming with both eyes open. The man had never said anything about how silent was a silencer.

When it came, the knock on the apartment door was soft and hesitant.

Faruk Kadumi could feel the last effect of the ether disappearing. He stood up and walked to the door. The knocking came once more, this time accompanied by a low urgent voice.

'Effendi has sent me.'

Faruk Kadumi opened the door. Saleem Arish brushed quickly past, closing the door behind him. He stood uncertainly in the hallway.

'Has Effendi phoned?'

'No.'

'He will phone.' Arish peered at the luggage. 'You are going away?'

'Yes.'

Arish sighed. 'I wish I could.'

He walked into the living-room, glancing around, then going to the window.

'A nice place.'

Arish turned from the window. He stood, stupefied.

Faruk Kadumi remained in the doorway, holding the pistol in both hands.

'Come away from the window,' Faruk Kadumi said.

Arish's mouth worked, but no words came.

'Move!' Faruk Kadumi said more sharply.

'Why?' Arish managed to ask. 'Effendi will make you –'

'Move.'

Arish began to walk towards Faruk Kadumi, hands extended as if in supplication. Faruk Kadumi retreated into the hall. Arish advanced, his eyes darting. He stood in the doorway.

'Turn around!' ordered the gunman.

'Please, no –'

'Turn around!'

Arish did as he was ordered.

'Please,' he whispered. 'I have money. Much money . . .'

Faruk Kadumi moved forward and placed the silencer against the back of Arish's head. He pulled the trigger. There was a small sound. Then Arish fell to the carpet. He made no other movement.

Faruk Kadumi stepped over the body, went to the kitchen and replaced the gun in the cupboard. Next he lifted the lid of the freezer. The neat rows of vials were frozen solid. Thawed, they

326

would be enough to cause a terror that would compensate for the fear he had felt since coming to this land of infidels. He closed the lid.

Then, once more stepping over Arish, he returned to the hall and picked up his bags. He paused to listen at the door, then released the catch and stepped outside. He closed the door behind him and walked to the lift. Moments later he had reached the street and hailed a cab to take him to Heathrow.

26

The safe house in Foley Street had been transformed by the time Morton and Shema arrived from Northolt in the ACC's car.

The half-dozen technicians Morton had requested from the London Embassy had arrived and established communication lines with the US navy headquarters in Ruislip, in the western suburbs, with Sixth Fleet HQ in Naples, and with the department of the navy in Washington. Since Wolfie and Michelle had returned, a link had been established with the GCHQ technicians in north London and their headquarters in Cheltenham. A separate radio link had been established with the USS *Independence*. The carrier was presently moving at full speed towards the coast of Libya. There were also permanently open lines to Danny in Tel Aviv, and with Matti's apartment.

The atmosphere was one of determined swiftness. Men spoke cryptically into telephones as they evaluated or conveyed information.

During the drive, the ACC had questioned Shema about the hotel bombers. She had given him names and descriptions, which he had called in to the Yard. Now, in a corner of the apartment, he continued to probe her, this time about Raza's sleeper agents in Britain.

'He'll need a network to distribute this anthrax,' the ACC said. He sounded nervous and depleted.

Shema looked at Morton.

He included them both in his sudden smile; to assure the ACC that he understood about his tensions, to reassure Shema he knew she would go on doing her best.

'Many of them are students,' she began. 'They are usually paid by the cabal. They mostly come to learn the language.'

The ACC broke off to pick up a phone. He gave an order to begin checking every language school in the country for Arab students – yes, *every* Arab. He rang off and turned back to Shema.

'How about safe houses?' he asked. 'Flats, a room above a shop? Anywhere?'

Shema frowned. 'I only came to London once.'

'Where did you stay?'

'The Regent Palace.'

The ACC did not bother to hide his frustration.

Shema closed her eyes. 'Wait. There's a place . . . I remember . . . it was on the road to the airport. When I left for Geneva, I stopped there to collect an envelope . . .'

Shema opened her eyes and looked at Morton.

'I am sorry, David. I cannot remember the name of the road.'

'Was it a main road?' the ACC pressed. He glanced at Morton. 'The chances are the safe house is still there.' He turned back to Shema. 'Can you remember what it looked like inside? A piece of furniture? Wallpaper or curtains?'

Shema shook her head. 'I cannot remember.'

The ACC breathed out heavily. 'Damn it, we're depending on you!' he said, his voice rising. 'There could be hundreds of thousands of people out there about to die.'

'I am trying to remember,' Shema said quietly.

'Then try harder!' the ACC snapped. 'There's someone out there with enough poison to turn this city into a wasteland. I want him caught before he does!'

'We all want him, Harry, for sure,' Morton said gently.

The ACC blinked his eyes tiredly as he looked at Shema. 'Sorry.'

'You're doing fine, Shema,' Morton said. Wolfie was standing beside a technician and waving at him.

'It's the GCHQ people,' he explained when Morton strode over. 'They've located Effendi's number. It's an apartment in Harrow-on-the-Hill. They've surrounded it.'

'No one's to go near until I say so,' Morton ordered crisply.

Wolfie grinned. 'I've already told them.'

Michelle turned from one of several VDUs set up in the living-room. 'Cheltenham says one of those incoming faxes was from Libya. The other from somewhere between Mexico City and Panama. They've narrowed down the receiving area to between Hammersmith and the Great West Road.'

Morton was already striding back to Shema.

'The Great West Road? Was that the road?'

Shema closed her eyes once more. After an age she opened them and said, 'Yes. There was an apartment block. We could not park. So I walked.'

'Try and remember,' Morton urged. 'How far did you walk? What did you pass? Shops? A pub?'

She shook her head. 'I'm sorry. It was three years ago.'

Morton turned to the ACC. 'Get every man you have into that road. Into every building. Into every room. Tell them they're looking for fax machines, and to check every deep freeze. And if they come across any bottles of perfume, not to touch them.'

To Shema he said, 'I'm going to get you driven down that road. It's surprising what comes back when you see something again.'

The only visible signs of security Faruk Kadumi could observe in the terminal area were the armed policemen patrolling in pairs, each cradling an Uzi. His bag checked, he felt calmer. In less than an hour he would be airborne, and bound for Paris. Once he was there he would be able to think clearer, make a phone call to Libya, and try and discover why he must go to America. In the meantime, he would go through Immigration at the last possible moment. Raza had said once in the departure area you are confined; there is no way out until your flight is called.

Faruk Kadumi continued to pace before the bank of telephones along one wall. He would leave making the call to Effendi as long as possible. But it had to be made.

Half an hour had passed. In that time Chantal had taken Danny's seat in Tel Aviv. Danny was now heading south into Egypt in the lead Two-12. With him were fourteen commandos. Close behind were the other five helicopters, each carrying the same number.

'The Egyptians have set up a refuelling stop at El Alamein,' Chantal was saying on the phone. 'They'll also provide a fighter escort all the way to the *Independence*.'

'Make sure they get properly thanked,' Morton said.

'Karshov's personally calling Cairo,' Chantal replied. 'But are you sure eighty-four men are enough?'

'We used less at Entebbe. And I'm counting on surprise. I'll also have Moeshe's people flying shotgun,' Morton replied.

Behind him one of the technicians was saying something to Wolfie. Across the room the ACC was speaking to the patrol car driving Shema along the Great West Road.

'They've started calling the Supreme Leader,' Chantal continued. 'After some blustering, he's taken it very well. Appleton's going to call him to say when all this is over, he can expect an invitation to the White House.'

Morton grunted. 'The surveillance net over Tripoli in place, Chantal?'

'An hour ago. There's a NSA K-12 and our own Watchboy. Also what the *Independence*'s putting up. The Supreme Leader as much as whispers a word to Raza, and we'd hear.'

'David!' Wolfie called out urgently. 'We've got a break at Heathrow. A call to Effendi's apartment.'

Morton hung up and strode over to Wolfie.

'What is it?'

Wolfie glanced at a notepad. '"The deliverer has been delivered." An Arab voice, male and cultured. Could be middle-aged.'

'Effendi say anything?'

Wolfie grinned. 'No. But he's been busy on the phone ever since, repeating the same message: "Collect and deliver." They're trying to trace the calls right now.'

'They get a location from where the airport call was made?'

'Terminal Two, ground side. He could have walked over from One or Three to make the call and walked back again. Or just taken a bus to Four.'

Morton shook his head. 'He sounds nervous, Wolfie. Just the message. As if he's scared of being traced. Someone like that would want to stay close to his departure point. What's going out of Two in the next thirty minutes?'

Michelle began to type furiously at her VDU. A replica of the

331

flight departure schedule at Heathrow appeared on the screen.

'A couple of charters –' Michelle began.

'He'll go scheduled flight,' Morton interrupted.

'There's a Lufthansa to Hamburg, Iberia to Barcelona and Malaga, Tunis Air –' Michelle continued.

'Get me their passenger manifests,' Morton told Wolfie. He stood behind Michelle and watched the flight numbers continue to appear on the screen. 'Also those for that KLM to Amsterdam, Swissair to Geneva and Air France to Nice and Paris,' added Morton.

Wolfie relayed the instructions into his phone.

Morton glanced towards the door. Shema had returned. She shook her head. He smiled at her to hide his disappointment and turned towards the men speaking quietly to their counterparts in Israel, Italy, the United States and on board the *Independence*.

Passengers on Air France 619 to Paris passed the last security hurdle before take off – the scrutiny of the Special Branch officer standing beside the agent's desk in the final departure lounge. Faruk Kadumi risked a smile. The officer nodded pleasantly, his eyes already on the next passenger in line.

Faruk Kadumi took a seat in the lounge.

Morton stood beside a fax machine with Shema, watching the Tunis Air manifest emerging. They scanned it quickly. Shema shook her head. Morton handed the sheet to a technician and instructed him to transmit it to Finel's computers.

Another manifest began to appear.

AF 619 eased back from the ramp and began to move out through the maze of taxiways to the runway.

Buckled in his seat, Faruk Kadumi stared out of the window. He felt the engine surge, then the Airbus began to speed down the runway.

Half the flight manifest for AF 619 had emerged when Shema grabbed Morton's arm.

'Him!'

She pointed to Faruk Kadumi's name.

'Who is he?'

'A doctor. He treats Raza's *Feydeheen*.'

Morton called to the ACC. 'We've got a prime target on the way to Paris. Can we recall the flight? It's Air France 619.'

'I'll try,' the ACC said doubtfully. 'But its being French, we'll have to go through Paris. It'll probably have landed by then.'

Morton reached for the nearest telephone and began to dial. 'Pierre?'

'*Oui?*'

Morton told Lacouste what he wanted done.

Fifty-five minutes later, AF 619 touched down at Paris-Orly. Ten minutes later it reached its pier. It took thirty more minutes for Faruk Kadumi's baggage to appear and for him to clear Customs inspection.

As he stepped towards the exit doors, two men emerged on either side. The older, a man in a sober suit, introduced them both.

'Police, doctor. Please come this way.'

With the practised ease of having performed the manoeuvre many times, they took his bag, at the same time lightly placing a hand each on his arms.

The incident did not go unnoticed by one of the baggage handlers. He had been instructed to watch for Faruk Kadumi and to hand him his ticket to New York. The handler called Marcel Bolot in Marseilles. The Corsican faxed the villa in Libya. Nadine retransmitted the message to the cabal's safe house in Mexico City.

As Raza had already left, the manservant did what he was instructed. He faxed the message on to Nuri at Sweetmont.

Realising the significance of Faruk Kadumi's arrest, Nuri immediately faxed the office of Ayatollah Muzwaz. From there a fax message was sent to Bolot instructing him to ensure Faruk Kadumi was freed. A sum of one million francs was promised for this service.

Fifteen minutes elapsed between the handler's call and the financial inducement being offered.

Five minutes later, the Concorde swept out of a leaden sky

and landed at Charles de Gaulle airport with Morton, Wolfie, Michelle and Shema.

During the short flight, Morton had been informed that Danny's force had reached El Alamein and the *Independence* was on station. The CIA had teams in Mexico City and Panama looking for Raza. In Tel Aviv, work had begun on the transponder. In Sweetmont surveillance had started on the Harmoos estate. There was no change in the condition of Miriam. When Matti had told him, he hadn't known what to say.

Lacouste was waiting at the foot of the steps as Morton emerged from the cabin. He had told the others to rest on board in preparation for the long night ahead. The pilot was already clearing a flight plan to Malta.

'How are things?' Morton asked as he reached the tarmac.

Lacouste spread his hands. 'We're mostly keeping him hot and cold.'

They walked towards Lacouste's chauffeured Citroën.

'When do the *Feydeheen* go?' Morton asked as the car sped across the tarmac and through a gate in the security fence.

Lacouste smiled sourly. 'Tonight at eight. Air France had a job getting a crew. They feared your people might try something. So we're giving the jumbo a full presidential escort.'

The car swept out of the airport and on to the ring road.

'That wouldn't have stopped us,' Morton said.

He looked out of the window. The rush hour was beginning. The chauffeur reached under the dash and pulled out a police flashing light. He reached out of the window and stuck it on the car roof. As the Citroën swung on to the emergency lane, a revolving blue beacon began to charter its course.

'What's your psychiatrist say?' Morton asked.

'Usual jargon. That he's stimulus prone, and with a strong element of blunting of normal emotional responses.'

Lacouste glanced quickly at Morton.

'Ideally, he'd like more time, David. A couple of days in that box of tricks, and our psychiatrist reckons Kadumi would remember things he never knew he'd even forgotten!'

Morton sighed at what might have been.

'Time we don't have, for sure.'

They rode in silence for the rest of the way to the aerial-festooned complex in the Paris suburb of Tournelles, to the headquarters of the Service of External Documentation and Counterespionage. Most people who worked there called it the Swimming Pool, because of the close proximity of a public baths.

The psychiatrist was waiting when they emerged from the lift into the sub-basement. He had a Chinaman's way of smiling, the wrinkles around his eyes remaining undisturbed. He bowed quickly and formally.

'Professor Wang,' he murmured in accented English. 'I am pleased to meet you. Will you come with me.'

The Chinese turned and led them to a small, cluttered office. There was a smell of chemicals; Morton glimpsed a pharmacy through a half-open door.

'Did the stuff from Tel Aviv help you, Professor?' Morton asked, leaning against the wall. Before leaving London he'd asked Chantal to put together everything they had on terrorist personality types.

Professor Wang sighed. 'He's outside the usual parameters. Older, more sophisticated. He's also a doctor.'

He turned to the desk and picked up a file. 'I've taken what we know and tried to produce in him *folie de doute* by increasing emotional stress.'

'Hot and cold,' Lacouste said cheerfully.

The professor nodded gravely. He handed the file to Morton, murmuring as he did so, 'A surgeon . . . it's really very sad.'

'It was his choice, Professor,' Morton said, scanning the few entries French Security had assembled on Faruk Kadumi. He handed back the file.

'How long before I can get to him?'

'Soon. Come, I will show you.'

The professor led them from the office down the corridor. He opened a hatch-like door at the end. Beyond were a couple of doors set into the wall. He opened the first one.

'Control room,' he explained, indicating the large table-height console in the middle of the room. Set in a wall was an observation window. 'He can't see or hear us.' He motioned for Morton and Lacouste to join him at the window.

In the cell beyond, Faruk Kadumi pulled a blanket around his shoulders, trying to keep out the cold.

'The control of physical stimuli is very important,' the professor continued. 'Change in temperature weakens resistance.

335

Right now he's going to feel like he's in an ice box. You watch.'

The professor turned and walked to the console. He pressed several buttons and checked the settings on the dials. Satisfied, he rejoined Morton and Lacouste.

They could see Faruk Kadumi's breath on the air as he stumbled to the cell door and beat with his hands on the ice-cold steel, moaning to be released. Then, wrapped in his blanket, he slumped on the thin mattress and continued to shiver and half-sob.

An alarm bell rang on the console. Professor Wang made fresh adjustments.

'Come, we'll wait in my office. It won't be long now,' he promised.

In the cell the cold had been replaced by an equally unbearable furnace heat. Perspiration ran off Faruk Kadumi's body and his hair was matted to his skull. The heat seemed to seep from the walls and floor, drying his lips and throat. The cell had also become darker, the solitary light in the ceiling now the merest glimmer.

Something was happening above him, a faint whirring sound began to fill the cell. Faruk Kadumi stared fearfully up into the gloom.

Openings had appeared in the ceiling. From them suddenly came lights so bright they burned into his skull. He felt as if his eyeballs were being shrivelled. Then the searing, terrifying light vanished as instantly as it had appeared.

In the semi-darkness, the heat once more began to be replaced by the chill.

There had been a period of silence in the office when the telephone rang. The professor listened and then handed the receiver to Lacouste. As he listened his face began to darken.

'Plastique?' he asked once. 'How many?' He put down the phone.

'They have started again. Little bombs near the Petit Port and Place St-Michel,' he said bleakly. 'Thank God, no one was killed. They gave a warning this time.'

'Perhaps it's to serve notice on your government not to change its mind, Pierre.'

'They've already moved the *Feydeheen* to the airport,' Lacouste said.

The professor lifted his arm to look at his watch.

'He is ready, please,' he said in the soft voice that reminded Morton of a mortician he'd once met in Hong Kong.

He told the professor what he wanted.

'I'll also need a couple of your strongest men,' Morton informed Lacouste.

While the professor went to the pharmacy, Lacouste made a telephone call. Waiting, Morton once more read Faruk Kadumi's file.

When the two thick-set detectives arrived, Morton gave them their instructions.

In silence, he led the way from the office.

After going to the control room to adjust the cell's lighting to normal brightness, the professor opened its door.

A blast of icy air swept over them as Morton and the others entered. They aligned themselves along one wall, saying nothing, only staring at the dishevelled and pathetic figure slumped on the mattress.

'Hello, Dr Kadumi,' Morton said in Arabic as he stepped forward. 'You know why you are here.'

Faruk Kadumi stared at him as if in a stupor. 'You know me?' he finally asked.

Morton nodded sagely. 'I know everything about you. Effendi told me, I know all about you and Arish.'

Faruk Kadumi continued to look at him slack mouthed. 'Who are you?'

Morton again chose to ignore the question. 'I know all about the perfume bottles,' he continued in the same level, steady voice, as if he was reciting facts that could not be in dispute. 'Raza has failed, of course,' he added. 'You are part of that failure.'

Morton took a step closer, judging the distance between domination and intimidation.

'I don't know what you're talking about,' Faruk Kadumi began, struggling to sit up.

'Yes you do. I know about your faxes. About what happened to

337

the girl in Athens. And Lila,' Morton resumed. 'You have been betrayed by many people.'

'No!' Faruk Kadumi's scream pierced the cell. 'No! You lie! You are a Jew! A filthy Zionist trying to trap me!'

Morton stared at him impassively.

'You will answer my questions?'

'No! Never!'

'Very well.'

Morton turned to the others and nodded. The detectives came forward and pinioned Faruk Kadumi to the mattress. From a pocket, the professor produced a syringe and a vial, its cork securely in place. He removed the cap from the needle and drove it through the cork into the tube and drew off a quantity of colourless liquid.

'We recovered this in Athens,' Morton told Faruk Kadumi. 'There's enough Anthrax-B-C here to kill several hundred people. You will be injected with it, then left here to die.'

The professor stepped towards the bed, holding the hypodermic upright and steady so as not to release a drop.

'No!' screamed Faruk Kadumi, struggling to break the grip of the detectives. They forced his head against the mattress, turning it so that he faced Morton.

There was a sudden smell of urine as Faruk Kadumi lost control over his bladder.

Morton crouched beside the bed.

'Dr Kadumi, I must inform you of certain facts,' Morton said in a suddenly deliberately dull and bureaucratic voice. 'No one knows you are here. You have disappeared off the face of the earth. No one can stop what is now going to happen to you.'

Morton remained crouching for a long moment, studying Faruk Kadumi's face as if he wished to remember it for ever.

The professor was standing behind him, syringe poised.

'Do it,' Morton said abruptly, rising in one swift, unbroken movement.

'No! What do you want to know?' Faruk Kadumi screamed. 'Please, do not do this! Please, oh please . . .'

He began to sob uncontrollably. The others looked at each other in silence, then at Morton. He continued to stare down without pity at the bed.

'The truth, Dr Kadumi,' Morton said softly. 'I want the truth. Do you understand?'

After a while, when the whimpering stopped, there was a tiny nod from the bed.

'Very well. Where did you stay in London?' Morton began.

When he heard, Lacouste slipped out of the room to call the ACC.

They had been going for an hour. The only pause had been for the detectives to escort Faruk Kadumi to the toilet where they had watched him change into the fresh underwear the professor had mysteriously provided. He had also adjusted the heat in the cell to make it pleasantly comfortable. Afterwards the psychiatrist had emptied the syringe of the distilled water.

A numbed acceptance had descended over Faruk Kadumi. He knew. This man knew everything. The relentless, driving voice told him that.

Early on, Morton had nodded for the detectives and the professor to leave the cell. He could hear them now, walking restlessly back and forth outside the open door.

Building from one question to another, he had meticulously and speedily discovered exactly how and where the Anthrax-B-C had been prepared. He had made Faruk Kadumi sketch the inside of the bunker and place it in relation to the villa. He had been pleased to see it matched what Shema had described. He had then taken Faruk Kadumi through his time in London up to the shooting of Arish.

'I had to kill him,' Faruk Kadumi whispered.

Morton nodded. It didn't matter, not right now.

'Who are the collectors?'

'I don't know.'

Once more Morton returned to the bottles of perfume.

'How many did you prepare in Libya?'

'A hundred.'

'And they were all taken to Athens by the Greek girls?'

'Yes. Except the one Lila took to Trekfontein.'

'That was the same potency as the others?'

Faruk Kadumi nodded.

Morton paused, calculating. One to South Africa, three to

339

England, at least one to the United States. That still left ninety-five unaccounted for. How many had been destroyed in the tanker fireball? Based on what had happened in Trekfontein, there could still be enough anthrax left to kill close to half a million people.

'How many bottles were you supposed to receive?'

'I was not told.'

'And what targets?'

Faruk Kadumi once again shook his head. 'I was not informed.'

Morton glanced at the door. Lacouste had come and gone again.

'Why were you going to America?'

'I was not told.'

'Were you going to Sweetmont?'

Faruk Kadumi stared at him tiredly. 'Where?'

Morton moved from against the wall. 'Rachid Harmoos. Were you told about him?'

Again Faruk Kadumi shook his head.

'I know him, of course. But I do not know what he has to do with this.'

'Ayatollah Muzwaz? Is he purely the money?'

'I don't know.'

Morton stared at him. Faruk Kadumi was still telling the truth. That was why it was an effort to conceal his own disappointment.

'David,' Lacouste was back at the door, beckoning.

He was white-faced with more than anger. He had a piece of paper in one hand.

'It is finished,' Lacouste said in a fierce whisper when Morton joined him in the corridor.

'What?'

'He's being released. Here!' He thrust the paper before Morton. 'The order is signed by the Minister of Justice personally.'

Morton glanced at the paper.

'Why, Pierre?' He handed the release order back to Lacouste.

'There was a call to the President's office to say there would be more bombs unless he is freed. The President immediately ordered he is to go with the *Feydeheen*. There is a car waiting.'

Lacouste glanced towards the detectives. He told them they would escort Faruk Kadumi to Charles de Gaulle Airport. He turned back to Morton.

'I'm sorry, David. I only hope you had enough time to get as much as you could. I really feel bad about this.'

Morton looked at him. 'Don't blame yourself, Pierre.'

Ninety minutes later, Morton and Shema sat squashed in the front of a Follow-me truck parked inside the heavy police cordon thrown around the Air France 747 on the tarmac at Charles de Gaulle. On the way to the airport, Morton had briefly stopped at a specialist shop Lacouste had recommended.

'Remember each face,' Morton said, as the *Feydeheen* stepped from the airport bus and climbed the stairs to the plane. Before they disappeared each gave a ritual clenched fist salute. Only Faruk Kadumi hurried on board without any bravado.

As the aircraft rolled out, Morton directed the truck driver to take them over to the far side of the airport where, beyond another security cordon, the Concorde waited.

After they boarded, Morton handed Shema the pair of throwing knives he had bought.

27

As the Concorde passed through Genoa air traffic control and headed east towards Malta, the ACC's face appeared on screen in the communications centre. He was speaking from the Operations Room at Scotland Yard. Morton had never seen the ACC look more tired or sound more triumphant.

'We've got them all, David. Twenty-seven of the little bastards. Students, girls mostly,' the ACC began. 'They each had a key to Kadumi's flat. By the time the first bint walked in, we'd removed the vials in the freezer and the two bottles and sent them to Porton Down. The scientists there say that even though the anthrax is diluted, it's still lethal. Anyway, we managed to get our own vials in place and everything went tickety-boo.'

At times the ACC could sound firmly anchored in another age.

'The collectors each took what they were supposed to from the freezer and walked out again,' he continued. 'We let them get well clear of the place and then nabbed them and we knew we'd got them all when the freezer was empty. The decontamination people are going through the place now.'

Behind him Morton could hear Shema exhaling with relief and the low voices of Wolfie briefing Chantal in Tel Aviv and Michelle reporting to Matti in New York what the ACC was saying.

'Are the collectors talking?' Morton asked.

'Some. They're proud as hell at what they'd been asked to do. Real little ayatollahs, some of them, filled with hatred. Reckon that even if we've got them, there's plenty more waiting in the wings to take their places.'

'Any line on targets?'

'Reservoirs and water pumping stations. London Underground and the Stock Exchange. Major department stores throughout the country,' the ACC said. 'A very wide spread to create maximum havoc.'

Morton asked: 'Effendi?'

The ACC nodded vigorously. 'A real hero. Once we picked him up and told him we were charging him, for starters, with conspiring to kill Saleem Arish, it was real save-your-own-skin time. He wanted to trade and naturally we said we'd listen. Right now Percy West and his people are promising him a one-way ticket to a country of his choice. The reality is that our Mr Effendi isn't going any further than the Scrubs or Pentonville once we've squeezed him.'

'Has he said anything about Harmoos?' Morton asked.

'Enough. Harmoos has been Raza's money broker. Percy's people have found all sorts of interesting documents in Effendi's apartment. Bank transfers from Colombia to Switzerland. Huge sums switched around Europe. Respectable evidence that ties in the drug cartels with Raza and Harmoos.'

'Hold a moment, Harry.'

Morton turned to the CCO. 'Get me Bill Gates in Washington,' then turned back to the screen.

'You were saying, Harry?'

'We've started to backtrack on what looks like a list of safe houses stocked with arms and explosives in this country and Europe. A full-blown terror network. We've got the Germans, the Dutch and the Belgians raiding. It looks like before we've finished, pretty well every country between Sweden and Spain is going to have to be combed.'

On an adjoining screen, the face of Gates had appeared.

'Good work, Harry,' Morton said.

'Good luck, David.'

Morton watched the screen from London rapidly darken, then turned to the image from Washington. He told Gates what the ACC had said.

'That's more than enough for me to declare war on Harmoos.' Gates's voice was crisp and businesslike. 'With this, I don't need a Surveillance Court authorisation. I can put together a joint FBI-DEA Task Force with local police backup and tear everything Harmoos owns in this country apart.'

'Bill, I don't want you to do that,' Morton said quickly. 'I don't want you to do anything.'

Gates's expression was stony. 'What the hell are you saying, David?'

'We still don't know how many bottles actually got into the United States, Bill,' Morton told the camera gravely. 'Even if you launch a simultaneous raid, there's no guarantee you'll be able to move fast enough to grab every bottle. By all means get a task force together. But they don't move until we are absolutely certain we have pinpointed those bottles.'

'What about Harmoos?'

'Again, do nothing.'

Morton watched the face staring out of the screen.

'I was never very good at doing nothing.'

Morton watched Gates run the back of a large hairy hand across his face.

'Trust me, Bill.'

Gates gave a quick, unexpected smile. 'In my book, you're still the one guy I do trust absolutely, David.'

For the next forty minutes Morton sat in his chair and slept soundly. Around him the technicians continued to maintain circuits to Tel Aviv and the *Independence*.

As the Concorde entered Maltese air space, the carrier radioed the news that Danny's helicopters were safely on board.

Shortly afterwards the plane swooped over the Dingli Cliffs, and cast its great delta shadow over the old Inquisitor's Summer Palace before landing at Luqa. The Concorde came to a stop close to a US navy Jet-Ranger helicopter.

Morton snapped open his eyes, stood up and stretched. He felt completely refreshed.

'Shut down everything except a line to the *Independence*,' he instructed the CCO. As he left the plane, Morton told the captain to prepare a flight plan for Kennedy airport. Then he led Wolfie, Michelle and Shema over to the Jet-Ranger.

The helicopter lifted into the warm night air and headed south. They were in total darkness, except for the streaks of white on the water.

344

An hour later the *Independence* rose like a cliff out of the heaving sea.

The carrier was completely blacked out as they passed over the fantail and drifted on to the flight deck, close to where Danny's helicopters were parked.

As he stepped from the Jet-Ranger Morton sensed the *Independence* coming to full operational readiness. Bracing himself against the motion of the ship's bow as she rode the swell, he glanced at the sky. It was inky black without a star.

A young officer in whites came running forward, and saluted. He wore mufflers and carried more in his hand.

'Colonel Morton?'

Morton nodded.

'Major Nagier and his people are in the movie theatre we're using as a briefing room. Briefing's at twenty-two hundred. Meantime, they'd like you in Cat-See.' He held out the mufflers.

The Carrier Air Traffic Control Centre was the nerve centre of operations at night. It had last been in action in the Gulf War, dispatching the *Independence*'s air armada against Iraq.

As they hurried from the flight deck a sudden roar of an aero engine running up to full military power disturbed the air.

'Seen this before?' asked the officer.

'Only on film,' smiled Morton.

'Not the same,' said the officer. 'Best get your mufflers on.'

They all huddled against the towering superstructure of the carrier's island rising six storeys above them. From along the angled flight deck came the shimmer of burnt-off fuel. The roar rose in a shattering crescendo.

Somewhere beneath his feet, Morton heard what sounded like two giant valves suddenly opening. Then came the impact of a solid wall of steam expanding itself against the catapult pistons. An F-14 Tomcat streaked past and lifted into the air. The air shimmering from its after-burner.

Moments later there was the sound of another engine running up.

One hundred and fifty flying miles away, from the window of Raza's office, Nadine watched the freed *Feydeheen* arriving by bus. They were tired but cheerful and were greeted as heroes.

Even hardened instructors embraced them and several of the camp's women staff kissed them.

With the *Feydeheen* was the official from the Ministry who had so angered Raza. While the men were being dispersed to their billets, he strode towards the villa. Nadine met him at the door.

'You have arranged for him to travel to America?' she asked.

The official nodded. 'He will be there in the morning.'

There was something about the man that made her dislike him. Perhaps it was his condescending smile, or the way he rubbed his hands together, a curious washing motion, as if he carried some secret or guilt.

'Is there anything else?'

'I'm to inform you these men will be permitted to stay here only for twenty-four hours,' the diplomat said with undisguised satisfaction. 'We cannot afford to antagonise world opinion by their continued presence.'

Nadine stared at him with contempt. 'Your concern will not be forgotten,' she said icily.

He turned on his heels and walked back to the bus. For one fleeting moment he had wondered what she would have done if he had told her the truth. But the Supreme Leader had personally ordered there must be no warning. And after all, a handful of terrorists were expendable when measured against the promises Appleton had made that soon the Supreme Leader would no longer be a pariah, but a welcome guest in Washington.

After the bus left, Nadine went to the broadcast studio. On the desk beside the Voice Throw console were the set of tapes Raza had made with her shortly before leaving the camp. Following his clear instructions, she began to activate the transponders he had positioned in Africa and Asia. Afterwards she would inform Nuri that Faruk Kadumi was on his way to New York.

In the Cat-See, the Air Operations Officer paused in his briefing of Morton to check one of the two monitor screens. They provided continuous infra-red pictures from the several cameras positioned around the flight deck. Dim red lights provided the only illumination in the Cat-See.

On the monitor a flight deck tractor towed an A6 fighter-bomber to the hook-up areas near the bowside catapult. Sailors secured the aircraft with chocks and chains. The tractor was unhooked and it trundled away to collect another plane.

One of the ensigns wearing battery-operated telephone headsets, recorded the arrival of the bomber on the Plexiglass status board completely covering one wall.

The Air Operations Officer turned back to Morton.

'As well as your own strike force, we're putting up both our Tomcat squadrons and our two F-18 squadrons, plus every serviceable A6. Hopefully, there won't be much left when they've delivered their punch,' the officer said.

On the monitor another fighter-bomber arrived on deck, fuelled and armed. Morton could make out the shape of the cluster bombs beneath the wings. Every Rockeye was designed to air detonate and release 1,500 bomblets, each containing an explosive charge capable of piercing reinforced concrete.

'Our Hawkeye's reporting all quiet in the target area,' continued the Air Operations Officer. 'What looks like a truck or bus arrived an hour ago. It's on its way out. Otherwise nothing.'

Six miles above the *Independence*, the twin-engined turboprop with its ugly-looking radar dome continued to fly a leisurely circle, its scanners probing several hundred square miles of desert.

Another fighter-bomber was being towed across the monitor.

'Weather going to hold?' Morton asked.

'Should be okay, but you can never tell. This time of the year wind can shift up to seventy degrees in an hour. That can play hell when it comes to keeping a final recovery bearing.'

'Tripoli still co-operating?'

The Air Operations Officer smiled thinly. 'Yes. It helps that they know we're here, and all the people we've got looking down on them. Come and have a look.'

Morton followed him into an adjoining room which was bathed in an unearthly green light from the scopes, radar screens and computer VDUs. Before each set a shirt-sleeved ensign with a headset. A senior chief petty officer wearing a master headset paced behind the ensigns, watching and quietly giving orders.

'Hold it, Tel Aviv,' he said into his lip mike. 'You can ask him yourself.'

The CPO handed a headset to Morton. He heard Chantal's voice.

'David, Moeshe's boys are on the runway. Do they roll?'

'Yes.'

'Okay. Now here's the other thing: we've picked up that woman's voice again and Raza's. He appears to be calling her from Aden. The technical boys place her in Bangkok.'

'What are they saying?'

'He's told her Tokyo will be the next to be delivered,' Chantal said.

Morton stared hard at one of the screens.

'Have Karshov call the Japanese Prime Minister. He'll know what to do.'

'You think this is a diversion? A bluff?' Chantal asked.

'I'll only know for sure when we reach the base.'

'Then it could be too late.'

'That's always a possibility,' acknowledged Morton, taking off the headset. He turned to the CPO.

'So tell me?' Morton said.

'Right.' The CPO nodded. 'Since the Air France jumbo left, Tripoli airport's been closed. Officially, their radar's gone on the blink. The truth is we've scrambled it.'

He turned to a large scope. A series of circles ran from the centre blip.

'The target area. Still no untoward activity.' The CPO pushed buttons on a keyboard. The screen cleared and remained blank for a moment. Then a splurge of dots appeared.

'The Egyptian army. They've got a regiment up on their border. No way Raza or his people can scoot that way. Same on the other side. The Tunisians are waiting. He can't go south, because the desert will get him. If he tries to make a break by sea, we'll spot him. We've got him all nicely boxed in for you.'

Morton smiled pleasantly. He'd heard that before.

From the villa's bedroom window Nadine watched the frost begin to crust the sand. It was too dark to see the sentries changing, but she could hear their low voices. Outside the door she heard the padding footsteps of a guard.

She turned from the window and went into the bathroom. While the tub was running she undressed, then sank into the warm perfumed water.

*

As he strode onto the stage of the carrier's movie theatre, Morton saw that Shema and Michelle were dressed in the same black fatigues and combat boots as the rows of commandos sitting in comfortable Pullman chairs. Wolfie sat beside Sam Goodman. Danny, who stood between two blackboards mounted on easels on stage, had chosen the major to lead a platoon.

One board was covered with a large sketch of Raza's camp, based on what Shema had described. The other board was covered with satellite photographs.

The row of helicopter pilots were staring intently at the photos while the commandos concentrated on the sketch. Morton picked up a pointer and tapped the sketch.

'Target. Raza's complex. One villa. Underground bunkers. Billets. Arsenal. A lab. The opposition. Anything between three-fifty and five hundred terrorists. Well armed.'

Morton paused to let them digest the size and strength of the enemy, and then turned to the satellite photos and addressed the pilots.

'Route to target is sea level to the coast. There are dunes up to sixty feet running for a mile inland, then flat scrub. Two miles from target there are hillocks.'

He turned back to the sketch map. 'The compound makes a good set-down point, but watch for crossfire. Hopefully it will be minimal.'

For the next thirty minutes Morton told them everything that Shema had told him. Next, he described the air strike that would precede the helicopter assault. He paused and motioned for Wolfie, Michelle and Shema to join him on the stage.

'Take a good look at them. They will be going in first with me. Major Nagier will lead the rest of you in. I don't want any mistakes. Pick your targets. We've got twenty minutes on the ground. That should be enough if everyone does his job. Questions?'

Goodman shifted in his seat. 'The chances are there will be women and children. What do we do with them?'

Morton glanced at Shema who gave a quick little nod.

'There *are* women and children. We don't know how many or where they will be. But let me remind you, you do not shoot unless they fire first. Then they become a legitimate target.'

Heads nodded.

Morton looked towards the projection box at the rear of the theatre. The lights dimmed and he turned to the movie screen above the stage.

'I want you to take a careful look at the faces you are going to see now.'

First on to the screen came a photograph of Raza.

'You take him alive,' Morton ordered.

Then followed the photo of Faruk Kadumi.

'Him, too.'

28

The voice of the Jet-Ranger pilot crackled in Morton's headset.

'We're at assigned altitude. Five minutes to coast.'

Morton keyed the mike. 'Anything on radar?'

'Sky's as clear as a nun's conscience,' the pilot reported. 'Still ten-tenths cloud, with sea haze extending well inland.'

'Any wind change?'

'Still light westerly. Ten knots off the sea.'

Wolfie, Michelle and Shema gave a final check to the straps of their parachutes and backpacks, and clipped their Uzis to their webbing. Attached to Wolfie and Michelle's belts were crossbows and panniers of bolts. Shema quickly checked the throwing knives she'd placed in the ankle pouch pocket in her trousers.

'It'll be no harder than jumping from that tower,' Morton told her.

Shema had described the training regime at the camp and the practice jumps that formed part of the assault course training.

She smiled. 'Easier. Raza used to have his instructors shoot at us with live ammunition.'

The co-pilot was in the cabin. He clipped his safety harness to a stanchion.

'Time to go, folks,' he said cheerfully. 'You'll get down a lot quicker than we took to get up here.'

Morton could feel the rotors struggling to maintain pitch at 14,000 feet. As the co-pilot opened the door, a red bulb glowed over the opening, and icy air filled the cabin.

'Line up,' ordered the co-pilot.

Wolfie would jump first, then Michelle, followed by Shema and finally Morton. He watched as each gave a last check to the chin straps on their jump hats. Through his headset he listened one last time to the pilot from the flight deck.

'Your battle strike force is presently over Egypt. Your other choppers have just lifted off from the carrier, and our strikers are lining up on the ramp. You're all set, Colonel.'

Morton gave an acknowledgement, then removed the headset and put on his jump hat.

The red light suddenly turned green and the co-pilot tapped Wolfie on the shoulder. He vanished through the door, followed moments later by Michelle.

'Once you're clear, just remember to count ten and pull the toggle,' Morton shouted in Shema's ear.

'Go!' yelled the co-pilot, tapping her on the shoulder.

Morton took his place in the open door.

'Go!'

He plunged into the void.

Nadine stood at the bedroom window. She wore one of Raza's robes she liked to sleep in when he was away. She wondered again where he was and when he would be back. She had not realised how much she would miss him.

Outside the bunker housing the broadcast studio and the laboratory, she saw the sudden flare of a match. The fool of a guard! Raza had forbidden anyone to smoke near the bunker because of the petrol stored above the ceiling to destroy the lab in an emergency. Picking up the Kalashnikov kept beside the bed, Nadine left the bedroom.

The frost-skimmed sand crunched under her feet as she ran to the bunker. She spotted the guard huddling in the lee of the building against the intense cold. He struggled to his feet as she approached, plucking the cigarette from his mouth. She smashed it from his hand with a furious blow from the rifle, and using the Kalashnikov as a club, she beat him mercilessly. Then, trembling all over, she turned from the half-senseless man and walked back to the villa.

In the bedroom, she put the gun down beside the bed, took her throwing knives from the top drawer of the bedside cabinet and placed them on top. She climbed into bed and dimmed the light to a mere glimmer.

Nadine had never been able to sleep alone in the dark since the time she had no longer shared a bed with Shema. She drifted into sleep remembering those nights in the refugee camp when they had lain together in the dark and listened to the men downstairs endlessly talking about how the day would surely come when their enemies would be driven from the face of the land.

Morton checked his compass. The camp was to the south. He picked up the lightweight scanner. When he had his back to the sea, small shadows began to appear on the screen.

'A small vehicle. Two men,' he murmured. 'About a half-mile ahead.'

'The perimeter guards in their Jeep,' Shema whispered.

From beyond the crescent-shaped dune they heard the low sound of a gear being changed.

Morton glanced at the luminous face of his watch. Fifteen minutes had gone since they had dropped. Thirty-five minutes before the air strike. He shoved the scope into his backpack, and at a crouching run he led them towards the sound of the engine.

Shema suddenly stopped, pointing to a pile of stones.

'Perimeter marker,' she whispered. The noise of the engine was receding.

Motioning for the others to wait, she crawled forward, feeling the sand in front and then turned and beckoned them. When they reached her, she signalled for Morton to kneel beside her, guiding his hand to the length of cable she had carefully exposed.

'Trip wire,' she whispered. 'It's linked to the monitor in the Jeep so that they know exactly where there's been a break-in.'

Morton motioned to Wolfie and Michelle. They unclipped their crossbows before melting into the night. The sound of the Jeep's engine had almost faded when Morton yanked the wire. Then he ran and crouched with Shema behind the heaped stones.

They could hear the Jeep racing over the scree, and see its sidelights rising and falling. It stopped a few yards in front of the wire. Holding their machine pistols, the two guards climbed out.

Suddenly they both pitched forward, guns flying from their grasp, already dead before the steel-tipped arrows stopped quivering in their backs.

From the Jeep a bored voice called out over the radio for the guards to report their position.

As Morton and Shema ran towards the vehicle, the voice was calling again to know what had happened. Morton picked up the hand mike.

'We crossed the wire by mistake,' he said in guttural Arabic. 'We've got a puncture and need to come in to fix it.'

'Okay,' grunted the voice.

With Shema and Michelle crouched in the back of the Jeep, and Wolfie beside him, Morton drove steadily across the shingle and sand towards the villa.

'The repair shop's at the back,' Shema called softly. 'You can drive right in. There'll be nobody there at this hour.'

Ten minutes later they entered the deserted workshop bunker and parked the Jeep. Morton checked his watch: twenty minutes to strike time.

The sound of the Jeep awakened Nadine. She lay in the semi-darkness, listening. The Jeep should be out on the perimeter. She reached for the bedside phone and dialled the radio room at the rear of the villa. The duty operator told her what had happened.

Sighing, Nadine put down the telephone and settled down to sleep, pulling the covers over her head.

At a crouching run, Uzi in hand, Morton followed Shema across the sand towards the villa. She held her weapon high across her body. Wolfie and Michelle brought up the rear, each with an arrow fitted in their crossbow.

'Kitchen door,' Shema mouthed in Morton's ear, pointing at a doorway to their right. 'It's always left unlocked for the outside guards to come and make tea.'

Morton pressed an ear against the door. Silence. He squinted through the keyhole. No one passed across his field of vision. He turned the handle and eased open the door. The others slipped in after him. Michelle closed the door behind her, slipping the bolt in place.

Shema pointed to two doors. 'One goes to the dining-room, the other leads to storerooms,' she whispered. 'The radio room is back there.'

Morton nodded and beckoned to Wolfie. While Michelle and Shema positioned themselves behind the door of the dining-room, Morton opened the one to the storage areas. He and Wolfie entered a stone-flagged passageway. There were arched openings with storerooms off them. At the end of the passage was a closed door: the radio room. Light escaped through the gap at the bottom of the door. Swiftly and silently they moved down the passageway. They could hear voices beyond the door. Two men.

Suddenly there was the scraping of a chair being pushed back and footsteps from inside the room. Morton and Wolfie edged back into the darkness. The air was filled with the faintly pungent smell of spices. There was a shaft of light as the door opened. Then footsteps were coming along the passage.

As the soldier passed, Morton glimpsed a short, thick-set figure holding two tin mugs in his hands. Tea time. Morton stepped out lightly behind him and made a whispering sound. The man turned and Morton drove the butt of his Uzi into the man's neck, crushing his windpipe.

Wolfie reached the half-open door. A soldier sat beside the table on which stood the radio, an assault rifle propped beside him. For one moment he stared in disbelief at the figure in the doorway. Then, as he grabbed for the rifle, Wolfie shot him, the bolt driving through the man's chest to pinion him to the chair.

Wolfie quietly closed the door behind him and went to help Morton drag the other dead Arab into a storeroom. Then they ran back to the kitchen.

Morton signalled to Michelle, who eased open the door of the dining-room. Through the arched windows, which covered most of one wall, came the reflected light of frost glistening on sand. Nothing moved out there. They stood for a moment, getting their bearings, their boots sinking into the deep carpet pile. The furniture was dark and massive, and on a wall hung the paintings Shema had described. She looked towards a door at the far end of the room and whispered, 'Wait here. I'll bring Nadine.'

Morton's Men flattened themselves against the walls and waited. The only sound was the click of Wolfie loading another bolt into his crossbow.

Minutes later Shema came back alone. She looked puzzled.

'Nadi's not there. Her bedroom looks as if she hasn't used it for months.'

It was the first time Morton had heard Shema use the diminutive name of her sister.

'Let's find Raza,' Morton said softly. 'He'll tell us where she is.'

Shema led them into an unlit corridor in the silent villa. Rugs cushioned their footfalls. They filed past several open doors, the rooms swathed in darkness. Shema mouthed that they were offices and a prayer room.

The corridor opened into a hall, from which other corridors led. All were in darkness except one, which was dimly lit. They stopped and listened intently, then crept across the hall towards the lit corridor. On either side were closed doors.

'Bedrooms for guests or domestic staff,' Shema whispered.

Slowly they moved down the corridor.

A door suddenly opened. A young woman stood there, dressed in a nightgown. Behind her was a soldier, buttoning up his trousers.

As Morton stepped swiftly past the woman and clubbed the soldier, Michelle slipped her hand over the girl's mouth. Wolfie helped her bundle the girl back into the room. She stared at them, wide-eyed with fright. She smelled of sex and sweat.

'Where's Nadine?' Shema hissed into the girl's ear. She remembered her now; she waited at table.

The girl's mouth wobbled in fear.

'Where's my sister?' Shema demanded again.

'With Raza?' Morton asked.

The girl rolled her eyes.

'Where?' Morton demanded.

'Bedroom,' the girl managed to say.

The soldier was groaning. Michelle yanked off the bed sheet and with Wolfie, tore it into strips which they used to gag and bind the prisoners.

Back in the corridor Shema led them into another passage. Here there were two doors, side by side.

'The first goes to Raza's office. The next is the bedroom,' she whispered.

Morton nodded and motioned for Wolfie and Michelle to stand on either side of the bedroom door.

Shema touched Morton's arm.

'Please, let me go in alone to get Nadi out.'

Morton hesitated, then agreed. 'We'll be right behind you.'

Shema turned the handle with infinite stealth, opening the bedroom door only wide enough for her to enter. She stood inside the door, holding the Uzi tightly in both hands, finger on the trigger, the snub barrel pointing to the huddle in the bed. Everything was exactly as she remembered it, the wardrobe, the dressing-table, the bed were all in the same place. The only new feature was a fax machine. She glanced towards the door leading to the office. It was closed. Raza had always left it opened.

There was movement under the bed covers.

Shema listened for a moment longer to the steady breathing and then walked slowly towards the bed.

In the dim light she could make out only one figure. She hesitated. Raza was alone. She looked quickly over her shoulder. The door was easing open.

Shema swiftly stepped around the bed and used the barrel to lift the covers quickly from around the figure's head. She stepped back. 'Nadi,' she whispered. 'Oh, Nadi!' and lowered the gun.

Nadine's hands grabbed for her knives on the night table.

'Nadi! It's me. Don't be scared. It's all right! It's me!'

Shema continued to whisper reassurance as she stayed her sister's hand. Nadine stared at her wordlessly. Shema put the gun on the bed and reached for her sister, embracing and kissing her and murmuring endearments. Nadine suddenly pushed her away, and looked searchingly into Shema's face.

'How did you escape?' she asked. 'Get here?'

Shema smiled, 'Later, Nadi,' and once more she held her sister close. Then she pulled away, looking towards the door.

'Nadi, we must hurry before he finds us.'

'What? What are you talking about?'

Shema stood up and picked up the Uzi.

'Raza. Where is he?'

'Where is he?' echoed Nadine. 'But I thought he had helped you escape?'

Shema shook her head. 'No, no.'

'Then how did you get here?'

'Later, Nadi. I'll tell you everything later. Just hurry and get dressed. We haven't much time.'

Nadine shook her head. She was beginning to feel calmer. She looked at Shema more carefully. Why was her sister dressed like this? And the gun. How had she got hold of a Zionist weapon?

'Come on, Nadi!' urged Shema. 'We've got to go!'

Nadine sat up. 'Go? Go where?' Her voice was firm. 'Why should we go anywhere? This is our home.'

Shema put a finger to her lips. 'Not so loud, Nadi. Raza could hear. We must go before the attack starts.'

Nadine slid out of bed and stood staring at Shema. The Kalashnikov was on the carpet near Nadine's feet.

'Attack? What attack?' Her voice was dangerously quiet. 'Who is going to attack us, Shema?'

'Please, Nadi, please. Commandos! They will be here very soon!'

Nadine grabbed Shema by the shoulders and shook her roughly. 'What are you saying?' she demanded. 'How do you know?' She whirled towards the bedroom door where Morton, Wolfie and Michelle stood silently watching.

'It's okay, Nadi,' Shema said quickly. 'They won't hurt you. They're here to help you.'

'Who are they?' Nadine asked.

'We're Israelis,' Morton said quietly.

'Zionists!' Nadine shouted.

'Nadi!' Shema cried. 'Stop this!'

As she moved to try and calm her sister, Nadine stooped and grabbed the Kalashnikov.

'Put that down,' Morton ordered. 'No one is going to harm you. Shema's right. We are here to help you!'

Nadine glanced from the door to Shema, and back to Morton, Wolfie and Michelle.

'Zionists!' Nadine shouted again. 'You brought the Zionists here!'

'Just get dressed, Nadine,' Morton said firmly. 'And tell me where Raza is.'

Now she understood. They had come to kill Raza. And somehow they had persuaded Shema to help. She turned to her sister, tears stinging her eyes.

'Why? Why did you betray him?'

'He is evil, Nadi. He has used us all!'

'No! No! No! I love him!' Nadine screamed.

Shema stared wordlessly at Nadine, and then moved towards her.

'Get back!' Nadine screamed, raising the rifle.

'Put your gun down, Nadine,' Morton commanded.

'No!'

'Nadi! Don't!' Shema cried.

Nadine stared for a second at the group at the door. Then she fired. The gun kicked in her hand and great slabs of plaster and wood flew from the wall and door, but Morton, Michelle and Wolfie had already dived to safety.

'You Zionist whore!' Nadine screamed at Shema. 'You betrayed us all. Die with them!'

Even as Nadine brought the assault rifle to bear, Shema moved. In one swift and continuous action she stooped and pulled out a throwing knife and hurled it. The blade buried itself in Nadine's chest.

Nadine stood for a moment, mouth open. Then she gave a little gurgling sound and pitched to the floor, the gun falling from her hands. She felt a hole opening; it was dark and bottomless. She was falling. No one could stop her.

Raza! she wanted to say. Raza! I love you!

Shema knelt over her dead sister and began very softly to weep.

From a long way away she heard the fax machine ringing and Morton whispering. Then Wolfie and Michelle were gently but firmly pulling her to her feet and helping her out of the bedroom.

Morton ripped off the fax message and shoved it in his pocket.

As they reached the outside of the villa, the air was filled with a sudden turbulence. It descended from the sky, leaving a fiery trail. Moments later came the first explosions from the far side of the camp. The air strike had begun.

Running for their lives, they reached a wadi and plunged down its side, carrying cascades of loose sand and scree with them. By the time they reached the bottom of the ravine they were half buried. All around them the earth heaved and split and orange tongues of flame destroyed the darkness. The first of the bombers passed only feet overhead.

In the wadi, time lost all meaning as the terrible bombardment lashed everything in its path, tearing away the sand around the bunkers like a living monster.

The villa exploded in a great cloud of smoke. Behind it the bunker housing the studio and lab erupted in a fireball which consumed the Voice Throw console and the freezer chest from which Faruk Kadumi had first removed the bottles of Anthrax-B-C.

Cluster bombs turned the parade ground into thousands of little craters. Scores of recruits and their instructors were pitched, lifeless, into them as they tried to run for the safety of the desert.

In two minutes – all it had taken for the air strike to complete its work – the great raging from the sky passed. For a few moments there was only the sound of flames. Then through their glow came the steady chatter of helicopters.

In the wadi, Morton and his Men dusted off debris. Then they scrambled back up the side of the ravine.

The choppers were coming in low over the desert and even before they landed, commandos were leaping out and deploying. The air filled with the crackle of small-arms fire.

Suddenly, from behind an outcrop of rock to the left of the wadi, came the deeper chatter of a heavy machine gun. Around the helicopters men began to fall. Others remained motionless.

Morton ran forward in a half-crouch, then dropped again. Wolfie wriggled alongside. Shema and Michelle crawled behind. Morton's machine gun delivered a withering fire across the parade ground and cries for medics began to mingle with the sounds of battle.

'I need a radioman,' Morton said.

'I'll go –' Michelle began, rising, but Shema thrust her down.

'I know this ground better!' She was up and running before anyone could stop her.

The noise of battle had deepened by the time Shema returned with a commando, a field radio pack set on his back.

'Get me Major Nagier!' Morton ordered.

The firing was intensifying as the radio man handed Morton the mike.

'Danny, we're behind the villa. Get your chopper over here. Scramble the others to take out those machine guns!'

'Roger,' Danny acknowledged.

The helicopters whirled into the air, then swept towards the machine guns and fired their missiles. The rock outcrop disappeared in a shower of splinters. Moments later the heavy machine guns stopped firing.

With the glare from the burning villa as a beacon, Danny's helicopter swept low and hovered close to where Morton's Men waited. Danny helped pull them on board, then the chopper pulled away and clattered over the battlefield.

Time and again the *Feydeheen* broke and scattered under the withering fire of the commandos, who moved steadily through the darkness in a merciless show of force. They took no prisoners.

From the helicopter Morton swept the area with his night-vision field glasses. He spotted a bunker built into the side of a dune at the far side of the parade ground, which appeared untouched. He handed Shema the glasses.

'What's in there?'

She shook her head, handing back the glasses. 'I don't know. It must be new.'

He turned to Danny. 'Get your pilot to drop a candle.'

The helicopter climbed swiftly to three thousand feet then released a 750,000-candlepower parachute flare. Sky and earth were lit by a dazzling eerie pink light as the helicopter swooped down towards the bunker and landed beside a platoon.

Goodman came running forward. 'Looks like a clean sweep,' he said. 'But no sign of Faruk Kadumi or Raza.'

'I know it,' Morton said shortly. 'Get your men and come with me.'

The parachute flare was fading but Morton saw that the dune rose in a crescent shape to a knife-edged ridge at least a hundred feet above the steel door to the bunker. No bomb could have penetrated such a barrier.

The firing became more sporadic, as they ran to the door. It was secured by a padlock and chain. Morton called for bolt-cutters and a torch. After a commando ran forward and snapped a link, Morton took the torch and opened the door. He stood transfixed by what he saw in the light beams.

There were row upon row of shelves stacked from floor to ceiling with explosives, fuses and casings: cases of Semtex and gelignite and drums of ammonium nitrate and black powder; boxes filled with concussive detonators used to trigger charges electronically; pressure release detonators that exploded when a predetermined amount of force was placed on them; bottles of prussic acid used in delay fuses. It was a bomb-maker's paradise. He turned to Danny.

'Get the napalm and a time fuse.'

Danny and Goodman sprinted to the helicopter and returned carrying between them a small drum.

'Get everybody airborne,' Morton ordered Goodman and the major led his men at a trot towards the helicopters parked in the centre of the parade ground.

There was a sudden movement in the scrub to one side of the dune. Morton whirled. In the torchlight he saw a number of Arab women and children rise and run in panic.

'Check the area,' he ordered Wolfie, Michelle and Shema. 'Get them out of here.'

He turned to Danny. 'A ten-minute setting should be fine.'

Danny clamped the time fuse clock to the drum and together they carried it into the bunker. When Danny had set the clock, they ran back to the helicopter. Wolfie, Michelle and Shema were already squashed among the commandos when they clambered on board.

'You did well,' Morton said.

Several of the commandos nodded tiredly as he picked his way up to the flight deck. As they lifted off, Morton called each of the other choppers on the radio to enquire about casualties. There were three dead commandos, eleven wounded, five of them seriously. It could have been worse.

'Fifteen seconds,' Danny called out from the cabin.

'Everybody brace yourself,' Morton ordered.

Moments later a pinprick of purplish-red light exploded to a glowing fireball hundreds of feet wide over the site of Raza's camp. The intensity of the light was so bright it lit up the inside of the chopper with the brightness of the sun.

No one spoke.

Morton could taste the brilliance of that light; it tasted like lead.

The shock wave from compressed air rocked the helicopter, bounced it upwards and then plunged it towards the ground. As quickly as it had arrived the shock wave passed. The helicopter was back in calm air.

When, an hour later, they landed on the deck of the *Independence*, the sky over Libya still glowed red. The glow remained even as Morton and his Men stepped from the Jet-Ranger at Luqa airport to transfer to the Concorde. Moments later a second helicopter landed with Goodman and his platoon. Carrying the bags with a change of clothes and their weapons, they too hurried to board the plane.

As the Concorde took off the fiery glow finally merged with the dawn of a new day.

29

The car jolted over another pothole and came to a stop outside a shack, which appeared to Raza to be held together with cord and nails.

The rain, which had fallen steadily since they had left Mexico City, had stopped, leaving only the humidity. Despite the air conditioner the inside of the car was like a sauna.

Every time he moved, Raza could feel the dampness of the upholstery against his dark three-piece suit. During the long drive he had regularly needed to wipe the gold-rimmed glasses he had adopted as a disguise.

The hand-tooled briefcase on the seat beside him glistened in the damp. Inside was his Chilean passport and documents stating he was a member of a Santiago brokerage with business appointments in Chicago and New York. The forged papers were purely for back-up. Raza did not expect to encounter any checks on his way into the United States.

The driver, who reeked of fiery jalopano peppers, turned and displayed a mouthful of badly discoloured teeth.

'Pilot ees inside, senhor.'

Beyond the hut, Raza could see the Beech-18 parked on the grass strip.

'Tell him I'll be there in a minute.'

The man shrugged and climbed out of the car. He was used to the ways of his passengers and the cartel paid him well.

Raza watched him waddle towards the hut, scratching his backside. The man was a peasant. He had even broken wind at table when they had stopped at the safe house on the way here. There had been a fax from Nadine waiting, saying that Faruk Kadumi was on his way to New York. He had sent a short acknowledgement.

As the car had passed through a succession of improvised towns and villages, he had begun to wonder why Nadine had mentioned nothing about the success of the London operation. He had tried to call her on the mobile phone the cabal had provided, but there had been only the long continuous sound that indicated the villa's number was out of service. That sometimes happened with a sandstorm. But this wasn't the month for sandstorms. Then, minutes ago, he had received a call from the cabal's chief operator in Mexico asking him to contact Ayatollah Muzwaz immediately.

Raza dialled the number in Iran. With the air conditioning off, the atmosphere in the car had become even more cloying.

The familiar wheezy voice was immediately demanding. 'You have heard?'

'I have been travelling, O Magnificent One,' Raza said.

'Then you do not know what has happened in London and Libya,' the Ayatollah said chestily.

Raza felt a sudden pounding in his head. The pain was back, worse than he had ever known it. He closed his eyes; the throbbing was still there.

'What has happened?' he finally asked, opening his eyes.

The Ayatollah told him, in that hard, driving voice. He told him about Effendi and Faruk Kadumi, about the death of Arish and the arrest of all the collectors. Finally he told him about the destruction in Libya. He spared Raza nothing.

'The Zionists,' the Ayatollah continued in the same harsh voice. 'They are responsible. Morton – he is behind it all. Yet you assured us he would be no threat. We made our plans on your assurance. We believed you. We trusted you.'

'He could not have done this alone,' Raza choked. 'The Supreme Leader must have betrayed us. The Zionists have corrupted him through their allies in the White House. The dog Appleton, he would be the one. He must be dealt with!'

'You were betrayed from within!' the cold, implacable voice continued.

'Within? I do not understand, O Magnificent One. Within?'

The Ayatollah wheezed before continuing.

'This woman of yours who was a prisoner in Germany. Our most trusted brother there has told us she has been released. She was seen boarding the Zionist plane to London. Later she was seen at the airport in Paris. She is working with them. She has betrayed you, we are certain!'

The pounding in his head was making Raza dizzy. The air was unbearably hot, yet the sweat trickling down his body was cold.

'Did she do it for money? Was she bribed or blackmailed?' the Ayatollah asked rhetorically. 'In the end it is of no consequence. She betrayed you.'

Raza wanted to scream. Then the moment passed. When he spoke his voice was flat.

'It is not possible. She is totally loyal –'

'Do not speak to me about loyalty!' the Ayatollah rasped. 'You assured us that everyone you chose would be absolutely loyal, would obey your every order. But look at that imbecile you sent to London!'

'I have already told you, O Magnificent One, that I will deal with him once he has done his work!'

'There is now less than a day left before we must give the signal for jihad,' the pitiless voice continued. 'Many of my colleagues feel we cannot risk that after your failure in London. Far from cowing our enemies, you have alerted them. They are now more vigilant than ever. We are all very disappointed in what has happened.'

Suddenly, Raza was shouting. 'Listen, old man, it is not finished yet! Do not judge me until it is!'

Raza broke the connection and, grabbing his briefcase, he climbed out of the car and ran towards the shack.

As the Concorde passed over Boston, Morton continued to listen to the arguments on screen among the group of advisers around the President of the United States, assembled in the basement Situation Room beneath the White House.

Danny, Wolfie, Michelle and Goodman stood in a tense group behind Morton's seat, knowing the fate of their mission depended on what was being said in Washington.

The arguments had started while the Concorde had still been 500 miles out over the Atlantic, and the President had called

Morton to add his congratulations over the thwarting of the biological attack on Britain and the destruction of Raza's base. Throughout the flight from Malta, the gratitude of Britain's Prime Minister had been followed by that of every European leader. Morton had told them all it was not yet over. The reminder had sparked the disagreement in the Situation Room on what to do next.

The focus of attention for those seated around the conference table was a model of the Harmoos mansion and the surrounding countryside.

Once more the Chairman of the Joint Chiefs had the floor. He had a stevedore's shoulders and a chestful of decorations. Morton watched him glance into the screen, then turn to the President.

'In my view the military should now take control of the situation. I recommend we air strike against the Harmoos mansion. A couple of missiles down his chimney pots or through the windows will do the trick. We showed what was possible over Baghdad. After the strike we send in Delta Force and kill anybody that's left.'

There was silence in the Situation Room.

'This is not Baghdad,' the President finally said. 'We don't know who else may be in the mansion. And there must always be a risk of a near miss. Baghdad also showed, I recall, there is no such thing as precision bombing.'

Ignoring the angry flush of his chief military adviser, the President turned to stare with extraordinary concentration at the collection of toy houses that represented the township of Sweetmont.

'There's also the doubt that a missile attack will destroy all the anthrax. I'm told that an explosion could actually spread the stuff.'

Morton watched the President look around the room, his haunted eyes settling in turn briefly on the Secretary of State, the Secretary of Defence, the Director of the CIA and the Chairman of the Joint Chiefs, who sat beside Appleton. The President's voice was heavy with foreboding.

'I don't have to tell you what would happen if a missile were to land on Sweetmont. We would have demonstrations which would make those staged during the Gulf War look like a kids' parade. Every pacifist in Congress would demand my imprisonment. And think of the propaganda we'd be handing our enemies abroad. How could we talk to China and what remains of the Soviet Union about human rights when they could say we're quite prepared to bomb our own people?' The President shook his head. 'There is no way I'm going to authorise that kind of force. There's got to be some other way.'

The Chairman of the Joint Chiefs folded his arms and sat back in his chair.

'Mr President,' the Director of the FBI said, 'I've got the capability to take out the mansion. My people are trained in anti-terror tactics, but before they go, we get the Civil Defence authorities to carefully evacuate the area. That way we eliminate civilian casualties –'

'We start that kind of evacuation and it's a recipe for mass panic,' interrupted the Secretary of Defence. 'I need hardly remind you that New York's on the doorstep. When these folk from Sweetmont start showing up in Manhattan, they'll create the kind of mass panic we haven't seen since Orson Wells said the Martians had landed.'

Morton heard the Director of the CIA clear his throat. 'We could hold them in protective custody until all this is over,' he suggested.

The Secretary of State shook his head wearily. 'Do that and after this is over we'll have every ambulance-chasing lawyer in town persuading those Sweetmont folk to file suit against the government for wrongful arrest.'

The President looked around the table once more. 'So, gentlemen, what do we do? Send in the FBI?'

As several heads began to nod, the President looked directly at the Agency's Director.

'Your people have had no direct experience of dealing with a situation like this, right? Let alone terrorists of this calibre?'

The Director gave a reluctant nod. Once more there was silence in the Situation Room.

Then, for the first time since the discussion had begun, the President directly addressed Morton. 'Given what you have heard, Mr Morton, how would you deal with the situation?'

Morton did not hesitate. 'With my own people. We have the capability.'

'You care to tell us how? And why you are so certain?'

'I prefer not to, Mr President. There are no absolutes in a matter like this,' Morton replied.

Appleton had half-turned to say something to the President, then changed his mind. Silence returned to the Situation Room.

'Very well,' the President said at last. 'Given what you have achieved, I intend to entrust the safety of this nation to your hands. You will, of course, continue to receive every support you need. Our resources and manpower are yours to command. And our prayers are with you.'

'Thank you, Mr President,' Morton replied.

After the screen had cleared he sat for a long time staring at it.

Dressed in protective clothing, Matti stood beside the City Center Emergency Room Director in the MICU cubicle, gazing at Miriam. She was in an exhausted sleep. Her bed was surrounded by monitoring equipment, machines that went click and ping and provided confirmation that the battle continued. Liquid was being infused into a vein in her arm from a bottle on a stand.

'I called London and spoke to Dr Cooper, like you suggested,' the Director said. 'She recommended we double the dose. It looks like it's working. In the past hour Miriam's vital signs have begun to stabilise.'

'She's a fighter, doc. That's the best shot she has.'

'You better believe it,' the Director said. 'You damn well better believe it!'

The Beech swooped low over the Rio Grande.

'Welcome to the USA,' the pilot said. He was short and wiry, with a face scarred with acne.

'Right now the Border Patrol radar will be trying to track us and pinpoint where we touch down. Adds to the excitement.'

Raza stared at him. Another of the world's cowboys.

'No sweat,' the pilot grinned. 'I do this three times a day. After Nam, avoiding the patrol's small beer.'

Raza turned and looked out of the window at the river below. Moments later they passed over the chain-link fence separating the United States from Mexico. On the razor barbs on top of the fence, shreds of clothing were visible, left by Mexicans who had tried to scale the barrier.

Minutes later the aircraft landed on the Texas mesa and taxied to where a limousine waited. The sun reflected off its tinted windows. The pilot reached over and opened the door on Raza's side of the cockpit.

'You'll have to jump for it, mister. The fee don't cover valet parking!'

Raza tossed his briefcase out of the door and waited until the plane was barely rolling before leaping to the ground. The pilot slammed shut the door and the Beech immediately swung round into the wind and gathered speed. By the time Raza had reached the limo, the plane was in the air.

As soon as he was settled in the back seat, the chauffeur drove over the bumpy ground on to a track. A mile later the track gave way to a road. After another couple of miles it merged with a freeway. Only then did the chauffeur turn and address Raza.

'Your ticket is in the wallet in the door. Mr Harmoos wishes you a pleasant flight,' he said.

Morton and Matti continued to walk around the high-sided van Swift Renovations had provided. On its side was the logo 'All Sounds of America Inc'.

The van was parked between the Concorde and an El Al 747, which had landed at Kennedy from Tel Aviv an hour before. That section of the airport had been closed and patrolled by police and Federal agents, while the equipment was unloaded from the 747.

'The FBI have a couple of hundred agents on stand by,' Matti was saying. 'The National Guard have their two best units on full alert. We've even had the navy offering helicopters. Everybody wants to be able to say they played a part.'

Morton nodded. Being involved would be a powerful plus for more funding later when it came to budget time in Washington.

'Helicopters could be useful,' he said. 'But keep everybody out of the area.'

Passing the van's tail gate, Morton could see Danny supervising how he wanted the equipment positioned. Half a dozen of the technicians from Matti's apartment were mounting a squat box onto a platform, which could be raised through a panel in the van's roof.

'Our ghetto blaster,' Danny said cheerily, patting the contraption designed to shatter glass or human eardrums with its electronic beam.

'Harmoos still suspects nothing?'

'Absolutely not,' Danny replied. 'Our man on the flight just called in to say Harmoos is spending his time trying to date the flight attendant. He's due to land at La Guardia in a couple of hours.'

'Anything new from the border?'

Danny checked a clipboard. 'The border patrol have so far spotted three illegal flights, but each time they got there, there was nothing but tyre tracks. Bill Gates has his people spread along the Mexican side. Nothing so far.'

'Tell them to keep looking, Danny. That, for sure, is the way he'll come.'

Morton saw Matti returning.

'This motel, how is it?' he asked.

Matti grinned. 'Better than you'd find on the West Bank – but only marginally. The sort of place where passing salesmen rent a room for the afternoon if they get lucky with a bored local housewife.'

'I take it none of them will be around?'

'No problem,' assured Matti. 'I booked everything for two days. And got an extra discount. That tells you the sort of place it is. Staff are the usual kind of sweated labour. The manager's a guy called Tom Benton, a real fawner. Nothing known on any of them.'

Morton watched more equipment coming out of the hold and being carried to the van.

'We won't need that second day, Matti,' he said. 'The sooner we get this over, the sooner you can get back to Miriam.'

Before Matti could respond, Morton had turned towards Wolfie, Michelle and Shema as they came down the steps from the Concorde. Shema had dark rings under her eyes. For most of the flight from Libya she had stayed alone in the Prime Minister's cabin. As he'd passed on his way to the flight deck, Morton had heard her praying for Nadine.

Together they walked towards the row of cars parked on the tarmac. On each door was stamped the All Sounds logo.

Several of the cars were already filled with Goodman's men. During the flight they had changed into civilian clothes and looked as if they'd stepped out of a Tel Aviv nightclub. Goodman, dressed in a bright sports shirt and skin-tight Levis, was loading the last of the musical instrument cases into a car boot. Each case contained a weapon and ammunition.

'How are you doing?' Morton asked Shema.

'Fine.'

He squinted at her. 'That I doubt. Okay, maybe.'

'She wasn't the sister I remembered. He'd destroyed her. But I'm not ready to talk about it.' The words came out in a rush.

They continued walking in silence.

Then Shema pointed to the logos. 'What do they mean?'

Morton shrugged. 'It's the best we could do. We're in the music business. The sort that provides the noise that covers up the lack of talent.'

They walked a little further before Shema asked, 'What do you want me to do?'

'When we get there, stay close to me. Everywhere I go, you go,' Morton said.

She turned to him. 'You know the law of the desert, David. It's the same for Jew or Arab. An eye for an eye. I want the chance to kill Raza.'

Morton held her gaze, then shook his head.

'There's more at stake here than personal revenge, Shema. And there are others with prior claims to you. If there is a chance, take it. But act within the rules of our operation. I not only want him dead, I want the menace he threatens destroyed. Eliminating that menace comes above all else.'

She looked away so that he could not see her face. Then she nodded.

Lou Panchez sat behind the wheel of one of the cars. He opened the passenger door.

'Want to ride with me? I've got the best selection of Kuwaiti music you ever heard,' he said.

Shema gave a little smile. 'That's the best offer I've had all day.'

Morton saw Danny standing on the van's tail gate, holding

one hand up and forming a circle with thumb and forefinger. Matti, already behind the wheel of his car, would lead the way.

In convoy, the staff of All Sounds drove across the tarmac and out of the airport. Twenty minutes later they were on the Connecticut Expressway and heading for the Stay-In-Style Motel.

As the United flight climbed out of Chicago for La Guardia, the attendant offered Raza champagne. He shook his head and closed his eyes. She stuck a red paper flag on the side of his seat, a reminder her passenger was not to be disturbed.

The terrible rage and consuming hatred that had accompanied Raza's headache on the flight from Texas had gone. He no longer felt that a hydra-headed monster, all with the face of Morton, was waiting to ambush him. As the plane climbed over the Illinois plains, he felt purged.

What had happened in Libya *was* devastating, everyone was dead, everything destroyed. The Zionists seldom took prisoners.

He would miss Nadine, of course. But he would find another girl to mould in his image. There were plenty.

And he would find a new base. He had found one after being driven from southern Lebanon, and again after that Satan-lover in Damascus had ordered him out of Syria, and later when Saddam had proved to be a false prophet. Now Libya's Supreme Leader had proved to be another follower of the American Devil. In time, he would be dealt with. Just as in time another true believer would offer sanctuary. Perhaps it would be provided by the rulers of Yemen or in Ethiopia. Or Sudan, or Somalia. There were still plenty of places where shelter could be found, where he could regroup and where men would flock to him. They always had.

What had happened in Britain *was* a disaster of the greatest magnitude. But to think further about it would be to waste time and energy.

Shema? He would deal with her. But only after he had completed what he had come to do. And whatever she may have told the Zionists, she could not have revealed to them what was to happen here in America.

In spite of all the setbacks, he would still succeed. Despite what had happened in Athens and London, the enemy could not be sure how many bottles he had left. Their uncertainty would be his strength. He would strike the way he always had – with a swiftness, a boldness, a ferocity that had so often in the past left his enemies helpless and terrified.

The prospect made Raza's closed eyes prick with excitement before he finally fell asleep in the first class section of the 747.

Morton's team settled in quickly. Within a couple of hours they had set up samples of All Sounds' range of amplifiers and synthesisers in the motel's conference room. The equipment looked no different from that of the brand leaders in the field; it had been purchased by the crew chief of Swift Renovations from a wholesaler in Queens.

While the display was being assembled, the chief had adorned the motel's lobby with cardboard mounted photos of groups using All Sounds gear. When motel staff mentioned they didn't recognise any of them, the chief smiled enigmatically, as if the fault was theirs.

Tom Benton, the hotel manager, had soon tagged All Sounds as a tight-fisted company. That would explain why its people only used the bar to buy soft drinks and chose the least expensive items on the menu and never made calls through the switchboard. A number were obviously musicians. They carried their instrument cases wherever they went. And they all seemed to be waiting for something to happen. The exception was their president, Mr Alexander.

He was a real dynamo: in and out, back and forth from the van that occupied several car spaces in the parking lot. Mr Alexander always seemed to be engaged in low-voiced conversations. He frequently nodded and said 'for sure'.

In some ways he reminded Benton of Mr Harmoos. Mr Alexander had the same driving urgency, the same ability to seem to be everywhere at once.

A minute ago he had been in the conference room, beaming benevolently. Now he was out by the van, talking animatedly to Mr Skorous, the company's vice president who wore his eye patch like a badge of office. With them was Mr Alexander's

374

assistant. She looked like one of those hauntingly beautiful Arab women Benton had sometimes seen with Mr Harmoos.

Come to think of it, there was something rather Middle Eastern about most of the All Sounds staff. They had that same reserved, watchful manner he'd seen in many of the Arabs who worked for Mr Harmoos.

The exception was Mr Harmoos' assistant, Nuri. Whenever he dropped in, he always had time for a drink and a chat. And he always stood his round and tipped generously. A couple of days ago Nuri had phoned to ask if there were any groups booked into the motel: a reunion, a conference, any kind of get-together. He'd explained Mr Harmoos was planning a staff party and didn't want it to clash with any other booking.

Watching Mr Alexander and the others climb into their van, Benton picked up the telephone. By the time the number was ringing the van had manoeuvred out of the parking lot.

Morton and Shema followed Danny through a sliding panel behind the driver's seat into the back of the van. There were half a dozen technicians already there, standing or squatting before the racks of equipment that covered both walls. The electronic beam gun occupied most of the centre of the floor.

'This console gives us push-button contact with Washington and Tel Aviv,' Danny explained. 'You want the President, you just push twice. We got a direct line to the Oval Office and his bedroom.'

Morton saw that stuck over the button to the White House was a paper strip with the words: *Appleton By-pass.*

Danny next indicated a small switchboard. 'CIA, FBI, National Guard. Again, just pick up a phone. No need to dial. We've got permanent open lines.'

He turned and pointed to a row of recorders along one wall. Before them sat technicians with headsets. Several spares hung from the wall hooks. Pinned to the side of the van was a large-scale architect's plan labelled: *Harmoos mansion.*

'Lou got hold of it,' Danny said. 'He sweet-talked the architect into believing he was going to profile him in some trade paper and walked away with all we'll need.'

Morton studied the plan while Danny continued, 'We've got

every phone point under surveillance. Our field crew's planted parabolics all round the place, in the cornfields and out back of the repair shop. We can switch from room to room to follow a conversation.'

'How about the shutters on the windows?'

Danny grinned. 'Harmoos must have been expecting the Mafia to come calling. Our people reckon they're made of rolled steel. Only way to deal with them is this.'

He stooped and opened a long case on the floor. Inside was an anti-tank grenade launcher.

'Incoming call on phone three,' called a technician.

Morton glanced at the plan. Phone three was in the kitchen in the Harmoos mansion.

A woman's voice answered.

'Is Mr Nuri there?' asked Benton.

'He is not available.'

'Can you give him a message?'

'What?'

'Just tell him Mr Benton called and we have a company booking for the next two days. Any time after that will be fine for Mr Harmoos' party.'

The woman hung up without another word.

In the van Morton looked at Shema.

'Lila,' she said.

'Exactly.' Morton smiled.

The call from that stupid motel manager had deepened the fury that had been building in Lila since she had arrived at the mansion.

These people were dangerous fools. First, Harmoos had left shortly before she had arrived. Then Nuri, the arrogant imbecile he had supposedly left in charge, had dared to tell her that Mr Harmoos had other interests to attend to. What could be more important than firing the first shots that would plunge the world into the greatest jihad ever visited upon the infidels?

Instead, look what had happened! The news from first London and now Libya was almost impossible for her to believe – if she had not heard it from that other imbecile, Faruk Kadumi. He had been told about the double catastrophe by Raza's man in

Algeria when he had changed flights there. Faruk Kadumi had arrived in Sweetmont in a state of collapse. After she had questioned him, she had sent him to the basement to help that other craven fool, Ismail. In a few hours they would have completed filling the vials. Then she would kill them personally – the way she would also like to kill Nuri. He deserved to die for his sheer stupidity in letting those two men into the mansion. She had made him check. The tyre company they claimed to represent had confirmed the names on the business cards were their employees. But Nuri, in his stupidity, had failed to check the physical description of the company employees against those of the men who had called. When she had told him to phone back, he had refused, giving her a withering smile and saying that would only arouse suspicion.

It would be a pleasure to deal with these people.

But for the moment they all had a part to play. Composing herself, Lila went to deliver Benton's message to Nuri.

The van continued its leisurely progress along the country roads around Sweetmont. In the back Morton and Shema listened to the conversation Lila had had after Benton's call. It had been recorded as taking place in the mansion's basement.

She had asked someone how much longer, and the man had replied it was very dangerous to hurry. Then a second man's voice, supercilious and condescending, had said that the speed of a camel does not always mean a good camel.

Morton looked at Shema. She quickly shook her head. She did not recognise either of the men's voices. Then a third man's voice grumbled that the sooner she left, the quicker they could finish.

'Wonderful thing, technology,' Morton said, positively beaming. There had been no mistaking the voice of Faruk Kadumi.

Wolfie recognised Rachid Harmoos as he came off the flight from Miami. A smile like that only came from a youth spent selling oriental carpets. And the bowing and scraping of the limo driver only came from someone assured of a hefty tip.

While the driver had hovered at the arrivals gate, outside the terminal Michelle stumbled as she'd passed his parked limo. The moment had given her long enough to clamp a disc-shaped transmitter, the size of a penny, under the limo's boot.

When the limo left the airport and headed for the expressway, Lou eased the Ford Tempo up through the traffic and dropped in a few places behind. Michelle tweaked the receiver to improve reception. From the limo came the voice of Harmoos making small talk with the chauffeur.

When they reached the freeway, Harmoos told the driver to raise the partition window. Wolfie and Michelle heard the sound of a phone dialling.

'*Aiwa*,' Lila said.

'I shall be with you in forty minutes,' Harmoos replied in Arabic. 'Is all in order?'

She made a guttural, mirthless sound.

'What has happened?'

She told him: about London and Libya; about the visit of the two men from the tyre company and the call from Benton.

'Get me Nuri!'

In the car they heard the phone in the mansion being put down, then picked up again almost at once.

'*Salaam alaikum.*'

'What's this nonsense with Benton, Nuri?'

'I thought after it is over, it would be good to take everyone for a celebration –'

'You are a fool, Nuri,' Harmoos interrupted. 'And I have no room for fools.'

Michelle and Wolfie looked at each other and smiled.

30

Two hours had passed. Raza's deadline was only five hours away.

In the van, Morton continued to monitor the operations activity – but for the moment he stood apart. In the end it always came to this: time. Suppose Raza did not come? So many times in the past Raza had made the preparations for others to execute. Morton felt the weight of that possibility bearing down like a physical burden. He knew he had done all he could.

Following a carefully planned route Morton had given him, the van driver continued to travel down one country road and up another. He frequently checked a large-scale map spread on his knees to make sure he did not take a turning that would bring him closer than three miles to the spot marked as 'T'. Around the letter, Morton had outlined on the map the target perimeter of the Harmoos estate.

The tension inside the van had noticeably increased after Morton had listened over a headset to Goodman briefing the platoon in the motel conference room. Afterwards he had called Tel Aviv and Washington to update Karshov and the President.

Danny had remained in constant communication with the FBI control van parked five miles to the west of Sweetmont. Assembled there were the Federal agents and National Guard units.

The panel behind the van driver's seat had been wedged open to allow a technician to use a camera mounted on a tripod and connected to a monitor screen. He was videoing all passing vehicles. On other roads in the area, two more Swift Renovations trucks were performing the same function.

The tapes were fed to the FBI van. There, a team of agents checked the registration of each vehicle while others performed the more difficult task of lifting from the videos faces captured by the cameras. These were then turned into still photographs and fed to FBI and CIA computers in Washington. Copies were also sent to Lester Finel in Tel Aviv. So far none of this investigation had produced any call-back to Morton.

An hour ago a technician in the van had filmed the limo as it entered the Harmoos estate. Minutes later he had stopped the camera as Wolfie and Michelle cruised by.

Since then the traffic had been light, mostly in and out of Sweetmont, until, in the past few minutes, the camera had started filming Day-Nite cabs converging on the estate. The entire fleet appeared to be heading there.

Squatting on the floor of the van, Morton continued to follow the fury that had started as soon as Harmoos had appeared at the mansion. His rage had begun in the hall, moved to the library, and then swept through the dining-room and on into the main lounge. It was like a hurricane, picking up force as Harmoos went from one room to another. Right now he was back in the library, and sounding like a man possessed.

'Those two men were agents of the Great Satan!' he raved. 'And how do you know they didn't plant listening devices. How? You fool, how?'

'I have checked the entire house, Mr Harmoos,' Nuri said nervously.

'Check again, you imbecile!'

In Morton's headset there was a crash of sound, so violent that it almost deafened him. In the library, Harmoos swept another line of fine leather-bound books to the floor.

'Check every shelf! Every book! Tear up the carpet! Check everywhere!'

'Yes, Mr Harmoos!'

Suddenly Lila's voice filled Morton's headset. 'This is a waste of time, Mr Harmoos! These men were only here for a few minutes. Nuri was a fool to let them in. But they never had an opportunity to leave anything behind so let's not waste any more time on this nonsense!'

In the van, a bountiful smile wreathed Morton's face. He

tapped a technician on the leg. 'I think we'd all like to hear this, Chaim.'

The technician switched the recorder to broadcast. From the speaker came renewed fury.

'Hold your tongue, woman!' roared Harmoos. 'You forget who you speak to!'

The van was filled with the sound of Lila's sudden anger.

'I know who I speak to – a fool. An employer of fools! Only a fool would have gone to Miami at a time like this. Only a fool would have chosen another fool like Ismail to do such important work. Be assured, when the time comes, such foolishness will not be forgotten!'

'Ismail,' Morton said. 'So that's his name.'

Another burst of fury filled the van.

'Be quiet, woman!' Harmoos thundered. 'Without me you would have less money for our cause.'

Morton was now on his feet, leaning against the side of the van, arms folded, the smile more beatific than ever.

'"Our cause"?' came Lila's withering voice. 'What do you mean "our cause"?'

They all heard her rage erupt as if it was fired out of the neck of a bottle.

'When did you last come and visit my people? Not your people. *Mine!* To see how *we* live. To hear the screams of the victims of the Zionists! When did you last share *our* pain? Hear the cries of *our* children every time they hear one of their planes? When did you last even hear a bomb fall? Or have to remember that if you can hear the explosion, you are still alive?'

Lila's voice was like a small storm howling through the house.

'Do you know what it's like to be buried for days wondering if you will be dug out? Have you ever seen children lying dead, all with bullets in their backs from running away from the Zionist guns?'

Morton looked at Shema. She was staring fixedly at the loud-speaker. The van continued to echo with Lila's words.

'Do you know what they did last Christmas? Disguised their bombs as gift parcels. They left them where they knew our children would find them. Not your children! *Ours!* You think your money makes up for that? You think because you contribute, it is everything? Do you have any idea what it is actually like to be there – facing them? Do you know that those the Zionists don't murder with their cluster bombs, die from dysentery or hunger? A thousand every month in Beirut alone. Even more out in the Beka'a! Do you know *anything*, you fool!'

There was the sound of a door slamming. There was no way for those in the van to tell if it was produced by Harmoos or Lila.

Shortly after a technician announced, 'Incoming call'.

Morton grabbed a headset and handed one to Shema.

The voice of the woman Matti had already identified to Morton as the maid answered.

'*Salaam alaikum*,' a man's voice intoned, and then hung up.

Morton looked at Shema. She nodded.

Raza drove exactly on the speed limit. The evening was heavy and overcast, like Beirut on a winter's day. From time to time he checked the map the hire firm at La Guardia had provided with the car. But the signs to the expressway were plentiful and the Sweetmont exit well signposted.

A couple of times a police siren had made his shoulder muscles tighten. But the cruiser had swept by, going the other way. Just to make sure, he'd tuned the radio to an all-news local station.

Coming off the Sweetmont exit, he continued to listen to a report that there was going to be a Middle East peace conference. He felt the blood rush to his face and forced himself to stay calm.

There could be no peace until the Zionists were driven into the sea. Saddam's rockets had shown what could be done. A few Scud missiles falling on Tel Aviv had all but reduced the Zionists to quaking terror. Only the American Satan had saved them. It was one more reason to deliver revenge on the Satan and his people. And after he had done so there would be no more talk of a peace conference.

Raza once more glanced at the map, then made a right turn. A van was coming towards him. Raza gave it a quick glance as it passed.

A mile further on as he slowed at an intersection to make another right, a car passed, with a young couple in front. Another mile beyond the intersection he turned into the Harmoos estate.

In the van Morton was soothing the mortified technician peering into the exposed innards of the video camera.

'It could happen to anyone, Benjy.'

'But it's the first time it's happened to me, Colonel. I checked the damned thing every half-hour. Then this.'

Minutes before the camera had jammed.

In the back of the van Danny was listening through a headset and nodding. He turned and called to Morton.

'Michelle got a quick look. He's wearing spectacles, but his build and skin colouring fit.'

Moments later Matti called in. 'Chrysler, blue two-door. Driver turned into the Harmoos spread.'

Morton smiled at the technician. 'You see, Benjy, it isn't that bad after all.'

Morton turned to Danny and asked him to have the All Sound cars go to their assembly point, and to inform the FBI control van what was happening.

Raza had gone immediately to where Faruk Kadumi and Ismail were at work. He had asked one question: how much longer? Faruk Kadumi had said they would be finished in one hour. Without another word, Raza had left and gone to Harmoos' study. Lila, Nuri and the millionaire were waiting for him.

'Everything, as you will hear, is ready,' Harmoos began. 'First let me say I truly regret these delays. But the Ayatollah personally recommended this wretch, Ismail.' Harmoos cleared his throat and then continued, his voice soft and silky. 'May I say also how deeply I regret your misfortune in Libya. Be assured, I will be only too honoured to provide the necessary funding to help you rebuild.'

'We will speak of that later,' Raza said. 'Just tell me what has been prepared.'

Harmoos nodded to Nuri, who consulted a clipboard. 'Each driver will leave here at two-minute intervals. They will go to all seven airports in the area. Waiting at each will be planes from Mr Harmoos' air charter company. They have all filed flight plans to the designated cities. These are Detroit, Chicago, Houston, Washington DC, San Francisco, Los Angeles and Seattle.

Men from Mr Harmoos' transportation company will be waiting at each arrival point to collect the delivery. At 8.00 a.m. tomorrow, local time, each delivery will be released at the designated targets. In Detroit this will be the main Ford assembly plant. In Chicago, the Wrigley Building. In San Francisco, the financial district. In Los Angeles the delivery will be made in Burbank. In Seattle our agent there will ensure it is released at the Boeing plant. In Houston the NASA facility. In each case we will use the water supply on the air conditioning system –'

'Each target has been carefully chosen to cause the widest possible panic,' interrupted Harmoos. 'The spread allows for a totally effective attack against totems America puts such store on: money, prestige, food and communications. And Trekfontein showed how effective a simple delivery method can be.'

'What about Washington?' Raza asked.

'Ah, Washington,' murmured Harmoos. He scratched behind one ear and smiled for the first time since Raza had entered the room. 'Please explain, Nuri.'

'In Washington, the delivery will take the form of a tiny remote-controlled plane launched in the vicinity of the White House. The guards will no doubt attempt to shoot it down. By their very action they will bring destruction to the Great Satan and those around him. Their bullets will hit the bottle and the liquid will be air dispersed over a wide area.'

'If they don't shoot?' Raza asked.

Nuri glanced at the clipboard.

'Then the plane will crash against the Oval Office windows. At this time of year they are always open. The President is a fresh air fanatic. The result will be the same.'

'New York?' Raza demanded.

'I will go there personally,' Lila said. 'Two vials dropped from the observation platform of the Empire State Building will create a dramatic effect.'

Raza frowned. 'I understood there are always guards on the platform to watch for suicide attempts. They could stop you.'

Lila shook her head. 'There's a ticker-tape parade through the city to thank the rescue services for their work on the bombed hotels. Everybody will be releasing balloons. The bottles will be tied to two. Time fuses will allow them to explode five hundred feet above the street. There'll be several hundred thousand people below. The result will be gratifying.'

Raza nodded and turned to Nuri.

'And I will drive overnight to Boston,' added Nuri. 'A couple of vials should take care of the students at Harvard.'

'You see,' Harmoos smiled, 'everything is taken care of.' He gave his ear a vigorous scratching.

In the van they all heard Raza's low sigh of satisfaction. Then Morton sat down before a console and began to punch buttons and speak softly and urgently into the phone. By the time he had finished the parking lot around the FBI control van had almost emptied, and across the country Federal agents and the National Guard were joining Swat teams moving to every designated target.

Morton began to prowl behind the technicians, like some impresario taking snatches of discordant conversations and shaping them in his mind into a whole that only he could see.

From the basement: '– will all this really make any difference?' Ismail asked.

'It will show the friends of Zionism the price they must pay. Now get on with your work,' Faruk Kadumi answered brusquely.

From then on only the sound of clinking glass came from the basement.

A parabolic picked up an exchange between Harmoos and Nuri.

'I heard them talking before they went to her room,' Nuri said. 'She still blames you for not being here.'

'Let her. My offer of money will concentrate his mind on what really matters. He is a pragmatist. He understands the rules. He will, of course, appease Lila because he needs her.'

'He already has. He has agreed she can kill Ismail.'

'But I hope not here. The wretch must first be driven to some other place.'

'She also asked to deal with Faruk Kadumi, Mr Harmoos.'

'And?'

'Raza said no. He said he must deal with him personally.'

And, from Lila's bedroom, had come the sounds of their love-making, followed by Raza telling her he wanted to sleep for an hour.

385

In the van Morton continued to listen, his face now composed in an unsmiling hunter's stare.

By dusk the All Sounds cars were parked around the van sheltering behind a clump of trees. Morton continued to talk by phone to the FBI control van. He gave a final order.

'Have those refrigeration trucks moved right up to your road blocks. Make sure everyone understands that when the time comes, it's work strictly for the Fort Detrick people.'

Across the crowded van, Danny called out that Wolfie was still reporting all was quiet.

Wolfie and Michelle were on the far side of the trees, looking out across one of the estate's cornfields. On the far side was the mansion. They had a mobile phone and their crossbows and a pannier of bolts between them. Each also had a Uzi.

On the edge of another ripening field, Lou squatted, keeping surveillance on the repair shop. Beside him was a PT-92 9-mm automatic with a double-stacked magazine.

Fifteen minutes after taking up position, Lou called in that the fleet of cabs outside the garage was moving. A minute later Wolfie reported they had begun to appear at the back of the mansion.

Morton looked around the van. 'Everybody set?'

There was a chorus of affirmation.

Danny opened a smaller box beside the grenade launcher. Inside were phosphorus shells, which on impact would produce a temperature of 5,000 degrees.

'Where's Shema?' Morton suddenly asked.

'She went out, said she wanted some air,' Danny said.

Morton pushed his way through the opening behind the driver's seat. Outside, Goodman and his men were opening their instrument cases and checking slide releases, peering into chambers and then rejacking slides to chamber rounds.

'Did you see Shema?'

Goodman nodded to the trees. 'Guess she went for a pee.'

'Help me find her,' Morton said tersely.

Michelle was waiting on the far side of the tree line.

'Seen Shema?' Morton asked.

Michelle shook her head, as did Wolfie behind her.

'Call Lou,' Morton told him. 'Maybe she's with him.'

Lou said he hadn't seen her.

'Maybe she's flipped.' Goodman was behind Morton's back. Morton turned.

'She could have changed her mind,' Goodman continued. 'Old ways die hard.'

Morton looked out over the cornfield towards the mansion. He remembered what she had said about the law of the desert.

'What are you saying, Sam?'

'She's not one of us, Colonel. She could have gone back to where, deep down in her mind, she never left.' Goodman's voice had a raw edge.

Morton continued to stare at the mansion. 'So what do you propose, Sam?' he asked as if he was genuinely interested in hearing.

'We go after her. When we find her, we kill her before she tells Raza everything she knows.'

Morton spoke softly to the cornfield. 'Go back to your men, Sam. Just continue with what you were doing.'

When Goodman had gone, Morton turned to Wolfie and Michelle.

'Go after her and bring her back. But remember she's still one of ours until I say so.'

He watched them slip into the corn, then he ran back to the van.

In the kitchen, Nuri came to the end of briefing the cab drivers.

'This is a chance for each of you to strike a blow against our enemies. But remember you will drive carefully and obey all traffic regulations. When you reach the airports you will be stopped by security before you are allowed on to the tarmac.'

Nuri began to move among them, distributing sets of papers.

'These are your clearances. They state you are delivering urgent medical supplies.'

He nodded to a pile of sealed steel boxes on the floor. Each was painted with a bold red cross.

'If anyone asks to see inside, you will point to the warning on each box that exposure outside a sterile laboratory will contaminate the contents. The warning carries the stamp of the appropriate public health authority, so there will be no problem.'

The drivers picked up their boxes and left the kitchen. As each did so, Nuri reminded them that Allah the Great and Good would protect them.

Moving almost silently yet with surprising speed, Shema reached the far side of the cornfield. She paused to get her bearings. Beyond was a wide sward of lawn. Then came a pathway. There were several ground-floor windows open and lights blazed in the rooms.

She felt calm and certain; the way she had always felt on a mission. Nothing would cloud her judgement or make her turn back. She was still a soldier, with a soldier's instincts to engage the enemy immediately and destroy him. Morton was right. A *Feydeheen* did not fear death. And now it mattered even less.

Crouching there, she remembered kneeling over Nadi, remembered the look in her sister's eyes – half-crazed and filled with blind hatred. Shema remembered all the others she had seen who had looked like that. The monster who could create such evil was indeed a destroyer.

Once more the guard, Kalashnikov in hand, came around the corner of the mansion and strolled along the path. She counted. As she reached twenty he disappeared around the back of the mansion. She began to count. Again at twenty, a new guard appeared from the front. It took him another twenty seconds to walk out of sight. The same as last time.

Checking both her throwing knives were secure in the waistband of her Levis, Shema sprinted across the grass to a window. The room inside was empty. She rolled over the sill and dropped lightly on to the carpet.

From the cornfield, Wolfie reported to Morton where Shema had gone. Then he and Michelle continued to creep towards the mansion.

In the basement, Ismail turned to Lila. Behind him the lid of the freezer chest was open. The table was littered with empty bottles that had contained the saline to mix with the Anthrax-B-C. The two bottles of Grecian Nights stood a little apart.

'I have been proud to serve the cause,' Ismail said. He wiped his hands on his trousers.

Lila had developed an unearthly composure. There was always this time of total disconnection beforehand.

'Why are you looking at me like that?' Ismail asked.

'Why do you think?' She could hear her voice suddenly tense with action.

A shattering thought struck Ismail. He could see death in her face.

'I would like to see Mr Harmoos,' he said, unnaturally loud.

'Stay still,' she commanded. She had casually reached inside her jacket and drawn out her gun, heavy and black, with a bulbous nose.

Ismail felt the room closing in on him, as if everything had suddenly been absorbed by that unwavering nose with its black hole pointing at him.

'Why?' he whispered. 'Why?'

Lila fired three shots in swift succession. One passed through Ismail's forehead at the hairline, scattering pieces of brain. The second removed his left eye. The third entered his mouth. For a moment Ismail remained upright as if impervious to the bullets. Then he sagged to the stone floor, his head hitting hard and sending the blood splattering.

Stepping quickly back to avoid the mess, Lila put the gun in her pocket, turned and left the basement.

Shema had reached the door of the room when she heard the unmistakable sound of a body falling. She opened the door a fraction and looked quickly into the hall. There were several doors, all closed except one, which was ajar. She saw a staircase leading down and, coming up, the sound of footsteps. Shema ran to stand behind the half-open door.

Some sixth sense, perhaps no more than an animal's instinct for survival, made Lila pause as she reached the top of the staircase. She peered into the hall. Everything looked exactly as it had when she had gone down to the basement. Yet she was certain there was something. Someone. Slowly, she reached for her gun, and then hurled herself through the doorway.

Shema was already moving, a diving, co-ordinated movement that had carried her several feet by the time Lila fired. The bullet smashed into the door frame.

In that moment Lila recognised Shema. She paused, stunned, neither able to accept nor understand. Shema's knife buried itself in Lila's neck.

As Shema moved back from the body a door further down the hall opened. Raza stood there.

In the van, Morton listened to Wolfie.

'We're close to the back. No sign of Shema. The third cab's rolling.'

Danny relayed the news to the FBI control van.

'Tell Morton we got the first two. No sweat,' the agent-in-charge replied. 'We just pincered them out. The Fort Detrick people have transferred the boxes to their bio-hazard truck. It's going to be –'

In the van they all clearly heard a new voice cutting in on the transmission.

'This is Mahmoud! Trouble! Men with guns –'

'Take him out!' came the crisp voice of the FBI agent. 'Just take him out now!'

Over the speakers came the sound of shots, followed by silence.

The agent-in-charge was back on the line. 'We have one dead cab driver. He was so close, he was on our waveband.'

'The box?'

'Secured.'

Morton turned to Danny. 'Think they heard?'

'I'll call Wolfie.'

Wolfie was already calling the van. 'Some sort of panic in the house. A couple of the guards are checking around outside,' came Wolfie's whisper. 'Shuttering's going down on the windows. All the cabs are beginning to roll at once.'

Morton spoke into his throat mike to Goodman.

'Sam, get your men up there fast. Matti, you and Lou as well. Watch out for Wolfie and Michelle. They're at the back of the target.'

Outside Morton heard the sound of running, then cars starting. Goodman's force would attack on two fronts. Half would sweep up the main drive, taking out the guard post, the barn and the workshop. The others would continue on to the mansion itself.

'And Sam,' Morton continued, 'Shema's in the house. Get her out of there – alive. Understood?'

There was a moment's hesitation. Then came Goodman's voice: 'Yes, sir.'

Nuri could hear armed men in the mansion, shooting while they rushed into position, as he ran along the edge of the cornfield, his Kalashnikov ready to give covering fire to the guard who was moving deeper into the corn. Suddenly the man was no longer there.

Wolfie's bolt had penetrated the guard's brain behind his ear.

Nuri stopped, peering into the darkness.

'Majid,' he called. 'Majid, where are you?'

'Here, come,' Michelle answered in Arabic.

Nuri whirled at the voice, rifle raised. As he did so, Wolfie shot a bolt into his chest. As he pitched forward, Nuri's reflexes caused his fingers to trigger the gun. The magazine began to empty itself into the earth.

At that moment a long burst of gunfire came from the one upper window of the mansion that had not been shuttered. Bullets raked the cornfield.

They caught Wolfie as he was crouching back into the corn.

Michelle heard him make a small disapproving sound, as if he were annoyed with himself. Even before she had rolled to his side, she knew he was dead. She grabbed his mobile.

'One down! One down!' she called urgently into the phone.

'On our way!' Morton responded in Hebrew.

Michelle began to wriggle closer to the murderous fire from the mansion. They would not expect that.

Raza turned away from the window from which the two men continued to pour crossfire into the field. It was the maid's room. She stood by the door, guarding Shema with a pistol.

Raza continued to pace around the room, oblivious of the gunfire. He took in the single bed, radiator full on, even though

391

it was summer, the bookshelf of paperback romances. He looked at everything except Shema.

There was firing now around the house.

'Why did you do it?' he asked in a calm voice as if he were enquiring the time.

'You betrayed us,' Shema said. 'You promised our people so much! And we believed you! When you said that to build a new world, the old one must first be destroyed, we believed you! When you said from suffering would come a better life, we believed you! Because of you, Nadine had to die! You killed her long before I had to. You killed all those people at the camp long before the planes and guns did! You have killed so many people with your warped philosophy and monstrous actions. You are not just mad, Raza. You are evil!'

He was standing now at the side of the window, peering out. There were lights on the far side of the field.

The men at the window leaned out, looking for targets. Suddenly one of them fell back into the room, a crossbow bolt in his head.

'Get that shutter closed!' Raza ordered.

The other guard tried to lower the steel shutter with the hand winch.

'It's jammed,' he cried.

Raza leapt to the window and yanked at the shutter. It fell a little way before another bolt struck it. He turned back into the room and glared at Shema.

'The Zionists,' he said. 'Is that what they told you? Or was it the Germans and the others who came to see you in prison? Did they fill your head with such poison?'

He turned from the window and walked over to her. Slowly, he reached out his right hand and touched her cheek. She stared at him defiantly. He looked at his fingers for a moment. Then with a speed and savagery that caused the maid to gasp, he yanked Shema to her feet and dragged her to the window. He spun her round so that she faced the cornfield.

'Morton!' he screamed. 'Here's your Zionist whore!'

Raza held Shema by her hair, forcing her to lift her head and expose her neck. With one furious blow he snapped the top of her spinal column. As her head fell forward he pitched her through the window.

As he stood in the opening behind the van driver, sweeping the mansion with his night vision binoculars, Morton saw Shema fall, legs and arms flailing, and her head at an impossible angle. He saw her hit the ground. As the shutter finally dropped into place, his van plunged on through the corn.

Pressing buttons on a console, Danny opened the roof and began to raise the electronic beam gun on its expanding steel frame. A seat like that on a tractor unfolded. Danny lowered himself on to it and pressed another button. The frame continued to extend until Danny and the gun protruded over the top of the van. He pressed a switch on the gun's control box. The gun gave a whirring sound and began to traverse.

Immediately there was the sound of glass in the mansion's windows shattering. In moments, the gun had taken out every pane. Danny increased the strength of the beam. It bombarded the shutters, creating an ear-piercing sound for anybody behind them.

Morton's van continued to plough through the corn. He could hear the fire-fight intensifying on the far side of the mansion. He climbed back down into the van, grasped the launcher and fitted a grenade. Hoisting the weapon on his shoulder, he clambered up the frame. He fired. The grenade exploded against the side of the mansion. A technician handed up a second grenade. Morton fired again. The grenade blew a hole in the mansion's roof. Morton let off two more rounds but the bumpy ground made it impossible to aim accurately. Below a technician continued to report progress.

'Major Goodman's men have cleared the workshop and barn and have joined up with the others. Matti and Lou are meeting opposition from the back of the mansion. The FBI and National Guard want to know when they can move.'

'They got all those taxis secured?'

'Checking, Colonel.'

The technician spoke into his throat mike, then called up to Morton, 'All secured, Colonel. The bio-hazard truck is already on its way to Fort Detrick.'

'Okay. Move them up,' ordered Morton.

The van had suddenly slowed.

Morton saw Michelle rise out of the corn, and jump on to the running board, holding the wing mirror for support. She directed the driver to where Wolfie lay. As the driver and a couple of technicians carried his body into the van, Morton fired another shot and blew out a ground floor shutter. He had his way in.

The van rolled forward.

Matti and Lou had worked their way round to the kitchen door. Goodman's platoon was round the far side and front of the house, pouring fire through several windows, the shutters of which they had removed with lumps of gelignite stuck to the window frames and fitted with short-delay fuses thrust into the explosive.

Crouching by the door, they nodded at each other, then kicked open the door, firing as they dived inside.

As they did so, one of Harmoos' men rolled a hand grenade across the floor from the shelter of the adjoining laundry room.

Matti and Lou died instantly.

Crouching beneath the ground-floor window, Morton heard the dull crumping sound from the rear of the house. He tossed a stun grenade into the room. There was a blinding flash and a concussive bang. Uzi in hand, he rolled over the windowledge into the room.

It was an office, with an English-style desk and filing cabinets. The explosion had blown open drawers. Papers were scattered everywhere. A body lay on the floor.

As Michelle scrambled over the window to join Morton, the gunfire continued unabated. They crawled towards the door, pushing the body before them. At the door they shoved it into the hall.

Immediately a burst of gunfire came from across the hall. The corpse twitched.

Morton's fingers moved gently around the trigger of his Uzi. The gun recoiled slightly as it fired. Across the hall, the Arab's face seemed to catch fire as the features disappeared.

In a crouching run, Morton and Michelle burst into the hall.

The sound of firing was even louder.

Out of the corner of his eye, Morton saw a hand raised. He turned and fired, hurling himself through the door behind the body of the Arab he had just shot. Moments later, behind him the hall filled with a blinding light. Then a terrible sound, followed by destruction and darkness.

He waited a few seconds for the grenade's shock to expand and expend, then ran back into the hall.

Michelle had shared the full force of the blast with the grenade thrower. His head was close to where hers should have been.

A door down the hall burst open and a massive figure stood there, hands raised.

'Do not shoot,' implored Harmoos.

The front door blew open behind him, and Goodman charged through, firing.

Harmoos began to spin and spread his hands under the impact of the bullets. Then he crashed to the carpet.

Commandos poured through the doorway. From the kitchen, Danny emerged, grim faced.

'Matti and Lou are back there, what's left of them,' he said. 'And somebody went out the door. Stepped through their blood. The footsteps are clear.'

'Upstairs!' Morton ordered Goodman.

The commandos followed the major up the mansion's main staircase. The sound of firing resumed as they cleared the bedrooms.

Morton and Danny moved towards a closed door at the end of the hall.

Danny grabbed a Kalashnikov from a dead Arab slumped in the hall and removed the magazine. Morton turned the door knob and Danny hurled the rifle into the room, towards the ceiling. Then in a concerted rush, they dived through the door.

A ragged fusillade flew above them and out of the doorway.

Morton adjusted to the room's light. It was a large drawing-room, a mish-mash of incompatible tastes: stuffed sofas and armchairs, European period furniture and velour curtains and oriental rugs. The shooting had come from near a credenza against the far wall.

Morton began to crawl further into the room. From behind a sofa Faruk Kadumi rose slowly in the half-darkness, hands above his head, a terrified look on his face.

'I wish to surrender,' he whimpered.

Morton and Danny rose to their feet, their guns trained on him.

'Where's Raza?' Morton demanded.

'He has gone. Moments ago.'

'The kitchen!' Danny shouted.

Morton bundled Faruk Kadumi across the room towards a commando.

'Hold him. If he even thinks of moving, shoot him.'

Goodman was coming down the stairs with the maid.

'We're secured, Colonel.'

In the distance came the sound of sirens.

'Everybody except Danny stay near the house,' ordered Morton. He ran to the kitchen, Danny at his heels. Matti and Lou lay just inside the back door. Still running, Morton and Danny reached the van.

'Set up that beam gun and work the field,' Morton said.

Danny climbed up on the roof and began to traverse the gun.

Standing on the bonnet of the van, Morton swept the corn with his starlight glasses. Nothing. Above him the beam gun continued to traverse. Then he saw something was moving towards the trees. He jumped into the van and ordered out the driver and technicians. Then he drove into the corn.

Halfway across the field, there was a bone-shattering jar. A tyre had blown.

Morton climbed into the back, grabbed the grenade launcher, and fitted a phosphorus shell. He stuck another in a pocket and took to the field on foot.

On the roof Danny was cursing fluently. The beam gun had jammed.

In the corn, there was no sound except the rustle of his own progress. Morton paused again to listen. The silence was total.

He was halfway between the van and the trees when the shots rang out behind him. He turned in time to see Danny falling from his perch on the roof.

Then the van was lumbering at an awkward angle towards him, smoke rising from its good tyre protesting at the uneven distribution of weight.

Morton knelt in the corn, bringing the launcher to shoulder level. The van was picking up speed, its headlights cutting a swathe through the stalks, the noise of the protesting tyres louder.

Morton stood up slowly, the lights catching his body.

The van had stopped about a hundred yards away, its engine smoking, lights still blazing. Someone was up on the roof.

'Morton,' screamed Raza. 'I still have enough anthrax to destroy you!'

The figure was standing, his hands moving.

'Nemesis,' murmured Morton, as he fired the launcher. 'Thanks be to God.'

The van erupted in a fireball. Morton fitted the second shell and fired again. There was another huge flash, then a roar as the corn ignited. Nothing – not even the last of the Anthrax-B-C – would survive the inferno. The threat was finally over.

Morton dropped the launcher and raced forward. To one side of the van there was a movement. He reached Danny, hoisted him across his shoulders and began to run towards the trees.

Overhead a helicopter hovered. It came low, making no effort to intervene, but following Morton until he had reached the safety of the trees.

Behind him the field was burning furiously around the remains of the van.

'You're going to be okay, Danny,' Morton said as he laid Danny on the ground. 'Everything is going to be okay.'

Given what had happened, the world learned remarkably little. It was a tribute, of sorts, to the skill of government and Intelligence agencies to hide the truth.

The destruction of the mansion and the death of Mr Harmoos were put down to one of those tragic accidents. A number of newspapers carried in their obituaries revelations of his secret passion for fireworks. The mansion, it seemed, had been a veritable arsenal of rockets and other pyrotechnic delights – which explained what sounded like gunfire that had accompanied its destruction when a box of rockets ignited. The ensuing fire had quickly spread to the adjoining corn.

As well as Mr Harmoos, among others who died was Dr Faruk Kadumi. Some of the wilder television reports speculated the disgraced surgeon was visiting Mr Harmoos to discuss an operation that might have solved the millionaire's constant battle to find a guaranteed cure for his obesity. In all, twenty-seven people had died in the conflagration, all of them Arabs.

National Guards, who happened to be in the area, returning from a field manoeuvre – never actually identified – had done their best to help put out the fire. Nevertheless, it had also destroyed one of Mr Harmoos' more modest ventures – the Day-Nite Cab Company. All the cabs had been at the mansion for the drivers' annual dinner with their employer. After, the vehicles had been totally destroyed and, facing an uncertain future, the drivers had opted to return to the land of their birthplace, Lebanon. The government had assisted them with passage. No one had actually checked whether or not they had arrived.

A week after the disaster, the Harmoos empire had been sold off to a private company called Swift Renovations. All efforts by the media to learn more about the company or its plans had met with polite refusals.

The day after the mansion fire, the Concorde had left New York. On board were eleven coffins.

A month later, the aircraft returned to New York to bring Prime Minister Karshov and a high-ranking Israeli delegation to the United Nations to discuss plans for the forthcoming Middle East peace conference. When the plane left, it carried an extra passenger. Dr Miriam Cantwell had been offered, and accepted, the post of Director of Surgery at the Jerusalem hospital where Ruth had once worked. Miriam had by then made a complete recovery.

She arrived on the night Israeli television carried two stories that shared the same top billing on other news programmes round the world.

The Supreme Leader of Libya was filmed being escorted by the President's National Security adviser, Brent Appleton, into the White House.

In Teheran, Ayatollah Muzwaz issued a short statement that he welcomed the peace conference on the Middle East. He added that he hoped his words would put an end to rumours that the mullahs had ever intended to wage holy war.

Morton saw both items on Danny's hospital bedside television. Danny was to be discharged in the morning, once more passed for active duty.

'It's a funny old world,' Danny shrugged, turning away from the screen.

'For sure,' Morton said. 'For sure.'

CIRCULATING STOCK
WEXFORD PUBLIC LIBRARIES
BLOCK LOAN
BUNCLODY
ENNISCORTHY
GOREY
TOTAL
NEW
PROJ
WEXFORD
DATE